SACRAMENTO PUBLIC LIBRARY
D0843527
04/13

# NECESSARY ILL

Aqueduct Press, PO Box 95787
Seattle, WA 98145-2787
www.aqueductpress.com

This book is fiction. Names, characters, businesses, organizations, places, events, and incidents either are the product of the author's imagination or are used fictitiously. Any resemblance to actual persons, living or dead, events, or locales is entirely coincidental.

Copyright © 2013 Deb Taber
All rights reserved.
First printing, March 2013

ISBN: 978-1-61976-022-6
Library of Congress Control Number: 2012951738

10 9 8 7 6 5 4 3 2 1

Cover Design by Lynne Jenson Lampe

Cover Acknowledgments:
Back cover:
Cloudscape over Desolate Road, Utah, Western, USA: Jay Lazarin/iStockphoto.com

Front cover:
Back-lit Ocotillo Blossoms at Big Bend National Park: Dave Hughes/iStockphoto.com
Cave 2: Alexandre Caron/iStockphoto.com
Foetus: Valerie Loiseleux/iStockphoto.com

Book Design by Kathryn Wilham

Printed in the USA by Thomson-Shore Inc.

# NECESSARY ILL

BY

DEB TABER

SEATTLE

# PART I

# SPREADER

## CHAPTER 1

At ten thirty on a weekday morning the restaurants are as empty as they'll ever be. One skinny kid who slips in and out of the restrooms is likely to be ignored. The perfect time for Jin to work.

Jin coughs inside the men's room, letting the sound bounce off the dirty floors, plastic urinals, and under the stall doors. The echo confirms that the room is empty for the moment, and all Jin needs is enough time to brush the doorknob with a single coating of the clear fluid it carries in a jar in its pack.

A man walks in as Jin scrubs its hands in the sink, soaping thoroughly between the two ten-second bursts of lukewarm water that the conservation faucet allows. Jin makes only momentary eye contact, enough to be polite but not familiar, rinses the rest of the soap from its hands, and exits before the effect of washing wears off and allows the poison it painted on the doorknob to mix with the oils in its skin. *Dirty hands spread disease*, says the sign above the sink. Now, in the city of Amarillo, they're fatal.

Jin finger-combs its shoulder-length hair into a more feminine style and moves on to the ladies' room.

Fifty-four restaurants in a small Texas town means one hundred and eight restroom doorknobs to paint with plague. A population of over half a million is far more than the fifty-four can support, and as Jin walks into the main dining area the lines are growing back toward the doors. Soon, that problem will be taken care of. For a little while.

In restaurant number thirty-seven, a lo-loc diner featuring yucca fries and pot pies made from the goat byproducts that the hi-loc establishments won't serve, a man walks toward the single-stall restroom before Jin, so it stops to order fries, presumably made from the field of spiny plants growing where the building's parking lot used to be. The girl behind the counter looks up and down its scrawny, sun-beaten frame and fills the yucca-fiber box to overflowing. Jin reminds itself to try to eat more. It shouldn't get skinny enough to draw attention, and the human brain needs more than greasy starch strips to function at its peak. Right now, the work is more important than hunger. Eighteen more restaurants including this one, thirty-six more doors to go, then it can return home to rest and eat real food, not grease-soaked filler and salt. It already hit the five hi-loc places in town in the morning, when dust and sweat didn't coat its skin and a now-discarded expensive jacket let it pass the hostess with muttered excuses of meeting someone who was already seated in the dining room.

The vortex of a toilet flush reaches Jin's ears, immediately followed by the rattle and squeak of a doorknob, no rush of a faucet in between. Jin watches the man from the restroom exit, wondering if he comes here often, knowing that if he does, the plague will kill him. Its eyes follow him until he is out of sight, committing to memory his particular hunch of the shoulders, the way he scuffs his right toe every few steps. When he is gone, Jin leaves its food for the prowling urchins that circle the diner and gets back to work.

The streets fill and empty like a pulse: foot traffic, bicycle traffic, and delivery trucks. Mostly tankers, shipping water from the low desert raincatchers and coastal desalinization plants, as well as the smaller box trucks and light SUVs of the local delivery services. Clouds of manure odor puff out of the smaller vehicles, indicating their owners are using personal fuel retrofits rather than corporate biofuel. Jin steps out into a momentary lull, listening to the barely contained hum of humanity from the surrounding buildings. It hums along a little, sounding down alleys like a bat, selecting the least crowded streets and passages without having to look.

Two men in dirty jeans and badly patched shirts stiffen as Jin nears. They don't look at it, but their change in posture is enough to let Jin know they've seen it. Travelers aren't common, so it tries to blend in, acting as if it has walked these streets all its life, pretending unconcern. It looks like a male now, so it should be safe from the common rapist. Even if it looked female, statistics say it should be safe with so many people around. A tingle in the back of its brain says that statistics don't know everything; the men suspect something. Time to run.

Instinct isn't always right. Jin forces itself to continue casually down the street, looking for a quiet place to rest. A man nods at Jin in passing, the same detached politeness Jin shows to anyone who bothers to notice it. Jin nods back. Keep walking, keep west. Just a few more doors to paint and then it can go home, down into the limestone fortress the Neuter Network has created deep beneath the desert of southeastern New Mexico.

A fist strikes between Jin's shoulder blades, and it crashes into the sidewalk. It pinches off the pain signals bombarding its synapses but can't quite staunch the flow of self-recrimination. It should have seen this coming. It should have avoided the contact. The two men who pretended to ignore it earlier grab hold of its arms while the one who struck it stands apart.

"I know what you are, you little bastard," says one of the ill-dressed men.

Jin says nothing, just kicks out at its captors. In answer, the two men grasp it tighter and lift the small body off the ground. The other man slices Jin's shirt open with his pocketknife, then stops, staring at the blank, bare chest.

"Jesus," he says.

"Never thought it would make such a difference," says the second man, twisting Jin's arm at a painful angle so that he, too, can see the smooth skin, unbroken by anything so unnecessary as a nipple.

A woman runs up hollering, waving a shotgun in the air as the first man claws at Jin's belt. The rest of the street is suddenly empty.

"Get off of her you perverts! If you lay one finger..."

She sees Jin and stops.

"What the hell?" she says. The barrel of her gun drops toward the dirt.

"You tell me," says the first man.

Jin feels a tug at its pants, then the hot air of the desert on its bare skin. It lets them look for a moment at the fact that it has nothing to hide, but enough is enough, and escape will be difficult if its pants are around its feet.

"Let go," says Jin.

"It's one of them, isn't it?" says the woman, her fingers tightening on her weapon. "Murdering beast. You killed my cousin's two boys. His wife, too, and you damn near killed *him*."

"Where?" Jin asks.

"You're not talking, worm," says the second man.

"Taos," says the woman. The men glare at her.

"Not me. Didn't do Taos," says Jin. "What disease?"

"He said you're not talking," says the man who so far has been silent.

The first man nods at him. "Help me get this thing's wrists tied together, and we'll see what we can do. Maybe we'll turn it into a girl after all."

Jin struggles against the stupidity of them all. Stupid not to ask what disease it brought to Amarillo. Stupid not to find out how to contract and how to cure the plague they seem to suspect is already in their city. They'll all die. If not in Jin's plague, then some other. The woman sees the sorrow in Jin's eyes and mistakes the expression for self-pity.

"You'll only get what you deserve," she says.

The men drag Jin with them down the street, barely letting its feet touch the ground. Finally, they've decided to make the scene more private, away from eyes hidden behind the windows all around. Stupid again, to move to a different location instead of just killing it immediately if they can't ask the right questions.

They toss Jin down in a dead-end alley, the asphalt digging into its chin and hands as it lands prone on the ground. No weeds grow up through the cracks in the asphalt here, but the churned, dry dirt tells it human, not animal, scavengers have picked the greenery clean. Jin backs toward the bricks that block the far end, readjusting its clothing as it moves and letting out whimpers that please its captors but are really meant to sound for outlets of escape. There is one, a door cracked slightly open with no human noises inside. Jin will have to go through the men to reach the opening, so it tests them for weakness, letting its posture ever so slightly mimic the man on the right.

Jin's thoughts slow and it breathes into the movement until the sensations in its body match the man's. It feels the tension and excitement the man is feeling: anger, anticipation, hate, fear, the lust for action. This ghosting makes Jin's face heat with blood and its body tingle with the sensation of an organ it will never have.

The second man is larger, but his rage is not as strong. He keeps glancing at the other two for reassurance. Third is the mostly quiet man, and Jin doesn't have to ghost him to know where he's thinking of putting his knife. The woman is of no concern, hardly even aware of the weapon in her hand. She is more interested in watching than being a part of the play.

The cornered animal act has brought Jin exactly where it wants to be. Using the leverage from the brick wall, it launches itself just to the right of the second man, diving low and rolling back onto its feet in a dash that takes it through the open door and into the quiet darkness, a place that feels much like home. Advantage regained, Jin decides to forgo painting the remaining doors. Silently, it works its way back into the crowded streets while the men crash through the darkness behind it, betrayed by their feeble senses. The plague is complete enough, and Jin has a long walk home.

The damp smell of rock and underground life gives way to the scent of disinfectant and purified air of the Network's research labs. An old, wrinkled neut looks up from the charts on its flexible screen when Jin walks in. A grin breaks its face into more wrinkles as it pushes a lock of wild gray hair back from its eyes.

"Bruvec," says Jin.

"How are you?" says Bruvec.

"Bad time, crazy city. Men attack, woman almost helps until she sees I'm no gen. Suspected plagues too."

"Danger to Network?" asks Bruvec.

"Doubt. Obvious outsiders. Everyone else ignored."

Bruvec nods. "Finish spread?"

Jin takes the nearly empty jar from its pack. "Few doses left."

"Put in the storage closet. Keeps?" says Bruvec.

"Not long. Sixty-day index, ten left," says Jin.

"Disposal cart, then. Sleep now, Jin. Beds are empty in the main room. If you're staying long, will set up a single."

"Showers?" says Jin.

"Everything empty. No one home but self and Net. And Keri, of course."

"Thanks," says Jin.

It scrubs down, inhaling the scent of chlorinated water, the last molecules of particulates that the filters can't pull out. It searches for a faint burnt taste or tingling sensation from the electrodialysis process, but finds none. Good. The desalinization equipment still works. Its muscles relax and tension vanishes like the steam. All is clean steel and white plastic here, plenty of recycled and recaptured water, and no germs allowed outside the labs. Spending so long up top makes Jin feel dirty most of the time. Down in the caves, the dust and mud are comparatively pure, and the living areas are free even of that inconvenience: a subterranean heaven.

Later, Jin lies on the soft white fabric of its cot, trying to forget the feeling of a man's hand tearing its clothes, his eyes staring with murder just because its body has fewer holes or lumps than he thinks it should. The squeak of the cot hurts Jin's ears as it turns over, trying to find comfort. The rustling of the sheets makes so much noise it barely hears the soft bare footsteps on the stone floor.

"You awake, Jin?" says Bruvec.

"Talk," says Jin.

Bruvec sits on the chair to one side of the bed, watching Jin with lively brown eyes far younger than its dark face. "Just wanted to know, what's next? Any ideas?"

"You asking for self or Council?" says Jin.

"Just self. Your plagues are always best. I remember suicide plague three years ago. Pure art."

Bruvec's wrinkled face stretches into a smile, and Jin relaxes into the covers. It is proud of that plague, not only for the arrangement of chemicals that worked to ease each victim into a simple, clean death, but for the number of people who fought the plague and survived. All they had to do was want to. Not the instinctual fight-for-life fear of death, but the determined choice to live, to put in the effort and the will to succeed that living required. Keeping up that fight for three weeks altered the subject's brain chemistry just enough to neutralize the virus. At the moment, Jin isn't sure it would have survived its own plague. It is too tired.

Warmth spreads through it, body heat trapped under the thermal blanket. The next plague should be big, as good as the suicide but different. Something new. A tickle at the back of Jin's brain makes it smile. It closes its eyes and visualizes the endorphins flooding its synapses. The pleasure of a new concept, a new challenge.

"Don't know what's next yet, Bruv. Might need study," it says.

"Studies are a problem. No volunteers," Bruvec jokes.

"Can tap into university databases, medical studies, find info, no big stink. Maybe go in, get close to gens, study direct," says Jin.

"Not again," says Bruvec.

Jin props itself up on an elbow, eye to eye with the older neut, watching the almost parental concern pull downward at the corners of Bruvec's eyes. Its umber skin is sallow from too many years without natural sun and cracked from its earlier years under that same star. Too much, too little, never just enough. That's why Jin seeks balance.

"I'm careful, Bruv. No one notices when I study. To them I'm stranger, maybe hanging around pickup stops, waiting for ride. Watch, learn, gone. No one cares."

"You won't die of plague, Jin. Stupid-brave."

When Jin gives no response, Bruvec shakes its head and pushes itself out of the chair with visible effort. Jin watches it leave, hearing its words echo internally as if finding a home for themselves in the folds of Jin's mind. The lights dim down at a whispered command, and it begins to slow its thoughts for the journey into sleep. Stupid-brave. Pure art. Stupid-brave.

# CHAPTER 2

The entire barn of chickens screeched in varying levels of annoyance and terror, yet even above that Sandy could hear her mother's screams. She wouldn't look, Sandy decided. If she couldn't help she shouldn't watch; yet she found herself pulling forward on her elbows to peer through the chicken wire at the floor below.

Four men surrounded her mother. Sandy recognized them from her trips into the city, delivering eggs and chicken meat to the local processing house. Now that she was old enough to drive, her mother had begun letting her do the runs on her own, and these men had openly stared at her, hungry for something that left her chilled.

They took turns at her mother as Sandy looked down from her hiding place in the third tier of chicken cages that lined every wall in the barn. Only the shadows and chaos hid her, and she tried to move as little as possible.

*If I'm still, they won't see me* she told herself over and over again. She'd been foolish to hide in a cage instead of running when the men had come through the door, calling her mother's name in tones that she hadn't heard since the last long fight before her father took Ronnie and left them to manage the Montana poultry farm on their own. As if the two of them could care for two hundred chickens and the small corn-and-squash farm that fed both the livestock and themselves on their own. She should have run, but she had been up on a ladder at the seventh tier and hadn't had time to climb down any farther before the chickens started screeching and drawing attention to her end of the barn.

Her mother's screams stopped, or fell beneath the volume of the chicken noise, and Sandy slowly drew as far back as she could in the cage. It wasn't meant to hold a teenage girl, and there was little she could do other than hope that the men would leave soon enough that she could somehow load her mother into the delivery van and get her to the clinic. She couldn't remember right now where the local clinic was.

"Let's get out of here. This is driving me crazy," said one of the men, his hands to his ears.

Two of the others started to leave, but the last one, the one who had been on her mother when she quieted at last, turned casually to face Sandy and smiled.

"Not yet," he said. "I like the looks of that chicken."

Sandy spun as best she could in the cage so that her boot heels greeted the men when they arrived. There was nowhere to run, but she could fight dirty. She was a country girl, after all, and had fought off the advances of a ranch hand or two over the years since puberty had filled out her body in a way that made men notice her as they never had before.

She was also hardly over a hundred fifteen pounds. After a couple of bruisings, one of the men caught her ankle and pulled, and she dropped to the barn's aluminum floor with a sound that hurt worse than the impact itself. She barely had time to feel satisfied that she had at least knocked him off the ladder in her fall, when the four of them were on her, tearing at her clothes and skin and hair. They had no weapons other than their own muscle, so she tore right back and screeched in the ear of the one who had complained earlier of the noise.

"Don't think she likes you," said a voice from behind the men.

They parted enough for Sandy to see beyond them to a serious-looking boy, about her age, who stood only a few feet away. Two of the men reached out for the newcomer, and Sandy used the distraction to fasten up as much of her undone clothing as she could. She silently thanked the unpredictable Montana weather that she had put on three layers that morning before coming out to feed the chickens. The men hadn't made it through the last of the fabric, taking time as they did to joke between themselves about "plucking the chicken."

The boy dodged their grip and landed a kick on one of the attackers. Sandy couldn't quite follow all of his moves, but he seemed to be landing more punches than he took until the two men who held her joined the battle. With one man down and the second limping, the new fighters descended on the boy with fierce determination and managed to pin him to the ground, facedown.

"I guess you like us better than she does then, don't you?" said one of the men.

He flipped the boy like he was no more than a pillow, and the limping one leered and brought over the bolt cutters that had been leaning against the wall. Sandy wished she had put them away when her mother had asked. She wished she hadn't been so sullen about any of her chores. She would have to tell her mother that, as soon as this was done.

"You're not quite girlish enough for my tastes, but with a little work, you could be pretty," said the man.

Sandy's view of the boy was obscured, but whatever they saw when they opened his jeans caused all of the men to step back in unison. Completely unaware of her own pain, Sandy launched herself at the back of the most aggressive man's knees, taking him down. The bolt cutters fell from his hand, and she took them in both of hers and swung wildly. She felt them impact something hard yet giving. Several times. But her mind refused to sort out the scene. All she knew was that hands were on her, and then they weren't, and there were sounds of other violence nearby, violence she wasn't causing herself so it didn't mean anything to her.

Then a soft voice said, "Stop. Over now."

Sandy looked at the boy, and then at the bruised and bleeding men sprawled at her feet. She jerked her eyes away from the boy's still-bared groin, then looked back again when nothing made sense. There was nothing there.

The boy let her look with a cold expression on his face, which turned to confusion when she smiled. She couldn't help it. He couldn't rape her if he tried, and that made him a friend, at least for the moment.

"I'm Sandy," she said.

"Tei."

Her smile faded as her heart began to slow.

"Mom?" she whispered, turning slowly only because so much of her didn't want to go in that direction at all.

Her mother lay quiet on the cold floor, and Sandy knelt beside her, feeling the bite of the aluminum through the thermal layers and her jeans. She checked for a pulse, knowing there was none, knowing little else beyond that.

"Do I call an ambulance?" she asked.

Tei shrugged. "Wouldn't do much good."

One of the men began to twitch and grunt.

"Want to leave?" said Tei.

Sandy glanced back at the chickens and shook her head, knowing there was nothing else to do but get back to work. Someone had to manage the farm. Someone had to do the feeding and the slaughter and the deliveries, and the few paid workers they were able to afford knew nothing about the business end of things. Her mother had always taken care of all of that.

Tei shrugged and began dragging the men outside, one at a time and with visible effort. Sandy looked from the men to her mother. They shouldn't be near her, so she went to help the boy—she couldn't help thinking of him as a boy, even with the evidence she'd clearly seen—and they got the men out to the roadside and left them there to live or die. Sandy hoped they chose the latter. A truck rattled past them without slowing, then another.

"What about her?" said Tei when they returned to the barn.

Sandy sat back down next to her mother. She didn't know what she was supposed to do. Call the police? The morgue? She knew how to handle dead birds, not people. The torn body in front of her hardly seemed to be her mother anymore.

Tei lifted her gently by the arm, then released her as soon as she stood.

"Called shock. Get you warm, maybe some water, then think."

He led her back to the house and gestured her toward the couch. She heard the sound of fabric rustling from the bedrooms, and a moment later he was wrapping her in blankets from her mother's bed. She wondered if he knew it was her mother's, or if he had just gone into the first bedroom he could find. It didn't matter. The blankets smelled like her mother, like soap and sweat and boiled corn, and feeling them surround her, she tried to tell herself it was like her mother's embrace, Mom telling her she was going to be all right.

She didn't feel all right, though, and her mother hadn't held her like this since she was eleven years old. Sandy hadn't wanted her to. Teenage snits, her mom had called it.

Tei handed her a wad of rough toilet paper for her runny nose and sat looking out the window as she cried. A motor started up in the distance, then faded.

"They're gone," said Tei. "Three drove, one died."

At the word "died," a fresh set of tears broke through Sandy. Not for the man, but for the finality of the word and what it meant for her and the body that used to be her mother. When her eyes drained dry, she looked at Tei.

"Will you help me burn her?" said Sandy.

"Private pyre?"

"I don't think we could afford a real cremation, and Mom always hated those anyway. She said bodies were supposed to return to the earth, not get packed into urns. I don't want to talk with anyone at the morgue, or the police. I think the man who died was a policeman's son."

"You saw which one died?" said Tei. Sandy wondered at his spark of interest.

"The blond one. I hit him with the bolt cutters so many times. He wasn't breathing when we carried him outside."

"Didn't know you noticed."

"I didn't either until now. So will you help?"

"If you want," said Tei.

She did. They sat in silence for a while, then Tei got up and came back with bandages and ointments from the bathroom. Sandy wondered if he was a thief of some kind. He seemed utterly comfortable rummaging around in someone else's home. The thought unsettled her a little, but not as much as it might have on another day. For now, she was grateful for his presence and the way he silently cleaned her wounds.

When he finished, she did the same for him, then she rose to go back to the barn.

"Wait. Take care of her tomorrow," said Tei.

"We will. But the chickens still need to be fed," said Sandy.

It was something to do, something that needed to be done, and nothing was worse than sitting in the living room feeling like her mother was about to walk in the door and tell her to get back to her chores.

She brought one of the blankets to the barn and draped it over the sickening sight of her mother's body. She tried to remember a childhood prayer, but could only come up with the *sh'ma*, and she saw no reason to "Bless the Lord's name forever and ever." She covered her eyes and sang it anyway, hearing the wobble in her voice, not knowing if her mother had kept up the practice of her religion in private after the synagogue in town had burnt down, or if the words would mean anything to her silent body even if she had.

Tei watched her curiously but asked no questions. When he saw where the feed was kept and how much she doled out to each cage, he took a bucket with him to the far wall and began to work on the chickens over there.

Squawks of hunger and anticipation vibrated the room in a familiar way. Sandy fed and cleaned and collected eggs and tried not to think about the cold, silent lump on the floor. She tried not to think of the strange boy who worked not so far away, who had frightened and beaten up rapists, yet who washed her cuts without a word and agreed to help her take care of her mother in the only way she could. She tried not to wonder what had happened to him, what gave him the inhuman body she'd seen. Her mind numbed by the day's events, avoiding such thoughts came easily.

## CHAPTER 3

Jin awakens as the room grows light, an artificial day radiating out from behind the limestone formations protruding from the wall. The pleasurable anticipation from the night before seeps slowly through the morning sludge of Jin's brain as it dresses in the loose white pants and shirt that are the standard of Home Cavern inhabitants. Thin arms and legs slide through the once-rough yucca fibers, softened and stripped into a thread almost as light and fine as cotton, then woven tightly for a smooth, warm fabric. The outfit feels natural to Jin, as if the topside clothing were an artificial skin it had to wear, while these are a part of its own nature. It tucks the thick socks Bruvec left for it into the pouch pocket at the front of the shirt. For now, the cool stone feels good under its callused feet.

Net nods as Jin enters the computing lab, too absorbed in its own screen to look up. Jin settles into a softly padded chair, enjoying the hum of electricity, the far-off buzz of the generators, and the companionable silence of Net.

After logging onto the Network intranet, Jin pulls up the spreader maps, animated to show the population drifts over the last half century, based on inhabitant-to-resource and -contamination ratios. Each half decade on the map is compressed into a single quarter-minute animation.

The US densities bleed from one city into another with only uninhabitable deserts, shrinking protected forests, industrial complexes, and landfills in between. As each area conquers its own challenges—low birth rates, limited water supplies, job shortages—the populations rise and lead to the same problems over and over again. Some new medication, invention, or waste-management program always solves the problem; some sort of disaster, human-made or otherwise, always brings the sobering resource shortage home again. Jin's stomach grows heavy as the current densities darken its screen again in the end of the two-and-a-half-minute cycle. No matter how hard a spreader works, the impact is always short-range. Even cities Jin has hit in the last ten years will likely need another spread in its lifetime, and in the meantime the waste piles grow higher, and biological and chemical contaminants permeate the soil and groundwater.

It freezes the map's loop as it ends the next round, seeking the black spots that indicate highest need and cross-checking the dates of previous spreads.

"Net, why no one hit St. Louis?" asks Jin.

Net's pale, broad fingers continue to click and type on the hundred-year-old machine it prefers, although Jin doubts the computer's insides are a fraction as old as its casing. Jin waits politely, hands off its own screen.

"Don't know," says Net after Jin has counted out two minutes in its head. "Lune was supposed to; hit San Diego instead. You want?"

"Can't. Grew up there," says Jin.

Net's pale blue eyes come to sharp focus on Jin's brown pair.

"Okay for you, Jin. You're careful, not bitter. Whole Council agrees. Run details by us first, but St. Louis is yours."

Jin shrugs, not used to special treatment. The only difference between itself and other spreaders is that Jin doesn't like to leave a mess. It has bad memories from its early days, but so does everyone. The doctors in St. Louis tried to say it was a girl, but the infant's brain and body disagreed. No one spoke of neuters back then; genders were the final word. For most people, they still are.

Jin pulls up a map of St. Louis. The familiar street names bring clear pictures in its memory, but an itch at the back of its brain is stronger. Memories of cloth tearing away from its body, fingers pressing into its skin, the sun burning into the pale brown places that haven't seen true daylight in over twenty years. With the memories comes an idea. Maybe it can temporarily cure St. Louis of a certain criminal element. Not the petty thieves and minor criminals that give a city life, but the kind of people who make the streets dangerous for neuters and genders alike. Jin usually doesn't target such a precise group; the Council reviews each proposed spread to ensure that all of the Network's plagues are designed to break evenly across racial, religious, social, and economic barriers—or balance each other out if the balance can't be accomplished in the same spread—although Jin knows that is often more easily attempted than accomplished.

The public statistics Jin pulls up for St. Louis show a graph of the area's violent criminals out of tune with its population's ethnic demographics. However, a deeper search of unsolved crimes, personal accounts, and out-of-court settlements shows a different image of the city's violent element, more in keeping with the appropriate balance. All Jin needs to do is study people like the attackers in Amarillo, find what sets them apart from others, then use that to target its plague.

The study starts with Jin's own body. It sets down its screen on a nearby table, closes its eyes, relaxes its muscles, and begins to let its awareness poke around inside. Like all neuters, in darkness and concentration it can sense its own internal workings as easily as a gen feeling a gust of wind on her skin.

Organs and systems are all normal.

Breath and pulse are steady at its average resting rate.

Brain chemistry is a neutral balance of aware and awake.

Sensation of calm is predominant.

This is the perfect starting place. As Jin calls up the memory of the attack, it can feel the production of serotonin slow, the muscles tense, a roughness of motion, and revulsion at the sensation of rough hands on its exposed flesh. It hears the sound of its shirt tearing open, the cushioned thud of its backpack falling to the ground. Jin holds the image there and scans its body again.

Heart rate is up.

Epinephrine and acetylcholine are entering the circulatory system.

Muscle tension is increasing.

The data is no good.

Jin knows without studying them that the attackers would have the same physical reactions, a similar biochemical signature to the ones it now shows. What it needs are real-time study subjects to understand the more subtle brain chemistry changes.

Net doesn't look up from its screen as Jin leaves the computing lab. The old neut loves computers, not humans, with the possible exception of Bruvec, who is nearly impossible not to love. Jin doesn't mind. Someone has to keep the systems running and secure, and Net is father, mother, and doctor to all of the machines.

Jin finds Bruvec in the medical labs, hunched over and squinting at a newly published volume on advances in oncology.

"Need study money," says Jin when Bruvec looks up.

"How much?" says Bruvec.

"Six weeks food, maybe five nights cheap lodge. Also new knife."

Bruvec looks at Jin with uncharacteristic sternness.

"What happened to old knife?" says Bruvec.

"Lost in Amarillo," says Jin. "Before attack, not during."

Bruvec shakes its head. "As if that's better. Money is easy, but Jin, take more. Passenger fare, more hotel. Getting too old to sleep with derelicts."

"Like to walk, Bruv," says Jin, ignoring the comment about its age.

Bruvec sighs and shakes its head. "I'll talk to Council, pull funds from spreader account. You'll have money in two days."

Jin nods and takes the short hike to the kitchen cavern. One advantage to living in a modified cave system is the lack of need for routine exercise. Just crossing from one facility to another is the kind of athletic adventure the people up top have to pay to attain. Jin trails its hand along the corridor wall, climbing over rock formations and skirting around the exposed holes that lead deeper into unexplored parts of the rock.

The scents of vegetable broth, warm bread, and woman reach Jin well before it passes the archway leading into the cooking and eating areas. Like all of the Home Cavern rooms, the kitchen is a hodgepodge of the modern, the outdated, and the ageless. Gracefully undulating sheets of thin limestone look like curtains surrounding the stainless steel ovens and grills. A woman sits at a plastic table, reading a paperback thriller that looks too fragile and ancient to survive many more turned pages.

"Hi Jin," says the woman. "Long time no see, don't you think?"

"Hi Ker. How's world?" says Jin.

"How would I know? I live down here, remember?" says Keri.

Jin sits down across the table from Keri, helping itself to bread from the loaf at the center of the table. "Okay, how's Network?"

"Let's see," says Keri, slipping a finger into the book to mark her page. "A bunch of our medics are helping with flood relief in Southeast Asia. I have no idea what the business end of things is like, but the recruiters have found two more neuts in the Southwest since you were last here."

Jin shrugs, pouring coffee for itself. Keri's the only one who gets excited over new neuters. She gets up and digs through the fridges and bins, her voice muffled by distance and rustling packages, but still clearly carried to Jin. The neut enjoys the woman's slightly rolling *r*'s and familiar Spanish-influenced staccato as much as the information it gains from the conversation.

"As far as spreaders go, you and Tei are the only ones home right now. It came in early this morning, with company, or so I hear. I haven't seen it yet. We have three in California and about ten spreaders scattered through the Midwest, seven on the East Coast, and the other twelve are on their way back in from various points. If you're asking about worldwide, I don't have the stats." She pulls a full plate from the warmer and sets it on the table. "Eat."

"Twelve?" says Jin.

"Twelve what? Oh, yeah, the other spreaders. I guess you didn't hear. Taylor died," says Keri.

"Plague?"

"No, though it might have had that too. We're waiting for one of the medics to get here for an autopsy."

"Bruv won't do autopsy?" says Jin.

"It can't anymore because of its eyesight. It complains it can't tell a lung from a gallbladder at more than ten inches away," says Keri.

"You hear what maybe killed Taylor?" says Jin.

"Just the usual. Violence and gore."

Keri reopens her book and flips through it to find her lost page. Jin stares at its food. After a while, it notices that Keri isn't turning pages anymore, and her eyes aren't traveling across the words.

"Who's coming for autopsy?" says Jin.

"I don't know, whoever's nearest. We've got one medic in Roswell now, two in Albuquerque, and several east of Amarillo."

Even without a neut's sharp senses, Jin's stiffening obviously attracts Keri's notice.

"What? Did something happen in Amarillo?"

Jin shrugs. "Nothing. Almost caught."

"Oh, Jin, you have to be more careful. Look what happened to Taylor, and there'll be more. Now that people are starting to learn that you exist, they're going to be after any neuter they can find." Keri's dark eyes cloud. "You all look so young and small that even if they can't tell you're not male or female, people will attack what they see as weakness."

"I'm okay," says Jin. "Worry more about gens mistaken for neut."

Keri stares into her book, her face almost a mask but not quite. In subvocal tones not meant for Jin's ears, it hears her say, "I didn't think you cared."

The sound of footsteps from the passageway echoes into the kitchen, and Jin is surprised to smell another female. Young, and probably fairly small by the lightness of her step. This must be Tei's "company." But Keri looks as surprised as Jin when she sees the neut guide a girl into the kitchen. After the first stare, Keri won't even look at her.

"How dare you bring that girl here, Tei! Where the *hell* is your brain? You don't know if she's safe, and now if you let her go, she might tell everyone we're down here." Keri's hands flick out in irritation. "Are you trying to kill us all? Because if you are, I'd rather die in one of your plagues."

"Finished, Ker?" says Tei, an olive-skinned neut with ragged black hair. A few generations ago, its ancestors may have come from Thailand or perhaps Cambodia, but the hint of soft Virginia accent that falls on Jin's ears gives away the neut's more recent origins.

Keri shakes her head and turns away to start preparing more food. Tei follows.

"Brought girl here for safety," it says. "Men tried to rape her, tried me too, only didn't give them time to figure how. She only trusts neuts."

Keri sets a plate in front of the girl, waving Tei and Jin away. Jin grabs another chunk of fresh bread and looks longingly at the plate it barely touched, but it knows better than to cross Keri when she has her mind set.

The two spreaders walk down a long, level tunnel toward the next main intersection, Tei's shoulder brushing the tunnel's left wall while Jin keeps far to the right.

"You recruiter now?" Jin asks.

"No," says Tei, then it shrugs. "Maybe. You ever sorry? For killing them?"

"Sometimes," Jin says, irritated to hear this question from another spreader, "but rather be spreader than pass off job to others, pretend deaths not my fault. Any who use brain can survive."

"Stupid to spread plagues, hoping no one dies," says Tei, exhaustion rather than accusation in its tone.

"Maybe. But everyone survives, maybe smart enough to live without damage," says Jin.

"Or maybe you not so smart," says Tei.

"Maybe not," Jin says, wondering why every neut thinks it's the smartest. No, not every neut, just every spreader.

It starts down to the labs, but a barely perceptible sluggishness in its brain tells it that the bread in its hand isn't nearly enough to keep it functioning as well as it must. It turns and hikes back, entering the kitchen cavern carefully so as not to upset Keri or the new girl. She's young, maybe sixteen or seventeen years old. Her long brown hair is recently washed and already springing up into curls, and she shovels quail eggs and toast into her mouth like she hasn't eaten in weeks. Jin warms up its abandoned plate that is still on the table, then sits. The girl glances up between bites. Keri ignores both of them as she bangs her pots and pans together in the storeroom. The girl's heart rate is quick, her breath rapid, but without any sign of anxiety or adrenaline.

"We smell to you?" Jin asks.

"What?" says the girl.

"You smell like girl. Not bad, just girl. Boy, man, woman, all have different scent. I can't smell neut. Wondered if familiarity or scentless," says Jin.

"Oh." The girl sniffs loudly. "No, all I smell is these weird eggs. Not at all like our chickens back home. Tei said you guys have heightened senses and stuff, but I didn't know how much." She pauses with the fork halfway to her mouth. "Hey, does it bother you if I call you 'guys,' or is there some other word I should use?"

"Guys okay, most neuts here don't care. Not he-she, though. It," says Jin.

"Isn't there something you'd rather be called than 'it'? Most people think of that as an insult," says the girl, already refocused on her food.

"But we are 'it.' Not male, not female, not other gender. No gender at all."

The reheated eggs are rubbery and unpleasant to swallow, but as Jin's body begins to absorb the desperately needed proteins, its brain sends out signals of pleasure entirely unrelated to taste.

The girl looks thoughtful. "I just remember hearing a rabbi talk one time when I was a little girl about how God isn't really male or female, not the way we understand them, but something beyond both. So I asked why we didn't call God 'It' instead of 'Him,' and he looked at me like I was trying to club him to death and told me it was disrespectful."

"Some neuts agree," says Jin, examining the girl's guileless eyes, "but word isn't disrespectful. Reminds people what we are."

The girl swallows the last of her eggs and starts spreading prickly pear-jalapeño jam on her toast. After the first bite, she coughs and gulps down her water, sputtering and wiping her dripping eyes. Jin silently places its own plain toast on the girl's plate and sets the jam-covered slices aside, shaking its head. It isn't sure if Keri did that to the girl on purpose, or if she simply didn't think that someone from another region might not expect the spices common to the New Mexico desert.

When her sputters die down, the girl continues, undistracted. "Why do you all talk so funny? Except for Keri, I mean. But she's a regular human—sorry, um, a gender. She told me it drove her nuts when she first came here not to have anyone who talked like her, but she was already used to Bruvec and Net, so I guess it wasn't that big of a deal. But she wouldn't tell me why you talk like that, only that most neuters do."

"Most here do. All know gen speech, use up top to blend in easier," says Jin.

"Yeah, that makes sense, so your doctor people can sound professional and not scare their patients. So are you just born talking that way?" says the girl.

Jin smiles. Genders are the ones who were born talking, especially this one.

"Brain works different. Faster, more efficient. This way more natural for us. Gets point across, not fancy," says Jin.

The girl shakes her head slowly, munching on the plain toast with caution, then enthusiasm. "Don't you ever just have casual conversations? You know, 'how's the weather,' even if you don't care how the weather is? Or telling someone about what you did all day even if it's not important?"

"Some do, maybe. Don't really know," says Jin.

The girl snorts. "What a lively bunch you are."

Keri bursts out laughing from the archway of the storage room. "You'll have better luck having a casual conversation with those crumbs on your plate than a neut. Won't she, Jin?"

Jin shakes its head and finishes breakfast. If the girl wants to learn about neuts, it will let her learn. But Keri is right. So much talk is tiring Jin out, distracting it when it really needs to be thinking about the new plague.

A study is one thing, but that will only give it the mechanics of the disease it wants to create. The delivery mechanism, contamination, and occulted antidote Jin always includes, these are the parts of a plague that take thought and time and the kind of attention to detail that few, even among neuters, can achieve. With a nod to the new girl and Keri, Jin clears its plate and heads through the shadowed passageways toward the labs.

## CHAPTER 4

She had fallen asleep in the field behind the barn again. That was the first thought the earthy smell and cool air brought to Sandy's mind. She was wrapped in sheets and blankets, though, and the steady hum of some sort of generator sounded just on the verge of her conscious hearing.

Underground.

Each morning had been the same since she had gotten here. The lights would gradually brighten at a preset time, waking her slowly. Next, the memories would come. Yesterday, her heart had begun pounding, and she'd had to open her eyes to reassure herself that the weight of all the rock above her wasn't crushing down, trapping her. Only going out through the doorway had eased her fear, and it hadn't truly left until she was in the kitchen with Keri, talking over sweetened tea and oiled toast.

Today she breathed slowly. Maybe it was better down here. Some part of her mind thought that she ought to miss the fresh air, the squawk of the chickens, her mother's gruff voice telling her to stop watching her shows and get back to her schoolwork or get up and start on her chores.

Now she had a secret world to explore, and Mom had never liked it when she lazed about in bed half the morning. She opened her eyes halfway, peering through a tangled curl that had fallen across her face.

"Ready to get up?"

Her eyes focused on the doorway, to the neut called Bruvec, an ancient-looking little person who might have been laughable if he—it—weren't so serene.

She pulled herself out from under the covers. The chill wasn't bad enough to make her shiver, but she pulled on the robe and slippers that had been left for her.

"Any plans for today?" Bruvec asked.

"I hadn't, I mean, I didn't know...what kind of plans can I make?" said Sandy.

She automatically returned the old neut's twinkling smile.

"Your choice," it said.

That didn't help much, considering she had no idea what there was to do in this place, let alone what was taboo. The neuts she had met so far were hardly helpful, speaking in their stripped-down sentences that she had to repeat to herself three times before she understood. Keri was little better, claiming she enjoyed the company then complaining that Sandy talked too much. Still, at least she was familiar.

"Can I go get some breakfast?" she asked.

"Of course. No food shortage here. Well, not much. We grow some, have funding to buy what's needed. You won't starve."

Sandy hadn't even thought of that. Growing up on the farm, they had never worried about a shortage of food, even if her mother was never able to get a contract with even the lo loc restaurants in town. Certainly, there were years when direct and grocery store sales were bad or a disease hit the flock and she grew sick of eating eggs and corn and squash every day, but starvation was never an issue as long as the snowmelt ensured plenty of fresh water for the area. Hearing Bruvec made her realize it was a likely option for her now. She had no idea how long the neuts would let her stay.

"Eggs and toast again?" said Keri, hardly glancing at the two of them when they entered the kitchen.

"Whatever isn't too much trouble. I can just put together something myself," said Sandy.

Keri whacked at her hand with a real wooden spoon. "Sit. I'll do it."

"Be nice, Ker," said Bruvec. "Girl's just trying to help."

"Mm-hmmm," said Keri.

Sandy sat down at the table, unsure what to do with herself. Bruvec sat across from her and poured tea from the pot that steamed between them.

"What you do before?" asked Bruvec.

Sandy told it about the chicken farm and school. She also told it about the things she used to do, back before her dad left and took Ronnie, her brother, with him. Sailing on the nearby lake and doing what her dad referred to as "fishing," though there hadn't been any fish in the water for decades. The only true fishing she'd done was on the trout farm down in Idaho.

"No chickens here, and lakes too small to sail on, mostly. No fish. But books and school if you want in computing lab. Only check out from Net for research, though," said Bruvec, with a stern look.

Sandy smiled. No watching her shows in her room, then. She'd forgotten to take her pocketscreen's charger when she left with Tei, and the battery was long dead. Her mother would have approved.

"I don't know. I think I need to do something more active, I guess. I just feel like..."

She didn't know how to describe it. Her fingers furled and unfurled, her legs bounced up and down beneath the table. She had the strong urge to go running down the corridors, to yell and beat her fists against the wall, not out of anger or frustration, but just because she needed to do *something*. Her mother had often talked of having cabin fever in winter, but this was worse. She felt cocooned.

"I guess I'd like to learn something. Not just schoolwork. A trade, maybe, something to do when I have to go back up into the real world," she said. She didn't figure going back to the chicken farm was an option, even if she wanted to.

"Down here's as real as anything," said Keri. "What, you think this is imaginary ham?"

Keri set the plate in front of her, and the salty smell made her stomach gurgle. Her family had never really kept kosher, since her father thought the whole thing was silly and her mother hadn't bothered to argue. Still, she never served pork at home. Hunger won out, and Sandy took a bite. With the taste of the meat, memories flooded back to her—her father, taking her and Ronnie out for a clandestine breakfast at the local pancake house, full of bacon and ham and sausage. Her mother, when the three of them came home, shaking her head in mock disgust and telling them that if they turned into pigs, she wouldn't be the one to clean the sty.

"What, too salty for you?" said Keri.

Sandy looked up, realizing she'd simply stared at the plate after the first bite.

"No, it's fine. It's good, actually. I was just thinking about my mom."

"Well, don't," said Keri.

The words were harsh, but the hand on her shoulder was gentle, resting a moment before Keri moved away. The knowing half-smile, half-grimace on the older woman's face told Sandy she was only trying to help, that maybe she knew something about that kind of pain. Bruvec watched the two of them closely, but Sandy couldn't tell what thoughts were clustering behind its eyes. It let her finish eating in silence, then took her out to show her around.

She already knew the path from her room to the kitchen and from the kitchen to the bathing areas. The former was a short, flat corridor, sealed and painted so it looked more like a hallway than a tunnel through rock. Lights glowed from the walls day and night, though Sandy hardly knew what time was so far from the sun.

The second corridor was more natural. Smooth stones had been set into the floor, clean and polished so the dust didn't stick to her slippers, but the walls were unpainted, sealed only to contain the dust and minimize the human impact to the environment around them. Dark holes led off from this corridor, not only to the sides, but also above her and occasionally below. Bruvec taught her how to keep three points of contact to steady herself as she crept around the largest of these gaping chasms. They were lit and marked so no one would stumble into them, but kept open for airflow and because some of them led to other settled parts of the Network caves.

Sandy couldn't shake the feeling that something was watching her from each of these dark holes, but Bruvec waited patiently ahead, so she stopped looking over her shoulder and followed. After a stop in the bathrooms to wash and dress, it told her to leave her pajamas behind—no one would disturb them—and follow. She pulled on her familiar worn sneakers and did as she was told.

Not much farther along the corridor, the stone tiles stopped, and the floor dropped first into sealed rock, then natural dust, dirt, and stone. Sandy looked back behind them at the light, growing dimmer as Bruvec guided her into the wilder caves. It handed her a flashlight and switched on its own.

"You see? Three floor-holes past where tile stops is teardrop hole."

Sandy looked where the flashlight beam was pointing. Sure enough, a hole shaped roughly like a teardrop on its side opened out from the left side of the corridor where the floor rounded up into the wall. It was behind a slight protrusion in the wall, so she hadn't been able to see it until she was past and looked back.

"Any trouble, go through there," said Bruvec.

"You're kidding. That hole is barely the size of my head," said Sandy.

"You'll fit. Watch."

It lowered itself to its knees and squirmed through the hole, arms first, then head, shoulders, torso, legs, and feet. Its flashlight beam flicked around in the dark as it squirmed through.

"See? Easy. Even old neut like me can do. You try," it called back.

"Are you sure there's room down there for both of us?" said Sandy.

"Both and more," said Bruvec.

She crouched down and aimed her light. There was a narrow tunnel, about four feet long, that seemed impossibly small. After that, her flashlight picked out what seemed to be the roof of a low cavern stretching away. Bruvec's eyes moved into her light's beam.

"See? Opens out back here, drops down into cavern. Room for all."

"I can't," she said.

"Must. Safety," said Bruvec.

"What did you mean when you said to go through there if there's trouble? What kind of trouble?"

"Any. Maybe workers come through looking for new places to dump garbage, toxics. Maybe gen on run comes down here in panic. Maybe Network attacked, all neuts here in danger."

"Has that happened before?" asked Sandy.

"Not so bad we had to hide. Usually find out about researchers and dumpers before they come, redirect to other areas. No gen on run gotten this far yet, but someday might."

"Tei told me what you do," said Sandy, settling on her haunches outside the tiny hole.

"You mean plagues?" said Bruvec.

"Yeah."

"Also tell you about medics, researchers, teachers?" said Bruvec.

"Yes," said Sandy.

"Then no more stalling. Climb in. We'll talk more when you show you can protect self."

Sandy took a deep breath and tried to do as she was told. Once her chest was inside the hole, she couldn't inhale fully and had to fight not to panic and hyperventilate. Bruvec coaxed her gently the whole time, reassuring her that she hadn't much farther to go, that she was doing fine. She convinced herself several times over that she was going to die, stuck there in the tunnel with her feet sticking out into the corridor. Keri or one of the neuts would find her there, her legs curled and desiccated like the Wicked Witch of the East. She hoped Bruvec had another way out.

Then there were soft, warm hands on her arms, guiding her hands so she could brace herself on the rocks below and pull, catching her as she came free from the tunnel and dropped the few feet to the cavern floor.

"See? You did," said Bruvec.

The proud smile charmed away her frustration and the complaints that had built in her throat on the way through. She picked up the flashlight from where she had dropped it and looked around. The cavern was large, though low-ceilinged. She had to hunch over so as not to hit her head on the highest portions, let alone the stalactites that hung down like dull, giant teeth. Bruvec pulled a heavy limestone-colored drape over the tunnel opening, blocking out the last of the feeble light that shone from the corridor.

The sound of running water startled her, and she swung the flashlight around to see a small, incredibly clear stream running slowly through one end of the cavern.

"Water there, food there."

Bruvec pointed to a long line of sealed cases. It opened one, showing her dehydrated food packets and seeds that could be sprouted in water to grow with very little light.

"Half of local Network could live down here for year," it said proudly.

"Only half?" said Sandy.

Its face clouded, but it shrugged.

"Can't save all, all the time."

The lingering sadness in its eyes told her that it didn't want to believe its own words.

"Do you really think we're in danger down here?" she asked.

"We're prepared, not paranoid. Danger comes anywhere. We do what we can, live lives. All anyone can do."

"My mother used to say the same thing."

Bruvec reached out and held her hand briefly, flicking off its light after she turned off hers, letting the darkness settle in around them. In the absolute black, with a warm hand in hers, Sandy cried. Not the shaking sobs she expected, just near-silent tears that ran down her face and made little thumping sounds when they dropped off her chin. Her nose started running, but she didn't want to sniffle and break the silence, so she let it run. Finally, sticky and soggy and feeling a mess, she smeared her face with her sleeve and breathed in deeply, slowly. She squeezed Bruvec's hand and let it go, savoring a moment completely alone in the dark. The old prayer she had said over her mother came into her mind again, and she hummed its high, eerie chant although the words meant nothing to her now.

After a short while longer in silence, she flicked on her flashlight and pulled back the curtain to the corridor. A few jutting rocks gave her footholds to climb up to the tunnel's mouth, and then she was squirming through, drained and dirty and feeling better than she had in years, possibly in her whole life. Sadder, too.

She turned to Bruvec, who was just pulling itself out of the tunnel behind her. She wondered if she looked as dirty and bedraggled as it did, then remembered her runny nose and suspected she looked worse. Bruvec smiled at her, though, like a proud parent or a teacher whose student has just passed a difficult test. She supposed she had.

She walked back toward the bathrooms, thinking of little but a hot shower and clean clothes. She had seen stacks of neatly folded clothing in a cupboard near the showers, and had seen Keri pull her own outfits from these stacks in the morning. If that was the way things were done here, she would follow along, though she wished she had brought more of her own things from home.

"What did you sing?" asked Bruvec from behind her.

She had almost forgotten it was there in her rush to the baths. It followed her in, and she stood awkwardly in front of the small mirror, turning so she couldn't see her smudged face.

"It's an old prayer, the *sh'ma*, that my mom used to like," she said.

"Pretty," said Bruvec.

"You're supposed to say it in darkness, with your eyes covered or closed. It's symbolic. My eyes were open, but it felt like they were closed, so it just seemed appropriate."

"Symbol for your mother but not for you?" asked Bruvec.

"I just like the sound," said Sandy.

Bruvec smiled. "Me too."

It left her then, to her relief. She had been afraid it was going to stay and try to chat with her while she showered. Neuter or not, she wasn't about to let anyone do that.

She pulled a towel from the folded stack with her fingertips, not wanting to dirty it before she had the chance to get clean. Her robe was still sitting on a shelf from that morning, so she grabbed it, too, and pulled the shower curtain closed behind her, letting the water rinse away the mucous and grime.

For the most part Sandy was left alone, and it was driving her crazy. She wandered into the computing lab, wondering if she should contact some of her friends. The few who were local would want to know where she was, and all of them would want to know why she wasn't in Montana anymore. Maybe they'd already heard about what happened to her mother.

She sat in front of a blank screen, already positioned in a holder for the best angle, and propped her chin up on one hand. Over in the corner, Net worked silently. Sandy stole glances at it from time to time.

With most neuters, Sandy couldn't help thinking of them as male or female. The gender she applied might vary from day to day or encounter to encounter, but there was something almost unavoidable causing her to think of them as "he" or "she." Nothing about Net was gendered. The spots and wrinkles that brought Bruvec's face to life cloaked Net as if it were made from fabric. Its short, solid frame carried extra pounds from years of being seated in front of the computer, bringing words like "pear" and "turtle" to mind. The round turtle eyes looked up from its screen and blinked twice at her.

"Help?" said Net.

"Oh, no. I was just daydreaming, I guess," said Sandy, but Net had already turned back to its own work.

Sandy played around on the intranet with her guest access code for a while, trying to find maps of the cavern system or anything else that might give her something to do. Everything she wanted seemed to be password protected.

She pushed back in frustration. She could access the shows she used to enjoy, but without the sound they were useless, and she was fairly certain Net would frown upon the music and dialogue cluttering up the silent lab. She didn't have a set of ear wires and wasn't sure she should ask. A rustle of fabric made her look up, and there was Net coming toward her.

"I'm sorry if I disturbed you. Look, I can go somewhere else if you want," said Sandy.

Net just shook its head and made a few selections on Sandy's screen, then went back to its own desk. When Sandy looked back at her screen, her mailbox was open to a new message. Net had sent her limited-access passwords to some of the Network files.

Smiling brightly at the oblivious neuter, she dived into the maps of the cave systems. They turned out to be essentially dull, nothing like the stomach-gripping walks through the tunnels themselves, where Bruvec had warned her to always keep track of her direction. Getting lost in the caverns was usually fatal.

There was little else of interest in the files she had access to, mostly general information that she had already learned from Bruvec and Keri and the somber neut named Jin. She printed out a few of the maps to take with her on an unfamiliar type of textured paper. She guessed the neuts didn't have access to the cow's parsnips that supplied most of the local Montana paper industry. With rough maps in hand, she left the silent lab.

So much of the underground world was silent, with the one constant noise being the inexorable hum of the generators. She meant just to get away from that noise, to go somewhere that she could think without being lulled by that steady undertone and its curious lack of any biofuel scent. She had her flashlight plus a spare for navigating the unlit tunnels between the common areas and the computing lab, so she found where she was on the map and set out to go a short way toward the surface.

She decided to take the path marked as the secondary entrance route, the one that led out into the wastelands near what was left of Lincoln National Forest. That way, she was less likely to be disturbed by any neuts coming home from their sojourns above, but still might be found eventually if she got lost.

The climb took most of her attention. The maps were full of cryptic symbols and notes that might have made sense to the neuter brain but for her were a complete mystery. There was no key or legend, just numbers and abbreviations and lines. She looked for signs of previous human presence and decided that the tiny column of three parallel lines at her current junction symbolized a ladder. She found slightly worn rocks that might be hand and footholds, so she climbed up and peered through the hole at the top.

A part of her knew that what she was doing was stupid, but it wasn't as if she was going far, and the path she was following matched the map perfectly so far.

The rock her foot was on cracked as she started to pull herself into the higher tunnel. Her fingers scrabbled at the floor and walls until she caught herself and landed, breathing heavily, facedown with her feet still dangling over the ledge. Getting back down was going to be hard.

She lay there for a while, letting the momentary panic fade. She inspected her hands for damage, but they were merely a little raw, not bleeding. She felt her nose where she had bumped it in her struggle, but again nothing was broken or bloody, and she realized half sheepishly that she was grinning.

Well, why not? This was fun. And despite the darkness, it was hard to feel like there was danger of any kind near. Danger of getting lost, yes, but she was going to be very careful about that. Human danger was far above her, and the animal life this far below the surface was limited to creepy-crawlies of the mostly nonpoisonous kind. Short of discovering something new, she was safer than in her own bed on the farm. Safer than she'd been in the chicken house, for sure.

The sound of slowly dripping water broke through her thoughts. She pulled herself to her hands and knees and crawled toward the sound. A chamber opened out ahead of her, just like on the map, and her jaw dropped open just a little as her flashlight shone around on stalactites at least five times her size, dripping slowly into a crystal-clear pool below. Each time a drop hit the water, ripples sent her light's reflection shimmering all around her. She wished suddenly that her brother was there to see it with her. Ronnie would have made up stories about creatures that lived in a place like this. He probably would have gone diving into the pool, too, no matter how shallow it seemed.

For a moment, she thought she heard his voice. But that couldn't be.

She froze, listening hard.

It wasn't a child's voice she heard, though by now, Ronnie would be old enough to have a lower register than she remembered. It wasn't the abbreviated speech of the neuters, either, though she couldn't make out individual words.

Sandy looked around for a place to hide. Shielding her flashlight with her hand and keeping its light away from the water, she sought out the kind of hole she could fit into without being obvious. There was no way to tell how close the voices were, or if they were coming in her direction.

She made the snap decision that it was worth taking the extra time to erase her footprints in the dust, but she had to uncover her light fully to do so. Fortunately, there were only a few spots with soft enough surfaces to hold a print, so she smeared them out quickly with her sleeve and squirmed her way feet-first into a long, curving tunnel that was just wide enough for her to breathe in shallow breaths. With her light off, she forced herself under control as much as she could and tried to listen above the sound of her pounding heart.

"Did you see that?" The voice was adult and male.

"See what?" Another man.

"I thought I saw a flash of light up ahead."

"Phosphorescence?"

"No. Looked like a flashlight that waved around and shut off. I just caught it out of the corner of my eye."

"Great. We've found one of those underground caverns with hallucinogenic gasses. I'll be sure to tell Cooper to name the gas after you."

"Knock it off, Weiler. The atmosphere readings are clear."

"Hey, you're the scientist. I'm just the engineer."

From the silence that followed, then the low whistle and exclamations of pleasant surprise, Sandy figured the men had found the cavern. She wished she could see them, then stopped the thought. At least there was no chicken wire or squawking.

"Will you look at that?" said the one called Weiler.

"Yeah."

"It'd be a shame to use this place."

More footsteps. Sandy held her breath, then let it out slowly when her head started to pound. If they found her, she would cry. Tell them she was a lost hiker and beg them to take her back to the top. She could say that she lost her provisions somewhere so they wouldn't question her about hiking with so little, but she had no explanation for her clothes. The comfortable linens of Home Cavern were hardly the kind of thing an experienced hiker would wear. Maybe if she cried some more, they just wouldn't ask questions.

She started working herself up into tears, which was harder than she thought it would be. She was scared, sure. With all that had happened recently she had reason enough to dissolve on command, but a part of the reason her heart still beat strongly was excitement. She had never been in a situation quite like this before. These men were researchers or some kind of exploration party, not murderers and rapists. While she knew there could be problems, it didn't feel like danger. It felt like fun.

"Look at this," said the man Weiler had called a scientist.

"How long do you think that's been there?" said Weiler.

"Hard to tell. I heard that back in the nineteen forties there were explorations deep into these caves, and again in the nineties, tens and the thirties. It's hard to tell the difference between footwear from two thousand on, so it could be from any of the later expeditions."

"It just doesn't seem right. This place feels like no one should have been here before."

"I thought you were an engineer, not a philosopher. I'm done with my readings. Let's go."

"Just a minute," said Weiler.

"Well, hurry up. I'm tired of eating this dried-up trash. Cooper said he'd buy when we got back to the surface."

"Almost done."

Barely audible electronic-sounding clicks reached Sandy's hiding place, then a rustle of equipment and the sound of the men's boots on the rock, drawing farther and farther away.

At the mention of eating, Sandy's stomach had produced a loud gurgle, but the rock around her must have insulated the sound, or the men had been too absorbed in their work to hear it. She struggled out of her hiding place, erasing her tracks again on the way out. Whatever the men were doing down there, Bruvec would want to know. She followed the paths back toward the populated caverns, moving as cautiously as her enthusiasm allowed. She felt like a spy returning from a mission. A spy who was very much looking forward to one of Keri's hot meals.

# CHAPTER 5

The sun quickly warms Jin's clothing and skin once it leaves the caverns. Above ground, foot travel is always enjoyable—the feeling of muscles stretching and contracting and the clarity of mind that comes with motion, making ready for the gathering of new information and the generation of new ideas. For now, there is no sack of death on its back. It is here to study and observe, to spend day after day just traveling and learning.

Raw desert gives way to shacktowns, where the poor are no longer driven off the arid lands, but instead have settled into makeshift homes pieced out of every material imaginable—broken cars, cardboard boxes, anything that can be found in the expansive landfills and pushed, dragged, or carried back to within walking distance of the rivers, streams, and rain collectors. Dying eucalyptus tree windbreaks separate the shacktowns from the blue-collar lo-loc subdivisions, complete with grocery stores, restaurants, and shopping areas. Beyond these, healthier breaks of various succulents give privacy and welcome shade to the larger estates situated far enough from the river that they must pay extra to have water shipped directly to their homes. Every home, rich or poor, has some attempt at a food garden, and this time of day a few children and older adults are out taking care of the plants, weeding and shifting canvas shades to protect the precious growing things from the sun.

There is so much the human mind knows, yet so much more to learn. In passing, Jin ghosts the people around it, not for the plague study, just to get to know them a little bit. Its stomach contracts as it ghosts the underfed shacktown children, but their synaptic firing is sharp and quick. Despite the hunger Jin feels in them, the youngest of the children are still strong and full of life. Only the pubescent ones begin to feel the effects of a lifetime of foul air and uncontainable waste, foods that are processed too much and water that is not processed enough.

In the heart of Carlsbad, everyone stays indoors, most of them crowding the long, rectangular buildings of the main water reclamation and processing facility for the area, counting the minutes left on the day shift. Others snatch a few last moments of sleep before they must awaken and prepare for a long night's work. Only a few people are out, mostly men who load and unload heavy plastic bottles from the trucks that line the streets, heating the already scorched pavement with their biofuel fumes of alcohol and animal dung. The local water business brings limited wealth, and the workers can't afford to waste their time, so they pay less attention to Jin than they do to the flies that fill the heavy air.

Jin continues north, back out into barren desert, listening to the music of the blood circling through its veins, filtering the smells that drift in from the landfills that lurk at the edges of its vision. The calluses on its feet thicken, and Jin feels them grow from inside and out. Even with all its awareness, the awareness of the entire Network, no one has yet figured out why gens can't feel inside themselves like neuts. Jin chills at the thought of not knowing its own body, not understanding where each sensation comes from. To have unknown pain, to be told of cancers eating away but not be able to locate and stop them; not to feel the heart rate increase, the white blood cells form and gather; not to be able to find infection and direct the immune system to create a cure from within… Terrifying.

Still, many neuts die in the plagues, too, and Jin understands. Spreaders infected from their own jars don't always realize the problem until too late, their minds focused on the dangers outside, not the ones they bring. But that is a risk, not the insurmountable barrier gens face between themselves and their own bodies. Jin thinks Tei may have been right. Spreading is a miserable life sometimes, but to maintain the health of the overall species, a certain amount of culling must be done. Here Jin's mind circles, step after step, as it moves toward the north, away from home.

Roswell looks empty as Jin crosses the city's southern border. The military institute fills the western half of town, while goat farms and trailer towns dominate the eastern section. Sandwiched in between, the main street of old downtown is preserved.

Jin peers into the windows in an effort to brand itself a tourist. High-priced plastic aliens stare back at it with their gaping black eyes as its ears scan the area for signs of activity. There are no street people, no poor people, no one outside without an immediate purpose. Even the tourists move from shop to shop with determination. A plague has been here recently, but something is wrong.

Jin approves of the location—spreaders must take care to hit near home sometimes or people might begin to suspect. But the Council is growing feeble-minded if it allowed a plague to take out the lower classes without a noticeable effect on others. It will have to ask Bruvec about that when it returns home; perhaps there's a balancing plague scheduled for the area, a common practice since not all delivery mechanisms can be demographic-agnostic.

In any case, the reduced population makes the area useless for a study. Bruvec was right, it needs passenger fare. Albuquerque is a long walk with limited food and money, and the area in between is almost entirely shacktowns, garbage dumps, and unshielded desert. Not the kind of place Jin needs. Not enough variety of humanity to study a city like the one it will target, the place it once called home.

Jin wanders along the main highway until it finds a screen advertising the local ride stop. Trucking companies with extra space in their cargo holds have listed their destinations and passenger fees. A pharmaceutical supply truck on the way from Dallas to Albuquerque lists a climate-controlled cargo area with cushioned seating for a reasonable fee, so Jin waits for that truck to come by.

The ride to Albuquerque should be a safe place to rest, but Jin can't relax. It never can sleep well away from home. There is too much unrest, too many people finding out the truth about neuters, or finding parts of the truth and making up the rest. It notices a crumpled flyer on the delivery truck's floor and straightens it out just to ease the boredom with something to read. The printout is from a group calling themselves "Citizens Against Generated Disease."

> In the 1980s, research groups reported to the American public that AIDS was the work of hate groups targeting homosexuals and drug users. Scientists denied these claims and the researchers were silenced, but were the claims ever really disproved?

Genders could think so close to the truth, yet still get the story all wrong. As far as Jin knows, humans didn't create the HIV virus; certainly not the Network, nor any other group Jin knows. The disease wasn't a product, but in a way, was the beginning. Some people of the late twentieth century thought that the major diseases of the time were nature's way of curbing the population. One neut decided the times were desperate enough that nature ought to be helped along.

Neuters didn't know each other then, didn't have anything like the Network. One neut named Rumbauch worked alone, studying chemistry, neurology, everything it could, as most neuts naturally tend to do. With their brains free from the constant mating dance that absorbs even a celibate gender's mind, other thoughts and drives must fill the time.

Rumbauch saw that the balance between the population and the available resources for a healthy life was out of hand and getting worse by the minute. The only population control left to the public was to shoot, knife, or nuke each other, leaving the vicious in charge and the rest dead or well on their way.

So Rumbauch became the first spreader.

A few years later, Rumbauch and other neuts formed the Network as a way to coordinate their varied interests, ensuring that the slaughter was balanced by contributions to the knowledge and health of humanity as a whole, as well as research into sustainable food and water supply and waste management. The latter failed to keep up with the growth, however.

The cheap paper of Jin's flyer tears as it turns to the back panel. So close to the truth, but the story is all wrong.

> How many innocents have died at the whims of these creatures who dare to walk among us with faces like ours, bodies like ours, yet no hearts to guide them? Men, women and children who have done no harm are slaughtered as casually as you might step on an ant. Who has given these people the right to play God? Only their knowledge of science, which separates them from true Godliness.

Jin tries to think of anyone who has done no harm, ever. Predators in every city pick off the wrong sort of targets, leaving survivors who only make things worse, less civilized. Controlled plagues are different. They strike only where they are most needed and stay contained within the area. The deaths are quick and virtually painless. Neuters know their biochemistry.

And in Jin's plagues, there is always a way out. Like the plague in Amarillo, where the death toll is already on the rise. No one needs to die from that one. All they have to do is wash their hands after using the restroom. The sign tells them. If they work at the restaurant, their training tells them. Mothers teach their children, even if they can't read. Common sense, cultural mores. Even most animals will clean after they soil. But enough people don't use their sense, so the population drops to a healthier level. All the best for the human race. Simple as that.

The truck comes to a stop and Jin finds Albuquerque is just what it needs—a real city, overcrowded with all types of people. It checks into a cheap motel and is grateful that the shower works. The filth from the truck and the foot journey are washed down the drain in quick, hot bursts, and Jin falls into bed before its hair is dry, smelling of strong soap and chlorine that doesn't quite cover the water's murky history.

The room isn't bad for the price. There is no need for a second shower to wash off invisible dirt or crawling insects from the bed sheets when it wakes up. Restored, Jin steps out into the warm evening and finds a tiny, overcrowded lo-loc diner. The wait for a table isn't long, but once there, the waitress takes nearly half an hour to come around. Jin is content to sit and wait.

The menu glorifies the locally produced foods, presenting them as if the diner served them by choice, rather than to avoid cross-country shipping costs and reliance on unstable food production in other areas, where the local population would take precedence over exports out to the desert dwellers.

"What can I get for you, hon?" the waitress says to Jin. "Soup of the day is corn chowder and the tamale plate's on special."

"Plain goat loin. Please," says Jin.

Saying the word "please" feels odd. It is out of practice with common grammar.

"Soup or salad?" says the waitress.

"Salad, no dressing. Water, please."

The waitress nods and weaves her way through the tables. Jin's saliva starts to flow. On the trip to Roswell it ate nothing but nuts and dried fruit. The brain wears down on travel food. For this study, Jin needs to be sharp, and without Keri there to play both cook and mother, it must remember to care for itself.

The salad greens make Jin's mouth ache in joy at the first bitter tang of meaty dandelion and kale. It takes a drink quickly so anyone looking won't notice the drool. The goat meat is gone before it remembers to breathe between bites.

Jin leans back into the booth's goatskin-covered plastic cushions, eyes closed. Pure real food is always bliss. Keri tries to dress up her cooking too often for its tastes, although it has never heard others complain. Jin's tongue may like the flavors, but its brain wants no distractions when it is on a study or spreading trip. Its body absorbs the food, the systems soaking up nutrients and breaking down everything into usable parts until there is only the slightest amount of waste.

The waitress catches Jin's eye and comes toward the booth, glancing over her shoulder. Even without ghosting, Jin can tell the woman is nervous. Her breath is quick and Jin can smell the sweat triggering her chemical deodorant.

"Get out of here kiddo, the meal's on me," she says.

"I can pay," says Jin.

"You're too young to be out on your own. There are some bad sorts around here," she says, visibly stopping herself from taking another glance behind her. "You just go home to your parents or whoever and be glad for the life you have, no matter how rotten it is. Go straight home. Now."

Her heart is ticking fast, her system overloading on chemicals she doesn't understand. Jin slides out of the seat, leaving a generous tip. Covertly, it scans the direction the waitress is once again checking. A young man, lightly bearded, spins slowly back and forth on one of the stools at the counter. His blue eyes are harsh and too bright, and when he sees Jin he grins nastily. Jin returns his cold, dead stare for a moment, then steps out into the city haze.

Neuter Network Archive
Pamphlet #CX75041-61
Sightings: AZ, CO, NM, TX, UT, CA
First Record: 12.18.75 Malfax, AZ
Origin Unknown

Citizens Against Generated Disease

Is God punishing us for our sins? One look at the world around you, and you will say yes. But ask yourself this: What sins have your children committed, to be cut down in their youth? What are the sins of the old storekeeper who fed his family for sixty years? Grave enough sins to cut them down without mercy, to target not only individuals but whole families, whole cities?

In the 1980s, research groups reported to the American public that AIDS was the work of hate groups targeting homosexuals and drug users. Scientists denied these claims and the researchers were silenced, but were the claims ever really disproved?

Citizens Against Generated Disease (CAGeD) is an organization founded to uncover and eradicate a group whose principles are so anti-society, so anti-life that they would dare to take the powers which God has named His own into their own hands.

How many innocents have died at the whims of these creatures who dare to walk among us with faces like ours, bodies like ours, yet no hearts to guide them? Men, women and children who have done no harm are slaughtered as casually as you might step on an ant. Who has given these people the right to play God? Only their knowledge of science, which separates them from true Godliness.

These are the people killing your cousins, your mothers, your husbands, your friends. We need your power to help us fight this menace so none of us will ever be CAGeD again.

# CHAPTER 6

The blue-eyed man leaves the diner about fifteen minutes after Jin. There is no expression on his face, yet he still looks cruel somehow. Just a turn of the eyebrows, maybe. He walks down alleys, poking in trash cans, while Jin watches from a distance, listening. An outsider wouldn't notice how its body moves slightly in keeping with his, its limbs performing mere ghosts of his movements. Most of the motion is internal, the intent toward action rather than the action itself, but the intent is enough to allow Jin's brain to process like his, to find his sensations. Blue-eyes' breath and pulse are within the normal range for a young male, his muscles tense, his motions quick. He's impatient, restless. He kicks rocks out of his way and stomps at pigeons. Brain chemicals don't tell Jin what he is angry about, they only say that he is angry, frustrated, in need of release.

He finds a sleeping cat, scrawny and striped, too lethargic to run. He picks the cat up, holding it in front of his face and glaring while the cat yowls. Jin kicks a rock into his heel, and he turns slowly, still holding the cat by the scruff of its neck. He smiles.

"Will you look at that, cat? It's my little friend from the diner. See, kitty, my little friend wants to rescue you from whatever horrible fate I might have in store for you."

His eyes are dilated, his brain a chemical soup of anger, slight fear, and anticipation. Jin continues to ghost his movements, locking them in memory.

"No, I don't think so," says Blue-eyes. "Not today, friend."

He throws the cat at Jin and slips away while Jin sorts claws from skin. He is quick and smarter than Jin suspected. It can't find any trace of him by sound or scent by the time the cat calms down enough to let Jin pluck the claws from its shirt and tangled hair. The cat sniffs Jin's mouth.

"Sorry. No meat left," Jin tells it.

The creature runs off and Jin walks down the shadowed streets, memorizing the layout of the city. It knows the maps already, but standing on the streets is different. It finds five good hiding places, three potentially useful shortcuts, and several dead-end alleys to avoid. It does not find any sign of study cases, so it turns back to take advantage of one night in an almost-clean bed.

At daybreak, Jin checks out of the hotel. Foregoing breakfast, it browses the public screens as well as the free rack displays in the entrance of one of the local grocery stores, the only place to find printed local news except the hi-loc drink bars. Flyers for "CAGeD" are joined by a group called "Killers Among Us" and an ad for a new bar in town proclaiming, "Gay's okay; worms go away." The schools all still teach the same drill: male and female are the only options for anyone other than worms. Jin is irritated by the misnomer. Worms are generally hermaphroditic, not genderless, but no one asked for its opinion on the matter.

It takes a copy of each flyer to file in the archives. The Network uses them to track the spread of information about neuts and what they do. So far, the consensus is that neuts are still safe from the masses of humanity for a while. Knowledge of them remains at the fringes of social awareness, highly inaccurate and relegated to rumor. The Citizens Against Generated Disease group doesn't know about neuts; whoever wrote about "worms" shows no evidence he or she knows about the plagues. Jin checks the "Killers Among Us" flyer.

> Now is the time to stand up. Now is the time to fight back. Among us are the killers—silent, deadly killers—and their next victim WILL be YOU!
>
> Who knows where the next disease will strike? Maybe the neighbor you borrow tools from is playing mad

> scientist in his basement. Maybe the paperboy went a little too far with his chemistry set.
>
> Because you DON'T KNOW, you will be UNPREPARED. That is why KILLERS AMONG US is here.
>
> KILLERS AMONG US has a full line of health and safety products from basic food and hand sanitizers to airborne agent filtering masks. We also carry ancient herbal cures that have been lost to mankind for hundreds of years! Contact us today for your sample catalog and FREE list of ten lifesaving tips!

Jin picks up an extra copy of the flyer for Bruvec. The old neut will get a good laugh. The address listed for the organization is in Albuquerque, but there is a chance no one in the Network has seen one yet. In the next market, Jin finds a few other old flyers that mention either neuts or disease, but the archives already have them on file.

The streets are full of the average workday crowd—delivery trucks belching a variety of fumes, bicycle couriers, maintenance workers—not useful at the moment for Jin's study. The Network already has that kind of thought pattern on file. After checking several alleys that hold only school kids cutting classes, Jin stops at a lo-loc clinic to check in with the Network. The receptionist hands it a tethered hardscreen, and Jin fills in its name as Jin Bruvec. All neuts in the area know Bruvec, and if the Network medic is in today, it will know what Jin is and why it's there. Reason for the clinical visit? Jin writes down "migraine." It risks getting tossed out without the receptionist even passing its charts to the doctor, but a headache is one of the few safe ailments to claim if the neuter medic isn't in. A neut can't even take off its shirt safely in front of gendered doctors. The lack of reproductive organs frightens people, makes them dangerous. Especially the medics.

Fortunately for Jin, when it was born its parents couldn't afford the series of operations that would have built a female out of their sexless child, so the doctors told them to raise it as a girl and tell no one about the difference. By the time the difference was overtly noticeable to others, Jin was on its own.

"The doctor will see you now, Jin."

The doctor's clothes and hair are styled to look female, but Jin detects no smell other than the acrid odor of the makeup the neut uses to make itself appear older.

"What?" says the doctor as soon as the door to the exam room closes. At least this clinic has real doors, unlike the curtained makeshift rigs in smaller low-income areas.

"About Taylor," says Jin. "Autopsy done?"

"Twenty-four stab wounds, died from blood loss," says the doctor.

"Figured cause. Any disease found?"

"None."

Jin takes this as bad news. The spreader, Taylor, was not weakened, just hit. Twenty-four times.

"Careful, Jin," says the doctor. "They…"

"What?"

The neut just shakes its head.

"Tried to make it 'girl'?" Jin asks.

The doctor nods. "Deepest cut, knife in to the hilt, judging from bruising. Ripped through intestines, punctured left kidney when Taylor struggled."

Jin leaves. There is nothing new to learn from the doctor. Genders fear what they don't understand, and the way they choose to understand neuters is to make them into something they don't fear. Women. As if carving a slit through the tiny neut urethra would suddenly give it estrogen and ovaries and an acceptable biochemical flow.

Jin wanders the city all day looking for trouble, finding none that suits its criteria. In a city like Albuquerque, with its bloated film and art industries and accompanying tourism, crowds are too thick for any criminals worse than thieves and pickpockets. Even the hidden nooks and crannies are far from private. As the sky darkens, the crowds thin a little. Jin is glad when it can finally stop pulling away from its own skin and walk without rubbing against other bodies. It walks down alleys, trying to draw out a subject. Keri said it looked vulnerable, yet so far no one has tried to take the advantage. *Come get me*, it thinks.

Perhaps it is too alert, too aware. It slows, then sits, slumped against a wall and feigning sleep. *Come get me now.*

The darkness deepens. Streetlights cast dirty shadows onto the asphalt, and Jin dozes slightly, its ears still open for sounds of trouble.

"Come on, sugar. Let me see what you got."

Jin follows the voice down the street to its left, turns right for one block, left again, then straight four blocks, and to the right. It smells two people, a woman and a man. Two hearts beat quickly. One flutters in fear, the other is strong with excitement and malice. Jin moves closer, and the scent of man grows stronger. It starts to ghost him, then changes its mind and switches to the woman. It must know her brain chemistry at the moment of attack. The man can be studied later, especially if Jin can get him to attack itself. It watches the woman closely, absorbing the ghosted movements into its mind and muscle memory for later study.

Her body is drawn in tight. Her eyes cast around for help, for escape. She can't see Jin in the shadows, its internal patterns becoming hers. Jin feels the adrenaline give them both strength. *Kick, bite, yell, woman!* it wants to scream. It stops that thought. It must study what is, not what it wants her to do.

The woman's whole body cowers from the man's right hand, and Jin feels the rush of electrochemical messages that stimulate terror. It cannot see a weapon, but its nerves send the message of warm gunmetal pressed into the side of the woman's throat. Hatred rips through the victim and she struggles in spite of her fear, finding courage in the pain where the brick wall bites into her back. Caught in the moment, Jin feels her strength and forgets itself. It becomes the woman. No longer controlling the ghosting, it struggles, kicks, and fights in miniature tremors, not realizing that the woman's limbs won't obey because they aren't connected to the messages its mind sends. It feels the woman's body tear and the small trickle of blood and other fluids, then the raw exposure and emptiness muted by shock.

"Thanks, bitch."

The man drops the woman to the ground and leaves, not bothering to hurry.

Self-hatred fills Jin, a feeling as if it is contaminated by some slowly decaying plague. It struggles to shake off the sense of the woman's body and come back to itself. Epinephrine residue courses through veins, both its and hers. *Stupid Jin*, it lashes itself. It allowed itself to get too caught up in the ghosting. It could have stepped in to help the woman somehow. *Just like gen watching others mutilate neuts.* But Jin won't just walk away like the attack never happened. It goes to the woman.

"You okay?" says Jin.

"Get the hell away from me, just get the hell out!" She flails at Jin, scratching and biting.

"Sorry. Really. Should have helped. Couldn't...didn't think. Sorry. Can I help now? Get you to doctor? Home?"

The woman scrambles deeper into the shadows, grasping around for something to throw. Jin backs away, searching for a sound to tell it which direction the man went so it can find him and at least try to complete the study. Maybe keep others like him from doing this again, let the human race strengthen instead of just grow. It hears the scraping of gravel as the woman runs off in another direction.

The search is fruitless. The man is long gone.

Jin finds a boarded-up apartment building on the edge of town that serves as the urban version of a shacktown and seems a safe place to rest. No sense in wasting the Network's money on another night in the hotel. The other transients don't bother it. One look tells them Jin has nothing worth stealing. A woman waves it toward an empty spot beneath a broken window. Jin sits, shaking, empty and cold. The woman in the alley was right to attack it. Only a sick person watches its fellow human being tortured without helping. It didn't even get the man so it could finish its study. Useless. Still, it has the woman's complete experience to work with. That will help.

The room is too crowded with foul-smelling bodies and their waste. Jin pulls itself up a broken staircase, searching until it finally spots an empty apartment on the seventh floor. It bends the broken lock on the door back into place behind it as much as it can, then sits with its back against what remains of the kitchen counter.

*Relax, remember.*

It feels itself back in the alley, not as an observer, but as the woman herself. Muscles and nerves creep inward from the skin as it feels the barrel of the gun at her neck. Lungs pull desperately for air. Chemicals trigger fear, disbelief. Bricks are solid and rough against her back. There is no way out. Desperation and the sound of tearing cloth. Panic cuts through the disbelief, and feelings become more detached. The sense of time slows. Air caresses her bared skin, and there is a momentary feeling of arousal immediately cut by hatred, pure and deep. An agonizing loathing of man and men and woman-self. The pain and disgust last forever, every movement etched with crystal clarity.

When the attack is over, the pain lingers. Revulsion makes the cycling of blood nauseating, and a complex firing of neurotransmitters carries to Jin the woman's guilt at not fighting harder, not getting away. Anger, humiliation, hatred, self-loathing, life-loathing.

Jin forces its breath to reach deeper and returns to itself. For a moment it is confused, looking down and finding no blood to wipe away. When it recovers enough, it eats and drinks a little from the supplies in its pack. As soon as the food settles, it turns back to the memory again, this time to focus on respiration.

Breath held.

Rapid, shallow.

Hold, gasp, hold. Not enough oxygen reaches the brain.

Gasp, cry, hold.

Ragged, uneven, shallow-deep-shallow.

There is not enough air to move the diaphragm. No air down to parts of her body the woman now wants to ignore.

No air.

Gasp, shallow breaths, cry.

Jin forces itself back out of the memory to eat, drink, and rest, then turns back inward to the woman's circulatory system.

Heart rapid, pulse strong.

Pulse weakens, circulation pulls in, saving strength for vital organs.

For a few seconds the system shuts down completely, then restarts.

Strong, sickening heartbeat, too heavy in the stomach.

Jin pulls back out and rests.

And slips back in, analyzing each system, separating chemicals and impulses, through the night and into day. It relives the woman until all of her reactions are cataloged, everything is separated and stored in its memory. The sooner it can get back to the Network computers and record everything there, the better. It never carries one with it—the brain is the most portable computer it knows. For now, it nibbles on a few more nuts and raisins, lacking the strength to find other food. Its water is nearly gone, but it is too tired to care.

Jin sleeps until dark, when a rattling at the door awakens it. An old man, reeking of alcohol, breaks through the lock and stumbles in. Jin wonders how he managed seven crumbling flights of stairs. It picks up its pack, and the old man tips his cap.

"G'day, kid, you got a smoke?"

Jin shakes its head and hands him a few of its remaining nuts and raisins as it leaves.

The early evening crowds are still thick when Jin enters the street. It has enough money left for two nights at a good hotel or several decent meals, then passenger fare back to Roswell. It wanders toward the outlying portions of the city, preferring food to a comfortable bed. A hi-loc grill is open, which Jin usually avoids, but in a tourist town like Albuquerque, it shouldn't stand out from the crowd. It pulls on the cleanest shirt from its pack and sits in a goat-suede-lined booth, ignoring the highly polished grain of the eucalyptus-wood table. Eyes closed, it checks over its body. Pulse is weaker than normal, glucose levels severely out of balance. Synapses fire too slowly. This is no good for a study trip. It must be quick and alert, or it will prove Bruvec right and not live long enough to die in one of its own plagues. No bravery, just stupidity and the stubbornness Bruvec says it is known for. It casts an eye down the flexscreen menu, past the peccary pâté with cactus fruit reduction and the hand-cut double-cooked queso-stuffed plantain. Its zooms in on the images of the restaurant's private greenhouse, where lemons, limes, and tomatoes are grown in the former parking lot. A rooftop vegetable garden provides the peppers, tubers, and other spices for the local dishes.

"Are you ready to order?" says a young waiter.

He has dark, friendly eyes and clothing and skin so clean Jin has to blink from the dazzle. It remembers to smile.

"Medium-well steak, spinach chard salad, no dressing, water and sage lemonade."

"I like a customer who gets right to the point. I'll have your salad out in just a moment. Uh, and restrooms are right over there if you want to wash up."

Jin looks down at its hands. The palms are clean enough, but the backs and wrists are full of dirt. Its face is probably worse. The sheepish smile it shows the waiter this time comes without thought.

As it passes the counter, a strong, familiar heartbeat catches its attention. Blue-eyes. The pulse has the same urgency as his had in the alley the other night. Jin looks down the barstools, but only a heavyset woman and her scrawny male companion, obviously tourists, are at the counter. Jin chooses the men's room and scrubs its arms, face, and neck as well as it can. It can't do anything about its clothes.

The waiter delivers the salad as soon as Jin returns. The greens absorb its full attention for a while, the thick grain of spinach and the sponginess of hard-boiled quail egg, the cool smack of red peppers and crunch of pecans, the iron being absorbed into its system. Ecstasy.

"How is everything?" says the waiter.

"Good," says Jin. Better than good. Suede booths aren't the only reason hi-loc places cost more.

"Your steak will be right out."

At the mention of meat, saliva floods Jin's mouth in preparation for the protein, the thick, nutrient-rich flesh. The peccary steak more than lives up to the anticipation, lightly rubbed with local seasonings and grilled slowly over mesquite flame. After the next spread, it should take a vacation. Let Bruvec give it plenty of money to travel to hi-loc diners throughout the Southwest, maybe move east into Louisiana and try the Cajun food. Study anything, as long as the food is good. It washes down the last divine taste of meat with sage-infused fresh lemonade, thinking further about taking that Louisiana trip.

"Don't worry about the check, your meal's paid for," says the waiter with a smile.

Jin wonders if it really looks that helpless to gens.

"Appreciated, but I can pay," says Jin.

"Not necessary. The guy over at the counter picked up your tab. Said you looked like you could use a friend."

Jin knows before it turns who will be sitting there, but it looks over at the counter all the same. The couple from earlier is gone. Behind a stout middle-aged man in business attire Blue-eyes swings around on his stool and stares at Jin with a sharp-edged grin. Jin thanks the waiter and picks up its pack, pushing past the new influx of diners to reach the counter.

"What you want?" it says to the man.

His eyes glint hard, sky blue with too-wide pupils. He smells of youth and man, his pulse even stronger than Jin remembers.

"I noticed you were new in town," he says, then deliberately turns back to his food.

Jin sees no point in talking to his back.

Everyone outside walks in small groups, clusters brushing against each other and bouncing off and on their way. Jin walks alone up and down the streets, listening, hearing nothing but the normal noises of a city at night. Human voices, the movement of rats and night birds. The animal sounds take over as the town falls away into junkyards and landfill. The stench of rot and the sounds of scavengers grow.

Jin weaves around the wastelands and back into the city's historic district. The streets are oddly empty with the vendors packed away, no silver-and-turquoise jewelry spread out on the sidewalks to attract the tourists. It continues to walk.

The city stretches farther than it remembers, completely surrounding the petroglyph monument, reaching out into what used to be plains. Film studios, museums, and hi-loc restaurants fill the streets as actors in tinted pedicabs and even private cars drive by. Tourists use their pocketscreens to fight over control of the high-res former traffic cameras to capture the celebrities' pictures and drop them to friends across the globe. Jin veers south, back into the wastelands, to find a spot among trash heaps as far as possible from the stink of the most recent garbage. With its pack laid out beneath its head, Jin lets its tired eyes rest on the few visible stars.

Hard dirt makes an awkward bed, and bugs tickle Jin awake every time it begins to drift off to sleep. Eyelash-legs crawl slowly up its sun-soaked skin, and Jin tries to send a shudder rippling down its body like a horse shaking off flies. Human muscles weren't made for that. Tomorrow, it knows it will itch.

Jin wakes up near dawn to cold, gray sky. It eats a handful of pecans as it rolls up its blanket, torn between savoring the morning and hurrying back to work. Voices creep in from the north, and Jin heads toward them, still chewing. Male voices, two men, both angry.

"If you're not out of my sight in five seconds flat, I'll shoot you where it hurts the most and watch you bleed to death slowly," says a man whose voice is edged with fury. Real fury, not actors rehearsing lines.

The footsteps of the other man stagger away, crashing through junk heaps in his hurry to disappear. Now Jin is close enough to see them. The first man raises his voice to reach across the wasteland.

"And if you ever touch her again, I'll shoot you first and warn you afterward!"

The yelling man is of no use to Jin. Anger is not the same as malice. It follows the other man until it is close enough to smell a woman on him. His heartbeat is rapid and he smells of sweat. The blood dripping from his bruised nose is nothing serious. Underneath the sweat is the strong odor of sex, but no trace of female blood or fear. The man is no rapist. Sex with another man's willing wife or girlfriend is of no interest to Jin.

It turns back toward the main part of the city. Old Town looks more familiar in daylight as the sidewalks sparkle with jewelry and tapestries. The air is full of the smells of grease, bodies, cinnamon, and peppers.

"Spare some change?" asks a filthy woman sitting on the curb.

Jin shakes its head and continues walking. The woman gets up and follows.

"Wait up a sec, will you? I can tell you're no billionaire, but I got kids to feed."

People walk by, ignoring the woman's pleas to Jin. Beggars are none of their business.

"Any little bit helps. My husband died in the plague down in Montgomery, and I ain't never been trained for no job. No one else to watch the kids."

"Sorry," says Jin.

Too late, it hears a man coming up on its left. He takes Jin's arm and a blade point pricks its side. The woman babbles on, leading Jin and its captor through the crowd. They follow her into a shop and out the back door to an alley filled with dumpsters. The woman still chatters while the man guides Jin along, his knife never leaving its side. Jin stops listening to the words, turning its attention to their bodies.

Pulses are on the high end of normal, blood pressure the same. The man is tense, holding Jin's arm and the knife in a steady, binding grip. Jin ghosts him, feeling his brain chemicals surge. Excitement, anticipation, the hunger of both stomach and hormones, wariness, desperation…

"You don't scare easy, do you?" says the woman. "That's okay, that's fine. We been watching you. Saw you around yesterday, the day before that. You've got no home, do you? Nobody looking for you. That's good, see, because we really want your help."

Jin transfers some of its attention to the woman, finding a similarity that comes from years of close contact or a family relation. They are probably brother and sister.

"Quiet, too," says the man. "I like that in a...hey, what are you anyway? Lily and I were trying to guess. You a boy or a girl?"

The woman glares at him, silent for the first time.

"Oh, Lil, come off it. Doesn't matter if they know our names, now does it? I tell you that every time. I'm Bill, kid. Billy and Lily. Kinda cute, right?" says the man.

"I think she's a girl. Boys get all sputtery when you can't tell, girls figure maybe they're safer if you don't know. Well, don't you worry honey, we aren't gonna hurt you like that," says Lily.

"Oh, I don't know, she might be pretty if we cleaned her up," says Bill.

Right there. Jin sharpens its focus on Bill. Something just shifted in the man, causing a reaction in the woman, too. It ghosts both, one after the other, and locks the patterns into its memory. This time it is careful not to become so fully absorbed that it forgets itself.

Excitement escalates in the pair, blocking out all fear. Now both are eager.

"Yeah, a little sport might be fun. Just 'cause we're doing our civic duty doesn't mean we can't have a little fun with it. Who's gonna know?" says Bill, and Lily smiles after only a slight hesitation.

They are still moving farther from the tourist and business crowds, closer to territory Jin knows. It puts on a show of fear and resistance, letting the gens think it is afraid to approach the derelict district. Lily nods toward a brick building likely to be empty this time of day while the resident squatters are scrounging for food. Jin hears rats, roaches, and pigeons. The breath of a couple of transients too far gone to notice them or care. A heart rate is up, but Jin can't tell if the sound belongs to Bill, Lily, or itself. It tries to separate them. The male and female smells are stronger, indicating both fear and arousal. Even Jin is showing minute traces of the scent of fear. These two are not stupid, and they have clearly done this before.

Anger floods Jin's system, entirely its own. It doesn't want its clothes ripped open, its body stared at again. Gens have no right to call neut bodies wrong or ugly or strange. It doesn't want to end up like Taylor. Part of its mind still records everything Bill and Lily are doing; another part prepares for a fight.

It considers whether to hit the man first and take his knife, or hit the woman before she can react. Her actions will be faster, Jin knows from the ghosting. She is the more dangerous of the pair, and it doesn't know if she has a weapon. Jin has bandages in its pack. Better to risk a cut in the side and hit the woman first. It shifts more attention to Bill. Chemicals flood his brain with daring. Jin throws itself at Lily, grabbing a handful of hair and stomping its heel into her knee. Bill's knee gets the same treatment as he reaches after Jin with the knife. Jin holds its sliced side with its left hand and runs.

Carrying the pack slows it down, but it needs the money and bandages. Familiar streets are just ahead, closer than the man and woman who limp after it, hurling curses. Lily stumbles and collapses, screeching. Jin didn't get Bill quite so well, and he limps along quickly, stretching his knife out ahead of him. The blade cuts Jin's bedroll from its pack. Another cut and one of the straps is gone, throwing Jin off stride. It uses the imbalance to swing the pack around off of one shoulder and full into Bill's face. He stumbles, still gripping his knife. Jin swings again, hitting both of his knees. He goes down slashing. Jin's small sneakers land a kick in his face, then stomp his wrist until the knife drops. Side bleeding, shins bleeding, Jin grabs the knife and runs.

The pain is only a slight sting as the adrenaline surge pushes Jin onward. It runs down alleyways, paying only the minimum of attention to its surroundings. It hears more than feels the crash as it falls to the ground beneath the weight of another body.

The knife it took from Bill breaks against the asphalt. Jin tosses away the useless hilt, wishing it hadn't buried its own knife so deeply in its pack. Ignoring the new wounds that open, Jin twists to face the newest threat. Staring back at it is a familiar pair of sky-blue eyes.

His grin is the same as it was in the diner. Jin tries to knee him in the groin but he twists, keeping Jin pinned down.

"Let go!" says Jin.

"In a minute. You being chased or something?"

"Maybe."

"Well then, let's get you off the street."

Blue-eyes takes Jin's pack and pulls it to its feet. It considers just leaving without the pack, but Home Cavern is a long way off. It has a little bit of money and food in its pockets but not enough for passenger fare, and certainly not enough to get it all the way home.

Blue-eyes leads it through a weed-filled lot, and both of them kick dirt over their tracks and the blood Jin leaves behind. Inside the building Blue-eyes enters, the air is hot and stale, empty of life except for the usual near-dead drunks who might or might not awaken after the day begins to cool. Blue-eyes sits and motions Jin to do the same. Jin wipes away some of the dirt with its not-bloody hand. Its left hand still holds its cut side.

"So, where is it?" says Blue-eyes.

He digs through Jin's pack as though he doesn't really expect an answer.

"Toss over bandages?" says Jin.

"Not likely. Where's the container? Or did you already spread your filth?"

"Can't answer if unconscious," says Jin.

"That's why you'll answer me before you pass out. Looks like you've had enough people trying to paw at you today, you wouldn't want me to do that while you couldn't even fight back," says Blue-eyes.

Jin leans against the wall. Blue-eyes digs through its pack thoroughly but quickly. His long fingers are sensitive to any lump in the first aid kit, in Jin's spare clothing. He rips open the hem of Jin's spare shirt and carefully cradles the speckled pills he finds there in the fabric.

"What are these?" he asks.

"Antibiotics," says Jin.

"Yeah? Why'd you hide them, then?"

"Thieves."

Blue-eyes laughs. "I'm not a thief. Not that kind, anyway. Take one."

He holds out the pills, careful to keep the fabric between them and his skin. Jin swallows one gratefully, closing its eyes. Designed by neuter medics, the drug instantly reacts to Jin's mucous. It half-forgets Blue-eyes, feeling the chemicals race to its wounds and block the infection already starting to grow. Bill's knife must have been obscenely dirty.

"That good, huh? I guess you were telling the truth," says Blue-eyes.

He continues his search. Jin's money and food are stacked to the side, the clothing and other items scattered. He sets the empty pack aside and looks at Jin.

"Well, I guess that just leaves you."

"Why?" says Jin.

It takes a chance and slips a packet of peanuts out of its pocket and begins to eat.

"Those the antidote?" says Blue-eyes.

"What?"

The grin on Blue-eyes' face finally disappears.

"You're probably smarter than I am, or they wouldn't let you work so close to home, so stop acting like an idiot. Get this through your head: I know what you are. I know where you're from and what you're doing here. I want you to hand over whatever kind of death you brought with you and get out of my city. I don't care if you bleed to death on the way home, just so long as you're out of my sight, permanently."

Jin sinks back into the wall.

"No plague," it says.

"Really? That's funny. You skulk around for three days, sleep in a hotel one night, an abandoned building another night, and out in the wilds another. What is this, tourism?"

Jin looks down at itself. Its left sleeve is already ripped, so it begins to tear off strips and starts bandaging its side. Blue-eyes doesn't stop it. Jin keeps its posture at ease, but as he twists left and leans forward to pick something up off the ground, Jin expands forward with an inhale, easing its right shoulder just ahead of the left. An echo of his, Jin's pulse grows steady and strong, but his quickened breath tells it that he is not as calm as he looks.

"Stop that!" says Blue-eyes.

Caught ghosting. The man knows too much about neuts. Jin wonders who was careless enough to talk, or if maybe Taylor was tortured before he was killed. Either way, if Blue-eyes knows about neuts, plagues, and ghosting, he probably knows more. And he was able to follow Jin without being detected. Jin decides that the truth is the safest thing to tell.

"No plague this trip. Just here to study."

It just wants to go home, shower, then head deep into the unsettled caves to study its memories in a safe, quiet place. Alone. It really misses being alone.

Blue-eyes' face heats red, then cools.

"Well, then. I guess you won't be needing this."

He stuffs everything back into Jin's pack and settles the bundle like a pillow at his back. He stretches his legs out, once again smiling without a trace of kindness or humor. Unable to think of anything else to do or say, Jin leaves him with everything it used to own and steps back out into the crowds and heat.

# CHAPTER 7

Bruvec took the news of Sandy's cavern encounter more calmly than she thought it would, while Keri went to the other extreme.

"That's it. You want to get yourself killed, girl, that's fine by me," she said.

She reached as if to snatch the plate of food away, but Sandy held onto it, meeting Keri's eyes with a grin. The woman released her grip so suddenly that Sandy nearly lost half the meal onto her lap, but fast reflexes came to her rescue, and she was back to shoveling food into her mouth before Keri had made it out of the kitchen.

"Ker's right, you know. Dangerous," said Bruvec.

Sandy concentrated on her fork.

"Your choice to come and go, but be careful, Sand."

Something in its tone sobered her for a moment.

"I will," she said. "I am. And next time, I'll take some food and water with me, so I'm better prepared in case I have to hide out for longer."

"Prepared is good. Not getting into situation is better."

"So what should I have done, then?" said Sandy.

"Did fine. Now let us handle."

"You know what they were doing there?" said Sandy.

Bruvec handed her a rough yucca-paper napkin. "Survey for new dumpsite. Probably toxic," it said.

"Toxic waste? You mean radioactive?"

"Likely. Been done for over century. Lock in lead or special glass container, bury and monitor."

"Is there a lot of stuff like that down here?" said Sandy, her appetite suddenly gone.

"More than you like to think, less than is truly dangerous. Mostly farther north, east. Have to come up with way to discourage this one. Maybe have to seal off connections to those tunnels."

"Can I help?" said Sandy.

Bruvec smiled at her and left. She decided to take that as a maybe.

Most of the work was boring. Bruvec called some neuter builders and painters in from some other part of the Network, and they worked quickly and quietly to scout out the tunnel systems for signs of the topside explorers. Once those were found, they began subtly reworking the architecture of the tunnels to alter the routes and guide markings.

The explorers would most likely have made electronic maps of their progress, so simply blocking off entrances wasn't effective. Instead, the crew built up the protruding rocks and carved back the niches. Not enough for the changes to be noticeable to the casual observer who had only been through the tunnel once or twice, but enough to obscure the tracking equipment and convince the gens that they were on the wrong path.

Sandy mixed the sculpting epoxy and watched as the neuts built up layer after layer of false rock. The stench of the acid used to deepen the crevices made her lightheaded, but Bruvec assured her the fumes weren't toxic.

"Maybe not, but they're sure strong," she said.

"We'll fix," said the neut she was nearest. "Need more epoxy. Less resin this time, more catalyst."

Sandy did as she was told with Bruvec's help and watched the final layer form under the neut's stubby fingers.

"Do you like doing this? Coming down here from wherever you live to build rocks?" said Sandy.

"Came up, not down," said the neut.

"Up? You mean there are caves deeper than this one?"

The neut said nothing.

"What's your name? I'm Sandy."

"En."

"N? Like the letter?"

"Yes."

"Is that one of your initials?" said Sandy.

En gave a slight shrug and picked up a brush. It thrust an open container into her hands and dipped the brush in, coating the bristles in a tannish powder. As Sandy watched, it dabbed the dust onto the rock section it had just completed, blending the new powder with the dust on the surrounding rocks. When it was finished, she couldn't tell the difference between the new rock and the old. Bruvec had assured her that short of extensive testing, no one would know the difference.

"How come the dust sticks like that and doesn't just fall off?" she asked as they moved on to the next section.

"Top layer had chemical attractant. Slight cling, like static electricity, only won't lose charge, helps confuse tracker readings."

Sandy watched closely when En reached the next section's final layer, and sure enough, the dust leapt off the brush to cling to the wall, just like fabric succumbing to static electricity.

By the time they were done with the tunnel leading into the cavern where she'd nearly been discovered, Sandy was yawning nearly every other breath. Even En took some time to stretch between sections, and the others around them seemed to slow and take frequent breaks as well.

Still, when someone called for volunteers to do a final sweep, Sandy set down her container of cave dust and was the first to reach the leader.

"You know what to do?" asked the neut in charge.

"Will you show me?" said Sandy.

It looked at Bruvec, who nodded. The neut shrugged and Sandy followed. The final step was simple: make sure all traces of the work and the crew were gone. Sandy swept and sprinkled dust over footprints. Just like the dust laid over the new peaks and valleys, Sandy realized that the powder seemed to absorb the chemicals odors. By the time she and the others had gathered the last of the stray brushes and other hints of humanity, the corridor once again smelled of damp rock and nothing else.

The cavern with the pool remained virtually unchanged, other than a narrowing of the entrance. Sandy wasn't sure which of the footprints the men had noticed before, but if they managed to get this far, they would already realize that something was strange. The crew wiped out all traces of themselves and the men, then sealed up the entrance that led toward Home Cavern.

En stayed behind to finish the face of the new closure.

"But that means it has to go all the way to the surface and back around to one of the other entrances all alone," said Sandy.

"It has other route," said Bruvec.

"Another route to where? There are other settlements that aren't part of Home Cavern here, aren't there?" said Sandy.

"Heard it tell you so earlier," said Bruvec.

"But it wouldn't tell me any more than that. Why?" said Sandy.

"You give out your address to strangers?" said Bruvec, gentling the words with a smile.

"Of course not. But if someone was helping me, I'd at least tell them what city I lived in."

Bruvec laughed, an infectious sound, and led Sandy back toward the settled part of the caverns.

"Good mind. Curious like a neut, only on wrong subjects," it said.

"What do you mean, the wrong subjects?"

"Not bad-wrong. Just not like neuts. We're curious about science, logic. You're curious about people."

"What's wrong with being curious about people?"

"Nothing. Just hard to satisfy down here. You interested in continuing studies? Maybe biology, psychology will match curiosity. Talk to Net."

Sandy was sure that Net wouldn't approve, but it gave her the passwords to access more Network files and a daunting list of publicly available college courses in human anatomy, microbiology, medicine, and psychology. The Network also had access to private courses from the most exclusive universities. She could only view, not participate, in these, so she suspected some of the access wasn't entirely legal.

"What more do you want? It's a free education that you wouldn't have otherwise," said Keri when Sandy asked her about it.

"Oh, I don't want anything more. It's just hard for me to picture Bruvec approving of anything illegal," said Sandy.

"Where have you been living these last few weeks? None of this is monitored, registered or otherwise legalized by any official office. Technically, I think we're not even governed by the state of New Mexico."

Sandy looked around her at the yellow-and-green kitchen decor that had become so homey she sometimes forgot it was several miles underground. She tried to think of it as part of a state and couldn't, yet some portion of her felt like she could push away the fragile limestone curtains and find herself looking out onto a street with children and animals and trucks.

"I can't believe that stuff isn't boring you stiff," said Keri. "I couldn't make it through half a lesson."

"Yeah, but you have the kitchen to keep you busy," said Sandy.

"You'll find something," said Keri.

She tried, but nothing seemed to work, so she found herself back in the computing lab with Net, alternating between listening in on a nursing course and dropping emergency room dramas to compare. The soundtracks were actually better in the lectures, but the drama show doctors were far better looking than the professors and most of the students.

She had finally screwed up the courage to ask Net for a set of ear wires so she could listen in comfort and privacy. When she saw a new drama listed with one of her favorite actors, Tom Liene, she dropped it onto her screen and started to watch.

The episode involved a burn victim being treated after somehow enduring fire, acid, and a chemical explosion. Liene played the handsome young doctor, of course, but she found the patient distracting her usually focused attention. She scrolled the file forward and checked the credits, but it wasn't a name she recognized.

She went back and froze on one of the shots, zooming and panning to take in the features.

The special-effects injury makeup obscured everything recognizable, but there was something familiar about the eyes. She stared at the screen for a while, burning the picture into her mind, then closed her eyes and ran through the faces of everyone she knew.

Jin.

It wasn't Jin. Sandy knew it couldn't be. But the look in the tea-colored eyes was the same as the quiet neut's, knowing and curious and guarded, with a touch of distant ego. The kind of eyes that made the person looking into them feel like she knew nothing about the world, and might be better off that way.

Sandy zoomed back out and continued watching the episode. Jin had been gone quite a while now, and she had seen the worry on Bruvec's face when she mentioned the spreader's name. Nothing was said, but the tension was building between Bruvec and Net and Keri. Others who came to Home Cavern were feeling it, too. The researchers kept to the labs, and visitors stayed only a day or two before moving on. The only upside for Sandy was that they avoided the kitchen, and that meant she was the one to take food from Keri down to the labs or into the corridor near the computing room for the visitors who spent most of their time there. Net wouldn't allow her to bring the trays any closer to its precious screens than that, despite the fact that all but Net's own personal system were entirely spillproof.

"What are you working on?" she asked each time she carried a tray down to the medical labs.

Most of the time the researchers muttered fairly noncommittal answers and hurried away with a sandwich in hand to pore over notes and graphs. One of the younger research assistants would occasionally take time to talk.

"Anything new today, Aflin?" said Sandy.

"Same old. Bacteria dies, bacteria lives. You?"

"Still living," said Sandy.

"Noticed. Still nuts upstairs?" said Aflin.

"Well, Net's still nuts, but I suspect that's been going on for most of its life. Everyone's still tense and getting tenser, though. I don't get it. If they're so worried about Jin, why don't they just go out and look for it?" said Sandy.

"Probably did. Bruv wouldn't panic without."

"I don't think I'd call it panic," said Sandy.

"That's because you can't ghost. Trust me, Bruv's worried. More than you see."

"What about you?" said Sandy.

"Worried? No. Don't know Jin, but if me, would just be out seeing city, happy I'm not stuck down here growing mold."

Sandy had peeked through the files on Aflin's project—research on molds engineered to break down discarded plastics faster and without unwanted chemical residue. As far as she could tell, the project was coming along successfully, but Aflin thought otherwise.

"Only two of five tests worked right," Aflin said. "One failure, two left indeterminate residue."

It put down its sandwich and went back to work, leaving Sandy with the feeling she had said something wrong. She waited around for a while, but Aflin ignored her, so she went back up to drop the empty tray in the kitchen.

"How long does it take to drop off a bunch of sandwiches?" said Keri.

"I don't know. How long does it take to get people around here in a better mood?" Sandy shot back.

"Sounds like you're shaping up to be a test case," said Keri.

"Can you blame me? Everyone around here is giving everyone else the silent treatment. I can't think of anything I've done wrong, but no one will talk to me, and everyone acts like it's my fault," said Sandy.

Keri turned toward the back of the kitchen, and Sandy slumped at the table, wishing she was sure she could find her way back to the surface without worrying about misinterpreting a map, and wishing even harder that she had somewhere to go once she got there. A cup of tea was set firmly in front of her, and Keri sat down at the other side of the table, her fingers wrapped around her own steaming mug. Sandy inhaled the scents of lemon and honey, warming her hands on the speckled stoneware.

"It isn't you. They're just focused on other things," said Keri.

Sandy told her what had happened with Aflin.

"Oh, that one," said Keri. "You definitely don't want to take that one personally. It thinks that just because it was better at science than the poor little gens it went to school with it should be some kind of celebrity down here."

"Really?"

"Oh, you should have seen it the first few days. It would come in here in a snit because someone actually made it clean the equipment. 'I'm *scientist*, not bottle-washer,' it said."

"What did you say?" said Sandy.

Keri shrugged one shoulder but her eyes gleamed. "I said, 'And now you're a cook. Don't forget to wash your own dishes.' Then I left. I have no idea how it managed not to starve."

Laughing felt good. She tried not to bond to Keri too much, never knowing when the older woman's sharp sense of humor would lash out in her direction, but of the people she encountered, only Keri and Bruvec seemed to understand. She tried not to think it, but the others seemed so cold sometimes they were nearly inhuman.

"Some neuts have humor. Even scientist neuts. You'll see," said Bruvec.

It had come upon her, sitting alone in one of the midsized caverns off the corridor between the sleeping areas and the computing lab. Sometimes she felt less lonely if she sat in one of these places, away from people who were too busy to notice her.

"I know neuts have as much of a range as gens, but why does everyone down here seem to forget that part of themselves?" said Sandy.

"Work. That's why they come. Also, don't know you. Takes us longer to get sense of connection with person than for gens."

"But if you can ghost them, shouldn't you be able to feel closer?" said Sandy.

Bruvec looked at her curiously. She had learned that look meant it was impressed by something she observed or learned, and she felt herself warm a little with self-conscious pleasure.

"Understand how ghosting works?" said Bruvec.

"I think so. Aflin explained it, and Keri filled in the gaps. Basically, the person ghosting gets to feel all the sensations of the other person, physical and emotional."

"Yes. Accuracy depends on skill, though. Practice," said Bruvec.

"Don't most neuts practice?"

Bruvec seemed to pull into itself. Sandy didn't have to be able to ghost to know what it was thinking. Jin was the best at ghosting. Jin was the best at everything, from what she had picked up from Bruvec and Keri, though Keri's attitude was more one of distant respect than affection. Even Net pulled its focus away from the computer screen and blinked its round eyes thoughtfully when Jin's name was mentioned.

The little neut hadn't seemed like much when Sandy met it. Less self-absorbed than the others, definitely. And those clear eyes that focused right in on her when they talked, yet seemed to take in everything else as well...Sandy smiled to herself. No wonder everyone was so worried about the spreader. Despite its bluntness and that sense she got that it thought it was smarter than everyone else, there was something magnetic about it. Maybe just the mystery.

"You miss Jin a lot, don't you?" she said gently.

Bruvec gave her that curious look again, then silent laughter broke through its face.

"You don't need ghosting! Thought-reader," it said.

"Not really," said Sandy, embarrassed she had said anything.

"Of course. Was joking. But you see emotion. That's difference between neut and gen. Neut can ghost all it wants, but if emotions only read as chemicals, then no connection."

"How can you feel another person's feelings and then not connect them to yourself?" said Sandy.

"Mystery of gen versus neut, maybe," said Bruvec. "Some neuts can, want to. Most don't bother, save time for other thoughts, other studies."

Sandy pulled the sweater she'd brought from home more tightly around her, wishing she could still smell the Montana air in its threads, even if that air smelled of chicken dung and bio-fuel exhaust.

"I wish I could help you look for it, bring it back," she said.

"Jin?" said Bruvec.

Sandy nodded.

The old neut placed its fingertips gently on the knuckles of Sandy's hand. She had seen it do this to Keri from time to time, but she wasn't prepared for the warmth in its rough hands, the hunger that human touch brought to her after so long without the jostling and casual pats and slaps and hugs she was used to in her life above. She barely had the strength to keep from clinging to its hand, burrowing into its shoulder like she used to do with her grandfather when she was small.

Instead, she held herself still, trying to feel the sensation like a neut would. Her medical readings had taught her how the nerves carried messages to the brain, how sensations registered from contact to consciousness, and she could picture it all in cartoonish drawings but she couldn't feel that pathway inside herself. Her brain just wasn't made for that kind of sensation.

"We all know some day it won't come back to caverns. Jin knows too, accepts," said Bruvec.

"But you don't want to accept it," said Sandy.

Bruvec patted her hand once, then lifted its own away.

"Not today."

# CHAPTER 8

Jin's feet drag on the Albuquerque streets. Too much has happened already this morning, and the small amount of money still left in its pocket is hardly enough for travel food, let alone passenger fare. The neuter medic at the lo-loc clinic will loan it money, if Jin can manage to reach it without another encounter.

The waiting room is the same, but the people seem dirtier, more desperate. Jin is, too. It uses the wait time to wash in the bathroom and top off its newly purchased thrift shop canteen, hoping the antibiotics left in its system will counteract any lurking bacteria in the tap water. When it returns to the waiting room, Blue-eyes is there, leafing through a magazine.

"Come on, kiddo, it's time to get you out of here," he says in a friendly tone. "Remember what I told you earlier? We need to go."

The receptionist looks up.

"The doctor will be with you in just a moment, Mr. Bruvec."

The grip on Jin's bruised arm tightens.

"That's okay, ma'am. I'll just take my little brother home. He gets confused when he's been out in the sun too long, but he's really fine," says Blue-eyes.

He smiles brightly at the receptionist with no trace of the coldness Jin has seen in his earlier expressions. The smile vanishes when he looks at Jin.

"No outside help. That's cheating," he tells Jin when they are back on the street.

Jin heads south, alone. One foot, then the next.

The first part of the walk is mostly city, but after a few miles this gives way to wasteland. Garbage piles up high and thick, tenanted by the homeless who don't like the city crowds. Jin sticks to the highways, not even attempting to flag down the delivery trucks to beg for a ride that it knows will be denied. At Tome, Jin turns east to cut through the deeper wastelands, but it can't get through. Expensive houses edge up to a massive double fence line that blocks the view, if not the stench, of garbage. Someday the cluster of eucalyptus trees growing between the fences might be thick enough to diffuse the smell, but not for many years yet.

It waits until late at night to walk through, hoping that the wealthy homeowners don't patrol their property with guns. Outside of the hi-loc areas, it walks during midday, when most of the population is at work or hiding from the sun. Each day is split into chunks, progressing at an infuriatingly slow pace. Jin refills the canteen whenever possible, rationing out the last of its money on food and water-purification tablets, then rationing the food and water down to the bare minimum for subsistence. It can't think. All the energy it has is reserved for walking south and east. Walking home.

Ten days later it reaches Cedarvale. The whole town is poor, but shows hints here and there of a more affluent past. Jin fits right in with the current population. Its body is wearing down to sinew and bone. It craves real food, vitamins, and rest in a place where it won't have to guard itself constantly. It camps an extra night in a small scrap of wasteland that is returning to a wild state, far enough away from the current dumpsites that the stink is hardly noticeable. Animals and other travelers have already stripped all of the cactus fruit, so Jin scrapes a prickly pear leaf with a rock and eats the withered but moist flesh raw. It is proud to only prick its hands twice during the process, even with the shaking. It decides to rest one more night before moving on.

Heat awakens Jin into dizzying sickness. Its stomach cramps and its blood simmers. Stifling the gag reflex, Jin forces last night's cactus back downward. It can't afford to vomit. There is nowhere to go to escape the sun. Mountains and forest lie to the south, but they are days away at Jin's current pace. It can't climb up to them anyway. It can barely stand.

It starts to think about giving up, but its body drives it onward in the direction of the far-off Cienaga del Macho River. The route to the caverns is longer this way, but there is a better chance of finding food and water. The Cienaga should be only a day's walk away. Jin tries to convert that time to its crawling pace, but the numbers get tangled and stop making sense.

Sudden darkness disorients it. After the sparkling glare, thunderheads make the world like night. Jin collapses in relief. The water will come to it. Electricity dries the air completely. A crack of thunder jolts Jin's brain into panic. It is on low ground, too weak to crawl any higher.

The rains come, soaking Jin and the surrounding dirt, pelting its skin like small stones. It tries to work its way up the closest rise, but the abused muscles won't crawl any farther. Jin tries to laugh, remembering Tei's mockery. Big-brain Jin drowns in a rainstorm. Funny.

Looking around, Jin forces its sluggish mind to track the paths of water, calculate the rate of rise. Even if the cloudburst lasts fifteen minutes, the water where Jin is won't be more than knee-high. Which does no good if it can't stand.

It pushes itself to a sitting position, as upright as it can get. Water that is knee-deep to a standing body is still below the neck of a person sitting, and cloudbursts in the area rarely last more than half an hour, usually far less. Jin sits still and concentrates on staying conscious as the water rushes past, rising. It catches water in its hands and drinks fresh liquid that has yet to touch the contaminated earth, then holds its canteen up for the sky to fill.

The flood stops at Jin's bottom rib, leaving its legs half-buried in sand and muck. Fortunately, the clouds remain. Its stomach is still empty, despite the fill of liquid, and its body has no reserves left to fend off disease. Black beetles float past, struggling to keep from drowning. Jin warns its stomach to hold on and carefully gathers them, hoping something more edible will float past. Nothing does.

It looks at the handful of bugs, and an involuntary shudder throws half of them back into the water. Jin gathers them again.

Deep breaths prepare its body for the coming meal, and it slams the whole handful down, trying not to feel the legs go tickling down its throat. The crunch of teeth on exoskeletons sends Jin's bile up. A quick swallow, and the ordeal is over. Jin tries to feel the tiny sparks of protein being absorbed into its system, but its senses are dulled. The sun sends heat through the clouds, and the wasteland steams as the water quickly sinks into the earth. Time to move on.

A withered prickly pear runs its spikes into Jin's leg, so Jin strips out the spines and eats the offending plant. It travels by night again, limping and crawling toward the fresher dumpsites, then into the shacktown that stretches the rest of the way to the river.

Despite being picked clean of edible food by the shacktown population, the riverbank shows more plant life than Jin has seen in weeks. It reaches the water just as the morning is heating, so it crawls under a cluster of cattails and sleeps.

The first thought Jin has on awakening in the muggy afternoon fills it with excitement: bath! It can wash itself for the first time since Albuquerque, not including the deluge out in the wastelands. Humanity rustles in the nearby shacktown, tending the local gardens and probably guarding the cultivated gardens and food animals, but no one is within sight for the moment. Blue-eyes has Jin's soap and clean clothes, but it doesn't have the energy to care. Carefully keeping an ear toward the populated areas, it removes its shirt and ties the sleeves to its legs. Standing still, it becomes a human fishnet.

Jin's first catch is illegal, only two inches long, but it forgets this until after it has already swallowed the fish whole. Sparse algae scraped from the rocks make a slimy but nourishing salad, and when Jin finishes bathing it sets more of the plant material out to dry in the sun.

Back under the cattails, it closes its eyes, feeling the algae being absorbed into its body, the fish protein and oils healing some of the damage from starvation. For the first time in weeks it rests well, not the fitful sleep of pained exhaustion.

Able to walk after rest and food, Jin follows the Cienaga del Macho to where it joins the Pecos River near Roswell, then turns south along the Pecos. With fish and algae and water weeds to eat, along with the fatter leaves and fruits of the nearby prickly pears, the journey is slow but possible. It must get home before malnutrition and exhaustion block access to the memories it has gathered to study. A pang of fear and frustration surges through Jin. The damage might already be done, the whole trip a waste. It can't check now. Even strengthened by the food and water it now has, it must save all of its energy for the walk. It decides to talk to Net about setting emergency food or money stashes in various cities. Maybe the Network can organize some sort of distress code so other neuts in similar circumstances can find their way home. It isn't the only spreader who has a tendency to find trouble.

Foot after foot, Jin heads south, resting every few hours throughout the night, truly sleeping only during the day. Another week and it will be down in the caverns telling Keri she's a great cook, letting her fatten it however she likes.

The city of Carlsbad is just ahead, the white streetlights reaching far out into the night. Jin walks straight through the city, just one more of the transient poor, blending easily with both the Hispanic and white populations as its shape and coloring share characteristics with both. It takes fewer rest stops now, anticipation pushing it onward. The dried algae is gone and the river nearby is stripped bare. There is nothing left that a human system can break down without spending more energy than the food can give. Jin searches the roadside vines and shrubs for fruit, but the birds and rabbits have left little, and humans have eaten the rest. It tries to share a rotten apple with a worm.

"Hey, get away from there," shouts a woman from the house where the apple tree grows.

Green apples are bad on a weak stomach anyway, Jin consoles itself. It is almost through the city now, almost close enough to imagine it hears the rustlings of friends underneath the earth.

A sign says no pedestrians are allowed on the freeway. Jin walks past, letting the darkness hide it. Only home matters. Lights fly by on Jin's left, horns honk as the water tankers thunder by, carting precious cargo from the desert collection units to the hi-loc communities.

"Off the road, moron!" someone yells from a high-up window.

Jin keeps walking, moving a little farther from the road. Running into cactus plants is painful and slows Jin down. It veers back closer to the road where the gravel is barren and level. Tires screech, more horns honk, and each driver feels the need to comment on Jin's presence. Oncoming headlights start making it dizzy. Jin grabs the guardrail and pulls itself along. Not resting since seeing the Carlsbad lights seven hours ago was a bad choice. *Foot after foot*, Jin reminds itself. Its head starts pulsing, and its eyes flood with blood-red light. *Pay attention to surroundings, Jin.*

Its ears pick out the humming motor and crunch of gravel, a passenger-size car slowly following, but only the chemical reek of commercial biofuel. Not a private car. Jin tries to walk faster, but it is going as fast as it can. The car stops, lights on top flashing red-blue-red. A state trooper steps out, flashlight held shoulder-high.

"Place your hands where I can see them, please," says a female voice. "Do you have any identification on you?"

"Stolen," says Jin, its voice harsh and cracking.

The lights stop flashing, then start again. Start, stop, start.

"I said, are you aware that this area is off-limits to pedestrians?" says the trooper, less polite this time.

Jin tries to come up with an answer to that, but the lights stop flashing and the world turns black.

# CHAPTER 9

Darkness is cut by screaming white. Jin blinks rapidly, trying to look around the edges of the flashlight beam. Its pupils pulse, uncertain whether to contract or dilate. Colored lights still flash in its peripheral vision, now more red than blue. Two paramedics get out of a truck.

"He's awake," says the trooper. "Took you long enough."

The paramedics gather to take Jin's pulse. Only then does it realize that its hands are cuffed.

"How do you feel?" says one of the medics.

His eyes are as blue as the Albuquerque man's, but his hair is dark and longer than Jin's, and he speaks with a slight Hispanic accent.

"Kid? Can you speak?"

Jin nods. They watch with raised eyebrows until it realizes they want proof.

"Yes," it says.

The medic nods to his partner, and they take Jin's blood pressure. Jin measures itself as they do.

"A little low but nothing dangerous," says the medic.

Their equipment is slightly off. Jin's pulse is lower than they say, but it will live. It looks around, trying to remember exactly how far it got before collapsing. There are still too many miles to go.

"Should we take him in?" says one of the medics.

The medics and the trooper look at Jin, clearly not believing it can afford a trip to even the lo-loc clinic, never mind the real hospital. It doesn't look rich enough to afford a toothbrush.

"No, you can go," the trooper tells them. "What're you on, kid?"

Jin shakes its head, scooting backward to lean against the guardrail.

"Just tell me," says the trooper.

"Nothing. Hungry, exhausted. Everything stolen. Just trying to go home."

"Where's home?" says the trooper.

"Whites City."

Nowhere else is close enough to seem plausible. The trooper looks closely at Jin's eyes. After a moment the flashlight's beam turns aside and she unlocks the cuffs.

"I'll take you down there. I'm about to go off shift for tonight, anyway. But you have to promise me I'll never catch you so much as jaywalking around here again. You really ought to not be out on your own like this. You've obviously seen a little of what can happen out here. I assume you won't be pressing charges against whoever stole your wallet?"

"No. Just want to go home."

"Get in."

Jin gratefully stretches out in the back of the patrol car while the trooper calls in to report her stop. The cheap plastic seat feels better than the softest bed Jin has ever known. It gives the trooper directions to a lo-loc community, a common stop for visitors but not shunned by locals.

"Sorry, hon, but I need you to sit up with your seat belt on. You'll be at home in bed soon enough. You out here with your folks on vacation?"

"Friends."

She nods and checks the rearview mirror to make sure Jin is strapped in.

"Yeah, summer break trips were always the greatest. Enjoy it while you can—it'll probably be the only time in your life you can afford one. You been down in the caverns yet?"

"No," Jin lies.

She tells it about Carlsbad Caverns the whole way there. Jin stifles an exhausted smile, knowing that the tourist caves are not even one-tenth of the local cavern system. The tours are all right for a family vacation, but the caverns Jin wants have soft white beds, food, and safety. And they are still too far away.

The trooper drops Jin off at a small apartment complex. It weaves through the grid of run-down buildings and permanent modular homes, wishing it had found a friendly cop just outside of Albuquerque. It won't reach home tonight, though Home Cavern feels close enough that it ought to hear the generators hum. It needs rest before tackling the five miles of open brush and low hills while trying to avoid tourists and park rangers. After that will come several miles more of winding trails through the darkness underground.

Jin finds an abandoned former garden plot, fenced in behind one of the buildings. It curls up on the barren dirt. The sound of bats returning to their roost wakes it a few hours later. *Almost home*, they screech in voices too high even for Jin's ears.

Early tourist crowds are already stirring when Jin awakens. It angles through them toward the gift shops, then casually drifts off the pavement until the road to the tourist caverns is out of sight. Loose rocks make hiking difficult, but the whole area is protected by the park service, so only small amounts of garbage clutter the landscape. The cool morning breeze against Jin's skin feels almost like the moist air of underground. It should have asked the trooper for food, it realizes too late. Its hands are shaking too much to peel cactus leaves, and its legs feel like toothpicks that might break with every step, but none of that really matters anymore. Home is so close. Jin sorts through a pile of sunflower shells that some tourists left on the ground, but all the seeds are gone.

Dirty clothes help Jin blend in with the sand and sagebrush. It reaches the cavern entrance late in the afternoon, sweat searing its skin where the sunburn has cracked all the way through. It doesn't feel the pain. Raw fingers find the hidden door with no help from its conscious mind. It taps a passcode and pulls carefully.

Real stone chiseled half an inch thick swings back on silent hinges. It steps into darkness, shuts the door behind it, and breathes in the welcome fifty-six degrees. Resting for a moment, Jin spreads its sunburnt skin into contact with the cool rock. Its brain sends a confusion of signals, not knowing whether the action is painful or pleasant, so Jin ignores them all. When its breath is slow and steady again, it gropes for the headlamps the Network always keeps near the entrance. The strap around Jin's forehead sends another torrent of mixed messages, but now it has to concentrate on the winding passage. Its body knows the route and pulls it through, sometimes on its belly, sometimes on its back, sometimes up on hands and knees, only occasionally on foot. It must have lost real weight. Squeezing through the tunnels has never been so easy.

Crickets scurry from its beam of light, making Jin laugh. Bad idea. It ends up with lungs full of dust, and the cough that echoes down the tunnel sends only one signal to Jin's mind: pain.

Swiss-cheese holes begin to dot the limestone beneath it. Jin finds the hole it wants and turns to face the rock wall to its right, dropping its legs down. It feels for the toeholds and begins the downward climb, knowing by the change of sound quality when darkness yawns open at its back. Dropped stones echo far away, fifteen seconds after leaving its hand. It works its way off of the climb and through a hole to the next level, which requires more belly-crawling. The thought of food and showers pushes Jin on. Its eyes have been half-closed since the beginning of the descent. At least malnutrition hasn't erased the route from its memory.

"Hey, dead or alive?"

A hand tugs Jin's shoe.

Somewhere along the narrowest part of the tunnel, it must have shifted into sleep. It is facedown in the dust, with uncounted tons of rock on every side.

Jin clears its throat and answers, "Alive, looks like."

"Smell like dead," says the voice behind it.

"Sorry."

Jin continues to crawl forward. It will shower someday. Soon.

"Hey!"

The voice behind it is angry. Jin must have dozed off again.

"Sorry."

Crawl on belly, on knees, climb down.

"Stop! You stupid? Turn right."

Jin feels its heart pound and forces the organ to slow. It can't afford the exertion, even if it was almost fatally stupid. A missed turn in the caves and its bones would be lost forever. It can't afford to stop paying attention just because someone else is near. It turns right and weaves around the s-curves, now in a standing crouch. The person behind it pushes, wakes it, forces it down the path. Finally, the tunnel opens out into a cave filled with artificial light.

"Longest two miles of my life," says the voice, disgusted.

"So? Almost last of mine."

Jin sits, eyes closed, with its back against the wall of the small chamber.

"What happened? You look like guano," says the other neut.

"Thanks. Go on. I'll rest."

It isn't someone Jin knows, or if they've met, Jin can't remember.

"Sure you okay?"

Maybe Jin nods before losing consciousness. It isn't sure.

"Jin," says a familiar, gentle voice, "wake up. Please."

A hand shakes its shoulder. It hasn't heard its own name for a very long time. Years? No, just miles. Jin feels the stone at its back and beneath it, and the cool air all around. So reaching the caves was not just a dream. Dim light reddens its closed eyelids. No one is pushing its foot, telling it to move on. The gentle voice knows its name. It must be almost home.

"You're awake. I hear you. Eat."

Jin's brain is half dead, not sending messages. It hadn't even smelled the food. It opens its eyes to Bruvec's gray-white hair and wrinkled forehead. Crackers and dried meat look Technicolor in the lamplight, and Jin's shaking hand casts a bird-claw shadow on the food as it grabs the protein first. It chokes on the meat. Too dry, too salty.

"Hi Bruv. Good to see you," says Jin when the coughing subsides.

"Jin...Jin!"

"What?"

Bruvec's eyes are wild.

"Oh. Pass out again?"

Bruvec hands Jin a canteen. "Drink and rest. Why so bad?"

Jin breaks the crackers into bits and sucks on the crumbs.

"Man stole everything. Knew neuts, guess he didn't like."

"Stole your sleeves, too?"

Jin lifts its shirt to show Bruvec the knife scab wrapped in what is left of the sleeve bandage. The cut oozes a little. Bruvec pokes the swelling and Jin nearly loses the small amount of food it has ingested. The antibiotics have long since worn off, and the cuts are severely infected. It can't concentrate hard enough to find the infection, let alone rally its immune system. Its left leg is swollen and stinging where the scabs opened as it crawled through the tunnels. Bruvec shakes its head.

"Sad sight. Go to med lab and have docs take look at you."

"Shower, sleep, and eat more first. Tell Ker to cook plain bird, little oil, lots of greens. Wheat, too, if available."

"No, Jin. You need docs."

Jin shrugs, still trying to chew, which hurts its gums. Bruvec helps it to its feet, and the two of them hobble toward Home Cavern. There is only half a mile to go, mostly an easy standing walk, just one steep drop and few narrow ledges, pits to avoid dropping into. When they reach the common rooms, Bruvec turns toward the medical chambers, but Jin starts for the showers.

"Jin, no."

"I know. To docs. Shower first."

"You'll pass out."

"Better clean unconscious than awake filthy. Food gave some strength," Jin lies.

Minutes later, Jin wakes up in Bruvec's arms as it carries it from the shower to the medics, dripping mud along the way. Jin watches gray-ringed puddles spread on white sheets while it waits for the doctor, wondering why it can't lose consciousness now. Wet hair drips down Jin's back, in need of cutting. Its side aches, its shin stings, and its feet burn. It wants real food, not stringy dried meat it can't even swallow. Where is Keri? It could handle some fresh fruit, if there is any around. Jin drifts into sleep, not a faint, where it dreams of chasing chickens it never catches. It walks on potatoes, too hot to eat, blisters moving up its legs. It falls into darkness after a wrong turn in the caves, landing softly in a place where finger-size ants crawl on its skin.

"It'll be okay," says the doctor's voice. "Needs antibiotics, rest, nourishment. Might have gaps in its memory. No structural brain damage but hard to tell yet what malnutrition has done."

Jin opens its eyes to see Bruvec nodding. A medic Jin doesn't know hands it a bottle of blue-speckled pills.

"One every eight hours, with meal," says the medic. "Six small meals a day from menu I'll give Ker, start with liquids only. Stay in bed. No walking, your feet are near gone."

"Bath?" says Jin.

"If carried to tub."

Bruvec grins. "Shall I carry you, highness?"

"Knock off, Bruv. Let Ker. You carried here."

Bruvec picks it up anyway, and Jin leans its head on the old neut's shoulder, wrapping its thin arms around the wiry body, listening to the beating heart.

"Can't stand you, Bruv."

"Me too, you, dumb Jin," laughs Bruvec. "But you so skinny, makes me look strong, carrying by self."

Jin sits on a bench in the shower, watching warm brown water swirl away. When the water starts to run clear, it puts its head back under and the flow turns brown again. Bruvec stands nearby to make sure it doesn't drown.

"Bruv?"

"Yes, Jin?"

"Scissors."

Bruvec leaves reluctantly, and Jin watches the water again. It refuses to pass out. Soap froths over its feet and legs as it scrubs, stinging the cuts until they go numb. It sits up, letting the blood flow back out of its head.

"Scissors, Jin."

Jin takes the scissors and grabs a handful of hair together, cutting as straight across as it can just behind the neck. It can barely hold its arms up long enough to cut. Suppressing the fear at its own body's disobedience, Jin sets a three-inch-long ponytail on the edge of the tub and rests a little before continuing to wash what is left of its hair. Bruvec reaches in and takes the tangle away, leaving a brown drip trail behind it. Jin closes its eyes, feeling tiny soap bubbles pop against its skin. It listens to their static sound. They smell so clean. It blows a handful of the bubbles at Bruvec when it returns.

"Silly Jin, act age," says Bruvec.

"You first."

It smiles, crossing its arms in the mockery of a corpse.

"Not *that* old," says Jin.

It turns the water off and stands to reach for a towel.

"Sit!" says Bruvec, handing the pile of absorbent cloth to Jin.

All the scrubbing wasn't enough. When Jin pulls the towel away, both the fabric and the tub are streaked with desert brown and the darker maroon of almost-clotted blood.

"Don't worry, Sandy will clean. She wants work. You rest," says Bruvec.

"Sandy?" says Jin.

"Girl Tei brought. You remember."

It hadn't known the girl was still here. Jin wonders what Keri has to say about that as Bruvec carries it to a private room.

"Not common rooms?" says Jin.

It usually sleeps there in the dormitory. Anyone who visits Home Cavern for a brief stay sleeps there, leaving the few private rooms for those who are at the Cavern on extended research or other longer trips. Realization comes with a dull, silent *oh*.

The private room is all clean white and silver. Even the limestone walls and floor have been whitewashed. A steel writing desk and bed frame match the simple gray rug on the floor. No color, nothing impure. Jin's skin contrasts, brown-red from natural pigment and the sun, almost the same color as its jagged, sun-lightened hair. It runs a hand over the blanket, leaving no dirt streaks. Perfect. It crawls under the covers and lets its wet hair soak the pillow.

"Thanks," it says.

"Night, Jin," says Bruvec.

Jin doesn't know whether Bruvec stays to watch as it drops into sleep.

"Oh good, you're up," says a voice from the doorway.

"Sand?" says Jin.

"Well, I used to be Sandy, but everyone around here seems to find the last syllable too much of a bother." She smiles and hands Jin a tray. "Your breakfast, your majesty. You know, you really do look like a queen or prince or something piled up on all those pillows, only you're way too thin. Royalty are supposed to be fat. That's how they show their wealth, right?"

"Sometimes," says Jin.

"Aren't you going to eat? Keri said I had to make sure you ate enough. She came in to check on you while you were sleeping and came back out practically crying. I can't see why. Sure, you're skinnier than when I last saw you, but you were kind of thin then, too. You'd better eat that before it gets any colder, though jackrabbit soup for breakfast seems kind of gross to me. Bruvec said it's what you asked for."

"Only edible thing docs will let me have," says Jin.

It starts to eat slowly, only paying half attention to Sandy's chatter, trying to feel the strength of its teeth on the small bits of meat in the soup, but its teeth are weak, and every bite hurts its gums. It chokes slightly, remembering the crunch of bugs, the slithering raw fish. Watching the food makes eating easier. Jin's body systems perk up, grabbing at the nutrients. The increased pulse nearly makes it feel sick again. Even so, the food is gone too fast.

"Well, you certainly were starving."

Sandy clears the bowl away.

"Thanks. More soon?" says Jin.

She pats its shoulder. It suppresses a flinch.

"Don't worry, I'll tell Keri you're hungry and see what I can do. If you need anything, just holler. I'm kind of on call here, so it's up to you to keep me out of mischief."

"Just need rest now."

Sandy's smile evaporates.

"Of course. I'm sorry to blather on like this; it's just been getting kind of boring here. I don't know enough to do any real research, but cooking and cleaning just aren't particularly exciting. I thought I'd try nursing, but you're the only patient I've got. So be a good patient and get your rest, all right?"

She dims the light panel on her way out, and Jin sinks into soft, white sleep.

Sleep, eat, repeat. That is all Jin does. It feels its body absorb the nutrients, feels its brain grow healthy again. Sleep, eat, sleep. Talk to Sandy.

"Talk to me?" Sandy laughs. "Don't you mean listen? I don't think I've heard you string more than ten words together since you got back."

"No gossip," says Jin.

"Yeah, I guess you wouldn't have picked up any where you were. Tell me about Albuquerque."

"Crowded. Even after last plague, six years ago. Water rationing, tourists everywhere. Good people, bad, most in between."

Sandy's eyes flash. "Oh, come on. There's got to be more to tell than that. I'm from rural Montana. All I ever saw of the country was out the sides of a passenger booth strapped on top of a water tanker when Tei brought me here. I want to know what the city's like. Any city, for that matter, as long as it's a real city and not just a big town. Is it true you've been to some hi-loc restaurants? Where else have you been?"

"Amarillo, last. Eugene, Lafayette, Baton Rouge. LA. All spreaders hit California and New York. Hardest to control."

"Where else? There has to be more," says Sandy.

"Fifteen years, many cities. Four per year, maybe. Different climates, different economies, same people everywhere."

"Still, it must be nice to travel. Are you finished with that?" says Sandy.

Jin shakes its head and pulls its lunch plate closer to finish the sandwich, grateful it is finally allowed solid food again. It stretches forward. The dizziness has been gone for three days now. Time to start strengthening again. When Sandy takes the plate away, Jin twists and rolls around in bed, hanging over the sides, stretching up and down. Anything that doesn't involve its feet.

"Are you sure you should be doing that? You don't want to rip your side open again. It's finally healing okay. Here, let me check," says Sandy.

Jin humors the girl, but its own internal examination of the wound is more thorough. A fine layer of new skin is forming under the scab, growing strong. There will be a scar, but Jin doesn't mind. Beauty is not a requirement for spreaders.

"Yeah, I guess you're okay. We can probably take your bandage off tomorrow. I'll see which one of the medics wants to deal with you this time. But I wouldn't plan on entering any bathing suit contests."

"Swim naked."

Sandy's eyes grow wide and her face heats red. "Oh, I didn't mean—do you really do that? All neuters?"

"Most here. No one self-conscious about what's not there. Outside, don't swim around people," says Jin.

"Yeah, I guess it's just hard to orient my thinking that way. Sometimes I think of you as a teenage boy, sometimes a slightly older girl. Just a bit older than me, I guess."

It realizes that Sandy is lonely. The only one of her kind around Home Cavern is Keri, who is always busy and not much interested in entertaining another gen. It ghosts Sandy slightly, testing the feeling.

"How old?" Jin asks.

"I'm eighteen, I think. It's September, isn't it? I just turned eighteen a few days ago. I hadn't even realized," she says.

"Happy birthday."

"Thanks. How old are you, anyway?"

Jin calculates.

"Thirty-two, maybe."

"Thirty," says Bruvec from the doorway. "Found you at fifteen, been here fifteen."

"Close enough," says Jin.

"Oh," says Sandy, flustered again. She takes Jin's tray away, smiling unconsciously at Bruvec on her way out.

"Need anything?" asks Bruvec.

Jin sniffs.

"Shower again. Smell musty. Hardscreen, maybe."

"What you need computer for? Rest brain, too."

"Boredom not restful."

"I'll bring you book."

"Really? Thanks." A paper book meant an older publication, and Bruvec rarely shared those treasures outside its own library. Unless it meant one of Keri's antique paperbacks. Jin hoped not.

"I'll carry you to shower now. Ready?"

"Let Sand, she's bored. Curious, too. Let her learn."

Bruvec nods and reaches out its hand. Jin touches the backs of the fingers lightly. Bruvec leaves, and Jin fidgets in bed. It hasn't had time to read a whole book in six years, other than for research. It stretches more, unable to rest.

"Bruvec says you want me to take you to your bath," says Sandy.

"You're nurse, right? Part of job," says Jin.

Sandy grins. "Well then, I guess I'd better do my job. Come on, patient. Off we go."

Jin lets her carry it, wondering why no one ever thought to bring wheelchairs to the Home Cavern clinic. Of course, there may never have been a need for them before. Sandy flinches and turns away when Jin starts to undress.

"Won't turn you to stone," Jin snaps.

"What?" says Sandy.

Her face is bright pink, and she looks about to cry.

"Sorry. From old legend. Ugly beast turns people stone if they look."

"But you aren't ugly! I mean, I wasn't really looking, but I never thought..."

Helpless, her eyes shift around to anywhere but Jin. She doesn't relax until Jin slides into the tub, then she looks only at its face.

"Okay to look at body. Sorry was cross. Most gens repulsed by neut looks," says Jin.

"You really don't mind? I guess it's just all so different from the way I grew up, you know?"

Jin sinks deeper into the warm water, letting Sandy ramble on about modesty, hormonal males, and her one experience at a public swimming pool. Maybe that's why most gens look at neut bodies in horror, but Jin doubts that. It has never seen them look at each other that way. It shakes its head to clear away the image of angry gens with too-blue eyes. It came here to get clean.

# CHAPTER 10

Sandy left Jin alone as soon as it was back in its room. She couldn't believe she had managed to anger Jin so soon after its return. She couldn't believe Jin would get so annoyed with her for trying to be polite.

She went back to the computing lab and asked Net if it could spare her a pocketscreen for non-research purposes, just this once. There had been no researchers there for several days, and she really wanted the kind of privacy that didn't just come from being ignored. She dropped a recorded drama onto the screen and hiked a short way to her favorite chamber. She closed her eyes and sprawled on the ground, letting the ear wires feed her the sound and her memory supply the visuals. If only she could block out the cold and the smell of rock, she could pretend she was at home on the couch, surrounded by friends, eating salty popped corn from last year's crop.

If she imagined herself in the basement, then maybe she could believe. She could even believe that the soft footsteps that reached her ears despite the wires were someone that she knew, someone she wanted to see.

"Homesick?" said Bruvec from somewhere to her left.

Sandy pulled the wires out of her ears, letting the sound reach out into the still air. She didn't bother to sit up.

"Most who come here don't miss home," said Bruvec.

Sandy wanted to say that she didn't miss home, she missed *people*—people who knew how to converse for pleasure, not information, who knew how to hug and joke and play—but she couldn't. Not to Bruvec, who was the only one who understood.

Instead she waited, feeling herself shut down until she was no different from the rest of them, detached and miserable and alone.

She saw Bruvec move slightly, and knew it was ghosting her.

"Poor Sand," it said, voice full of sympathy. "But wrong."

"Wrong?" said Sandy.

"We don't feel so alone. You need more than me, more than Jin. You need gens."

Sandy pulled herself upright, trying to think what it would be like to be back home, to be in the world of natural daylight and noise and life. She shook her head.

"I do. I need that, but I can't go back there," she said.

"Why?"

She stilled the flutter of panic in her chest. Up there were murderers, rapists, and all kinds of other dangers. Her mother was gone and Dad and Ronnie where God knew where, and she still didn't want to explain to her friends what happened, especially now that she had the Network's secrets to keep.

"I'll tell Jin I'm sorry. I'll get back to work here. Really, I'm trying," said Sandy.

She started to leave, but Bruvec gestured for her to wait.

"Your choice. Always," it said. "But don't just run off. Network is afraid you might tell."

"You don't trust me?" said Sandy.

"Do. But you need bonding with others now, and sometimes secrets come out."

She wanted to argue, but she knew it was right. She did have a tendency to babble sometimes, especially now that she so rarely had a listening ear.

"I would never tell anyone on purpose," she said.

"Know. But stay for little while, okay? I'll work, find way to make better," said Bruvec.

Sandy couldn't help herself. She hugged it briefly, then went to return the screen to Net and seek out Keri.

Keri was in one of her moods, moving nonstop around the kitchen, checking ingredients and ovens. Sandy knew better than to get in Keri's way. To do so was to risk being swatted with some sort of kitchen implement.

"About time you showed up. You're late for taking Jin its meal," said Keri when she noticed Sandy hovering in the entry.

"Already? It just ate about an hour ago."

"Three hours and counting. Where did you learn to tell time? The tray's in the warmer, though it's probably dry as a bone by now. If Jin complains, you're taking the blame," said Keri.

"It won't complain," said Sandy.

"Not out loud, but that doesn't mean it's not thinking about it. Go."

Sandy waited until Keri strode to the other end of the kitchen before she grabbed the tray out of the warming range. She didn't mind Keri's sharp words, but her hand still had a tiny red mark from the day before, when she had stepped between the cook and her bubbling stew. The sharp thwack of the metal whisk hadn't hurt so much as startled her, but the gesture had seemed so automatic that she wasn't sure Keri would be able to stop herself from doing it again, and the next time she might have something sharp in her hand.

Sandy mentioned that to Jin when as she sat watching it eat, trying to keep the conversation away from the bathtub and the day before.

Jin took a swallow of tea. "Ker won't hurt," it said.

"Oh, I know she doesn't mean to hurt me. I just think sometimes she forgets that there are other people around her, and I'd hate to be forgotten when she was carrying a knife," said Sandy.

"How she copes," said Jin.

"With being a gen down here?" said Sandy.

Jin nodded.

"I don't think I can handle it much longer. I don't see how you stand it, living with hardly anyone around," said Sandy.

"Don't see how you stand up top," said Jin.

"Oh, the crowds can be overwhelming sometimes, like when my friends and I would go to movies in town on a Friday night. But it's just people. And out on the farm it was just me and Mom and the ranch hands who worked the fields and the slaughterhouses. That wasn't crowded at all."

"You worked slaughterhouses?" said Jin.

"Ugh. No. They stank worse than the henhouse, and that's saying a lot. I just liked having the other people around. On holidays, I'd bring them lunch or dessert. That was the only time I actually went out there."

Jin looked down at its own tray, and Sandy got the impression it was stifling a smile.

"Yeah, I'm a regular serving girl," she said.

Jin's smile formed for real, and Sandy relaxed. It had forgiven her, at least partly, for her earlier mistake, though she still wasn't convinced she'd said or done anything wrong. Jin was the one who assumed she was turning away from it because it was ugly. She had never said that, never even thought the word.

But she had thought it looked strange. She didn't want to use the word "wrong," but it was there in her mind. The unbroken body had certainly not looked right, and Sandy could no longer think of Jin as a young man or woman. It was something else, and she really wasn't sure anymore how different from her it was.

"Tell me about being a spreader," she said.

"Why?"

"I just want to understand. Tei told me what it did before it brought me down here, just so I wouldn't feel betrayed or misled when I found out."

"Told you that?"

"Yeah. It told me about that before it told me about the Network. I think it was testing me to see how I'd react to the concept before it trusted me enough to tell me about the Network. I'm still not sure why it did."

Jin shrugged. "Instinct, maybe. Smart doesn't always mean rational."

"So tell me about what you do, then."

"You already know."

"I know what you do and a little bit about how you do it, but I still don't understand how you *can*," said Sandy.

Jin sighed as if it had been through all of this too many times before. It set the tray over on a side table and stretched its body, twisting and reaching in ways that made Sandy worry about injury, but it always seemed fine afterward and she didn't want to test its patience by insisting that it stop.

"I'll talk if you take me out," it said.

"Out where?"

"Anywhere but kitchen, baths, labs. Cave somewhere. Quiet."

"How am I supposed to do that?" said Sandy. "Those pathways require the kind of climbing that you can't do yet. The medics would kill me if Keri didn't get to me first. Even Bruvec would rip me apart."

"Not Bruv."

"You don't know what this place was like before you got back home. It was so upset it hardly spoke more than Net."

Jin raised its eyebrows at this but said nothing.

"All right. I'll take you. Just let me get this tray back to Keri and scout out a route that's not too difficult. I'll be right back," she said.

She took the tray back to the kitchen, ignoring the dirty dishes that Keri would scold her later for neglecting. The path to the cavern Sandy normally used for escape would be impossible to reach with the makeshift wheelchair Net had rigged up from equipment in the research labs. The little cart could hardly handle the trip to the showers. Sandy scouted around for other caves that were easier to get to, but they all required some climbing or more crawling than Jin looked ready for. She went back to its room.

"How much do you weigh?" she asked it.

"Don't know. You've lifted before," it said.

She had, but that was just to transfer it from the bed to the cart, from the cart to the shower bench. Now, she lifted Jin straight up off the bed, testing its weight.

"Would you be able to hang on if I carried you piggyback?" said Sandy.

They tried, and after some scrambling, Jin was settled in with its arms wrapped loosely around her neck. She let it back down onto the bed, laughing.

"You're just like my little brother. He always wanted a piggyback ride, but then he was too much of a showoff to hang on tightly."

"Will work?"

"I think it'll work. Let's go," said Sandy.

She pushed Jin on the cart for the first part, then let it ride on her back for a short, precarious climb down to another tunnel level. She left Jin resting there while she hid the cart down a rarely used corridor, just in case anyone came looking for them.

From there, she carried Jin again for a short distance until they were at a spot where they could turn on a lantern and brighten the room without the light being seen from above. She had to practically force Jin to stay off its feet once the lantern was lit, but it finally gave up and settled against the rocks, looking up at the stalactites above.

Sandy sat near it and shook out a blanket over both of them, reminded of the times she and Ronnie would play explorers in the cellar, setting up camp for a long winter's siege. Jin closed its eyes and drew in a long, slow breath, its face softening into a look of contentment.

"Missed this," it said.

"What, the smell of wet rocks?" said Sandy.

"And silence."

Sandy sat as still as she could, trying to see the cavern the way Jin did—something to come home to. The caverns comforted her too, but only in a lonely way, like a house that was empty but full of familiar things.

She let Jin absorb the place in silence for a while, then asked it again about the spreading.

What she got was little more than Tei had told her. Slow but steady population growth and resource shortages and the black-and-white contrast of life and death held against the colorful panorama of individual choice. She still didn't understand how they could live with themselves after spreading a plague, but she became fairly certain she didn't want to know.

She was sitting next to a killer, but one so unlike the men who had attacked her mother that she would have taken its hand for comfort had she not known that it didn't want her to. Instead, she changed the subject, telling Jin about the men she had found exploring for dump sites and her part in the work crew that reformed the tunnels overnight.

"Anything since?" asked Jin.

"I don't think so. Bruvec said people were watching the trail, but so far no one has come down there. It sent word out for other neuts not to use that pathway anymore," said Sandy.

Jin just looked thoughtful.

"Why would they do all that work and then not come back?" said Sandy.

"Takes time. Maybe lost funding, waiting for approval," said Jin.

Sandy supposed it was right. Still, she wanted to find out if the ruse had worked. If the changes they made weren't enough, there could be toxic waste a short hike away from where they all slept. She drew the blanket tighter around her.

"Do you know someone named En? It was the neut I was helping on the project, and it said it lived somewhere near here, somewhere farther down."

"Don't know. Probably artist cave," said Jin.

"There's an artist's cave down there?" said Sandy.

"Enclave of artists," said Jin.

Something about that sent a thrill of excitement down Sandy's throat. So there were neuts who weren't scientists and researchers. She had thought the work crew were simply more laboratory types with construction experience. The ones she met certainly acted little different from the Home Cavern dwellers. Still, something about the idea pleased her.

"I think I saw a neut on a video," she said.

Jin looked at her, waiting.

"I was watching a show, and one of the actors—it was in heavy makeup, so I couldn't tell—but it reminded me of you. I think it was a neut," said Sandy.

"Not me," said Jin.

Sandy was about to protest that she hadn't meant that when she realized Jin was teasing her. She smiled and shook her head, wondering if she would ever stopped being surprised when Jin or the others showed a sense of humor. She wasn't sure she could handle staying with them long enough to find out.

# CHAPTER 11

"Jin! Did the doctor say you could be up already?"

Jin shows Keri its bare foot.

"Almost healed."

Keri shudders at the thick layers of scar tissue and calluses. Jin shoves its foot back into the slipper. At least they aren't so badly swollen anymore. It sits at the kitchen table, chin on its hand.

"Any news?" it asks.

"You mean Sandy hasn't talked your ear off yet? She's sure talked mine off about you. Be careful with that girl; she's pretty fragile for all her act. If you had a gender, I'd say she had a crush on you."

"She's curious. I answer."

"Maybe. What do you want? More plain goat and kale? Don't you ever get sick of that stuff?"

"Good for healing. Feeling better now; make fancy if you like. Small bit of lamb, maybe," says Jin.

Keri glares at it, but Jin just smiles blandly back. They both know Jin only eats lamb or beef when it wants to build up extra energy for a trip.

"So you're planning on going off again so soon, are you? What do Bruvec and the doctors say?"

"Not going out, just into deep caves," says Jin.

"Even worse. Now you get to go beat yourself to death in your mind, as if both it and your body haven't already taken enough. Do you want to end up like Taylor or Nuin?"

"Nuin too?"

"Nuin too."

"Same way?" asks Jin.

"It was definitely stabbed to death, but there were signs of some disease too. I just hate to see you go out there. It's going to get worse. Stay down here, and let the masses run the world dry or figure it out for themselves. Let them live or die on their own, but stay out of it where you're safe, Jin."

"No."

"Why not? Do you like your job so much that you wouldn't be happy not spreading disease?"

"You know that's not why."

Keri turns back to her cooking. Jin smiles, ghosting her frustration and her concern. She knows better than to argue with it, but still she tries. Her stubbornness is what Jin likes most in her.

Jin trades in white pajamas for tan travel clothes and new shoes. The shoes are a full size bigger than it used to wear, but that can't be helped. The damage to its feet will never completely heal. A small food pack, a pocketscreen, and a canteen are all it carries.

It circles cautiously around the outer passageways. The Carlsbad Caverns tourist caves are several miles north and west of Home Cavern and nowhere near as deep, but sometimes researchers and explorers come closer than Jin would like. It listens carefully, headlamp turned low. Only rock and water distort the hum it sends down the passage. Narrow corridors force Jin to shape itself around protruding rocks. It worm-crawls on its stomach and back, this time without losing consciousness. It climbs down notches cut into bare rock until the crevice opens out into a large cavern where the only sounds are dripping water and the occasional scuttle of insects.

Jin strikes a lantern it picked up from one of the Network's stashes, and the whole cave takes on a warm, orangish glow. It switches off the headlamp and pauses to breathe in cool air, slightly colder than home without the generators to add a few degrees. All possible shades of brown and gray surround it. A clear pool sits at the base of a glistening pillar with an army of stalagmites at its feet. This is better than anything the tourists take pictures of. Jin sets the lantern in the center of the room and wanders. Muscles relax now that it is finally alone, safe, and mostly clean, aside from the travel dirt. It touches the rock formations lightly, praising their beauty. Nowhere in the world is like here, so silently breathtaking. It sits against a rock, drinking water and absorbing the view for a while. Above it are rock curtains so thin that light shines through them. So many tunnel openings lead out of the chamber that Jin feels like a mouse in a giant block of Swiss cheese, hungry to begin.

Pacing sets Jin's mind in motion and warms up its muscles. North, south, north, south. The monotony of the eleven-step path lulls its brain into the memories it wants to explore. It pictures itself walking through the Albuquerque streets, Lily on one side, Bill on the other, his knifepoint just below its ribs. Jin's muscles remember ghosting their movements. Now it acts out the movements fully, living Bill from start to the knife-cut, at which point the connection is lost. Jin runs through the action a few times, helping the memory grow stronger. It doesn't usually wait so long before processing. There are several gaps; it can't tell yet if the memories are gone from malnutrition, or if the ghosting was interrupted during the study.

After a few initial runs, Jin narrows its focus slightly, concentrating on the time between Bill and Lily deciding it is a girl and the moment it kicks Lily. The length of time is still exhausting and has several small gaps. It focuses on the circulatory and respiratory systems, giving each one two runs through, then adds in the memory of ghosting Lily. Most of the time gaps fill in. Jin just lost focus on him to concentrate on her for those moments. Over and over, it runs the scenario, taking only short rests in between. As chemicals flood through its system, it enters them into the pocketscreen, adding standardized equations for the hormones and gendered thought patterns its neuter brain can't supply.

Once circulatory, respiratory, nervous, and endocrine systems are cataloged on the pocketscreen for both gens, Jin compares the data to the attacked woman from the alley. No good. The reactions are too similar. Nothing strikes it as useful for creating a disease. It rests and eats, clearing its head. After a brief nap, it splashes its face with water from the cavern pool and begins again.

Too many instructions from the nervous system tangle together. Jin can't sort man from woman from self. It backs up and tries to recapture the feelings first; it can trace the chemicals afterward.

Bill: *excitement, sexual arousal, stab of both, tension, contained excitement, growing arousal, (gap), distrust, excitement, (gap), heightened arousal, uncertainty, eagerness, surprise.*

Jin runs through his reactions twice more, but the two gaps remain. Frustration can ruin a study, bleeding into the memories and altering the data. Jin sits and watches the reflections in the pool until it is calm again. Then it eats and thinks.

That first gap—had Jin done something to cause the distrust that followed? Who or what did Bill distrust? It, Lily, something in the environment, or maybe himself? Jin runs the scene a few times in its head, just the regular, nonkinesthetic kind of memory. The gap occurred just before they entered the building. Right before that moment, Bill slowed and leaned in. The gap means nothing, he just mistrusted the building.

Jin still feels like something is missing. It uses its visual memory to fill in.

Just before the gap there is a slight shiver through him. A trickle of sweat runs down his cheek. Fear? It runs through the chemistry again.

*There.*

He has the slightest shift in body and attention, angling toward the door. The sensation is not fear, but guilt. Just a tiny shred, but the guilt is there. Jin catalogs the feeling for potential use. Now it can dig more deeply into the specific chemical balance and firing patterns in each subject's mind.

Remember, eat, log, sleep. The familiar routine comforts Jin. Food is starting to get low. Soon it will have to go back and ask Keri for more.

Nothing stands out as a route toward a plague. The biochemical reactions of victims and attackers are too similar to each other, too similar to reactions that could be caused by everyday events. A plague built on such data would kill at random, worse than random, leaving alive only those who didn't react to any kind of stimulation.

Jin will have to return home and transfer the study onto one of the larger screens. The pocketscreen's display, even when unfolded, is not enough to keep the layers of information sorted appropriately, and Jin's own memory is still sluggish. Even if it weren't, a stronger brain than humans possess is needed to actively use so much data at once, a brain that doesn't have to keep up with functions such as breathing, moving, staying alive.

Before returning home, Jin lies beside the pool, letting the cool, still air relax it. The sweat of frustration dries, and all thoughts of Albuquerque drain away. It takes the walk back to Home Cavern slow and easy. The bright white of home hurts its eyes; the steel glares. Everything is too bright, too clean. The cave dirt on its pants is a stain, an eyesore.

"Net," Jin says in greeting.

"Jin."

Net nods it toward a screen at the back of the room. There is a small cluster of researchers near the front, but they are silently absorbed in their work.

Jin drops the memory from the pocketscreen and begins to chart out the studies, one by one. For so many years, it has studied the human body and brain. Now, with just its memories and ghosting, it knows by feel exactly where brain and hormonal activity is clustered. It could draw the equivalent of the most advanced magnetic scans from the data it holds.

Jin calls up a file with its own neurochemical charts to compare. The system already has records of its brain functions in a range of emotions and activities. It splits the screen four ways and begins to compare the attackers, the alley woman, and itself, chemical by chemical, signal by signal. Each subject shows different amounts of the hormones and neurotransmitters, but the basic components are the same.

Jin unrolls a second flexscreen from a nearby charging tube and links it to the first screen. It shifts its displays, arranging the chemicals in chronological order from the memory sequence, running left to right in squiggling lines like a seismograph, using the width of both screens. The data becomes an unreadable mess when Jin tries to overlay and compare two charts, never mind all four. It clears the display, rearranging the output to cover all four available flexscreens.

Chemicals line the left side of the contiguous screens, with vertical bars marking five-second segments of their flow. The display looks like a music score out of some fevered composer's nightmare.

Net sets a plate near Jin, but as far from the equipment as possible.

"Ker insists," says Net.

Jin nods and continues filling in lines, tracing chemicals, and refining the charts. Its fingers are not fine enough to get the detail it wants on the touch screen, so it switches to a brush. Net looks over its shoulder.

"Strange music."

Jin pushes back and eats while staring at the chart. Net stares too, but it is more interested in making sure that the crumbs stay away from its precious hardware.

"Anyone in Network researching sound waves?" says Jin.

"Eus dot wave."

Jin calls up the file "Eus.wave" to find that the most current sound research is being conducted by the Network branch in the Mediterranean. Nothing in the file is quite what Jin needs—mostly old research on sound's general effects on neurotransmitter activity. Jin decides to send a message in case there is something that hasn't been dropped into the Network intranet yet.

The reply might take seconds or weeks, depending on how active the project is, so Jin gets back to work. It color codes the charts and tries overlaying them again on a single screen. Big, bold strokes of major chemicals like epinephrine, norepinephrine, cortisol and acetylcholine blot out the white background almost entirely. Except in Jin's control chart, they are all too similar. That's good, though. Bystanders can potentially be sorted out by that difference. Timing and duration of minor neurotransmitters show noticeable differences between the victim and attackers, but Jin still doesn't have enough data.

It needs some deep cave time again to catalog its own experience as a victim under attack, if enough attention was left between ghosting to notice anything of itself. It also should have retrievable data from the attack in Amarillo and the face-off with Blue-eyes in Albuquerque. That might be enough to isolate what it needs. If not, it will have to go out and seek new attackers. Sandy and Bruvec won't like that. Keri will probably chain it to its bed.

Jin takes its plate back to Keri and fills a pack for its return to the deep caves.

The trip is short. Reliving its own memories is easier than constructing from ghosted body patterns. Back in the computing lab, the new data takes half a day to chart. Jin as victim, Jin as killer. It sorts through the Network files for records of other spreaders; after all, the intent of a plague is the same as that of an attack. Their brain patterns nearly match Bill and Lily's if Jin removes the major chemicals of stress and fear, and of course the hormones that separate neuts from gens. Already, it can feel the deeper portions of its mind begin to fit these patterns together into something that will become another healing disease.

Data from the few moments of ghosting Blue-eyes adds grace notes to Jin's sheet music of malice and fear. Aside from the stress reactions and hormones, there are other differences Jin notices between gens and neuts, all concerning duration of the chemical flow. It removes most of the neuter charts, bringing forward the woman from the alley. All of her chemicals spike higher, faster.

It stares for a while at the screen, then saves everything and shuts down. It returns to the private room Bruvec is still keeping for it and sleeps, thinks, and sleeps for three days.

There is no mail from the Mediterranean project yet, so Jin studies the scant amount of data it has for Blue-eyes. He shows no adrenaline, even just after attacking Jin. The chart is a pattern of average daily life: walking, talking, thinking. Just to check, Jin charts itself as it sits. Practically the same. Seems odd for a man to throw someone to the ground and steal their belongings with such a balanced biochemistry. He hadn't seemed so calm at the time.

His major chemicals chart into long, thin lines. The rest are short dashes, all overlapping. Like Jin's chart. Like the other neuts whose files Jin has pulled.

But he smelled like a man, and had the beginnings of a beard.

Okay, so he smelled like a man. He also knew about neuters and spreaders and that the base of the Network was somewhere near Albuquerque. Probably the exact location. He knew about ghosting. He looked for a plague and he took Jin's pack.

Jin calls up the visual memory of him leaning back, smiling. He says something, watching Jin. It says something and stands. Its mind's eye sees what it didn't notice then: Blue-eyes' body gathers and stretches forward as he inhales. He was ghosting.

Can a man learn to ghost? Probably. All he has to do is shadow a person's movements and shape his body as they shape theirs. But would he have the sensitivity to alter the chemical flow in himself, or to understand and use the data?

Jin calls up more neuter charts—medics, recruiters, and artists. Spreaders differ slightly from the other groups. The knowledge of self as a killer permanently alters some of the chemical patterns.

Blue-eyes not only thinks like a neut, he has a spreader brain. All of the patterns match.

# CHAPTER 12

Each day, Sandy wandered farther up the pathway toward the surface. She traveled the main route up toward Carlsbad Caverns National Park on most days. The path was well used and well marked by the passage of many feet. There were plenty of twists and turns and places to get hurt or lost, but Net had rigged up a charger for her old pocketscreen and given her full access to the Home Cavern maps. Between those and the directions she had coaxed out of Jin, the way seemed clear.

Too clear.

Gens could find the entrance any time and come down exploring, looking for recreation or a place for more waste or any number of things.

"Not likely," Jin had said when Sandy had voiced her concerns.

"Maybe not, but it could happen, couldn't it?"

Jin had merely shrugged and said something about a special locked door at the entrance that gens couldn't find. Sandy remembered from her own trip down that Tei had seemed to open a hole in solid rock. She hadn't seen how it managed the trick, and she doubted any of the tourists would either, even if they followed a neut through the desert to where the entrance lay.

Still, Sandy told herself that she was monitoring the pathway for any danger. As Jin got better and spent more time on its own work, she climbed even farther, all the way up until she imagined she could feel the air warming around her so near the sun. At that point she had to admit to herself that she no longer worried about intruders. She just wanted to see if she could do it—find her way out of this blackness and get back into the open air.

The climbing made her sore, but already she could see her muscles starting to change tone and the roundness her mother had still called baby fat melting away. The day she touched the back side of the door that led out to the surface, she rushed back to the tunnels nearly giddy with the accomplishment.

She couldn't tell Bruvec—it would worry about her leaving. She wasn't sure how Keri would react, but when she got to the kitchen, something stopped her from saying anything.

"You look a wreck. Where've you been?" said Keri.

"Just exploring," said Sandy.

"You've been doing a lot of that lately. Deciding to become part mole?"

"I think I'm all mole by now. Sometimes it feels like if I try hard enough I'll be able to see in the dark," said Sandy.

"Moles don't see. Other senses," said Jin.

Sandy turned to see it standing behind her in padded slippers and its usual white and tan clothes.

"I guess you don't need me to bring your food on trays anymore," said Sandy.

"It will if it keeps missing meals while spending every waking moment in the computing lab," said Keri.

"Net says can't eat there anymore."

"I'm surprised it let you eat in the lab even when you needed to," said Keri.

Sandy watched the two of them, the easy conversation. Maybe it was still the endorphins from the climb washing her brain, but for the first time in quite a while, she felt utterly at ease in Home Cavern. It almost felt like a place that deserved to be called Home.

Smiling to herself, she decided to keep her journey to the surface a secret for a while. Eventually, she would ask Jin how to open the door, either with or without telling it why. She was fairly sure it would know either way as soon as she asked.

Or sooner.

Jin followed behind her as she wandered the corridors, heading toward the computing lab to drop more shows now that she had her own screen back, or perhaps to the showers to see if Keri had been exaggerating about her appearance. She hardly noticed Jin's presence behind her until it spoke softly.

"You miss sun, don't you?" it said.

Sandy stopped walking and glanced up and down the corridor. They were still in the well-lit areas, and they were alone. She looked at Jin.

Jin's mouth twitched in a fleeting smile, and it pulled a daddy longlegs off of Sandy's sleeve, holding the insect up by two legs as the others struggled helplessly in the air.

"Don't live down this far. You've been near surface," it said.

"I wasn't trying to leave, honestly. I just wanted to see if I could find the way by myself."

"Good. Best to know way around."

"You won't tell Bruvec?" asked Sandy.

"Why? Bruv won't mind."

"I think it would. It says the Network is nervous about me being here, and even more nervous about me leaving."

"Not Network. Council. Don't worry," it said.

She wanted to ask it what the difference was and why exactly she shouldn't worry, but it seemed to think the subject was settled.

"Jin?" said Sandy.

Jin waited, eyes expectant.

"I know you said you like it here, and I like it too—really, now more than before, I think—but can you really stay so long without sun and rain and all the smells? I think that's what I miss most. Other smells than dust and rock."

Jin nodded. "That's why spreader, not researcher. Part of why."

"So does that mean you'll tell me how to open the door and get outside?"

Jin hesitated, then shook its head.

"Why not? You made it sound like me going up there wasn't such a big deal," said Sandy.

"Wait. Tomorrow, if no answers on project yet, we'll go."

Sandy let Jin handle Keri's usual complaints while she waited out in the corridor. It endured the verbal torrent placidly and accepted the overloaded bag of snacks that Keri forced on it. Then, not far outside the high-traffic areas, it opened the bag, pulled out a water pouch for each of them and a small packet of something else, then tucked the bag into a dark hole.

"Remember, third on right," it said.

Sandy tucked the food and water into her waist pack. "What happens if we forget?"

"Next week, bad smell. Ker won't forgive for month."

That was the last it spoke to her for a couple of miles. They were three or four miles below the surface, but with the way the path wound around and only occasionally had straight climbs, it took hours to get anywhere at all. Plus there was the crawling and the inching through narrow tubes. By the time they stopped to rest, Sandy was fairly sure she had forgotten how to walk upright. For the next leg of the journey, she chattered on to Jin about what they might find at the surface, whether the day would be dark with clouds or hot and sunny, full of smog or rain.

Jin occasionally answered a direct question, but most of the time it was silent. She wondered why it had decided to come at all, or if it was just there to make sure she didn't run away. It ought to know her better than that by now. They all should.

The last mile they traveled in utter silence other than the sounds of their bodies against rock and the air passing into and out of their lungs. The elation she'd felt on her trip alone wouldn't come, and she wondered if she had done something wrong, something to make Jin angry with her again.

"Shh, listen," it said.

Sandy wanted to tell it that shushing someone who hadn't spoken in hours was silly, but she did as she was told.

"Hear that?" Jin asked.

She strained her ears as hard as she could and held her breath, but all she heard was her own heartbeat, pounding from the latest exertion. The next time Jin shone its light her way, she shook her head.

"That's why both come," it said. "Not safe to open door without knowing other side. Could be person out there."

"Is there?"

Jin was silent again for a while, then shook its head.

"Animal of some kind. Maybe coyote, maybe cat. Hard to tell."

"How can you tell any of that at all?" said Sandy.

"Told you before, better hearing. Can't hear breath or heartbeat, even though rock is thin; can hear footsteps, voices, sometimes paws."

"Then how do you know nobody's out there, or that the coyote or whatever it is isn't a person? Coyote footsteps can't be much louder than a heartbeat."

"Depends on surface. Heard body brush up against rock, not footsteps," said Jin.

"That could have been human."

Jin shook its head and refused to argue more. Instead, it knocked on the door with a sequence of taps in various places.

"Show me that again!" said Sandy.

It did, twice more, then let her try.

This time, when the latch released away from her hand, they stepped out into the bright, hot air.

Sandy closed her eyes to the shock of the sun on dry earth and let her body warm quickly while she tasted the air and smiled at the reddened darkness behind her eyelids. Eventually, she opened them.

Jin had its hand over its nose. Sandy inhaled as deeply as she could. The wasteland scents of rot and rust were strong, but so was the smell of warmth, and that was what she was after. They wandered slowly, a short distance from the mouth of the cavern. With the carved door shut behind them, Sandy realized she would have to rely on Jin to find her way back in. She had no idea if the lock pattern was the same on the outside as the inside, and the face of the rock looked the same from several angles. She couldn't be sure exactly where they had come out.

But Jin was nearby and there was no reason to worry. She had the urge to stretch out on the ground and she gave in to the impulse, squirming like a pup in the heated dirt. Jin laughed, and Sandy laughed back, louder and longer.

"Oh, I needed this. I swear, I don't care how well Keri feeds us down there, until she can put sunshine on a plate I'm not impressed."

She looked over at Jin.

"What's wrong?" she asked.

"Nothing."

Sandy sat up. "Something. I can tell, Jin. Just because I don't ghost and I can't hear what people mutter under their breath all the time doesn't mean I don't know when someone's unhappy. Do you want to head back down?"

It looked at her, seemingly unable to speak, then turned its back on the direction it had been facing.

Sandy looked out toward the east to see what it had seen. There was a city not too far off. She could see high-rises poking their tops over the line of garbage heaps. Not skyscrapers like the pictures she had seen of big cities, or like Denver when the tanker drove through on the way here, but large enough to show her the juxtaposition of living people and their garbage.

She watched the buildings as the sun lowered. It was still far too bright for the evening lights to be coming on, but she tried to imagine the people she couldn't see. Talking, laughing, eating. Holding each other for comfort or for fun. She smiled and hugged her arms to her chest, but her mind crept back toward the silent neut behind her. She tried to imagine those buildings as Jin saw them. People consuming, reproducing, wasting, polluting. Eating up the land until the plants were all gone and building up trash heaps until they blotted out the sky. She shivered in the heat and shook her head to clear it.

That wasn't the way she saw things, no matter what Jin might have to say. She had looked up the statistics herself in an effort to understand, but the concept of population versus resource ratios just didn't seem dire to her. They would manage. Maybe not forever, but it really wasn't so bad.

She was glad to be gendered, to be able to see those families in her mind instead of what they would become. Still, she also turned her back on the cities for the closer vistas of garbage and the mountains rising beyond.

"Okay, Jin," she said. "Let's go back."

It showed her how to find the right surfaces to tap and the pattern that released the silent lock so they could pull the door open and climb into the darkness. They paused a moment for their eyes to adjust to the sallow beams of their flashlights, and Sandy turned back to once again tap out the pattern on the door before pulling it shut a final time behind them.

She could come up without Jin now, perhaps inching the rock open slowly so she could scout the area nearby for danger before she stepped out onto the desert above.

She knew she wouldn't. As barren as the landscape was between the junk piles, she had seen how close the world was pressing, and she wouldn't risk the sanctuary of the neuters' home. Her home, for the time being.

# CHAPTER 13

From: MediWaveP/nnw
To: Jin/USHomeCav/nnw

Try Prof Dair, BakhP.ugr in Germany. Info file nnw/resonance. Write Dair for access. For access to MediWave files, code is Bruvec birth name. Tell Bruv hi. Ask if need more.

Gar/MediWaveP/nnw

Finally, word from the sound research project is in. Jin finds Bruvec in the medical labs, its face thrust into a microscope.

"Question," says Jin.

"Anything for you."

"What's birth name?"

Surprise accents the lines in Bruvec's face, making it look older and younger at the same time.

"Don't remember?" it says.

"Never knew."

Bruvec laughs. "Oh, *my* birth name. Thought you wanted yours."

"You know mine?"

"Know everyone here," it says.

"Yours is access code for file I need. Gar in Mediterranean says hi. Know it?"

"Gar lived here, way back. Grew bored with our caves, went to Greece. Swims daily in sea, so it says."

Jin's skin tingles as it pictures the warm, sparkling water.

"Spreaders ever get vacation?" Jin asks.

"Except you. Fifteen years you never ask. You okay?"

"Maybe. After St. Louis, maybe take time off?"

"Any you say."

Jin nods and turns to go. A light hand stops it.

"Jin," says Bruvec, "never told you name."

The MediWave project files compile years of study on how sound affects the human brain, thoroughly cataloged and cross-referenced. Brainwaves, chemicals, stimulated areas, sound wave size and shape are all analyzed and documented. Jin has to re-arrange all of its study charts again, moving chemicals up and down on the screen to correspond with pitch frequencies. According to the project files, tiny amounts of most mood-related brain chemicals can be triggered by chords or other note combinations and progressions. Only barely able to read music, Jin patches the notes into its chemical charts, unsure whether it is creating a psychological symphony or just plain noise.

"Hi Jin. Keri sent me to force feed you, so don't try to resist," says Sandy.

"Minute."

"You have exactly fifty-seven seconds."

Jin continues charting, carefully pasting the unfamiliar chords over the chemicals it knows like its own pulse. Soon it will need to find help with the instrumentation. It drags its fingers across the screen, now healed enough from the sunburn that the skin no longer cracks every time they bend. The screen goes blank, and Jin finds itself looking through it to the table beyond. Sandy pulls her hand back from the edge of Jin's screen.

"Sand!" yells Jin, loud enough to draw looks from the few others in the lab.

"Calm down, Jin. I gave you a full minute, and it's not like everything isn't automatically saved. All I did was put it to sleep. Everything will be fine. Eat. Look, Net even let me bring your food inside."

"Not hungry."

"Stop acting like a spoiled two-year-old. You were dangerously malnourished, and everyone here wants to make sure you don't lose too many of your valuable brain cells. I can just imagine what carrying on a conversation with you would be like after brain damage. It'd take two hours to get three words out, and they still wouldn't make sense. Eat."

Jin knows when to give in. It takes the plate and chews with slight exaggeration.

"What? Did I actually get through to you? I'm going to have to tell Keri about this one. Hey, are you okay? Or am I too late and the brain damage has already set in?"

"No. Just reminded of someone. Mother."

"You remember your folks?"

"Lived with them fifteen years."

"I guess that makes sense; it's just that nobody talks about their past around here. It's like no one ever had parents or brothers and sisters. Did you? Have brothers or sisters, I mean."

"No."

"I have a brother. I think he's still alive, somewhere up there," says Sandy. "I don't really know, though. He was living with my dad when my mom and I were attacked."

"Miss your dad?" Jin asks.

"No, not really. Well, no more than I did before. I hardly saw him after the divorce. I remember he used to laugh a lot when I was a kid. Were your parents together or separated?"

"Together."

Jin eats slowly, offering Sandy some of the carrot sticks Keri has heaped on the plate. She must have spent a lot of Network funds to have those shipped down from Colorado. The girl rolls a chair over and watches Jin eat.

"What was it like, growing up neuter? Did other kids make fun of you?"

"Not at first. Little kids somewhat neut anyway. Teasing started in fourth grade. Other girls turning into women. By age fourteen, all but me changed."

"So that's when the other kids noticed something was different?"

"Was loner before. Talked stupid, they said, but smarter at schoolwork than three together. Talked more like gen then, but brain often leapt ahead, left out words. Tried not to stand out. Kids called me stupid. Nickname 'Slow Jin' started young. Teased that I must be stupid or drunk."

"Your parents named you Jin? I thought you guys came up with your own names. They're all a little unusual."

"Jennifer. Jen became Gin-with-G for teasing. Name stuck, fit better than Jen."

"Well, I suppose if all you got was teasing, that wasn't so bad."

"Boy named Brad Huxley left dead fish in my locker. Knew him by smell. No one else in seventh grade wore musk, smelled musk on fish, fish on him. Chased him after school, threw fish in his face, punched hard few times and ran. Broke his nose, bruised throat. After that, kids teased from distance."

"Didn't you have any friends?"

"One. For while."

"What happened?"

"Hung out after school, mostly she'd talk, I'd listen. Pretended crush on boy so she wouldn't suspect. Embarrassing. One day we talk about future. I say I want to study animals. She admires, but I see she feels bad about wanting to teach. I tell her teaching's good."

"There's nothing wrong with that," says Sandy.

"Yes. She never told me about teaching."

"Huh?"

"Her face just like yours. You know neuts hear well. She subvocalized, like talking to self inside throat. Lips don't move much, mostly tongue forms words with hint of air. I heard. After that, she's uncomfortable."

"I can see why. Do all neuts hear that well? I thought you could only hear muttering and whispers."

"When young, yes. Learn control later, tune out. Now I use just enough to keep safe, track studies."

"Not safe enough, apparently," says Sandy.

Jin shrugs and turns back to the dark screen. Now that the plate is empty, maybe Sandy will let it work.

Sandy looks at the screen with a knowing smile. "I'll be back in a couple of hours with more food. This time, maybe you'll listen when I tell you to eat."

Jin watches Sandy leave the lab. Having gens around Home Cavern is awkward, like a little bit of the outside world is pressing into the Network core. It has to wait until the sound of Net and the others working lulls it back into the lab's sanctuary before it can work again.

Ups and downs and a sense of counterplay emerge in the charts, but Jin doesn't have enough knowledge of pitch to really hear the difference. It continues until all of the charts are done.

"Net, who's home in artist caves?"

"Which art?" says Net.

"Music."

Net types for a few seconds, then shrugs. "Last population data months old. Don't report often, but sound studio just finished. Should be plenty there."

"Thanks," says Jin, and heads for the kitchen.

---

"Again, Jin?" says Keri. "You know, it wouldn't kill you to take some time off. It's not like anyone up there will miss you."

"After this spread, promise I'll take vacation," says Jin.

"Where are you going this time? How many days?"

"Now or spread?"

"Now," says Keri. "I'd rather not know where you take your plagues."

"Deep caves to see artists. Week, maybe."

"They have food there. Why do you need to bring any?"

"Don't know I'm coming. Don't need extra mouth there."

"Kind of you to think of that," says Keri tonelessly.

"You all right?" says Jin.

Keri nods.

"Then why you look guano?"

"Well, at least you don't beat around the bush."

"Didn't mean to be rude," says Jin.

"No, Jin. It's fine. It's just...Bruvec."

"Bruvec?" Jin's stomach drops. "What's wrong?"

"Nothing new," says Keri, sitting. "It just seems to get more fragile every time I look at it. It doesn't work on much of anything anymore."

Jin brushes the back of Keri's hand with its fingertips. "Not so bad, Ker. Bruv has earned rest."

"More than anyone. But sometimes I catch it looking so sad when it thinks it's all alone. So weak."

"All grow old, Ker. Bruv still has life left."

"It had better. I don't know what I'll do with myself when it's gone."

"Why change? This your home, Bruvec or not. You'll miss Bruv, everyone will, but you're part of Network, much as any neut. Always have place to live, any work you want."

Keri gives a short laugh. "That's good, because I couldn't live anywhere else now. I'm probably the only gen in the world who knows about you and still wishes she was neut, but I'm a woman and always will be."

"What's this talk about being a woman?" says Sandy. "Or is this a private conversation?"

Jin looks at Keri. Her privacy, not its.

"Nothing, Sandy. I'm just moaning to Jin about my miserable life down here. You'll find yourself doing the same if you're here too long."

"Nope," says Sandy, flashing a grin. "I'll just get Jin to tell me stories. It can spin a good one if you ask the right questions."

"Must have been the starvation that altered its brain," says Keri. "Used to be the only person around here who talked less than Jin was Net."

Sandy collapses into a chair. "Like I said, you just have to ask the right questions. So, Jin, what are you up to?"

"Trip," says Jin.

"Can I come?" says Sandy.

# CHAPTER 14

The hand on Jin's foot feels familiar, but this time no one is pushing to wake it up. It crawls forward and pulls itself to standing. No sound comes from up ahead. Jin's headlamp shines into the pit at the center of the room, and all it has to do is scale down there and knock.

"Ow! You did bring a first aid kit, didn't you? My poor knees will never be the same again. Why didn't you tell me there would be so much crawling? The way up to the surface is nothing like this," says Sandy. "Plus, I think I've gained weight. Any more and I'll never squeeze back through that last section."

"Shh."

The rocks are unstable here. Any abrupt noise can cause damage, and Jin has no wish to bury itself alive. It shows Sandy how to find the hand and foot holds, then begins the long climb down. When its feet hit a solid surface, Jin taps Sandy's foot to tell her to slow down. She releases the wall, and they crouch to pass through a short tunnel. Jin taps the rock ahead of them lightly, twice high, once low, then pushes forward and steps into a large phosphorescent chamber. Sandy follows, gawking.

With the door shut behind then, Jin switches off its lantern. As soon as their eyes adjust, violets and greens become clear. Deep purple crystals shimmer in intricate patterns on every wall between patches of blue-green phosphorescence.

"It's like...being underwater," Sandy whispers, "only I can breathe."

She takes long, slow breaths as if to be sure.

"Beautiful?" says Jin.

"Yes, very. Beyond beautiful." She traces part of the pattern with her hand, not quite touching the surface. "It's a fish?"

"Artist wanted ocean here. Brought."

"Can I touch it?"

"Once. Can't too often, body oils cause crystal growth to change. Everyone gets one touch."

Jin ghosts Sandy as her hand caresses the crystals. It can't stop a shiver, the sensation is so delicate. It echoes her sigh, her feeling of ache and longing, like ghosting a person in love. The gen kind of love, with ripples of pain and sadness. Jin imagines graphing that sensation onto its music charts. The result would have to sound glorious.

"It's amazing," says Sandy.

Jin almost echoes her, it is ghosting so closely. It shakes itself to release the connection.

"Tell me," says Jin.

"Like it was alive. For some reason I expected the crystals to be cold, but they're not. Not warm, either, but so many tiny textures all at once! I've never felt anything so complex and gorgeous in my life. Why? What was it like when you touched it?"

"Haven't."

"You've never touched the crystals? But you just said that everyone gets to do it once. Why not you?"

"Waiting."

"For what, your deathbed? Do it Jin, touch them before you go off and kill yourself on one of these trips. If you don't, you'll regret it."

"Can't regret if dead."

"Fine. I'll regret it for you," says Sandy.

"Maybe on way back," says Jin.

"You're impossible."

Jin has Sandy push on a small portion of the wall that is not covered in crystal patterns. A door clicks, and the two duck into a warmly lit cave, blinking until their eyes readjust to the light.

"Kind of anticlimactic, isn't it?" says Sandy.

"No. Look at walls."

Jin guides her toward the side of the cave. At first glance the walls look natural, brown and white limestone with dark and light patches. On closer look, every square inch is covered with intricate line drawings, interlocking and overlapping. Tiny specs of color separate to the eye when viewed at a short distance. The rock is not truly brown, but covered in flecks of purple, yellow, green, red, and blue. White and gray lines trace the images and dreams of nearly a hundred years' worth of artists.

"Look at this one, Jin!"

It stands next to her. With its head turned sideways, a full panorama of the Rocky Mountains stands out. It can almost believe there are tiny skiers hidden in the slopes. Sandy steps back, blinking.

"But how can that work? I know they're there, but I can't pick them out until I'm about three feet away."

Even Jin, who has seen the pattern before, can only pick out where some scenes interlock, especially those painted by different artists. Within each drawing, the colors and shapes blend so well that everything is undefined from more than a few feet back. Even up close, it has to know how to look.

"Wow. If their music is anything like their art, I don't know if I'll ever leave," says Sandy.

Jin lets out the soft breath that serves as its rare laugh.

"They won't mind me being here, will they? I mean, no one in Home Cavern except for Keri seemed to care, and that was just at first. But it all seems so private here," says Sandy.

"Because we're alone. Most neuts don't need much privacy for living, just for work. Otherwise, just mind own business."

"Yeah, I guess. It still throws me off, though. I didn't believe Bruvec when it told me to help you bathe when you were recovering. I'd never want a stranger bathing me. Too embarrassing, not to mention creepy."

"Not even nurse?" says Jin, ignoring the uncertainty in Sandy's voice. It can tell she's still bothered by their conversation in the shower rooms, but it has no idea what to say to her about that.

"Well, I'd put up with it, but I wouldn't like it."

They follow the cavern wall, which curves off to the left. Sandy's hands keep reaching toward the paintings, almost but not quite touching. They stoop through a narrow tunnel spiked with phosphorescent plants, then straighten as it opens out a little. Lanterns aren't needed at all anymore; these passages are meant for regular use. The tunnel ends in a modest-sized amphitheater. Seats carved of gypsum and lime glitter in the dim light.

"Where is the light coming from?" says Sandy.

"Ceiling."

"But the whole thing is evenly lit rock! I don't see any place it could be coming from."

"Whole ceiling false. Giant diffusion panel; lights behind. Remember, everything here is art."

Sandy shakes her head in disbelief, but continues following Jin down the aisle toward the stage. It shrugs.

"Talk to designer," says Jin.

"If anyone's here. I haven't seen or heard a soul except for you and me since we left home."

They cut across the empty stage into the darkness behind, through tunnels lit by a dim blue glow along the floor. Jin stops at a patch that glows green instead of blue and pushes on the wall just above the glow. Metal clicks on stone, and a door releases into Jin's hand. It steps in, with Sandy close behind.

The lighting is brighter now as they head down a short hall into the green room, the lounge where the actors would wait to go on stage. Last time Jin visited the artist caves, this had been the common gathering place whether or not the artists had a show going on, mostly because the room connected directly to the kitchen.

The inside of the green room is full of furniture, mostly velvet-covered and framed in plastic painted so convincingly that Sandy tests with her thumbnail to check for real wood. Rich jewel tones dominate. Even the rock walls are painted burgundy. At the far end of the large chamber, a group of people talk and eat. Their plain clothes contrast with the lavish setting. Sandy awkwardly tries to compose her face, but Jin can see her surprise. It ghosts her for a moment, feeling wonder, slight fear, and much joy.

Ghosting a gen's other emotions—besides fear, anger, and hate—is rare for Jin, and it finds them enjoyable. Gender emotions have a different feel from neuts'. Estrogen, testosterone, progesterone, and androgen give a strange flavor to everything it feels.

Others in the room are aware of the newcomers. Jin can sense their curiosity, but apparently the policy is to let guests make the first move. Jin scans the group, noticing a smaller subgroup in which the heads nod slightly, the feet tap the floor, and one neut's long fingers beat out rhythms on its leg.

"Musicians?" Jin asks them.

One of the foot-tappers turns to them.

"Welcome. And woman, too. Who?"

"Jin. Woman is Sand."

The neut grins. "Not much sand down here, afraid. Only rock and dirt."

The others roll their eyes and groan.

Sandy smiles tentatively. "My name is Sandy, actually. You have a lovely home down here. You should really give Home Cavern some help, it's so sterile and white and boring."

Laughter surrounds her.

"We try. Sneak up when others sleep, play music, make art. They chase us back down, send art with us. Forgive rudeness. I am Rouelle. This is everyone else."

A young neut drags a couch over, and the travelers sit while others gather to hear their story. The room fills quickly as neuts from deeper in the artist caves hear something unusual going on. Soon every seat is full. Sandy strokes the velvet cushions, finally able to indulge her sense of touch. Jin watches as several of the others ghost her, smiling.

"Do tell how woman comes here. Usually only see gens up top. Forgive us, Jin. Your story soon," says Rouelle.

Jin is happy to oblige. Sandy is far more interesting than itself. All it ever does is work. Or it used to. Now it just eats and sleeps.

Sandy tells a brief version of her story while all the gathered neuts share her emotions. She skims over her pain at losing her mother and gives an exaggerated account of nursing Jin. She tells them stories she has only heard third-hand—Jin passing out in the tunnels, Jin eating bugs to stay alive. The tales generate a hum of subvocalized comments and questions. Spreaders rarely come to the artist caves, except as new recruits who have not yet chosen their work.

Rouelle looks at Jin. "Seen you before. Five years ago, Bruvec brought you as guest?"

Jin nods.

"And three years ago, too," says an unusually tall neut with the smooth speech of one who spends much of its time with gens. "You didn't talk to anyone, just sat for two days in the Painted Cavern. I saw you. I'm—"

"Tom Liene!" gasps Sandy, turning to get a good look at it.

The silence turns her face red.

"I mean you are him, aren't you? You look just like him, only you're not really a 'him?' I used to have the biggest crush on you two years ago—and I have no idea why I just told everyone that. Jin, will you please teach me how to stop talking?" she says.

The others laugh, and the tall neut pats Sandy on the shoulder. "Down here, everyone calls me Slim."

Jin looks from Sandy to Slim. The neut's hair is dark and short, but longer than the blunt cut that seems common in the artist caves. Gens would easily mistake it for a lanky young man, about seventeen to twenty years old. There is grace in its presence, and charisma. Jin finds itself liking the neut without knowing why.

"You know it?" asks Jin.

Sandy takes her turn to laugh.

"Oh, Jin, I can't believe you don't know who he—I'm sorry—*it* is. Tom Liene is only one of the hottest young actors out there. Just because you literally live in a cave doesn't mean you can't watch its movies and shows. Look, there's a screen right over there."

"That's okay, I don't need people to know my work. This is just family around here," says Slim. "So what brings you two down to our less-than-humble home?"

"Need musician help," Jin says.

"Of course. Jaunty tune to lift spirits? Melodrama background for creating plague?" says Rouelle.

Jin hands it the printout of its charts. Rouelle looks them over carefully.

"Can you make?" says Jin.

"Busy piece. You wrote?" says Rouelle.

"Computer wrote, mostly. Convert brain chems to sound waves with Greek program. Want to hear, see if sound causes same chems to release in others. Use in next plague, maybe."

"Hmm. Never been part of plague before. Specific instrumentation?"

"Your choice."

"Want to see studio?" says Rouelle, standing.

Sandy and Jin follow, with Sandy casting several backward glances at Slim. Each time she does, she blushes.

They climb a short set of stone steps from the green room and continue on a slanting path. Jin calculates that the studio is directly above the stage, though with all of the twists and turns in the path it can't be sure. Rouelle knocks a pattern that unlocks the door, then presses firmly. Inside, it seals the door behind them, cutting out all sounds from below including the far-off hum of the generators.

The colors on the studio walls are more neutral than any they have seen so far in the artist caves. Instead of rough rocks, a textured acoustic shell surrounds them.

"Too much sound damages rock, caves collapse," says Rouelle, "and we make too much sound. Shell protects structure, vents sound out by bouncing along special tracts, waves small enough not to damage."

One side of the room holds three organs, two pianos, and a pile of electronic keyboards. Other instruments and cases lie about. Marimbas, tympani, and bells are clustered together at the far end.

"Here." Rouelle leads them to the keyboard area and plays a short piece. "This okay for your song?"

"If no trouble, maybe try few different instruments, see which you think best suits piece."

"Could take few days."

Jin nods. "Brought food so we don't take yours."

Rouelle looks horrified, though Jin suspects it is exaggerating.

"Not wise to offend Cook. Sure your Keri is fine, but this is artist home. Don't you know food is art too?"

"It's not like you eat that much anyway," says Sandy. "No one's going to starve by sharing a few meals with you. You heard our friend, don't offend the cook."

"Good," says Rouelle, ushering them back toward the door. "See you in few days. I usually stay here while working, but make selves home. Green room or chamber next door if you feel social. Someone there will find beds for you."

Jin and Sandy find themselves back out in the corridor as Rouelle seals itself inside the studio. Sandy looks around the dim corridor at the branching pathways of nondescript rock.

"Well, I hope you remember how to get back there, Jin. It's all a maze to me."

As soon as the two make their way back to the green room, Slim comes over to them. It nods as Jin explains their need to stay a few days, then disappears to see about their lodging. Exhaustion from the trip down hits Jin, and it begins to sway until Sandy notices and forces it to sit.

"You just rest here, and I'll see if I can scrape up something for you to eat. I think you damaged your body more than you realize, so don't keep trying to be so active. You haven't recovered."

"Don't get lost," Jin tells her.

---

Waking in a colored room is strange for Jin. The light blue bedspread snags on its rough hands. Next to the bed is a set of clean white clothes in the Home Cavern style of a wraparound shirt and loose pants. Jin picks them up and wanders out in search of a shower and breakfast. Its bare, calloused feet slap the cool stone floor, but the sensation hardly reaches Jin's conscious mind.

It tries to follow the sound of water and voices, but so many caverns bounce the sound that it can't find the right set of tunnels. It finally runs across Sandy, dressed like a neut in tan pants and a matching shirt.

"You find showers?" asks Jin.

"Sure, I'll show you. Only they're not showers here. They have this big communal bath made to look like a running river with tide pools, but it's all artificial and the water's heated and filters itself. It's amazing." She laughs. "They were as curious about my body as I was about yours that first time, only they were totally open about it, asking questions until I felt stupid for trying to hide and just gave up and joined them. You'd be proud of me. Here we are."

They step into a large chamber permeated by what Jin could almost mistake for natural daylight. The scents of plants and fresh earth mingle with the ever-present odor of damp rock. Someone must have brought the soil down bucket by bucket.

Jin hangs its warm nightshirt on a hook and puts the clean clothes carefully on the shelf above. It can feel its pores open to let in the steam.

"Whew, it's warm in here," says Sandy. "I'm going to head on to breakfast. I'll be checking with Cook later on to make sure you've eaten. See you in the green room in a while?"

Jin nods, only half paying attention. It inhales, feeling the heaviness of warm, humid air on its skin. Carrots and potatoes are planted in large arcs along the artificial riverbanks. It walks carefully on the stepping-stones so it won't crush any.

"Grab snack if you're hungry," says a neut in one of the tidepools. "Beans ripe there, some carrots if you want to dig. Carb basket on table."

Jin's body isn't quite ready for food yet. Still, it plucks a green bean from the vine just to feel and smell the freshness. The scent engulfs Jin and saliva rushes over its tongue. It bites down, feeling the fine hairs on the vegetable's green skin, the cool damp inside, the crunch and the tickle as rough bits cross its tongue.

"Been a while since ate one?" says the neut.

Jin finishes the bean and slides into the pool. Age shows in the other neut's roughened hands, though its face is still unlined and young. Its eyebrows carve a sharp up and down, and the nose is more than slightly hooked. Not pretty by gen standards, but that doesn't bother Jin. The neut is probably a few years older than itself, but far younger than Bruvec or Net.

"Jin," says Jin with a gesture toward itself.

"Pelin," says the other neut.

Warm water flows over their bodies, the steam forming a curtain that billows between them. Pelin hands Jin a small soap cake that smells like tangerines. It cleans its skin and hair, then leans back to find that the rock beneath its head is padded. With a sigh of contentment, Jin settles in.

"You like our luxury?" says Pelin.

"Now, yes. Not permanently."

"I know spreaders generally prefer more sterile. Sandy says all is white where you live."

"White and silver. Kitchen has some color. Ker says all kitchens must have yellow and green. Don't know why."

"Why two gens there?"

"You heard Sand's story?"

Pelin nods.

"Ker is different. Lived there longer than me. Found on street corner as little girl when Bruvec still lived up top as recruiter. It and Net pretend gens, then. Orphan arrives, they take her in. Later, city gets rough, they're attacked, move to tunnels with girl. She grows up knowing Network. Chooses to stay, cook for us."

"Why attacked? People find out they're neuter?"

"No, gens didn't know about neut. Thought they were both same sex, maybe male, maybe female. Don't know."

Pelin nods. It climbs out of the pool, touches Jin's shoulder, and disappears into the steam. Jin resists the urge to wash its shoulder again, thinking how happy Sandy must be here, where people are always touching like she does. It moves to a bigger section of still water now that the others have all gone to breakfast. In the solitude, Jin breathes easier and begins to relax.

"There you are!" says Sandy. "I thought you'd have drowned by now. Come on, it's time to eat. The cook here is great. No offense to Keri, but they really do make everything into art here. Well, come on, get out."

"No."

"Jin, come on."

"No. Need time alone."

"Fine. Suit yourself. But you need to eat."

Steam rises from Jin's flat chest and hairless legs. If there weren't so many people around, it would love to take its vacation here. The Pacific Ocean would never be this warm or smell this good.

Bits of conversation echo through the tunnels. Not enough sound to be considered loud, but enough to bother it. It swims back and forth under water for as long as its breath holds out.

"Anyone in?" says a voice.

Jin decides not to answer. The lights dim into their night setting. Jin looks up at pinpoint stars set in unfamiliar constellations. Sleepily, it wonders what the designer intended the star shapes to be. The sky turns slowly as Jin floats, the hum of the star projector hidden by the rush of water. It climbs out of the pool and spreads itself on a towel on the ground to continue watching the stars travel. A moon rises, in crescent phase but wearing sunglasses. A fan kicks on, the warm breeze drying the last of the water from Jin's skin as it comfortably rests between waking and sleep.

At lunch, Jin gathers with the others in the green room as dishes come from the kitchen at random. Everyone takes what they want without formality. Something smells meaty and filling, so Jin lifts up a portion to find moussaka with lamb and sharp cheese.

"How such fresh ingredients?" it asks.

"We have a shortcut to up top. Whoever does the shopping packs the food into coolers on a cart, which we lower down a shaft and then roll into the kitchen. There is plenty of supply money from sales," says Slim.

"Artwork sales?"

"Some," says another neut. "Most recent wealth is from book-to-movie animations, lots from screenwriting and outside artists."

"Outside artists?"

"People like me," says Slim. "Some who don't like cave living, and others who just can't create without being around gens. Other actors, mostly."

"Which other actors?" asks Sandy.

"Wouldn't you like to know," says Slim with a grin.

No matter how hard Sandy prods, it won't answer her question. They tease each other like siblings until Jin's laughter leaks out.

"Wow, Jin," says Sandy, "I don't think I've ever seen you smile this much at anyone except maybe Bruvec."

Jin can't help itself. Few of the neuts it knows have such enthusiasm. Slim's is contagious, and Sandy feeds off of it. Perhaps being around others is not always so bad.

"Tell, Jin, about spreading," says Pelin.

"Yes! Must be adventure," say others.

"I'll say," says Sandy. "It had better be a good adventure when Jin comes home more than half dead."

"Last trip no fun," says Jin. "Creating disease is most interesting part. Spreading good for travel."

It reluctantly sets aside its dish and sits up to tell the story.

"Created one maybe eight years ago. Great sugar plague, hit LA on Halloween. Lace candy with special chem; harmless alone. Person eats too much, feels queasy. Nothing happens if stop there. Keep eating contaminated candy or any other sugars, feel worse. Only those who ignore body signals die."

"Kills many kids," says one neut.

"No. Kids smarter. Higher initial threshold but most stopped when sick feeling started. Most deaths were teens and adults."

"But what about all of the kids left without parents?" says Sandy.

Jin sees the flicker of pain in her eyes, rapidly blinked away.

"Kids stronger, more resourceful than most think," it says softly.

After a moment, Sandy nods. "Tell them about the Amarillo plague, Jin. I thought that one was good."

"You know signs in public restrooms, say 'wash hands'?" says Jin.

Many of the others nod, a few who have spent most of their lives underground just shrug.

"Doors leading out of each restroom in each restaurant are painted with chem. Activate chem by touching door or knob without first washing hands. Immediately enters bloodstream, can't pass to others, death within three weeks. Wash hands first, no plague. Washing rids fingers of trigger element, chem can't stick."

"Serves them right for eating out," says Cook.

"Sandy says there is way to stop your plagues, even after catching. True on this?" says Pelin.

"Yes. Stopping is more complex, since easy to avoid plague in first place. Element normally found in fingertips reacts with chem, even after in bloodstream. Keep hands clean, away from mucous membranes, chem dies out, person lives."

"Sounds a little too easy," says Sandy.

"No. Ever have cold? Hard not to rub eyes, nose. Even healthy people touch face often. Also, no one knows this will cure, or might try harder."

"Isn't there any way you can warn them? Send out rumors about how to cure the disease after it's planted?" says Sandy.

"No. Goal still to decrease population. Try to preserve any who figure out for self while not excluding less intelligent if they simply follow directions."

"I suppose," says Sandy. "It just seems like that could kill off a lot of good people who were simply careless."

"Probably did," says Jin. "Careless can make dead faster than anything, good people easily as bad. But all types of people still alive, both Amarillo and elsewhere. Next plague might be different."

The others wait silently as Jin explains what it wants Rouelle to do. If the sound waves in its music can be made safe enough not to kill the general public, the next death Jin spreads will be airborne. Not as a pathogen, but as music.

"Yikes. Sounds like a tough job," says Slim.

"Now see why I'm so tired?" says Jin.

No one laughs.

⁂

That night, Jin wakes in the dark, not at all tired anymore. Sandy sleeps soundly in the next bed. Jin gets up quietly so it won't disturb her and steps silently down the tunnels, through the green room to the kitchen. Only one neut sits there, writing.

"Snacks in fridge," it says.

Jin picks out an apple and some cookies and heads to the baths. Daylight is on for the plants, but the cavern is empty. It sits on a rock with its feet in the pool, watching the water form slight ridges that flow around its ankles. Jin hasn't tasted homemade cookies like this in five years. Keri's are too sweet, but these are rich with peanut butter and oats, only mildly sugary. The texture feels good in Jin's mouth.

"You mind some company?" says Slim.

Jin gestures to the rock beside it, and Slim joins it with its feet in the water. Jin offers it a bite of the apple. Slim takes a taste and hands the fruit back.

"I don't usually like them, but you were enjoying it so much, I thought I'd try."

"Always enjoy good food. So little out on road," says Jin.

"You seem the sad kind of quiet, Jin."

"Just self. Maybe all spreaders this way. Job is killing. Can be happy, not lighthearted."

"So quit."

"No. Needs doing. Rather do myself. Less guilt."

"How's that?" says Slim.

Jin speaks slowly, trying to pin down the right words.

"If not taking part in killing, might pretend I'm not involved, not responsible. Isn't right. Am involved because I'm aware, see need for deaths, condone spreading. Would rather have full deed on conscience than push aside, let someone else take blame."

"Even if you've already done your share? You can be responsible for the deaths you've already caused, but even spreaders get to retire," says Slim.

"Sometimes have nightmares of all people on earth's surface. Buildings, cars, all too heavy for crust. Earth crashes in, caverns buried in debris. So I walk up there, see what empty land we have, try to prove to self we're not that bad yet. But empty land disappears or gets buried in garbage, wastes away as desert. Drives humans crazy."

"Humans were crazy to begin with; don't you know that?" says Slim.

Its quiet voice settles gently, not drifting past the curtain of steam.

"Can't tell for sure. Wasn't alive before resources got scarce," says Jin.

"Me neither, but I read. Humans have always been crazy. That's why I became an actor. To try my own way to stop the craziness, choosing films that carry a message out to a broad audience. Or maybe I just wanted to join in the insanity."

"Through film."

"Film, television, all of the unreal worlds that come alive through the arts. They can be as effective in some ways as your plagues."

"No. Over time, maybe, but we're too close to edge. Change goes too slow. Large-scale death is only hope now."

"The cities just fill again," says Slim.

Jin swishes its feet in the water. It has run the figures, again and again. Without control, the population will outgrow the available resources in a few generations, with quality of life growing worse and worse.

"Maybe just ego, but still think world is better with me than without," says Jin.

Slim lightly touches the back of Jin's hand. They sit together, sharing the silence and Jin's cookies until the early morning risers begin to wake up with the artificial daybreak and rustle about in the tunnels around them.

# CHAPTER 15

Sandy couldn't believe she was living in a cave with Tom Liene. It never felt like a dream, and she had always been too sure of her own mind to question her sanity, but the whole world of the artist caves seemed surreal.

The green room always smelled like fabric and rich cakes or cheeses, the studios reeked of paint or clay, but the world around her sounded like a *world* again. Messy and noisy and rich and full of life. People laughed around her, and it didn't matter that they were neuts who could calculate her heart rate just from standing next to her in a room. It didn't matter that she was a curiosity to them. They asked questions, and she answered or the other way around, and when she asked if she could watch some of them create their art, they either said yes or no, but they never made her feel inferior or unwelcome. Some of them even hugged her once in a while.

Tom Liene did. Or Slim, as it insisted on being called.

"If you see me up top, I'm 'Tom' and 'he.' I come down here to get away from that, to be who I am among people who won't bother me over the way my body is formed. I need to remember who I am, to be a neut as well as a human being."

"Do you think you'll ever tell people up there what you really are?" said Sandy.

"Not what, just who. And I don't know. I kind of doubt it."

It stretched out beside her on the stage of the empty amphitheater. Sandy loved the way its thin wrists and ankles stuck out from its sleeves and cuffs when it did. She tried to adjust to Tom as a neut, as Slim, but her teenage daydreams weren't that far gone in her mind. She couldn't help imagining what it might be like for him to kiss her.

It, not him, she reminded herself.

"Do you have lots of friends up there?" she asked.

"As many as anyone, I suppose. I like people. I like to meet them, to talk to them and hear what they think, but the connections are never quite real when you can't be yourself, and the only ones I can really be close to are other neuts."

"Don't any gens know who you are?" said Sandy.

Slim smiled at her, an expression of innocent teasing that had made it famous among the beauty-hungry world of casting agents and directors.

"Well, I can think of one," it said.

Sandy smiled back, determined not to blush this time and partially succeeding. It was right. She knew, and she was very much a gen.

"Want to help me run lines?" it said.

"Sure. Does it matter that I have no idea what that means?" said Sandy.

"Yes, but we can fix that," said Slim. It handed her several pages of a script. "You read Catherine's and the doctor's lines. Don't worry about acting or trying to get into the scene. Just read them as naturally as possible, and let me know if I get any of mine wrong. Okay?"

Sandy looked over the pages. "Sure. Can I try acting a little bit if I want to?"

"As long as you stick to the lines. Ready?"

She began, trying not to remember that when she had daydreamed about this moment, they were on a film set rather than an underground stage. And that in her fantasies, the actor across from her was a man named Tom, not a neut named Slim.

They ran through the scene a second and third time, and Sandy began to relax. This was the way things were in the world. Maybe that wasn't such a bad thing.

Jin seemed restless. Sandy watched it pull away from the other neuts and disappear for hours at a time. It sometimes came back covered in dust, or at least with enough smudges on its pants and back to show that it had sat somewhere in the unfinished caves, no doubt alone and thinking whatever thoughts spreaders had in their heads while they waited for a plague to come together.

She found it seated in Painted Cavern one day, too far away from the walls to see the drawings.

"Are you all right, Jin?" she asked.

It nodded.

"Are you sure? You look tired. I can help you back to your room if you need to rest," said Sandy.

"No."

It rubbed its temples, ran its fingers into its straight hair, and looked up at her, face framed in its hands.

"Dreams again," it said.

She sat down across from it in silence. She tried to slow her breathing, the way Jin said it did when it began an internal study. She imagined herself mirroring its position, feeling the way the skin tightened on her fingers as they straightened into her hair. She tried to imagine that hair feeling thick and straight like Jin's, rather than her own unruly curls. Nothing happened. She could sense Jin's emotions better by watching it than she could from trying to ghost.

"Want to run away with me?" she said. "Just for a few days. We could go up, get some sun, and by the time we get back, Rouelle will be done making your music, and you can get on with the next step, whatever that is."

"Sun won't help." It sighed heavily, leaving the rest unsaid.

Sandy knew it well enough by now to understand what it didn't say. Only the plague would help. It would sleep less and less until the bodies began to fall, until the newsdrops reported mortality rates on the rise in whatever town it was targeting this time. Sandy couldn't remember. She had never cared much for geography, never given much thought to leaving Montana until the day her mother died.

She imagined those people, their bodies relinquishing the patterns of breath and blood, lying still and stiff for the fire that would turn them to ashes for their loved ones to bury or keep or toss to the winds the way her own mother's ashes had gone. She wondered if Jin pictured those bodies as the numbers rolled in, and fell asleep with their stillness lending quiet to its mind.

She decided she would never ask.

She sat for a while longer in silence, but the chill of the rock all around her began to creep into her muscles and bones. She shook off the dust and left the spreader alone. It had said it preferred things that way, she reminded herself, and it wasn't like it wanted comfort from her.

On her way back to the green room, she ran into the older neut who often seemed to shadow Jin around the caves. At the moment she couldn't remember its name.

"You seen Jin?" it said.

"Out there," Sandy gestured toward the back of the amphitheater and the tunnel to Painted Cavern.

"Pelin, no," said Slim, coming through the backstage curtains.

Pelin's face took on a stubborn look.

"Come on, Pel. You can help me and Sandy rehearse. If Jin's out there, it doesn't want to be bothered."

Pelin's eyes flickered from Sandy to Slim, and it nodded.

"You were coming to help me rehearse, weren't you?" said Slim.

"Always! But I thought you were supposed to be up top shooting today," said Sandy.

"I was. Albuquerque mandated rolling brownouts to conserve power for the hospitals and businesses that really need it. The film commission's arguing that they fall into the latter category, but they won't win that fight for a while yet. We're scheduled to start back up in a couple of days."

"You still don't know part yet?" said Pelin.

"Oh, I know my role. But two days is plenty of time to forget, and I wouldn't want to let the synapses calcify, you know," said Slim.

"You act, I'll watch," it said.

This seemed to be the response Slim expected, but Sandy felt sorry for the neut. It seemed as lost among the artists as Jin was.

"Come on. You can read the doctor," said Sandy. "That way I can concentrate on Catherine. Who knows, I might not even need to use the script."

Pelin took the paper and stood a short way off stage. Sandy grinned at Slim and let it start the lines. She had been running through them in her room for days, trying them out with different inflections and emotions, just as she had watched it do when they rehearsed.

Pelin read mechanically, and it tended to skip words as its eyes got ahead of its place in the script. Still, Sandy gave it her best and came in at the right times, even catching Slim in a minor slip.

When they were done, Slim shook its head and took the script back from Pelin.

"You're right. And you've been practicing," said Slim.

"So was I any good? Was I at least better?"

It appraised her thoughtfully. "Better, yes, but your work is still raw, and your voice isn't trained. Do you think you would like to come up with me when I go back up to shoot? I'll see if I can find you an acting class or workshop to take. There's usually one or another going on in the city."

"I'd love to, but I can't afford an acting class. I left the farm with nothing—we had nothing to take, unless I wanted to get on the truck with a chicken under one arm and a bundle of corn under the other," said Sandy.

"Live chicken?" said Pelin.

"Live and loud and probably mad as hell," said Sandy. "And angry chickens are mean."

"Don't worry about the money. It's just one class, and I have plenty to spare."

"I'll ask Jin when it gets back," said Sandy.

Both neuts gave her a quizzical look, but she didn't say anything. It felt right to ask Jin. She was still trying to take care of it, and it might need her, at least to make sure it got safely home. She didn't like the look of the circles under its eyes.

"You'll need story—why you show up with young girl," said Pelin.

Slim laughed. "You've been reading too much gossip, Pelin. No one's going to care if I show up with a young woman. I happen to be seen in public with young women all the time. It helps with my image."

Pelin gave it a disgusted look and stalked off the stage. Sandy noticed it went back toward the main areas, not out to Painted Cavern and Jin. She was glad of that. The neut seemed to have even less sense than she did about when to leave people alone.

"What's it getting so upset about?" asked Sandy.

"I don't know the whole story. It might tell you if you ask, but I would wait for it to calm down a bit. It'll be fine."

"Do you think people will really care that you're seen with me?" said Sandy.

"Oh, a few gossip threads will probably write stories about it. Who knows, you might become a big mystery story for them. Unless you want me to tell everyone you're my sister."

Sandy laughed, comparing its lanky body to her own curves and short stature. "I don't think they would believe that. I'll take the mystery if I can get it."

"Good. Let me know as soon as you can if you're coming. I'll check into classes and see if I can get you into a good one."

She wished Slim would offer to teach her itself, but she hated to ask. It was busy, and wouldn't always be there. Up top, it might not have time for her at all. She realized she had little idea how these things worked. She had watched all of the regular behind-the-scenes programs and followed the dispersion of Hollywood throughout the Western states as different parts of the pre- and post-production were farmed out to cheaper sources. The Hollywood culture itself hadn't left California until, over the last five years, the power shortages chased the ancient studios out. Now she wondered if Albuquerque was going to lose its film industry as well. She would hate for that to happen, now that she was down here with Slim.

She looked around the now-empty stage, wondering if she might have whatever it was that could make her a successful actress. She stood silently, straining her ears for any sign of the neuters around her, but either they were all somewhere else, or they were being quieter than gen ears could hear.

She turned to the empty seats and delivered her lines, full of laughter and sadness and fury. It didn't matter that they made no sense without Slim's compelling voice in between, or that the emotions she chose didn't go with the scene. This was her first chance since she'd followed Tei away from home to do something for herself, and she was going to enjoy it for whatever it was worth.

# CHAPTER 16

"Songs finished," says Rouelle. "You listen, I must eat."

Its eyes are red, the circles underneath them deep and shadowed. Slim shows Jin how to use the local sound system while the others gather.

"Which one first?" says Sandy.

"Doesn't say," says Jin.

It selects one of Rouelle's creations and turns the volume up. The alley woman is first, three hundred seconds stretched into an eternity of pain and distress. Every second Jin ghosted is prolonged, agonizing. It can almost smell the garbage in the alley and feel the day's leftover heat radiating from the asphalt. Violation rips through the listeners note by note.

Jin wonders how it could possibly have stood by and let the man do these things to her. Sandy curls around herself, tears flowing down her angry face. Someone talks gently to her but she shakes her head. Slim sits motionless with its head in its hands, and Pelin watches Jin. Jin finds itself irritated by the other neut's gaze.

"Play again," Pelin says.

"Don't you dare!" says Sandy. "I don't want to hear that awful thing ever again. Please, Jin. That sound is terrible. Don't make me listen."

"You want to hear other?" Jin asks her, ignoring Pelin.

"No. But I will anyway, just give me a minute to catch my breath."

When Sandy is ready, Jin plays the second track. Though this one is longer, the time doesn't stretch so much. Again Jin sees the rocky street and dirty alleys, only this time it is the one carrying the knife. Sensations flood through its brain, more intimate than ghosted memories. It feels the excitement, arousal, and cruel intent, more clearly even than when it was conducting its study. The music distills and clarifies.

"What you think?" says Rouelle, shuffling back into the green room with an uneaten sandwich in its hand.

"True art," says Jin.

"So you'll use somehow in spread?" says Pelin.

"Maybe. Right now for more study. So many same chems in attackers' and victims' minds, like notes on paper. Finite number, all available to everyone. Only patterns, progressions, dynamics separate hunted from hunter. Music helps sort differences."

"Good. Exhausting work. How you live with memories?" says Rouelle.

"Just do. Maybe someday have you play my song, then we both know."

"Someday," says Rouelle. "Now, must get clean."

The whole group moves toward the bath cavern, feeling the need to wash away the psychological dirt of listening to cruelty. Sandy recovers herself in the water, splashing and joking with the others as she shakes off the effects of the music. Jin floats on its back, absorbing peace from the water. It should probably head home in a few hours. There is still a lot of work ahead of it.

"Jin, can I talk to you for a minute?" says Sandy.

"Talk."

"Would you mind making the trip back by yourself? I hate to run out on you like this, but I'm really happy here, and I don't feel like I'm in everyone's way like I do around Keri and Net, and—"

"Don't mean to make you feel in the way."

"I know, but I can't help it. The others said it was okay if I stayed here. They like having me around, sensing my reactions and emotions. Slim says it'll be nice to have a gen around so people can see how their art might affect me. It's even taking me for acting lessons! I really do hate to have you go alone, but if you're okay with it, I'd like to try."

Jin looks up into Sandy's hopeful brown eyes.

"Not good. Learn cave routes first, then choose," it says. "Isn't like surface route from Home Cavern. No maps, no markers."

"Why? Someone can always guide me back to Home Cavern if I need to go. Or up top. You heard Slim, they have a shortcut to the surface, so if I go back with you I'd be learning a maze I didn't even need."

"Find someone teach you surface route right away. Not safe to rely on others in emergency."

"So if someone agrees to teach me how to get out, you'll let me stay?"

"Your choice, not mine. Just suggestion," says Jin.

"I know," says Sandy, but her voice is less than certain. "You'll tell Bruvec and Keri and the others? You think Keri'll be mad?"

"Probably yell for hour," says Jin.

"Well, tell her I said not to yell at you. It was my choice," says Sandy, her voice firm.

"She knows. Will yell anyway. You know Ker."

"Yeah. I'll miss her too. You'll come back and visit, though, won't you?"

"Probably need more from Rouelle soon," says Jin.

"Good, then I'll expect you. Who knows, I might take up some art form of my own. I feel better when I'm doing something, you know?"

Jin knows. It drops its feet down until they touch the bottom of the pool. After saying its good-byes and packing up its few belongings, it quietly heads out toward Ocean Cave and the silent tunnels beyond.

"Jin, wait!"

Sandy catches up with Jin in the Painted Cavern, panting. The bag she thrusts at Jin smells so good it almost has second thoughts about leaving.

"Cook wants you to have this. And I wanted to say, well, so long, for one. And you had better touch the crystals in Ocean Cave, or I'm coming after you, and I'll—well, I'll sit on you until you do."

"Thanks."

Jin does pause in the phosphorescent glow to enjoy the sight. Its hand lingers just above the crystals, not quite touching. Instead, it recalls Sandy's hand, lightly caressing, full of wonder and surprise.

Muscles Jin hasn't used in several days protest the first part of the climb, then stretch out their kinks and settle into the motion. It shuts off its headlamp and feels its way through utter darkness for part of the crawl, enjoying the solitude while its mind toys with the possibilities of Rouelle's music.

The trip home is over too fast. Jin finds itself in well-lit caves before it is ready to deal with friends again. Keri walks through the passageway toward it, her hair damp from the shower.

"All right, where'd you lose the girl?" she says.

"Stayed below," says Jin.

"With the artists?"

Jin nods, bracing itself for the invective.

"Well, I'm not surprised. She wasn't happy here, much. Only when she was pestering you. I'm just surprised she let you leave without her. She must have really liked the people down there to let you go so easily."

Jin just looks at her blankly. No wonder Keri and Net get along so well. No one can figure out either one of them.

"So what are they like down there? I've heard all sorts of stories about the artist caves, but I always figured a lot of it was just talk. Is it really that different?"

"Yes."

"So why don't you stay there too?"

"I like here."

Keri shrugs. "Yeah, home is wherever you're used to being, I guess. Any luck with your research?"

"Think so. Just need more time."

Net is in the computing lab, as always, when Jin walks in. Jin calls up its charts, studying the Blue-eyes sound wave file. The trip certainly didn't improve its music reading skills. On paper, his file doesn't look much different from any of the others. Maybe it should have stayed longer with the artists, asked more questions and learned to read music a little better. At least it could have brought more than two charts for Rouelle to work with.

A vague sense of discomfort stiffens Jin's spine and shoulders. It tries to stretch the tension out, then realizes there is an external cause. A new person has entered the room, and when Jin catches its eye momentarily they both immediately look away. Wordlessly, the other neut takes a seat as far away from Jin as possible. Jin returns to its own files, but the sound of tapping and dragging fingers grates on its nerves. Net's typing has never bothered it, nor did the group of researchers. Only another spreader can make it feel this way. After a few minutes, Jin can't think of anything but the sound of the other neut's breath and movements. Irritated beyond reason, it leaves the lab.

It is too restless to sleep, so it tries to walk off its frustration in the less-traveled tunnels. It shouldn't have let the other spreader drive it away from its work. They don't harm each other. Jin doesn't even know this one very well.

It tries to analyze the reaction, recalling stories of people, gens even, who sense danger from another person without knowing why. Maybe the animosity between spreaders is the same. They sense a wrongness in each other, the intent to kill, and are particularly sensitive because their own bodies send off the same electrochemical signals. They are protecting their home territory.

Jin laughs at itself. Home Cavern doesn't belong to any one spreader. Certainly not itself. But its brain keeps turning over the theories, and it knows that much of human behavior is biological, not rational. It has read of scent chemicals causing unconscious awareness. Perhaps certain sounds could have a similar effect. A brain that responds to certain auditory frequencies might also send out minuscule amounts of that same sound. Brain waves and sound waves aren't so very different.

Back in the computing lab, Jin forces a smile at the other spreader as thanks for the inspiration. It searches the MediWave files for any reference to the human brain broadcasting sound waves. Nothing. The only data relates to how sound affects the brain. And the body. Jin studies those files for a while, until it gets an idea that just might work.

A few medics are at work down in the test labs of Home Cavern. Several researchers conduct experiments at the far end, and the spreader from the computing lab creates its newest plague in a small lab at the west end. The small labs seal tightly, so it and Jin won't disrupt each other.

Jin chooses a lab at the far end of the east wing and signs out the equipment normally used for recording experiments. After connecting the large hardscreen to speakers, Jin calls up Rouelle's files. It splits the playback display, then calls up the file of sound it recorded itself. The quality isn't as good, but for the sounds Jin needs, the recording will do. It seals the door, excited.

After relaxing enough to normalize its vital signs, it plays its own tones on a looping cycle. The rough sound of generators fills the lab, their sonic and subsonic frequencies electronically altered to match the information Jin finally was able to dig out of the studies done by Professor Dair in Germany. As the track plays through the first cycle, Jin notices a slight elevation in its pulse, breath, and heart rate. Nothing more.

"Spare a few minutes?" it asks a researcher who stands chatting with a small group in the main lab.

"Sure. Anything's better than dyeing more mold. What?"

"Lab sixteen east. In few minutes I'm doing self-experiment. You check in every four minutes, have crash cart ready. If I wave, no problem. Leave immediately, seal door behind."

"Any risk to me?" says the researcher.

"You stay to listen, yes. Leave fast, no. If I'm unconscious, shut off sound first, then resuscitate."

"Okay, see you in four. East sixteen."

"Wait ten minutes for first check. Need setup time."

"Sure."

Back in the lab, Jin seals the door and starts Rouelle's song of the attack, also looped. It tries to lie still on the room's single gurney and relax, but the music makes it fidgety, so it starts to pace. After the first cycle through Rouelle's song, Jin starts the modified generator sound alongside the music but at a barely audible volume. Its agitation increases. Its pulse builds, its heart rate increases, and it starts to sweat. As Rouelle's music builds toward a climax, Jin has a hard time catching its breath. Epinephrine, cortisol, it can no longer grasp the names of the chemicals that flood its brain. Its breath comes in short gasps, and its heart rate escalates to near pain.

It chokes. And stops.

Jin's heart still pounds, but the pain is less. It looks at the lab door, which is still closed. The researcher has not come in to check on it yet. Jin tries to figure out why the sensations stopped, but the music and undertones fill the room, and its heart rate begins to spike upward again. Sweat flows freely, and it can't hold still as it realizes what the interruption was. Just the song looping back to the beginning, resetting to a time before the slow build of the altered generator sounds could coax Jin's body into a heart attack.

"Oh good. Still standing," says the researcher from the doorway. "See you in four?"

Jin waves it away, then staggers as the sound builds on the next loop. This time the pain is worse. Rouelle's music plays on in the background, and Jin's heart tries to burst through its ribs. It claws at its clothes to release the pressure, fingernails leaving red scratches across its throat and chest. Its hands shake. It can't hit the right part of the screen to stop the music. Its fingers are too damp to register the contact. Sweat gets in its eyes until it can't see. Flailing, it grips the whole screen in both hands, squeezing until one finger holds down on the power button long enough to shut off the machine entirely. Exhausted, it falls back onto the gurney.

Heart rate slows, pulse still high. Breath slows.

"Tough test?" says the researcher.

Jin nods and waves, unable to speak.

"Need anything?"

The researcher looks doubtful when Jin shakes its head, but the door seals behind it in silence. Jin concentrates on breathing, not thinking. Its shirt is shredded, and a long line of blood seeps from the left side of its chest into the fabric.

But the experiment worked.

Jin's heart rate shoots up again until it forces itself to control its excitement. The plague will work.

It sterilizes the lab for the next researcher and cleans and bandages its wounds. At least no one can question the scratches in the private showers of Home Cavern. Jin trots back to the living quarters, its brain spinning wildly with plans.

"What's with you, Jin?" says Keri. "You're acting kind of funny."

"That a smile, Jin? About time," says Bruvec.

A grin pulls at Jin's mouth against its wishes. It ducks its head down toward its plate as the Home Cavern regulars gather around the small table in the kitchen.

"Tell," says Net.

"Found! New plague, different from any before. Far as I know, anyway. Works great."

"How do you know?" says Ker. "I thought you were too self-confident to test your plagues on animals before releasing them into the population."

"Self."

Bruvec slaps the table.

"Ha! Call head docs, Jin finally gone crazy."

"Not crazy. Only way to test. Now need to make real version."

"Sure, Jin," says Bruvec. "Experiment worked great. How's being dead feel?"

"Didn't let kill me, obviously. Just far enough to prove point."

Net slams its cup down and stomps off toward the computing lab. Keri does the same toward the back of the kitchen, where only newcomers or the foolhardy would follow.

"They're right, Jin. Don't try so hard to die. Maybe need vacation now, not after spread," says Bruvec.

"No. Fine, really. Whole test was safe, had researcher stand by for help."

"So, tell, what's new plague?"

"Picks off attackers, malicious intent. Always high proportion of population. When recorded frequencies meet sound patterns in attacker's brain, waves interact. Create stress, heart attack."

"Won't hurt general population?"

"Tried first test without attacker brain chems triggered by Rouelle's music. Slight increase in heart rate and blood pressure, nothing dangerous."

"Maybe danger for people with already high blood pressure."

"True. Needs refining. Will go see artists tomorrow, get help."

"Don't know, Jin. Seems uncontrolled," says Bruvec.

"Some risk, but plague actually protects people who don't die. Leaves them safer from each other for while."

"Maybe," says Bruvec.

"Want to make St. Louis trip soon as plague ready," says Jin. "Maybe few weeks, depending on musicians. Okay with money?"

"How long for spread?"

"Not long. Walk to El Paso, two days. Passenger fare two days, same back. One week, spread and check. Money for three weeks, just in case?"

"Twice that to be safe. Last time you left half what I gave here. And catch ride from Whites City. Carlsbad, at least."

"El Paso is only two days, easy pace. Half of journey underground, no danger. Besides, can't walk to Carlsbad. Caught on no-access road last time, cop might remember."

"From Whites City, then," Bruvec says. "Or hire car."

"No need, Bruv. Please." Jin can hardly believe it is encouraging the use of a private car service. The Network is rich, but not extravagant.

"We'll talk when you get back from artists."

"Good. Take care of self, Bruv."

"Only if you do same."

# CHAPTER 17

Sandy stumbled into the sunlit haze and caught her breath—or tried to. After having nothing but cave dust to filter out for so long, her lungs were caught off guard by the city smells of exhaust, garbage, and excrement. She ran a few steps to catch up with Slim, not wanting to get lost alone in what seemed to be a rare blend of hi-loc and lo-loc community.

A dirty sweat that wasn't entirely from the heat coated Sandy's skin, but she refused to complain. Slim led her down a concrete sidewalk—something they didn't have in her part of Montana—and up the steps of a small but well-maintained house.

"We can clean up here," said Slim, its half-stifled smile telling her more than she wanted to know about the state she was in.

"I don't know if the clothes I brought will fit in around here," said Sandy.

"Then you'll make a fashion statement. We're not staying here anyway. This is just the stopping point."

"Too bad Jin didn't know about your house here when it was on its way back to Home Cavern," said Sandy.

Slim's face lost its humor, and it shook its head.

"I wish it had. We need more spreaders like Jin, but I don't think there are any. We can't afford to lose it now."

"What do you mean? Keri said there are plenty of spreaders throughout the States and even the world. Tei didn't seem that different from Jin to me," said Sandy.

"I don't know Tei," Slim admitted, "but I've met a few others. The ones who do the job for long enough forget sometimes why they do it."

"You mean they start to actually *like* what they're doing?" said Sandy.

"No. They don't kill for the pleasure of killing, or at least I've never known one that did. They just become so involved in the science and statistics of the job that if you asked one of them about how the people were affected, they wouldn't even know what you meant."

Sandy shuddered. She wanted to ask Slim if it had known many spreaders, but the itching of dirt and dried sweat suddenly seemed more important. She poked through the hallways to find the bathroom, wondering just how many spreaders there were in the area and if maybe one of them had started to spread a plague she had contracted from the smog.

Just as she had lathered up her skin with soap, the power went out. She let out a huff of exasperation and quickly rinsed and shut the water off. The cool water felt good, just dripping from her skin in the darkness, despite the chemical smell. So different from the underground baths of the artist caves.

She wondered if it was that she was growing older, seeing more of the world, or if living with the neuters had changed her so that she noticed these small differences in sensation that she hadn't ever thought of before. She smiled at the way the light came through the windows, casting shadows in the hall, and found Slim in one of the two bedrooms, packing a small bag of clothes. It tossed an empty bag her way.

"Here. You can put your stuff into something that isn't covered in cave dust."

"I didn't realize the brownouts reached all the way out here," said Sandy.

"They never used to. I need to check and make sure there aren't driving restrictions before we head into the city. Anything you need?" it asked.

*A hug, maybe. Something resembling a normal life*, thought Sandy. *For you to be male and interested in me wouldn't hurt either.*

She was pretty sure she had been careful not to subvocalize, but Slim reached out to her in what she could only interpret as a brotherly way, gave her a one-armed hug, and dropped a quick kiss on the top of her head.

"You'll find your way," was all it said before frowning at a pocketscreen as it checked on traffic. One of the burdens of being a rich actor with a private car, she guessed. "Looks like we're clear to head into the city. Do you have everything?"

She didn't. She dumped her extra pair of jeans and a few other items into the new, far more stylish bag and nodded. Seeing Slim climb behind the wheel of a car almost made her laugh. It looked much more like a man now, in topsider clothes and with its hair combed back and to one side. On closer look, she was pretty sure it had added a little bit of makeup to broaden its cheekbones and square its jaw.

"So I guess I should be calling you 'Tom' now," said Sandy.

"I'm Slim until we get there. If you forget and call me that later on, no one will probably notice—although usually it's the bigger men who get called Slim," it said.

"Or Tiny," Sandy said, remembering one of their huge farmhands. She had never known his real name.

She settled back into the seat as the car pulled into the slow-moving delivery truck traffic that eventually fed them onto the series of smaller highways leading to I-25 and the southern outskirts of Albuquerque, where the local film industry proclaimed itself Hollywood's new home. The countryside they passed was an endless array of shacks, lo-loc communities, and junkyards. The closer they got to the city, the more construction she saw. She tried to remember scenes like this from Montana, but there were no hi-loc neighborhoods with upscale shops, just utilitarian lo-loc wares where the farms left off and the pseudo-urban areas began. She used to laugh at the neighbor's cows contemplating their reflections in the glass of the strip of shops that bordered their pastures. Now, she wondered what the cows saw reflected there. More pasture grass, maybe, but darkened by the window tint and impossible to eat, or just a wall of something blank and smooth that blocked their paths and held them in the same small square, fighting for grazing rights with all of the other cows. At least her chickens had their own spaces, their own little three-by-three cages that were cleaned as often as she could manage, and were comfortable and warm.

"You want to drive for a while?" said Slim.

"What?" said Sandy.

"You're watching the cars ahead of us as if you could weave this car through them and out the other side."

"I am? Sorry, I was just daydreaming. I wasn't trying to criticize the way you drive."

Slim laughed. "Don't worry, I'm not offended. And I'm serious. You can drive if you want to. I don't mind."

"Maybe on the way back," said Sandy.

If she drove she would have to watch the road. For now, she was content to sneak glances at Slim, her imagination fighting between the image of it as a man and the reality of its neuter nature. The sun was nearly down, and the whole world looked unfamiliar and wide and open after the caves. She eventually closed her eyes and drifted in and out of consciousness until the sound of the engine shutting down and the key scraping out of the ignition brought her out of her reverie.

"We're here," said Slim.

Sandy looked around the well-lit parking lot, only halfway taken over by the local residents' garden.

"Where's here?" she asked.

"An apartment a few of us keep. There's usually an extra bed open. Meryl's still back in the caverns, so you can have its spot for tonight, at least. Come on."

Slim led the way up several flights of stairs and into a large apartment. Magazines and a couple of empty coffee mugs were scattered around, along with what Sandy now recognized as "sides"—the parts of scripts actors used to rehearse. A neat pile of technical-looking equipment sat in one corner, and a long-haired person wearing jeans and a tank top stepped out of the kitchen with a brownie halfway to its mouth.

"Tom! Thought you were going to get back here days ago. Hello."

The last word was directed at Sandy. She was pretty sure the person was a neut, and even more certain that it was waiting for some sort of signal from Slim to indicate whether or not they could speak freely.

"Anyone else around?" said Slim.

"Just Phazy. In case you couldn't tell by all of the camera equipment taking up valuable real estate." It indicated the cases Sandy had noticed. "Call me Lancaster," it told Sandy.

"I'm Sandy. Nice to meet you."

Lancaster still looked at Slim.

"She's all right. I just brought her up from the artist caves for some acting lessons," said Slim.

Lancaster flashed a real grin at Sandy this time.

"Why didn't you say that right off? Forgive me, I always get twitchy if I'm in front of gens without my makeup on."

Sandy looked at it more closely. "Lancaster…you're not Heather Lancaster, are you?"

"In the flesh, though not as much of it as some directors would like to see. Problem is, I've got nothing to show them. Now who's Slim pawning you off on for these so-called lessons, hmmm? One of the rankest amateurs, I'll bet."

"Lanky thinks it's the only one with any acting talent up here on the surface," said Slim.

"You bet your hormonally deprived ass I am! And for calling me Lanky, I'm giving her the last brownie."

Before Sandy could protest, Lancaster had reached back over the counter that separated the kitchen from the living room and had the crumbling sweet halfway into her mouth. Slim laughed at the look of surprise on her face.

"I guess I'll just have to starve, then. Looks like you two are getting along fine. Wake me when the next batch is done."

Lancaster tucked its arm into Sandy's and pulled her onto the couch. "Come on, gen girl. I need some brain-picking time with you to keep my performances real. It's so rare I get to talk to someone who can help me finesse my act."

"Don't keep her up too late. She's in the ten o'clock class with Christoph Zin tomorrow," said Slim.

Lancaster waved Slim away and turned back to Sandy. After only a few minutes of Lancaster's enthusiasm, she found herself forgetting that the person next to her was a neut and not a girl her own age. It was probably ten years older, at least, she told herself, but soon she was calling it Heather and spilling her guilty secrets about her old crush on Slim and the other actors she'd had images of in her bedroom back at home.

Eventually, Lancaster stretched out and pulled away from the huddle they'd formed to keep their voices from disturbing the other two neuts in the apartment. Its voice dropped some of the girlish pitch, and Sandy felt as if she could see its face almost shift, losing the pixie quality and fading back into the childish androgyny of a neuter.

"Thanks," it said. "That was really helpful."

"You mean it was all an act?" said Sandy, fighting to keep the heat back from her face.

Lancaster looked at her in surprise.

"Of course. I said that, didn't I?"

Sandy thought back. It hadn't exactly said it was going to study her, but she supposed she could have construed its words that way.

"It's all right," she said.

Warm fingertips touched her arm. "No, it's not. Look, I'm sorry. I didn't mean to make you think I was anything other than I am. I thought you knew that being a neut meant I'm not interested in any of those things from a personal perspective."

Any of those things. Love and crushes and secret desires. Sandy was glad she hadn't told it about her more recent thoughts since meeting Slim. The way its profile in the sunset shining through the car's windshield had made her throat tighten, just knowing that she would never find the man she thought Tom Liene had been, that she might never feel as comfortable with any man as she did with the neuts who had no real interest in her. She was nothing but another subject to study.

"Sandy," said Lancaster.

"I'm just tired," she said.

"You can stay in Slim's room. I'll stay with Phazy," said the neut.

"If it's all right, I think I'd rather just sleep out here on the couch."

Lancaster gave her a look as if it was going to argue, then shrugged and silently let her be. At least she now knew why it had referred to the gen acting teachers as amateurs. They acted for money, for fun and maybe fame. She wondered if the other neuts turned their personas off when they came home, and how much of Slim's patience and concern was just an act, a charm it put on because it thought it should. At least Jin and Keri and the others in Home Cavern never pretended to be anything they weren't. She fell asleep wondering if she should have just gone back to that sterile whiteness, then slept fitfully, dreaming of getting lost in the caves and hearing laughter subvocalized all around her.

"You're quiet this morning," said Slim as they drove toward the city.

Sandy nodded, still looking out the side window.

"I should have warned you about Lancaster, but we both thought you knew," it said.

"How could I have known? I can't ghost, I can't hear subvocalizations, I can't even think as fast as you do, and I certainly can't analyze someone else's body chemistry by mimicking their movements or breathing the way they breathe."

"That's not quite how it works," said Slim.

"I know. But it doesn't matter," said Sandy.

"I'm sorry."

They drove in silence for a while longer, until Slim pulled off of the road. Sandy looked around, but they were in what looked like an empty lot, no acting studios or sound stages in sight.

"Come here," said Slim, holding its arms out to her.

"I'm not a child," said Sandy.

"No. You're less of one than I am, physically—even emotionally. I'm not trying to patronize you, and I don't know if this will hurt more than it will help. You need human contact right now, gen contact, but I'm the only one that's available." It put a hand on her shoulder. "Please, Sandy. I can't care in the way you want me to, but I do care."

"How much of this is an act? A way to learn more so you can use it in your art?" said Sandy.

"None of it. And all, I suppose. We're just living our lives, Sandy, same as you. Sometimes we don't know how you think, either."

Sandy let it hug her, then. Not because she particularly wanted to, but she was tired of struggling. After a moment of resistance, she tried to relax into the comfort of the human body next to hers.

It wasn't right. Slim's embrace should have felt warm, like a friend's or relative's hug, at least. Instead, she felt as if there were a plastic film between them. Jin would probably describe it as something that stopped a contact-induced biochemical reaction. Sandy wasn't sure if the barrier was mental or physical, but after a moment, she pulled away.

"I can't," she said.

It dropped her off at her acting class and went on to the film studio. She was far too early for the class to begin, so she wandered the nearby areas, watching the neighborhood wake up and the shops come to life. She considered ditching the class to go lose herself in the flow of the city, but by ten o'clock, the streets were crowded with more people than she had ever seen in one place in her life, and the relative emptiness of the classroom was a relief from the pressure and heat.

She sat through demonstrations on gesture and diction, her mind more focused on the way Lancaster had opened her so easily than on the instructor's methods. When she was called up for a demonstration, she nearly refused, glancing frantically at the exit.

That wasn't the person she wanted to be. That was the girl who hid in a chicken cage while her mother was killed in front of her.

She stood at the front of the room and looked out into the eyes of the rest of the class. Warm and teasing eyes. Faces as frightened and determined as her own. Gen faces, gen eyes. She turned her attention back to the instructor and mentally crumpled up that flimsy plastic barrier. Here, she might embarrass herself with awkward mistakes, but no one would know what she was thinking. She was safe inside her own skin.

The class time flew by after that, as did the time she spent browsing through the city after class, waiting for Slim to finish its shoot. By the time she got back into the car, long after dark, she could look at her former crush and let it be what it was. Slim had treated her the same way it treated Pelin and Jin and everyone else in the artist caves. Lancaster would be a different story, but Sandy could handle it. And when they went back underground at the end of Slim's filming, she would have plenty of stories to tell.

# CHAPTER 18

The dark silence of Ocean Cave clears Jin's mind. All thoughts of plague, of music, of Bruvec and Blue-eyes drain into the porous rock. It feels its own breath, heart, and blood; the patch of scar tissue on its side; the vanishing scabs on its legs. Being alive feels good, leading Jin to wonder if being dead feels good too, in its own way, at least until the last of the nerve impulses die out.

Jin rolls slowly to its feet, feeling the fluids and bones shift as it rises. It braces itself for company and presses open the door to Painted Cavern. Only one figure waits inside.

"Hi, Jin. Sandy and Pelin wanted to come too, but I reminded them of your love of crowds, so now you're stuck with just me as your welcome back committee," says Slim.

"Thanks."

"Your gratitude is overwhelming. Sit here with me for a moment. I was just deciding whether this volcano is ready to blow. What do you think?"

Jin tilts its head to see the painting properly. This version of the Rockies is painted from a different angle than the section it had shown Sandy. The browns separate out into green trees and reddish earth patched with snow.

"Not volcano. Pike's Peak," says Jin.

"They'll be awfully shocked when it erupts, then," says Slim.

"Who?"

"The sea serpents. See here?"

An interlocking but thematically unrelated painting depicts dragons coiled on dragons, making up a whole ocean. A single small ship lists dangerously to one side.

"Don't worry, giant panther will save."

Jin points to the picture above, a panther bigger than the mountain range, swirled with reds, blues, greens, and purples. The cat looks poised to gobble Pike's Peak in a single snap, then lap up the ocean to wash the mountain down.

"Good to have you home, Jin."

Jin looks at Slim, unsure whether the other neuter is making an assumption or an invitation.

"Given the choice, you would never leave our baths, except maybe when Pelin gets too close," says Slim.

"It always like that?" asks Jin.

"Pelin? It loves anything new. It will cling to you, wring dry all your stories, and move on. It's kind of a professional sycophant. All artists need fans, and Pelin fills our need. Don't let it bother you. It's harmless."

"Odd, though. Always touching."

"Many of us do that. Didn't you notice? Maybe we watch too many movies or spend too much time around gen actors and artists. We pick up nasty habits like enjoying human contact from time to time. We'll be even worse now, with your friend Sandy providing a bad influence."

A hint of a smile finally breaks through on Jin's face.

"Want her to leave?" Jin asks.

"No! We love her. Poor Jin, you have no taste for the wild life."

"Yes, prefer sedentary lifestyle of being attacked. Know why *they* try touching."

"Poor Jin."

This time Slim is not smiling.

Rouelle looks through the new charts with Jin in the green room. After a moment, it calls over a percussionist, a neut Jin has seen but never met. They mutter together for a long time while the drummer pats out rhythms on its leg, hitting accents with its feet and head.

"Several different music styles, all embedded with undertones, never repeating exactly. You in?" says Rouelle.

The drummer nods.

"We can do," Rouelle tells Jin. "What undertones?"

Jin directs it to another chart on the intranet. The musicians huddle again, the rhythm of the drummer's hands, feet, and head never stopping.

"Simple enough. What effect this have on people?"

"None for most," says Jin. "For some, cause heart attack. Don't play frequencies same time as song you made last time."

"Which one?"

"Second. Makes listener's brain chems simulate attacker's, become vulnerable to frequencies embedded in new music."

Rouelle's eyes widen, and the drummer glances between them uneasily. Jin senses that Pelin has silently come to stand at its elbow, following the exchange intently. The two musicians start off for the studio, picking up a couple of other neuts on their way out. A hand touches Jin's shoulder, and Jin doesn't try to stifle the annoyance in its features as it turns to face Pelin. Standing near, Pelin is much smaller than Jin had thought. The top of its head barely reaches Jin's nose, and Jin is not tall itself. It waits for Pelin to speak.

"Come to baths with me, Jin? For talk."

"No."

Pelin shrugs and settles into the velvet cushions, pulling Jin down with it.

"Okay, here then. Tell me more of music plague."

"Nothing more. Just heart attacks."

"Won't hurt others? Any?"

"Shouldn't. Can't test much."

Pelin stares at Jin's throat. Jin presses back into the arm of the couch to avoid the hand reaching for its collar. Pelin persists, touching the end of the thin scab visible above Jin's shirt. The hand is surprisingly gentle in contrast to the harshness of Pelin's face.

"Tested on self, didn't you?"

Jin slides out from the touch to stand beside the couch.

"No volunteers."

"I'd volunteer. Other spreaders need volunteer tests too?"

Jin stares at the other neut. "You want to die? That's why no volunteers. Creating death, not playing games."

Slim slips an arm around Pelin's waist, swinging it up off the couch and around toward the kitchen door. The motion is dance-like, and Pelin takes the interruption good-naturedly.

"Don't bother Jin, Pelin. It's our guest, remember, and tired from the journey. Go suck someone else's blood for a little while."

Jin cringes at Slim's words, but apparently this is a joke between them. Pelin smiles at Slim, who gives it a genlike peck on the cheek. Pelin slips out from the taller neut's arm to join Sandy as she enters the room.

"Jin!" says Sandy.

She shakes Pelin off absentmindedly and rushes over, stopping just short of throwing her arms around Jin. Pelin settles into a couch at the far end of the room, looking hurt.

"How long have you been here? I didn't even realize Slim brought you in already. This is great! How long will you be staying? I've been helping Slim run its lines for its next project. I'm getting the hang of acting, and of course Slim is fabulous. You've got to see it!"

Unable to contain herself any longer, she squashes Jin into a hug. After a few muffled grumbles and halfhearted struggles from Jin, Sandy lets go.

"You just missed Jin telling us all about the new plague Rouelle is making for it," says Slim.

"Well, what are we all standing around in here for? Jin, you can tell me about the plague while I show you to your room. You'll stay with me—I have my own room now. Then I'll fill you in on what everybody else has been doing. You'll love this—I'm even learning to bake a little. Cook's a lot more lenient than Keri."

Pelin starts to follow the two of them out of the room, but Slim intercepts it again, letting Jin escape with only Sandy to deal with. Sandy refrains from touching it further as they walk down the passageway to her room. In fact, the bubbling energy seems to slide out of her altogether and they walk along in silence for a while. Jin still gets the sense she is happy to see it, but something is different, too.

"Sand, what you think of Pelin?" says Jin.

"Huh? Oh, I don't know, kind of like a lost chick that won't get out from underfoot, I guess. Why?"

"Don't know. Makes me uncomfortable."

Sandy laughs, but only a little. "Oh, poor Jin. Forced into being social again. Well, I'll promise not to make small talk. I won't even ask you about the weather."

"No weather in caves."

"That's what we all love about you Jin, your sense of humor."

Jin spends most of its time avoiding Pelin and floating in the baths. It agrees to watch Sandy rehearse with Slim and is surprised to find that she does take to acting quite well. Both of them flow from self to character easily, with Slim's portrayal of a young man so convincing that Jin finds itself sniffing for traces of testosterone.

The two of them coax Jin to the baths after rehearsal, where Sandy commands the center of attention by giving back massages to anyone who doesn't complain. Jin lies facedown on a grassy area, slightly apart from the noise and splashing. The steam relaxes it, and the noise of the others fades in and out of Jin's awareness.

Eventually, it realizes that the voices have been gone for a while and someone has turned the lights to their evening setting. Orange and purple clouds are projected on the upper portion of the walls and the light is golden and warm, a cross between sunset and candlelight. Jin rolls over onto its side to take a better look and finds itself staring into a pair of ice-blue eyes a few feet away on the grass. Short wisps of dark blonde hair splay across its cheek, and the eyes are guarded but hopeful. Pelin.

"What, Jin? So bad that I want to hear you talk?"

In this light, Pelin's eyes are a piercing blue framed by high cheekbones and a clear complexion somehow made cruel. The bend of the eyebrows, the hook of its nose, the beginning of frown lines around its mouth.

"Want me to go?" Pelin says, hurt again.

It starts to stand but Jin grabs its arm, pulling Pelin back down and itself up to a seated position in one motion. It stares hard into the bewildered face, then closes its eyes and calls up a memory for comparison.

"Stop, Jin. You're hurting."

Pelin's voice is different, smooth rather than harsh. Jin loosens its grip on Pelin's arm, but doesn't release.

"Where you from?" demands Jin.

"What you mean? Live here. For twenty years, maybe more."

"Where before?"

"Born San Diego, family moved to North Dakota when young. Why?"

"Any other neuts in family?"

Pelin responds with silence, but its face goes through a dozen changes. Jin automatically notes the brain chemistry and sound wavelength for each one. It almost begins ghosting, figuring it will get more information that way, but just as it moves to begin, Pelin speaks.

"You met *him*, didn't you?"

Its eyes are narrowed but dropped so Jin can't read the expression. The disgust in Pelin's voice is enough. Jin lets go of its arm.

"Almost killed me," says Jin.

"Takes more than that weasel to kill you, Jin. Where is *he* now?"

"You heard story when Sand and I first came. Man stole pack, forced long walk. Called Albuquerque 'his' city."

Pelin snorts. "That's Brat, all right."

"Brat?"

"Parents named it Brett, I always called Brat. Used to be joke, now wish I called it worse."

Pelin looks up at Jin, its eyes brighter than before. When Jin doesn't speak, it sighs and wraps its arms around its knees. Jin sits in a mirrored position, waiting.

"Truly sorry it hurt you, Jin. Hoped it had killed self by now. Hates everyone. Tried to be spreader but plague killed too many, too homogenous. All low-income, mostly black-Hispanic. Made gens think of hate crimes, racial genocide. Council forbid from spreading again, not that it wanted to after that. Wasn't happy in research, medicine, business, teaching. No interest in art. Own plague killed its best friend. Hates gens because it has to hide, hates neuts for making it killer."

"Network doesn't make killers," says Jin. "Spreaders choose own path. Bruv even discourages, usually. Can quit after trial run, no questions."

"Brat knows. Probably hates self worst of all. That's why it takes hormones. Doesn't want be neut anymore; can't be gen. Now is neither; likes best that way."

"Gens there afraid of him," says Jin, remembering the look in the Albuquerque waitress's eyes. "Has cruel face."

Pelin sighs and brings its head down to its knees. "Runs in family. So now it's 'he,' and I stay here, hiding. Trying same thing. To negate self, only using opposite of hate. Attach self to others, love them, be absorbed. That way don't have to think of self, don't have to be Pelin."

"Why? You not so bad," says Jin.

Pelin brings its head back up with a trembling smile.

"Know. Annoying like crazy, but not so bad I send strangers off to die. No. Am too much like Brat. Can't really hate it. I killed, too."

"You were spreader?"

"One job, trial like you say, year before Brat's. Were close siblings once. Have no stomach for killing, Jin. Believed cause was right, went in, did job, wiped out half of Denver. Got back to caves fast as possible, threw up for two weeks, wanted to die."

It fingers the green beans growing nearby, pinching a stem but not quite plucking the bean all the way off. Its hand drops back into the dirt and it meets Jin's eyes.

"Still see bodies every night. Horrid plague. Something went wrong; victims felt no pain, I made sure, but kept throwing up blood. They were so scared."

Jin nods. For years it forced itself to watch the deaths it caused, trusting the compassion triggered by the horrors to keep it humane. Maybe it should try doing that again, at least occasionally, to remind itself what the rest of the world might feel.

"Admire you, Jin. You have strength. I couldn't stand guilt. Still can't."

Jin hesitates, then lightly places its fingertips on Pelin's shoulder. Pelin leans into the touch for a moment.

"Thanks for bringing Sand. She helps when everyone sick of me. Ghosting her relieves guilt. Forget self for while again. She's good."

"Not good to forget self too much."

Pelin nods. "But distract me for while, please? Tell about Roswell. Anywhere up top. Not Albuquerque. Haven't been up top since my plague. Tell about land, buildings, people. Just so I know world is still there," says Pelin.

Jin leans back, looking up at the fake sky, and tries to form landfills and deserts and shacktowns into words.

By the time Rouelle is finished, Jin is almost sorry to leave. Rouelle drops the coin-sized hardcopy music chips into Jin's hand, looking refreshed and tremendously pleased.

"This one a pleasure, Jin. Just sad I can't put own name on. Rouelle would be famous!"

"What about Miko?" says the drummer.

"What about you?" says Rouelle, winking at Jin. "Here. Miko is good promoter too, made press kits and list of distribution channels."

"Thanks," says Jin.

Miko bows to Jin, its hands still tapping out rhythms Jin can't comprehend.

Slim, Pelin, and Sandy walk Jin to Painted Cavern to say goodbye. Sandy starts to say more, but Slim pulls her back, grinning, and clamps a hand across her mouth. Jin steps into Ocean Cave alone. This time it hardly stops on the journey, arriving home in just a few hours, happy and ready to go.

Keri insists that it stay the night to rest and eat before starting out for St. Louis. Jin grudgingly agrees with her logic and cleans a plate of steak and peas before letting her help it pack food for the trip.

"So, are we going to lose you to that artist group like Bruvec thinks?" Keri asks.

"Bruv says? Must be true."

"They certainly do put you in a good mood down there, I'll say that. And Sandy is so busy she hasn't even bothered to send a message."

"Sure she misses you," says Jin. "I won't leave here for there. Artist caves nice, but need to travel. Need our labs here in between."

"You never were the settling type. They're going to force a vacation on you soon, though, if you don't decide to take one of your own accord."

"Talked to Bruvec. After this trip, two weeks off."

Keri shakes her head. "I'd ask for more than that. You may think you're okay, but I can still see the bags under the circles under your eyes."

Jin savors the clean white bed that night. It may not have one again for quite some time. In the morning, it decides to eat breakfast with Keri before searching out Bruvec for the travel money.

"Sorry, Jin," says Bruvec when Jin finally tracks it down.

"Okay, found you now."

Bruvec shakes its head.

"What? Not get funds?" says Jin.

Impossible. The Network is rich, and Jin asks for so little. Unless Bruvec asked for too much.

"Tell Council I'll take whatever they give," says Jin.

Bruvec shakes its head. "Truly sorry. Trip delayed."

## CHAPTER 19

Jin has nothing to say. It just stares.

"Sorry, Jin," says Bruvec again.

"What? We don't spread plagues now?"

"Not forever, Jin. Just wait."

"How long?"

"Few days, week maybe," says Bruvec.

It lowers itself stiffly until it is sitting with its back against the cave wall. Jin sits across from it after a moment, trying not to show impatience and well aware it is failing miserably. It can almost hear the notes of its own frustration.

"Remember you had to check with us about plague in hometown? Council wants to review," says Bruvec.

"So, what? Can't go 'til they say okay?"

"Yes."

"Why couldn't they say earlier? What's problem?"

"They like music plague, like a lot. That's holdup. Maybe want to send others in, watch St. Louis. If works okay, might spread to larger area."

"How big? Whole Midwest? Could take a while."

"Silly Jin. Think this plague needs in-person spread? Can go bigger than Midwest, maybe whole country, then whole world if trial goes well. Others would help monitor, not isolated spreaders anymore. Big business Jin, big breakthrough. Proud?"

Jin tries to sort out what it is feeling. Not proud. Mostly worried. For one thing, a worldwide spread with a single target group would throw off what little balance remains in the human race. For another, spreading a single plague so far is too impersonal.

More like a random disease of nature than something human, something created in the passion of discovery, shared as a way of helping the species survive. Survival has to be the goal. Otherwise, all of this is just murder.

"Don't like," says Jin. "Council isn't looking at long-term."

"I'll tell others you say so."

"You're Council now?" Jin shakes its head. "Too sedentary for you. Just last week you chased me around caverns."

"You mean this morning. Yeah, getting old. Happens to all, maybe even you someday."

Jin can tell Bruvec doesn't believe this. It is still convinced Jin will die violently on one of its spreading trips. Jin figures it is probably right.

"When does Council meet again?" says Jin.

"Tomorrow night. Can't say how long decision will take."

---

Bruvec comes to find Jin in one of the wild caves a week later. "Council is excited," it says. "Start soon as you like."

"What conditions?"

"One person with you at all times, three others follow separately to observe."

"Who?"

"Three observers unknown to you, Council picks. Travel companion you pick, subject to my approval."

Jin looks at Bruvec standing before it and knows what Bruvec wants it to say, but the neut really is too old to be away from the safety of Home Cavern for long, and Jin plans to do much of its travel by foot, as always.

"Sorry, Bruv, can't be you."

Bruvec nods but its face doesn't agree. "Know. Just never tried spreading, always wondered if I could handle."

"You couldn't, friend," Jin says, gently touching a curl of its nearly pigmentless hair.

They walk back together to the main caverns so Jin can pack, and Jin ghosts its friend along the way. The blood is sluggish in

Bruvec's veins, and its breath rasps a little in its lungs. Just a few years longer and no one will ever be able to ghost Bruvec again.

"Meet three o'clock tanker at Whites City stop day after tomorrow. Arrive St. Louis in three days, short layover in Kansas City," says Bruvec.

"No," says Jin.

"What now? Just do," says Net, trying to hand Jin a printed itinerary.

Bruvec holds out a hand to hush Net. "You not find travel companion yet?"

"Found. Go get it today, leave day after tomorrow."

"What's problem, then?" says Bruvec.

"Told you. Catching ride from El Paso."

Net walks off. Keri stays and listens, pretending to be invisible next to the kitchen counter.

Bruvec sighs loudly. "Okay, Jin. Why? Why wear out feet when trucks go faster? You make self old before time, soon look old as Bruv."

Jin goes around the table and crouches by Bruvec's chair so it can look up into the older neut's downcast eyes. Its fingertips lightly stroke the back of the wrinkled hand. After a moment, Bruvec lays its other hand on top of Jin's.

"Have to go my way, Bruv. Life no good if just rushing around killing. Promise to ride whole way from El Paso to target, but let us walk first part. Better for Pelin, too."

"It really agreed to come with?"

"Yes. Its need to see world again is stronger than guilt."

"Stronger than fear, too?" says Bruvec.

"No. But bigger fear is spending whole life as nothing. It lives with artists but has no art. Was spreader, couldn't spread. Any change, even risking death, is better than knowing it turned away from own life."

Bruv brushes Jin's knuckles with its fingertips.

"Spreaders always smartest, Jin smartest of all. Someday maybe make world a better place."

Jin just shakes its head. It can't really picture the world any better; that will take researchers and scientists to figure out how to scrub the air and water and make the waste stop piling up. Jin just hopes to keep things from getting worse for a while.

Painted Cavern seals behind Pelin and Jin. Slowly, their eyes adjust to the phosphorescent ocean world. Pelin turns, both of its hands dancing lightly over the crystals, only an eighth of an inch from touching. There is a smile on its face, though its eyes flick around as quickly as its elevated pulse. It is obviously reliving ghosted memories.

"Who?" asks Jin.

"Mix. Right hand relives Sandy. Picked up from you just now. Left hand sometimes me, sometimes…"

"Brat?"

"Mmm. Down here just once together, when it first came."

"You can tell whose ghosting I show from just watching?" says Jin.

"I know Sand. Has very distinct movements, you repeat well."

Jin lets Pelin have a silent good-bye after they push open the door leading out of Ocean Cave. It hasn't been this far out of the artist caves for nearly half of its life.

"Which way to El Paso?" it says.

The first half of the trip to El Paso is underground. The cavern system stretches far beneath the surface the Guadeloupe Mountains into the Cornudas. Without the danger of breaking chemical jars on the difficult path, Jin can relax and enjoy the rough terrain while Pelin absorbs the idea of going to see new places.

They emerge from a small cave in the hillside around the middle of their second day. The true cave entrance is hidden by a thin stone door with the standard pattern-sensitive lock. A short tunnel leads out into the brightness where El Paso's suburbs spread deep into the Cornudas Mountains, where terraced gardens take full advantage of the shade and rainfall of the higher elevations. Junk heaps and wastelands line the roads connecting the lo-loc suburbs to the hi-loc city, where truck and pedestrian traffic is visible. Pelin clings to Jin's elbow, its breath shallow and quick.

"Just ignore," says Jin. "Don't try ghosting anyone. They'll leave alone."

Pelin releases Jin and adjusts its sunglasses. Its pale eyes are more sensitive to light than Jin's, and it hasn't seen true sunlight in nearly two decades. The heat turns the sunscreen on its skin into a nauseating potpourri of coconut and perfume, but Pelin seems oblivious as it gawks like a tourist at the masses of humanity around it. Jin walks far slower than its muscles want to go so Pelin can take everything in.

"When will others be there?" asks Pelin.

"Observers not meeting in El Paso, they go straight to St. Louis in three days, maybe. We won't see, won't know who they are unless accidentally cross paths."

Pelin is distracted by a group of laughing boys. Jin sees it ghost and almost stops it, then shrugs. Pelin's business, if it wants a sensory overload. Jin's main concern is the unanswered question of whether the plague will affect people with already high blood pressure. It would rather not have its new friend become the test case. Not on its first trip out in so long.

Jin uses the walk into the city to teach Pelin all of the edible plants it knows. Jin shows it how to prepare and eat prickly pear leaves and fruit, explains how to peel and weave yucca fibers into something useful after the flesh is baked or fried.

"Okay, just don't make me eat bugs," says Pelin.

Jin digs into its pack and pulls out a bag of cookies. They are one of Keri's jokes, oat-nut clusters shaped like bugs to remind Jin of its desperate meal after the flood.

At sunset, Jin and Pelin watch the sky turn fiery orange as they rest and eat fruit and more bug-clusters. Jin watches its cookie carefully as it eats, not sure if Keri's humor runs as far as adding a real bug at the center. When the sun is down, they walk onward.

Just after midnight they cross into the city proper and use some of Bruvec's money for a room.

"Thought you didn't stay in hotels," says Pelin, dripping wet after two short bursts from the hotel shower.

"Bruv gave too much money, cash and credit. Knew I'd spend just so don't have to carry with. Also, El Paso transient laws are strict. Can't afford time in jail, maybe having packages confiscated. You done in shower?"

"Go ahead. Haven't used real shower in long time. Feels like how I remember rain, but timer won't stay on long enough. Think we'll see rain this trip?"

"Not here. St. Louis, maybe. Set alarm for seven? Have to get to stop early or we'll miss passenger pickups."

"Done. Night Jin."

"Night."

St. Louis is busier, dirtier, and a little more crowded than Jin remembers. Wastelands push in at the city fringes, and the stench of rot and smoke fills the particulate-heavy air, just like any city in need of a spread. The main passenger stop is in the part of town where Jin wasn't allowed to go as a kid. The place looks the same to Jin as the day it left home.

It walks with Pelin to the local music distribution center, and they hand the package Miko prepared to the receptionist on duty.

"Local band?" she asks without interest.

"Compton Heights," says Jin, giving the neighborhood listed in Miko's publicity packet.

"Thank you," the receptionist says.

She puts their envelope on a stack, then turns her attention to her screen. Spreading a plague is never this easy. Pelin tugs Jin's sleeve, anxious to leave the scene.

Outside, the two neuts wander slowly through the streets. Jin can't help focusing on Pelin's nervous breath and racing heart. It hardly notices the faces and forms surrounding them.

Rouelle said everything they needed was in the packages, the right words and names certain to get the tainted songs played on the sampler sites and dropped like wildfire. They deliver five more packages to lesser upload centers throughout the city in different formats—rock music, a college station, country, popular, classical—giving a fake local band's name and history for each one. One more for the instrumental music network piped through hi-loc shopping areas. Each song is completely different, but all carry the same death tones. Packages delivered, there is nothing to do but wait.

"We anywhere near where you were born?" asks Pelin.

"No. Getting closer," says Jin.

Pelin nods, and they walk in silence for a while. Jin hadn't realized it was heading home until Pelin asked. It turns left instead of continuing straight down Olive, still toward the verge communities where hi- and lo-loc meet, but not toward home. There's no more need to consult a map. Jin stops at an office building. A yellow sign burns through the smog with the name of a bank's offices, three dentists, and a few lo-loc restaurants and a mixed market with local produce, textiles, and art. The top four floors are an office share/dormitory for independent workers, mostly order fulfillment and customer service.

"Jin?" says Pelin.

"Used to be school. Football field under that end of building." Jin points.

"Parents still live near here?" asks Pelin.

"You know where your parents live?" says Jin.

Pelin smiles, shakes its head. "You have any siblings?"

"No. Unless parents had kid after I left. Were probably afraid to try again. You older or younger?" says Jin.

"Than Brat? Older. Four years," says Pelin, leafing through the pamphlet rack in front of the market. "At least won't run into *it* here."

"No, seemed rooted in Albuquerque," says Jin.

"Um, excuse me, miss?" says a woman's voice. "I, that is, are you Jin? I mean Jen? Jen Morales?"

Jin turns. The woman is about its age, but looks much older. The body has little fat, but not much muscle either, and sags a bit. She's sad, maybe. Definitely tired. Brown hair, jeans, and a button-down shirt; a tan shoulder bag newer and more stylish than the clothing. Her voice triggers Jin's memory. It listens hard for subvocalizations. The woman repeats Jin's full given name.

"Shaney," says Jin.

"You remember! How are you, Jen?"

"Still called Jin. This is Pelin."

Pelin smiles and nods a shy hello.

"Nice to meet you, Pelin. I just can't believe you're here, Jin! Um, do you two want to get some food or coffee or something? Maybe catch up a little? I've been, well, I guess a little out of sorts lately. It would be nice just to sit and talk. Maybe you can tell me where you've been these last few years. Fifteen years, isn't it? Since you left?" She smiles weakly.

Jin absorbs the scent of sweat, the biochemical signature that spells out Shaney's nervousness. It looks at Pelin, who gives a barely perceptible shrug to show it's willing to do whatever Jin wants. Jin agrees to join Shaney for lunch. Meeting a new gen might be good for Pelin.

Shaney's chatter leads the way through the crowded streets.

"Jin and I went to school together. Kindergarten through part of tenth grade. We didn't really stay close, but we sometimes got together, especially in junior high school."

"Told you about Shaney," Jin says to Pelin. "Nicer than others, kept secrets."

Shaney blushes. She tries to hang on to her composure, but her eyes grow bright and a single tear escapes. She sniffs and swipes at her face.

"Sorry. It's been an interesting couple of months."

The three cluster into the entry of a lo-loc cafe to wait for a table. Jin had told Pelin the same story it told Sandy. Shaney was the friend it had lost through not being careful enough about keeping its differences secret. Either she had grown up enough to no longer be afraid of that difference, or time had dimmed the fear from her mind.

"You live near here, still?" Jin asks.

"I just moved back. I'm staying at my mom's house until I find a place of my own. For me and my son."

The tears threaten again. Jin refrains from ghosting, wanting to allow Shaney the privacy of her own emotions until she chooses to share them. It remembers her just like this, when the early signs of puberty would send her into tears for reasons Jin would never understand. Back then, it would have ghosted her to feel close.

"Jin showed me your old school," says Pelin.

Its eyes are also bright with tears.

"Stop ghosting," Jin subvocalizes.

"Yeah, that was the first thing I did when I came back, too," says Shaney. "Go see the old school. Only they tore it down two years after we graduated and built that monstrosity."

"You still teaching?" asks Jin.

"Of course, you would remember," says Shaney. "No, I'm done teaching. I want to do something where I only deal with a limited number of people."

"Why?" says Pelin.

Jin jabs it with an elbow.

"Because that way it won't be so hard when two-thirds of them die," says Shaney.

"Disease?" says Jin, already knowing the answer.

She nods. "My younger son, my husband, nearly all the boys in my class, and half the girls. The doctors said maybe the virus had some sort of hormonal component, that maybe testosterone somehow made the boys more vulnerable to disease. I don't think he even knew. My older son managed to pull through, though. My mother found the two of us wailing on her porch in the middle of the night. I'm still not sure how I got him all the way here."

Jin tries to keep the sick feeling down in its stomach by calculating the odds, but there are too many variables. The queasiness spreads upward from stomach to brain. Pelin pulls away from them, not enough for Shaney to notice, but the distance makes Jin shiver.

"You lived in Amarillo," Jin says.

"You heard about our plague, did you?" says Shaney.

A hostess leads them to a table before Jin can answer, then leaves them to turn their menus over and over in silence. Jin wants to tell Shaney it's sorry for her loss, that it knows sometimes death is easier when the family can all go at once, when no one is left to mourn. Still, it's glad one son and Shaney survived. A world needs people who can be friendly to outcasts.

"I—" says Jin.

"Thanks," says Shaney, as if she's heard and said the words too many times before.

A spike in Pelin's pulse draws Jin's attention. The Soundwave plague can't have started, not so fast, and Pelin is far too gentle to feel the effects so sharply, unless high blood pressure really is going to be a problem. Jin doesn't realize it is ghosting until its own pulse slows with Pelin's to the most relaxed Jin has ever felt in its friend. Only then does Jin turn fully to see it staring out the window. Even a gen could feel the awe in Pelin's voice when it speaks.

"Look. Rain."

Fat drops quickly cover the sidewalk. Jin nudges Pelin to shut its gaping mouth before Shaney starts to ask questions. Jin had subconsciously heard the rain start, but to it the sound is just background noise. To Pelin, the rain is a miracle.

"Pelin loves rain," Jin explains to Shaney. "Too much time in the desert."

Shaney looks around.

"I need to go. My son will wonder where I am."

Her pulse rises, her breath coming way too fast. She pulls a pen out of her shoulder bag and scribbles something down on the buckthorn-fiber napkin. Jin remembers the texture of the paper from its childhood.

"It was good to see you again, Jin. Nice meeting you, too, Pelin. Um, here's my number. If you want to get together sometime while you're still in town, call me."

Jin tucks the napkin away and switches to the other side of the booth, watching Pelin watch the rain.

"Poor woman," Pelin says. "You'll call her?"

"Don't know."

Pelin turns away from the window. "If yes, be careful what you say. Please don't bring up Amarillo."

Jin nods, and the waitress finally arrives to take their orders.

For two days, Jin and Pelin wait for the Soundwave music to air. Curiosity and the nostalgia of being back in St. Louis get the best of Jin, and it calls Shaney. At least it can thank her for her kindness when it was young, and maybe say good-bye this time before it leaves St. Louis for good. Shaney's mother answers the phone.

"Jen, is that you? Shaney told me you were back in town. How are you?"

"Okay. You?"

"Oh, I do all right, thank you for asking. Let me get Shaney for you."

Pelin flips through the hotel entertainment listings, chuckling to itself.

"Hi, Jin," says Shaney.

"Hi. You have spare time?"

"Too much, unfortunately. When do you want to get together?"

"Evening okay?"

"Today? Yeah, that should work. Do you want to just come over? My mom would love to see you. Maybe you could even meet my son. I told mom you looked just like I remembered from high school."

"Seven o'clock?"

"Okay. Do you remember where the house is?"

"Yes."

"See you at seven, then. Oh, would you like to bring your friend, too?"

Jin glances at Pelin, now exploring the screen's remote.

"No, just me."

"All right, see you soon. Oh, and Jin?"

"Yes?"

"I really am sorry for, you know, just kind of dumping you off back then. I hope you can forgive me."

"Don't worry, Shaney. Already forgiven."

Pelin is watching the screen with a big smile on its face. Jin hangs up the phone and watches. Pelin gestures on the remote, splitting the display into three different channels, and turns its grin on Jin.

"These are neut shows," it says. "One in big screen from our cavern. One on left topside is artist in Italy, other one local."

"Who from your cavern?"

"You didn't meet. But Slim has guest role this episode."

Jin sits on its own bed, watching the screen. Slim's part is small, but the recorded laugh track hollers and cheers the moment it steps into the scene. People are obviously expected to know who it is. It looks very male in the costume and makeup, which Jin finds disturbing.

"You're seeing friend at seven?" says Pelin.

Jin nods.

"Good. Leaves plenty time for food. I'm starving."

On the way through town, they walk through a small park where scrawny trees try to convert a city's worth of carbon dioxide into oxygen. Pelin picks up a caterpillar and lets the creature crawl on its hand for a while.

"You like topside?" Jin asks.

Pelin nods.

"Maybe others will let you deliver artwork, you can travel more."

Pelin shakes its head. "Not like you, Jin. Don't need travel. Is okay now and then, maybe. Not good to forget sky and sun, but caves are home. I like home."

At the restaurant, Pelin excuses itself to go wash the caterpillar residue off its hands while they wait for their food. A few feet away from the table, it hesitates and turns back.

"Which I look most like?"

Jin examines its clothes, hair, and build.

"Could be either. Women's might be safer. I have to use here, since some might remember me."

Pelin nods and follows Jin's advice. Over food, they each keep an ear on the restaurant's music system. So far, they recognize nothing as part of the plague.

They wander the city all afternoon, stopping to browse both lo- and hi-local stores and public areas that are playing music. Finally, when they stop in a crowded coffee shop, a song comes on that makes Pelin sit up straight and silent in its seat.

"This one?" asks Jin.

Pelin nods. "Recognize Rouelle's work."

Jin ghosts Pelin, monitoring its heart and breath carefully throughout the whole length of the song. Its lungs are constricted, the veins and arteries are tight, but although its nervous system is under stress, Jin detects nothing stronger than it felt in El Paso. Jin forgets to pay attention to the rest of the coffee shop patrons, not noticing whether any of them react. It is ghosting so fully it forgets itself until self-recrimination intervenes. Selfish, not to want its friend to die in its plague. Pelin has the chance to live or die just like everyone else.

The song ends, and Pelin's and Jin's hearts and breath return slowly to normal. Jin releases its focus on Pelin's movements and lets its own normal heart rate return. Finally, it remembers to take a look around them.

"None dead," says Pelin. "Man over there had trouble, recovered."

"Wonder if song is too short," says Jin.

"Maybe he was just high risk already. I'll ghost, see what blood pressure returns."

They spend the next twenty minutes in silence. Pelin ghosts the man while Jin contemplates how it can raise the dosage if the songs are not effective. If the Council will let it try again. Pelin decides the man just has high blood pressure, probably not combined with an attacker mentality. They wander back out into the growing dusk, where Jin parts ways with Pelin to go find Shaney.

Shaney is jittery when it arrives, rushing back and forth through the kitchen, asking three times if it wants anything to drink. Her mother puts a hand on Shaney's shoulder to calm her, smiling at Jin. Jin always liked Margaret Lewik. A practical woman. Her husband died in a car accident when Shaney was very young, so Jin never knew him, but it always suspected Shaney must have inherited her nervousness from his side of the family.

"Let's go downstairs," says Shaney.

"Your room looks almost the same as in junior high," says Jin when they reach the muffled chill of the small home's basement. It remembers to speak slowly and use the gen forms of grammar.

"Yeah, except the posters are gone. Remember the big Art Pinolde poster I had over there? And all the rock bands?"

"Same colors, though."

"Yeah. So, I talked enough about me yesterday. Tell me what you've been up to. Where have you been living?"

"Travel, mostly. Like to see new places. Otherwise, I spend time in New Mexico."

"What part?"

"Near Roswell."

"That's not far from Amarillo, really. If I were going back there maybe we could get together occasionally, only I don't think I'm going back. I'm sorry, Jin. You must think I'm just an awful person. First I stop talking to you completely, and now I'm unloading my entire miserable life onto you in two days."

"Always considered you a friend, Shaney."

"Really? Even after I walked out on you in the ninth grade?"

Jin shrugs. "You didn't talk to others about me. Didn't make fun, or join others against me."

"Still, it must have been awfully lonely for you. I never saw you talk to anyone else except when it was necessary for class."

"Was fine by myself," says Jin.

"You have other friends now, though, don't you? I mean there's Pelin, of course. But others, too?"

"Yes."

"Um, I hate to ask this, but just so I don't embarrass myself, is Pelin a he or a she?"

Lying would be easiest at this point, but Jin feels Shaney has earned some amount of trust. If the news about neuts is beginning to seep into general knowledge, maybe recruiting a few more sympathetic gens who know neuts as people and can come to their defense is a good idea.

"Pelin isn't either," says Jin. "Not everyone is a man or woman."

Shaney's eyes grow wide and her mouth drops open like Pelin's did watching the rain. The reaction only lasts a moment before her composure reasserts itself. Shaney has inherited some of her mother's practicality after all.

"You mean Pelin's an androgyne?"

"No. Androgyne literally means 'man-woman,' like a hermaphrodite. Pelin is neither. Completely sexless."

"I don't understand," says Shaney.

"Hormone balance and physical structure are different. No reproductive system. No gender."

"But wouldn't he—uh, she—"

"It."

"Wouldn't it still have to have either two X chromosomes or an X and a Y?"

"Actually, there's much greater variety of chromosomes available. X, Y, O, Z, N, probably few I can't think of right now. Some people have more than just one pair, too. Called chimeras."

"Come on Jin, that's not possible, is it?"

"Of course. You've heard of double-Y?"

"Yeah. Those are the men that usually turn out to be sex offenders, aren't they?"

"Few do, not as many as you think. There are other combinations, too."

"So you're saying Pelin has an extra chromosome?"

"No, Pelin has just regular pair, but with significant difference from standard X or Y. We call chromosome N, for neuter. Causes different structure in some organs, in pelvic bone. Mutation is linked to other characteristics too."

"Like what?"

Jin realizes it hasn't been cautious enough. It wants Shaney to understand, but it can't give her anything that could link neuts to the plague that took her son and husband. No more science, nothing about neurology or ghosting. Shaney's face turns red, and once again her tears threaten to leak.

"I said, 'like what?' Jin."

"Physical characteristics. No puberty, no growth spurt, slightly different build."

"But wouldn't that make Pelin not human?"

"It seem human to you?"

"I hardly know it well enough to judge."

"Assure you, it's human. More than some men and women I know."

Jin feels Shaney's tension and fear. She keeps her jaw clamped tight in an attempt not to subvocalize. Jin tries to ghost her, but for the moment, she is so still that other than tension, Jin can pick up little. Shaney is still frightened of the unknown, now more than ever. But what Jin doesn't feel is her pulling away from it. It thinks back over what it has told her. Surely it gave enough information that she should figure out Jin is a neuter too.

Shaney's mind has gone other directions.

"So it could be true," she says, digging through her bag.

"What's true?"

"This."

She hands Jin a pamphlet. It hasn't seen this one before, either in the archives or its travels. It sits on the bed, shoving aside the memories linked to the sensation, and reads.

## Don't be Fooled

What you don't know can't hurt you…
if you're already dead.

This is what they depend on, what they need to survive. The secrecy, the ignorance, shepherding us quietly to our deaths.

They walk among us everywhere as if they were normal people. Do normal people unleash death onto whole cities? These people know the consequences of the plagues they bring. They know exactly how and when you will die. They know who their targets are, and we can't fight them because we don't know they exist.

Until now.

Look more closely at the stranger passing through town. Is it a man? A woman? A boy or girl? Look more closely before you decide. This person, this pestilence in human form, may not be any of the above.

Androgynous beings have populated the earth for nearly as long as mankind. Unable to reproduce, these mutants simply lived out their lives and quietly died, causing no harm to the rest of us. Later on, modern medicine came to their aid, allowing them the choice to become full members of human society.

Some of these creatures have accepted this opportunity. Others, however, have turned against us, banding together to destroy a society in which they have chosen not to take part.

Often highly gifted in science, these pseudo-humans develop diseases and spread them among the population. They treat human beings as breeding stock which must be deliberately and mercilessly culled. We have never stopped them because we had no reason to suspect. A single investigator, however, has risked his life many times over to study their habits, gathering inside information on them for years.

Now he brings this information to you to ask for your help. Spread the word. Pass this message around. Share, copy, even if you don't believe. End the secrecy. Question strangers, choose your health professionals carefully.

Most of all, stop the death. Please, protect our society.

More literature to follow.

KnowMore.LearnAndLive.dbf

# CHAPTER 20

Sandy had once imagined that she would stay on the farm all her life, but her mother wouldn't even let her finish that thought out loud.

"You have better things to do with your life," she would say.

Only now did Sandy realize her mother had been talking about herself, and that those "better things" were never going to happen for her. Sandy hoped she would never have the same to say for herself.

With Jin gone from the caverns, Sandy had talked Slim into taking her up for more acting lessons. She rode tour buses between the acting studio and its apartment, where she and Lancaster tip-toed around each other until it left for a shoot somewhere in South America. Phazy's silence was different, more tolerable, stemming as it did from the wide and barren gulf between technicians and actors, regardless of gender or its lack.

Each night as she waited for the tour bus, she checked the job ads and the rooms for rent. The former were of little use, since her experience on a chicken farm was irrelevant in Albuquerque's urban sprawl. Even the outlying farms wouldn't be able to use her; she knew nothing about kale or goats. The room ads were more of a daydream, since she was still dependent on the charity of the neuts.

"Hey, beautiful, need a ride?"

She turned to see Slim grinning at her from its private car two lanes over, stuck in the same jackknifed-water-tanker gridlock that had delayed the tour bus for half an hour so far. She half-closed the pocketscreen and dodged the fenders that impatiently inched forward on the streets.

"Are you trying to gain a reputation for picking up strange women, or just studying how to flirt?" said Sandy as she got into the passenger seat.

"Just because I'm not personally attracted doesn't mean you're not beautiful," said Slim.

"I am, aren't I?" said Sandy.

She couldn't help herself. Class that day had gone spectacularly well, and the instructor had a surprise for them at the end of the lesson.

Slim laughed, its sunglasses hiding the impish flicker Sandy knew by now was in its eyes.

"You're in a good mood," said Slim.

"I have an audition tomorrow. Christoph set one up for everyone who scored high enough on their monologues. I have head shots and everything!"

She pulled up the photos on her screen. There she was, captured on film in a variety of poses and settings. Smiling, angry, sexy, frightened.

"There's more once the photographer uploads them to the dropsite," she said. "And he gave me a list of agencies that specialize in placing extras. He said the work is boring, but it pays well if I can get the right kind."

"He's right. Do you feel like celebrating?"

"I do," said Sandy, flipping her hair back the way the acting coach had said made her look daring and carefree.

Slim laughed. "All right, your choice. Dinner, dancing, movies, whatever you want."

It glanced over at her when she didn't answer.

"What's wrong?"

Sandy shook her head and turned the air-conditioning vent away from her. She wished she had a jacket.

"I was going to say dancing. I haven't been in so long, but then I thought, what if the music..."

"...is Rouelle's," Slim finished.

"I know it can't be. Jin just took the packets to St. Louis centers and they're probably not even playing there yet, let alone dropping nationally. But if it can come up with music that kills, couldn't somebody else do the same? And they could target anyone, not just the people that Jin's plague targets," said Sandy.

Slim eased the car around the jackknifed tanker, careful not to hit the men who were carefully trying to work the truck back into a drivable angle without damaging the dented tanks further and risking a spill.

"Everyone knows that death can come at any time, Sandy. You are just more aware of the danger than most. But you aren't a cave dweller. You need to be out here to live, and you need to remember not to hide from life just because you know it's going to end."

"That sounds like a line from one of your movies," said Sandy.

"Probably is. But if you want to dance, let's dance. You've accomplished something you set out to do, and you'll get a lot more of that done now that you've decided to stay up top."

"You guys are really annoying when you do that," said Sandy.

"Do what?"

"Listen to people subvocalize."

Slim reached over and tapped the bottom of her screen. The apartment listings leapt from thumbnail view to full screen.

"I didn't. I'm just literate sometimes."

Sandy glanced down at the apartments she had highlighted, then tried to read Slim's face. It wore the mildly bemused expression that seemed to come habitually, but there was some pride there as well. She couldn't tell if it was proud of her for finding work, or for looking for a place to stay.

"I think everyone will be more comfortable once I'm out of your apartment," she said.

"We do like having you there, Sandy, even Lancaster does. It just has no idea how to make up to you for betraying your trust, and it isn't sure it wouldn't accidentally do the same thing again."

"I know. I'd rather see if I can learn to get along with it when we're not sharing the same space," said Sandy.

Slim nodded. "Just don't call it Lanky."

Sandy laughed. She still didn't feel much like music and dancing, but dinner sounded good. After being spoiled by Keri and Cook, the actor neuts were terrible in the kitchen, baking everything from boxes and powders and cans. They didn't even participate in the community food gardens, so fresh produce was nonexistent in the house. She missed the corn, meat, and eggs from the farm, and the occasional real beef from the Montana lo-loc restaurants.

"You pick the place," she told Slim. "As long as the food doesn't require adding water just to make it look like food again," she said pointedly, "I'm hungry enough to eat anything."

Slim grinned at her and soon after pulled the car into a crowded hi-loc lot. They received a few double glances and open stares when they were seated in the dim dining room. Slim did, at least, and then the watchers' eyes would slide from it to her, often hardening with jealousy or widening in surprise. Let them stare. She had earned the treat, and Slim was the only friend she had in the area to celebrate with.

"You're still thinking of Jin," said Slim after they had ordered.

Sandy nodded, unsure whether she could say more in a public place like this.

"It's not alone," said Slim.

Sandy looked at it gratefully. She hadn't been sure when Jin had changed from being irritated by Pelin to enjoying the older neut's company, but the simple fact that it had a friend was a comfort to her. It wouldn't die starving and alone.

"Neither will you," Slim whispered.

It shoved the basket of fresh tortilla chips toward her and pulled the salsa around to where they could both reach. It dunked a chip and held it up, hand beneath to catch any drips.

"To a brave young star," it said, toasting her with the chip.

Sandy reached for a chip and returned the toast.

"So, tell me about your audition," Slim said.

Slim seemed impressed by the director when she mentioned who it was, then checked over the list of agencies her instructor had given her.

It tapped the third name down on the list. "Check with this group first. They have a steady client base, and I know one of the casting agents pretty well."

"Neut?" said Sandy, under her breath.

"A woman who helped me when I was first starting out. Let me see your screen." It added a name next to the listing, then said softly, "She places a lot of us. Neuts. She doesn't know, but I'd rather have you working with us than anyone else I've seen come through lately."

"Do you really think I might get to work on a project with you someday?" said Sandy.

"Strange are the ways of the world, my friend."

Sandy glowed with pleasure for the rest of the night. She slept in Slim's room now, no longer hiding out on the couch to nurse hurt feelings. In some ways, it was like being back with a family again. She fought the urge to whisper to Slim as she had to Ronnie when they were kids together and would sneak into each other's rooms late at night to hatch plots and make up stories.

Ronnie would be fourteen by now. She hadn't seen him since he was ten. Maybe she should look her father up the next time she had a free day. Her mother must have said at some point where they went. If she dug deep enough, she might remember.

She rolled over in the sagging single bed, barely able to make out Slim's form in the amber light that bled in through the window from the street below. The neut, no matter how it tried to be kind to her, wasn't Ronnie. She wasn't even sure how her brother might react to her after so much time apart, but he would be a gen and a relative, and that had to count for something.

Unless he was dead. She finally let herself think that it could have happened. Dad and Ronnie could have been attacked like she and Mom were. Or they could have gone to Amarillo or some other town where the Network spread plagues.

Sandy kicked off the sheets and stretched out, rubbing her eyes. She was grateful to the Network and the artist neuts for their generosity, but she wished they would just let her be for a while. Their thoughts were in her head now, their fears and their solutions. She found herself wondering if she would ever be like other gens again.

When the paychecks from her first bit roles—mostly as a crowd extra and a few lines in a tourism commercial—began trickling in, Sandy put down a deposit on a room. She had three roommates who shared the tiny kitchen and living room and a bathroom full of cracked tiles, but she had her own bedroom with a lock on the door, and she could crawl into bed at night and listen to the hum of insects and feel safe.

She met only two of her roommates her first week in the place, though one of the women assured her that Jeremy was "a nice, quiet guy, really funny, hardly ever home." They weren't sure what he did for a living, and Sandy started to wonder if he was a neut who left to go down to the caves for research or art. She wondered if that would be awkward or comforting.

When she finally met him, it was neither.

"Hey, new girl," said a male voice when she walked into the apartment after a long day's casting call.

She froze at the sound. His laughter grated against the walls in a way she had thought only neuts could detect. Maybe it was just her imagination, but something about him brought on strong memories of the men who had attacked her on the farm.

"Don't just stand there looking like a stunned possum. Grab a beer if you want and come in. I'm Jeremy."

"Jeremy?" she said.

"Yeah. What's the matter?"

"Nothing. Just tired is all. Nice to meet you," said Sandy, then she fled to her room, locking the door behind her.

She pulled out her screen and tapped Slim's number, but the message said it was unreachable. Of course. It had gone back to the caverns for the weekend, promising to get word to her if Jin and Pelin were back early. She would have gone with it if the opportunity to do a commercial hadn't come up. Nothing exciting, just sitting around a restaurant drinking tea all day, but it was money, and the work was fun. She met tons of people that she might or might not ever see again, and everything was friendly and superficial and had nothing to do with science or death.

Jeremy had nothing to do with science, but he reeked of death.

That was stupid. She wasn't a neut, and even a neut couldn't tell what a person was like just by hearing his voice. She should probably go back out into the living room and apologize to him, but she just couldn't make herself go. She decided it was something in his voice that reminded her of the men who had attacked her, but they had all been dark-haired with sunburned white skin, while Jeremy had light hair and olive skin that tanned instead of burned. The tone of his voice was the same, though, or something in it. She couldn't know for sure, and she felt like a fool, but she pushed her dresser in front of the door and checked the locks one more time before she was able to crawl into bed and go to sleep.

In the morning, she regretted giving in to her fears. Her mouth tasted like a sewer from going to bed without brushing her teeth, and her skin felt oily and heavy. She cautiously slid the dresser away from the door and tiptoed out to the bathroom.

Normally, the girls left the door unlocked in case one of them really had to use the toilet while another was in the shower. They hadn't used the right to intrude since Sandy had come to live there, and Marie, the older of the two, assured her that she never would. This time, though, Sandy locked the door behind her and set her phone on the shelf above the towel rack with the setting on one-touch emergency dial. She soaped quickly between the allotted one-minute water bursts and dressed with an eye on the lock.

Jeremy came by while she was brushing her teeth, the door open so she could catch Marie on her way out to work.

"I see you got your beauty sleep," he said, leaning against the door frame so she would have to squeeze past him to get out. "Any time you want that beer, you just let me know."

Sandy nodded and muttered something unintelligible around the mouth full of toothpaste. She hoped he would take it as a sign to go away. He stayed a moment longer, then looked her up and down in a way that made her feel the need to jump back into the shower for another scrub. She waited for a few seconds after he left before walking through the doorway that now seemed heavy with taint. The feeling lasted until she was out of the building with the city laid out around her, a fresh list of rooms for rent on her screen.

# CHAPTER 21

Too many years among the neuts of Home Cavern have deprived Jin of its ability to lie convincingly to people it knows. Privacy is respected there, and it hasn't had this much direct contact with a gen other than Keri and Sandy for over a decade. It takes a deep breath and hands the pamphlet back to Shaney, ghosting her just enough to gauge her reaction to its statement.

"Shaney, pamphlet is designed to make people hate what they don't understand. Neuts are just—" it pauses and takes a deep breath, slowing its brain to accommodate the unaccustomed gen speech patterns, "—a scapegoat...a new group to pin troubles on instead of Jews, Gypsies, immigrants, people with different color skin or different shaped eyes."

"So you're saying nothing in here is true? People like Pelin don't spread diseases?"

Her brain reels with anger and hate so violent that the Soundwave plague would kill her for sure.

"There are...small amounts of truth. Neuts exist, mostly in secret. Isn't—it isn't safe being different. Some choose to get operations, hormone treatments, turn themselves into near-gens," says Jin.

"Gens?"

"Genders. Male and female. Some treatments make significant changes, others are just cut and paste. Neut chromosomes are normal—a normal human mutation. The only real difference is we can't breed. Not interested, besides not having the proper biology."

Shaney's mind finally grasps the obvious. She takes a step backward, then another, staring at Jin. For a moment, Jin thinks about trying to hum in pitches that might trigger a slight relaxation in Shaney's mind, but the thought of manipulating its former friend repulses it. Instead, it speaks softly to her.

"Thought you already figured out I'm one too. We're just people, Shaney. Yes, some neuts kill. So do some gens. But not all neuts, and certainly never because we're trying to take over from gens. Many neuts are doctors, business people, researchers, teachers. Pelin is an artist, not a killer."

That is only a small lie, easily told. Jin ghosts Shaney again, feeling her anger creep higher. Betrayal. That is the song her chemistry is singing. The truth must stop there.

"And what are you, Jin? You said you travel a lot," says Shaney.

The gen speech patterns wear its energy down. Continuing this way seems too exhausting, but it presses on, for Shaney's sake. "I do research, mostly. Psychology. I…travel to find new subjects and keep up with current advances."

Shaney nods, releasing some of her tension. "I remember you wanted to do research. Wasn't it something about finding animals no one ever discovered before? Cryptozoology or something?"

"I found them. Neuts. Learned from them, from myself. Now I study the minds of neuts and gens."

Shaney's shoulders slump, and Jin releases the ghosting to study her from the outside. Her hands shake slightly as the panic clears out of her system. Jin turns the talk toward Shaney's new job search, hoping to find safer ground.

"I don't know. There's nothing that feels right, you know? I put together resumes and letters, then at the last minute I don't send anything out. I don't know what I want to do with myself anymore," says Shaney.

"I think you'll be happier teaching again. That was all you ever wanted to do. Just take time off first, maybe. Try subbing for a while, maybe tutoring. Get used to being with students again."

"Maybe. It's just too soon right now."

Footsteps thunder down the basement stairs, barely softened by the worn carpet. A few seconds later, the sound of a video game invades Shaney's room. Shaney follows Jin's eyes to the door.

"That's Seth. My son."

Jin wants to ask Shaney if it can see him, this child who had contracted the Amarillo plague and lived. He must be strong and intuitive. Shaney sighs as if to force all her fear and frustration out of her lungs in one breath.

"You want to meet him?"

Jin nods, unsure whether this is what Shaney expects, and follows her to the den. A skinny, brown-haired adolescent boy stares intently at the video screen. He looks up at Jin and his mother for the flicker of a second, then is back to his buttons. After every burst of activity, he rubs his fingers vigorously on the legs of his jeans. Jin can see the worn spots that indicate the habit isn't new. After the game ends, he excuses himself to the restroom with another quick glance at Jin. Sounds of scrubbing come through the closed door.

"He has mild obsessive-compulsive disorder," says Shaney quietly. "It got worse as soon as his brother got sick. Nothing that really disrupts his life. The psychiatrist said it's becoming really common for kids these days to be obsessed with cleanliness. The cause is partly neurological and partly just a reaction to the environment. But you probably knew that, being a psychologist."

"I read a few reports about the increase in cases. Interesting, but not my field," says Jin.

When the boy returns, Shaney's hand flutters toward his shoulder, almost touching, then pulls back. She sighs and motions Jin to come with her back up the stairs.

"I just want to touch him, hug him all the time, but he gets so upset and has to wash and change clothes. I have a scheduled 'touch-time' with him in the evening like the psychiatrist suggested, but it's still hard for me, especially with Jason and Dale gone."

"Your husband and other son?" says Jin.

Shaney nods.

"Your gesture," says Jin, imitating Shaney's hand fluttering over Seth, "reminds me of a friend."

"Another one of your sexless people?"

"No, a woman. We went to see artwork together. She really wanted to touch the paintings. Instead, she felt the air above them. Seemed to help her."

"It does," says Shaney. "But it's never enough."

---

Back at the hotel, Pelin is once again sprawled in front of the room's screen.

Jin tells it about Shaney's son and her similarity to Sandy. It pulls a copy of the pamphlet Shaney found out of its pocket and hands the paper to Pelin.

"You know where from?" Pelin asks.

"No. Albuquerque wouldn't surprise, though. Writer knows more about us than most. All information accurate."

"Accurate? You 'band together to destroy a society in which you have chosen not to take part' lately?" says Pelin.

"Know what I mean. Basic info is correct despite negative spin. Also, is aimed at more educated readers than other flyers I've seen."

"Could be Brat, maybe. Was always twisting words to suit self. Why now? Been out there for years."

"Maybe scared," says Jin, sitting on the empty bed. "Searched my pack, found nothing. Maybe was afraid I'd already spread, it might catch. Or afraid something was still in pack it didn't recognize."

"Aren't flyers supposed to be local?" asks Pelin.

Jin shrugs. "So is music. Brat probably knows paper catches eye more than newsdrops, since so little competition."

Pelin nods, thoughtful. "Can we do anything about?"

"Don't know. Usually just ignore. Pamphlets like this been around for ages, only usually not so informed."

"Bad news," says Pelin, looking back through the text. "Loaded with words keyed to trigger negative emotion. Will affect people almost like Rouelle's music does. Be screaming for all our deaths."

"Makes no difference. Can't do anything until plague finished here, future spread decided by Council."

Jin turns on the screen's audio and drops the latest local music mixes. They listen for over an hour, hearing no hint of the Soundwave songs. Restless, they walk through the city until even the bars are closed. The next day is the same.

By the following day, Rouelle's music is in the air. Jin walks down the street, feeling vibrations from a dark-tinted delivery van raise its heart rate slightly. Later, it gets the same feeling from the speakers in a mall. It is still worried that Pelin's tension and distorted feelings of guilt and imagined malice about its own long-ago plague might make it susceptible to the undertones, but although Jin's ghosting detects an increase in anxiety, there is never any real trouble.

One man drops to the ground nearby and a few heavyset women gasp for air, but as soon as the song is over the women move on. The man doesn't. Neither does a young woman they see later in a grocery store. Jin buys a cheap pocketscreen from a vendor before heading to the passenger stop with Pelin. Whoever else the Council sent will complete the study. Time for them to go home.

Jin reads the obituaries on the truck. Only thirty-two deaths from cardiac arrest are reported in the downtown area. That seems to indicate the plague isn't fatal for people with high blood pressure, but a plague that hardly kills more than a day's worth of industrial accidents is a waste of the Network's resources.

It will have to wait for further reports. Rouelle said the full effects might take a while. First exposure might not kill someone with occasional malice, but repeated saturation should catch anyone with a strong tendency toward acting on cruelty. Sound waves will suffuse the air and linger there to catch people for minutes, even up to an hour after the song is over.

As Jin checks national news on the screen, Pelin quietly watches Kansas and Texas roll past through the makeshift window in an air-conditioned box van, craning its neck at an awkward angle to see the sky. Jin automatically scans the distance for rises, valleys, and trees. Any place not covered with man-made housing or junk. Tiny vegetable gardens are crammed between plastic shacks made out of old septic tanks that are sloppily glued together. Still, these people are wealthy, in a way. They have their own homes, and the gardens to feed them.

Jin turns away from the yellow and blue plastic domes. On the other side of the road are bigger gardens, then houses and apartments as the gardens grow larger. Older kids dash across the interstate to steal dinner from these larger gardens, dodging back with full sacks among the trucks and tankers that speed upward of one hundred miles per hour.

Jin rolls its head backward, stretching its neck. Riding wastes away the muscles, and Jin craves its time alone in the wastelands. Walking gives it time to look around, to let the people and the land inspire new ideas. Otherwise, the plagues are just chemicals sitting in a lab, waiting to kill.

Pelin remains silent on the walk from El Paso into the mountains. While Jin enjoys the evening air and the long-awaited stretch of its muscles, Pelin looks longingly at the people around them.

"You okay?" says Jin.

"Homesick, I guess."

"Just few hours to cave entrance. Time goes fast, you'll see."

"Not homesick for underground. I miss people. Have good friends there, even if sometimes tire of me. Belong in artist caves, Jin. Not adventurer like you."

After the sun sinks below the horizon, Pelin continues.

"Don't really belong down there either. Have no art."

"You have empathy. More than any I've known. You're probably good as Sand to show artists how gens will react to neut work."

"Maybe. But I create nothing."

Jin cannot answer. It will lie to protect itself from Shaney's hate, but it can't lie to make its friend feel better. Spreaders are not taught how to give comfort, except whatever kind of peace can be found in death. It wishes it knew the words to trigger release of tension in Pelin's mind. Instead, it leads the way back into the darkness of home in silence.

## CHAPTER 22

Sandy tried to talk to her other roommates about Jeremy, but they laughed at her worries. Marie took her aside later on and whispered in a way that would have been comical had her concerns not been real.

"*Si*, I agree with you, Sandy. He frightened me when I first met him, but I am older than he likes, I think, so I don't worry no more. You, though, you're too pretty to be around him."

"What about Brooke?" said Sandy.

Marie waved dismissively. "Brooke! She's always with her boyfriends. Any of them would knock him down flat, and he knows this. You lock your door when he's around, you hear me?"

"I will," said Sandy. "I do."

She did, and she kept looking for another place to stay. She wished Slim would get back from the caverns so she could ask to stay with it for a few days while she sorted things out. She could hardly think straight just knowing Jeremy was out there. She tried to be rational. He just reminded her of the men who attacked her, that was all. Bad associations. But every time she tried to make herself step into the room with him, something frightened her back behind locked doors. Finally, she caught a tourist van over to Slim's, hoping it had gotten back and just hadn't called her yet.

"Not here," said Phazy when she knocked on the door.

Unlike the others, it didn't bother with gender speech patterns unless it was at work.

"Could I maybe just hang out here for a little bit? I hate to bother you. Look, I'll make you dinner or something if you like. I just can't be in my apartment right now," said Sandy.

It opened the door farther and stepped back to let her in. On the couch sat Lancaster, looking for all the world like a stylish young female model, except for the way it devoured the junk food in front of it. Its eyes turned slowly from the wall-size screen to Sandy.

"Hi. You're back," said Sandy after an awkward pause.

"Well, don't just stand there in the doorway. Out or in," said Lancaster.

Sandy figured she was already more than halfway in.

"I'm really sorry to bother you," she said.

"No bother unless you keep interrupting my show. Don't mind the makeup. I just got back from a screen test," it looked down at itself, then grinned back at Sandy. "Don't mind the cleavage, either. Fake, you know."

"Of course," said Sandy.

"Said you'd cook?" said Phazy.

"Do you have anything to cook with?" asked Sandy.

Both neuts waved her toward the barely-used kitchen in a gesture she took to mean she could use anything there. They hardly had anything for her to work with, but she found a few of the quail eggs that Lancaster kept around for its cake mixes and was digging for spices when Lancaster shut off its screen and stood with its elbows leaning on the counter, watching her.

"Peace offering or nervous tic?" it said.

"What?" said Sandy.

"Cooking. You trying to make friends, or just hoping to fry whatever's bothering you to bits?"

"Mostly frying," Sandy decided. "But if it works as a peace offering, I'm willing to try."

Lancaster came over beside her and sniffed at the eggs just beginning to sizzle. Sandy tossed in something she thought might be paprika, though like half of the other spice containers on the shelf, this one wasn't labeled.

"So you decided we aren't monsters," said Lancaster.

"I never thought you were." Sandy looked at the almost feminine face. "I love Slim and some of the other neuts down in the caverns, it's just—"

"You think of Slim as Tom. A man," said Lancaster.

Sandy shook her head, sprinkling something that might be chives into the pan. "I used to, when I first met it, but I haven't thought of it like that for a long time. And I certainly never thought it was a monster."

"So just me, then."

Sandy wanted to take Lancaster's hand and sit down with it, reassure it so that pitiful tone would leave its voice, but she thought if she did, she might start thinking of it as a woman again.

"I never disliked you because you were neuter. I just don't like being used for my gender any more than you like being hated for yours."

"Lack of gender, you mean."

"You know what I mean," said Sandy. "Truce?"

Lancaster held up a plate and Sandy slid two eggs off the pan. Instead of sitting down to eat, it disappeared into Phazy's room for a minute, then came back and held another plate out to Sandy. She slid two more eggs off the pan and kept the last one for herself. Lancaster sprawled back on the couch and started to eat, then sat up a moment and twisted its arms around as if trying to reach its back.

"Help me get this off, will you?" it said.

Sandy suppressed a smile and helped the neut remove the bra and false shaping. She even scratched its back a bit in the places she knew would be itching from the elastic.

"Ah, much better. Don't see how you can stand wearing one all the time," it said.

"You get used to them," said Sandy.

"Not if I don't have to. You really don't have a problem with neuts as people, do you?" it said.

"I told you. A neut saved me from being raped, probably saved my life. Neuts have been taking care of me since then, and I haven't done a whole lot for any of them."

Lancaster looked her in the eye, and something about its face was more serious than she had seen from it before.

"You know what Network does?" it said.

"Not everything. Just the research and the medics and teachers and spreaders. Something about business or investments, too, I think."

Lancaster turned the screen back on and flipped the display to computer. Sandy saw the familiar backgrounds and data displays of the Network portals.

*

Neuter Network Archive File #SDR939913SWP
Data report, St. Louis trial
Soundwave plague
Jin/USHomeCave Rouelle/USArtCav

Population before release: 1,667,923
Total deaths 9.19-10.06: 600,452
Standard deaths equivalent time period: 2,024
Estimated plague deaths 9.19-10.06: 598,428
Remaining population, midnight 10.06: 1,067,471

Demographics of deceased:
Gender: 43% male, 55% female, 2% neuter, hermaphrodite, transgender or other.
Ethnicity (based on predominant genetic traits): 38% Caucasian/Anglo, 24% African, 19% Hispanic, 9% Asian, 5% Native American, 5% Other/undetermined.

Pattern of spread: 17% of deaths occurred 9.19-9.22, 19% occurred 9.23-9.26, 28% occurred 9.27-9.30, 26% occurred 10.1-10.2, falling to 10% from 10.3-10.6.

Outlook: Requires further study for continued effects. Potential for worldwide distribution.

Council endorses continuation of above plague. Spread confined to Midwest until supporting studies made. Cities listed below scheduled for spread at earliest convenience. Council commends talents of those involved with creation and distribution. Drop recommended for further spread to avoid suspicion.

Cities approved for Soundwave spread as of 10.15.77:

Chicago, IL
Cincinnati, OH
Cleveland, OH
Columbus, OH
Des Moines, IA
Grand Rapids, MI
Green Bay, WI
Indianapolis, IN
Knoxville, TN
Madison, WI
Minneapolis, MN
South Bend, IN
Springfield, IL
Springfield, MO

Continue running all other spreader activities normally, excepting cities listed above.

⁂

"You know what this means?" said Lancaster.

Sandy took the controls and scrolled through the full text of the message again.

"Rouelle's music. Jin's plague," she said, sounding almost like a neut herself. "The music worked?"

She knew the numbers meant success, but still she felt she needed speak the words in question. Lancaster's eyes widened a bit when she mentioned Jin and Rouelle by name. She guessed Slim had never told its roommates how much contact Sandy had with spreaders.

"I thought the artists didn't consider themselves part of the Network. How do you know about this?" said Sandy.

"We all work with the Network. That's basic self-preservation. We don't all see things the same way, and we choose not to involve ourselves with the Network's behavior, particularly the spreading. That doesn't mean we don't have access, don't keep track of what's going on."

"So you know about Soundwave, then," said Sandy.

"I do now. What do you think of the plague?"

"I think I'd feel a lot safer in my own apartment if those tones were on the radio here now," said Sandy.

She hadn't meant to speak with so much venom, but her nightly struggle to listen for the sound of the lock rattling at her door had exhausted her. If Jin's poisoned songs could let her know once and for all whether Jeremy was worth fearing, she could sleep again, and as tired as she was, that didn't seem wrong.

Lancaster looked at her steadily, its eyes changing from disapproval to understanding. It leaned toward her, the front of its shirt gaping now that it had nothing there to fill out the fabric. The hand it laid on her shoulder was gentle and reassuring.

"You can stay here tonight, if you need to. Tomorrow, I'll come with you and see if we can find out what's going on with this man."

Sandy nodded, grateful for once for the neuter's empathic skills. Meryl, their fourth roommate, was still in the caverns with Slim, so Sandy crawled into the bed that still felt like hers and slept soundly until long after sunrise.

She only had a half-day shoot the next day, so she crept back into her apartment for a change of clothes and was on her way out when Jeremy opened his door.

"There's the little mouse. You got a new boyfriend you're spending time with?"

"I'm late," said Sandy, trying to walk instead of run toward the door.

"I heard you were some movie star's chip," said Jeremy.

He caught up to her in a few long strides and grabbed her hair playfully. He laughed and let her go when she pulled away, but a moment later, his hand closed on her shoulder and he spun her around to face him.

"I just want to say hi to my roommate face-to-face," he said.

She still didn't like the look in his eyes.

"Hi. Now I'm really late. I have to go."

His eyes narrowed, and his face lost the teasing look, but he didn't move as she backed up two steps and turned toward the door. She was more than halfway to her shoot location before she realized she had no idea whether or not she had locked her bedroom door.

The shoot was another commercial, this time for one of the powdered food mixes she despised. For once she actually had a few lines, which meant more exposure and more pay. She tried to shake off the worries of home and get into the part, but the director kept looking at her when she called for another take, and Sandy was pretty sure she was on the verge of getting fired. Finally, the director tossed her bleached ponytail back over her shoulder and yelled at the cast to take five.

"You're new around here, aren't you?"

Sandy looked over at a boy about her age—if she could trust looks anymore—who stood blowing thick curls of inky hair out of his large gray eyes. She smiled at him without meaning to. Very cute, she thought, then hoped she hadn't subvocalized the words, just in case.

The boy laughed. "I don't usually stun the girls speechless. I'm Nick."

"I'm Sandy. Sorry I'm so distracted. Roommate problems."

Nick glanced back over his shoulder. "Yeah, you wouldn't believe one of mine. She thinks she's an opera singer and practices at two thirty in the morning. Every morning. I tried to tell her that the opera closed down decades ago, but she's convinced it'll reopen with all the Hollywood types here and she wants to be ready."

"Are you waiting for someone?" said Sandy.

"Huh?"

"You keep looking back over your shoulder," she said.

"Oh. Yeah, I'm usually on the crew here, but we ran short on extras, and I was expendable, so now I'm part of the cast." He sat down next to her. "Normally this is the time I'd be running around following orders, but they said they didn't need my help. You looked like you might."

"Not unless you can tell me whether my roommate is just an annoying creep or a dangerous one," said Sandy.

"Hmmm...I'm not really a good judge of people. You seem nice, though. Are you?"

Sandy turned a real smile on him. She wasn't sure if he was just spouting lines at her, but he had hit on exactly how she felt. She didn't trust her own judgment and wanted someone to walk up and tell her whether they were what they seemed or not. Lancaster might be able to help her with Jeremy, but with Nick, she would just have to talk to him a little, maybe let time tell her if she was right. Of course, she might not ever see him again after the shoot, but if he really was on crew, then it was likely she would. Good crew members were much harder to find and keep than extras.

When the PA called them back and Sandy got to her lines, her face was no longer shadowed with worry and she felt she could act like the confident young woman she was supposed to portray. A few more takes, and her part was done. She even imagined the director looked at her more kindly when she was through.

Nick was nowhere to be found when she gathered her things to leave. Disappointed, she caught the last tour bus headed out to the neuts' apartment, hoping Lancaster would keep its promise about going to see Jeremy.

Lancaster met her at the door with a look Sandy couldn't decipher on its face. It let her in and turned on the screen without thinking, logging on to display a message from Slim.

"Your spreader's back," it said.

Jin had reported in from El Paso, which meant it would reach the artist caves within the next two days.

"You're going down?" said Lancaster.

"Of course! I wouldn't miss Jin's coming home. And poor Pelin! It's first trip out, and they were gone for three weeks. It's probably exhausted."

"Pelin went out?"

Sandy laughed. "You should see your face. Yes, Pelin decided it needed to see the world up top again. Jin chose it to go with it to St. Louis."

Lancaster turned away, shaking its head. Sandy didn't have to be able to hear subvocalizations to understand that it knew Pelin, or at least had met it, and must have assumed that Jin had some sort of magic trick to get the shy neut out of the caves. And the skin of a camel to tolerate it that long.

"You could come with me if you want," said Sandy.

Lancaster shook its head. "Slim will meet you at the house near the surface route. I have a shoot on Monday. Don't worry, we'll deal with your roommate when you get back."

Sandy hesitated, wondering if she should stop at the apartment to pick up a few things for the trip. She decided against it. She could get anything she needed from the neuts at the artist caves, and if she'd left her room unlocked that morning, Jeremy had probably already been through anything personal she had there.

Besides, she wanted to be there the minute Jin and Pelin walked through the green room door. No doubt Slim would make her wait again with the others instead of going to greet the travelers ahead of time. It just didn't understand that she knew Jin well enough now that she wouldn't go running up and grabbing it into a hug or anything else the spreader might find offensive. At least, she didn't think she would. She smiled to herself as she headed to the southbound passenger stop. Perhaps they did know her well down there after all.

# CHAPTER 23

Great cheering breaks out when Jin and Pelin return to the artist caves. Cook calls a celebration, serving mulled wine and more snacks than anyone can possibly eat. Pelin looks relaxed and happy now that it is home, though the low angle of the lamplight picks out more lines on its forehead and around its mouth than Jin remembers from before the trip. Jin shows the plague report and instructions for further spread to the group, which sets off another cheer.

"This first plague even victims can enjoy, eh Jin?" says Rouelle.

"I don't care if they enjoy it, as long as those malicious creeps can't hurt anyone else," says Sandy. She shudders, not entirely intentionally.

"Not all victims are like men who attacked you, Sand. Anyone can have malicious or violent intent under correct circumstances," says Jin.

"So, Jin, if the Council is spreading the rest of this electronically, what are you going to do with yourself?" says Slim.

"Don't know. Maybe travel farther north and east, thinking up new plague. Bruv said to take vacation."

"That doesn't sound exactly like a vacation, Jin," says Sandy.

Jin shrugs. It doesn't feel like relaxing and eating its fill anymore. Its mind is still humming in agitation from the encounter with Shaney. Work is better than rest.

"Why not find source of anti-neut pamphlet?" asks Pelin. "Maybe those travels will give you ideas. If not, at least is something to do while Council decides on spread. Might help keep Network safe."

"True. But no idea where to start," says Jin.

"You were one who pointed out—may already know where pamphlet came from. If not Brat, might know who did."

"You really think sibling wrote?"

"Can't tell. Deliberately stylized writing voice, certainly not unlike Brat. May know nothing, just a thought."

"What?" says Sandy. "Somebody slow down and translate for those of us who have no idea what you're talking about. Whose sibling?"

The others glance at Pelin, then look away. Most of them know about Brat. Some of them were once his friends, but the choice of whether or not to explain the history to Sandy is not their business. Pelin sighs.

"Had neut sibling, now it thinks it's male. Hates Network. Doesn't like killing with own hands but probably wouldn't mind if we all died."

"And where exactly is this pleasant human being?" says Sandy.

Pelin looks at Jin.

"Albuquerque," says Jin.

Sandy starts in at full blast. "Albuquerque? My God, Jin, are you completely stupid? Don't you think the guy who tried to kill you last time is still going to be there? Do you think he won't recognize you? You can't possibly walk back into that city. If you won't listen to me, maybe Bruvec will stop you. I thought you were supposed to be its friend, Pelin! How could you even suggest such a thing? Jin, please, please, please tell me you two were just joking. Going into a city where a maniac hates you in order to find another maniac who hates everyone like you is stupid, pointless suicide."

"Only one maniac," says Jin. "Pelin's sibling is one who stole my pack."

As the others calm Sandy down, Jin decides that Albuquerque is a good idea. It will just plan ahead this time and stash emergency supplies in and around the city before it gets close enough to encounter Brat. Pelin is right, seeking the author of the pamphlet might help the Network, and traveling with a purpose will certainly help Jin. It needs to find a new direction, to think up new lines of plague. If the spread of Soundwave is successful in a multicity format, the whole job of spreading moves into a larger scale. Less personal, more effective. Jin isn't sure if it likes the idea, but it will prepare anyway, just in case.

Jin decides to walk most of the distance to Albuquerque. Bruvec, despite its protests, understands and brings Jin two new pairs of walking shoes. It also gives Jin the names and locations of friends in Santa Fe, Albuquerque, and Alamillo in case of trouble, not knowing that Sandy and Slim have already done the same. Jin stashes dried food, money, antibiotics, and vitamins throughout its clothing, too, just in case. Its pack is stuffed with full travel equipment including a new bedroll, water purifier, and first aid kit.

"We all still worry, Jin," says Bruvec. "Might find some way to leave you bare again."

Jin shakes its head. It won't underestimate Brat again, and the artists have given it travel gifts as well. Pelin brought it a whole bundle, including a gold ring shaped with a bat head to pawn for money or use as a weapon in a fistfight. Jin scratches at its finger beneath the ring, unused to wearing jewelry. From Cook and a few of the others is a tiny airtight pouch shaped to fit under Jin's tongue. The pouch contains a two-day supply of protein and vitamin powder. Bruvec smiles when Jin places the contraption in its mouth.

"Looks uncomfortable."

"More comfortable than eating bugs," Jin says, shaping the words with minor difficulty. "Should tell Cook to make for all travelers."

"No one staggers home starved but you."

"Some don't get home at all. This could help."

Bruvec shrugs, ending Jin's argument the way they usually end. Still grumbling to itself, Jin begins the long hike to the surface.

Because time is not important, Jin decides to take the trail through the Capitan Mountains and the last protected nondesert wilderness area in the state instead of walking through the wastelands, cities, and shacktowns. It hands the ranger a steep entry fee and pins the badge on its backpack that says it has paid the price to enjoy some nature. Once Jin passes beyond the barbed wire fence, the air seems cleaner, and the stink of rotting wastelands fades away. A few rangers wander by on patrol, but as long as Jin keeps the badge clearly displayed, they don't bother it.

At night it lies awake watching the few stars it can see beyond the bleed of city lights and smog, thinking of the Kansas septic tank shacks and the tall multipurpose buildings of St. Louis. If the statistics hold, the Soundwave plague could reduce the entire population of the country by about one-third. Maybe the world, if the Councils in other countries agree. But what then?

The question keeps Jin awake. Somehow, the balance between living bodies and the resources they need always seems to tip away from the ideal. Jin has no skills or interest in waste management; it leaves that to the researchers who focus on the refuse humanity creates. But can it switch its focus from death to birth prevention? The results would be longer lasting, but the thought makes it feel slightly ill.

This is not just life and death. Everybody dies someday. But regulating birth means making a decision that affects the living, taking away a choice they normally have. Someone would have to decide who gets to have children and who doesn't, and Jin doesn't want to be that person. No neut should. No gen, either. That has happened in the past, and always with a biased focus and results ranging from disagreeable to reprehensible and disastrous. But if that is the way for the species to survive, then maybe somebody has to make that choice. Someone who will balance the factors, not favoring one ethnicity, gender, wealth bracket, or any other group above another.

Jin tries to bore itself to sleep by thinking of the possible ways to solve the problem. Regardless of ethics, the biology of selective birth control could be done. And with propaganda neck-deep and painstaking detail to balanced demographic ratios, maybe the Network could pull off the job without pitting gens against each other. They would need the help of a skilled word artist, but that is exactly what it is heading to Albuquerque to find.

Disgusted with itself for even entertaining the idea, Jin rolls over and closes its eyes. Would gens really prefer to live with that choice taken away? Jin doesn't understand how that could be possible, but the point is moot for the moment. Soundwave is doing its job well, and at the end of the spread, there might be enough resources left to ensure comfortable survival for another generation.

Jin opens its eyes again. Even in this nature preserve, it can still hear the swish of tankers rumbling their way through the mountains and the shouts of another group of campers nearby. The air and water are heavy with dirt, the stench of the wastelands seeps subtly into the atmosphere, and well over half the people it passes in its travels are hungry. The end of the human race won't come during its lifetime, but it has run the projections and has no doubt that death for all of them is coming soon enough if nothing is done. Before it drifts off to sleep, its last conscious thought is to wonder if that is such a bad thing after all.

Jin stashes a portion of its supplies outside a thrift shop in Belen, a midsize city just outside of Albuquerque's suburban sprawl. The rest of its supplies have already been scattered around the outskirts of the metropolitan area, except the money and weapons Jin keeps in its pockets to use during its stay. It doesn't dare rely on the Network's connections. It has no idea how many of them Brat knows.

It walks toward Albuquerque at a leisurely pace, with no real plan in mind. It has never tried looking for a specific person before. Somewhere in its mind Jin had almost pictured Brat waiting for it at the city limits sign, perhaps picking his teeth and nails with the broken blade Jin took from Bill.

Maybe coming here was idiotic, like Sandy said. Brat might know nothing about the pamphlet from St. Louis. There is no solid connection to Albuquerque at all. But every time Jin thinks of the words, it pictures eyes even bluer than Pelin's and a voice that grates like sandpaper against its skin. A voice to match the frail blond stubble that is all a neut on hormones can grow.

What it needs is to find the best place to distribute literature that is designed to cause outrage and indignation, and have those words reach people with enough time and enthusiasm to act on the ideas. It sets out toward the nearest college gathering spot.

Sure enough, Brat is there in a lo-loc cafe that offers a bank of screens and power centers, setting a new flyer on the overflowing local news rack. He pins one up on the bulletin board above, too, covering a roommate wanted ad. He smiles to the girl at the counter and waves. She smiles back with obvious insincerity. Jin creeps in closer. As soon as Brat is out of the young woman's sight, she turns to her coworker.

"That's the guy I was telling you about. Don't you think there's something really creepy about him?"

Jin watches Brat's back tense for moment, then sag as he continues walking away. The hormones have had no effect on his hearing. Jin waits for him to disappear around the corner, then picks up one of the flyers.

"I sure hope you're taking that just for entertainment value," mutters the counter girl as Jin walks past.

Jin nods, not looking up.

"Creep," she mutters under her breath.

Jin wonders if the trace frequencies sent out from its spreader brain chemistry make her feel that way, or if something about it looks as cruel as Brat. Someday maybe it will have a chance to continue the sound wave research, focusing this time on brain emissions, maybe see how different spreaders really are. It takes the flyer to the campus library, now a public library, as only the campus laboratory buildings are still actively used as classrooms. The lecture halls are used by local theater and tour groups since the lectures are all dropped on the students' private screens. Jin rents a screen booth in the library for an hour and checks the news from St. Louis.

Soundwave-related deaths continue there on a low scale. Most of those who would respond to the tones are already dead. Jin wonders if the ones who are dying now are targeted by their rage at losing loved ones. It tries not to search for Shaney's name in the obituaries but continues to be relieved when it finds nothing. The newsdrops say a mass cremation was recently held and a memorial date is set for the following month. The stoic citizens blame the mass of heart failures on an unusually cold autumn, and the more flippant wear T-shirts proclaiming, "My heart stops for St. Louis," but the majority of reports say local doctors are still searching for answers. Jin doubts they will know where to look.

The other cities from the Council's list all show signs of activity. Grand Rapids and Madison have the least. Springfield, Indiana, has a mortality rate near thirty percent, and cities that were not directly hit but are in close proximity with the target cities are also showing signs of activity.

Jin checks the national news to see what spreaders are up to across the country. A plague in Tampa is blamed on undercooked seafood. Jin has doubts that one truly started with a crustacean. One of the Home Cavern spreaders, a neut who calls itself Din, likes making plagues that copy old diseases like malaria or the Black Death. Tampa is probably seeing Din's version of *E. coli.* Two of the other spreaders haven't reported in since the Council approved Jin's Soundwave project.

A random sampling of news from major cities in each region shows that heart attack cases are up all over the country. Denver, Philadelphia, even LA note an increase in fatal heart attacks significant enough to be considered newsworthy. Jin scrolls through to the LA entertainment news.

> Publicists won't say when or if America's hottest new band, Rate, will tour the Los Angeles area. In a rehash of publicity stunts from the late 20th century, Rate members are staying in hiding. No publicity photos have been made available, and the band's management says none are scheduled to be released. Even the members' names are a mystery, and no live performances, local or otherwise, are scheduled.

> Some accuse the band of making music so terrible they are ashamed to show themselves, but with their first song topping the drops across the nation, Rate is probably laughing harder than the critics.
>
> An update on the band's website says the next single as well as the full album will be released by the end of the year. Maybe by then they will come out of hiding.

Jin smiles to itself. The rock music version of Soundwave seems to have stretched beyond the Council's prescribed limits. A quick scan shows that Rate has hit most of the country. Enough drops of that single, and no one will have to bother spreading the other versions. The waves will be in the air around every kid who doesn't use ear wires. Still, spreading a few of the other versions might be prudent, just to ensure the demographic balance.

Someone takes a seat in the booth next to Jin. Despite the designation of the screen booths as "private," the flimsy wall panels do no more than block direct glances at the neighboring screens. The faint smell of man reaches Jin's nose. Too faint. Jin leans back, not bothering to wipe its screen, even as Brat leans back as well to get a view. The pseudogen is wearing his mock-friendly smile.

"You must have a pretty strong death wish. Or did you just come back to keep me entertained?" he says.

"Following your writing career," says Jin, holding up a copy of his pamphlet.

"Ah, yes. You like those? Oh, wait, don't tell me. You're here to execute me for betraying the cause, aren't you? I guess I should have gone underground. Oops, I'm sorry, that's your job."

"Not here to kill. Vendettas not sanctioned, remember? You would know."

"I wondered how long you'd take to figure that one out. What gave me away?"

"Why you write these?"

"I don't think I'll answer that unless you speak like a human being. I know you know how."

"Already speak like human," says Jin.

"Apparently the subject is open to debate, but if you want to quibble, I'll rephrase: I might answer your question if you ask using complete sentences following the officially acknowledged rules and norms of American English," says Brat.

"Fine. Why...are...you writing these pamphlets?" says Jin.

"Good. Next time without the pauses. I write them because I think it's only fair that people are aware of any threat to their lives so they can fight it if they choose. I'm not encouraging them to hunt you down. I just want people to know why their friends and families are dying. What they do about it is their choice."

"Nice speech. Writing used words selected to spark emotion, action."

"What did I say about the way you need to speak if you expect me to answer you?"

"Not question. Statement."

"Well, you could at least throw in an occasional conjunction. Come on, let's go for a walk."

"Where?"

"No deserted buildings. I just don't trust people not to eavesdrop if I sit in one place too long. Since it looks like neither one of us is going to kill the other just yet, you might as well tell me your name."

"Jin," it says as it follows him out the door.

"Jin. I seem to recall you using Bruvec's name last time you were here. Is the old bitch of a bastard still alive?"

Jin isn't sure how to respond. It can't ghost Brat without him noticing, so it can't tell whether his anger or his calm is real. His hatred of Bruvec is real, though. His eyes dilate and his nostrils flare.

"Oh, cut the innocent act. Of course I know Bruvec," says Brat.

"Just never heard anyone who didn't like it before."

"Everyone has enemies. Speaking of which, don't tell me you came all this way just to ask if I wrote a couple of words. What do you have in mind for my city?"

"Nothing."

"Just like last time, eh? Then why is the rate of fatal heart attacks up about a hundred fifty percent since you were here last?"

"Heart attacks often increase with season change."

"Don't give me that. We haven't even had the first snow yet."

Jin shrugs. "Happening all over nation. Was just reading about in newspaper."

"And you expect me to believe that you and your Network had nothing to do with it."

"Doesn't matter. Question, though. How you…how would you…feel about a change from population reduction to growth control?"

"Congratulations. You now speak like a politician. What the hell do you mean?"

"Control breeding instead of killing," says Jin, not quite believing itself. "Would reduce population too slowly but has longer lasting effects. Keep spreading until population reduced to sustainable level."

"I thought you kids avoided that sort of thing on the grounds that it was distasteful to your nonexistent morality. You have approval for this project?"

"No. Still many kinks. Your talent for propaganda might be only way to pull off without causing more damage."

Jin hesitates at the edge of campus, but Brat continues walking. "Your project sounds interesting, but the answer is no. As long as spreaders still exist I won't touch anything to do with the Network. And somehow I doubt you're about to go renegade on them," says Brat.

"No. My home. Friends, like family. Just because you don't like doesn't mean they're bad people. If birth reduction works, then maybe slowly phase out spreading."

"Just what the hell do you think it is you're doing? Selling computer chips? You can't phase out mass murder; you either are a killer or you're not. You, Jin, are the worst kind of killer because you don't see anything wrong with what you are."

"No. Know who I am, what I do. You're one trying to be someone else."

Without warning, Brat shoves Jin to the ground. It rolls, dodging the steel-tipped boots that fly at its face. Jin is crouching to spring at Brat's knees when a voice cuts through the air.

"Brat!"

Jin recovers from its startle faster than Brat does. It knocks a familiar knife out of Brat's hand and ghosts him as he grabs his wrist and stumbles. The chemical residue of anger is complicated by a tangle of emotions Jin can't quite sort out. Brat stares behind Jin at the source of the voice.

Jin doesn't have to turn. It isn't truly surprised.

"Brat! You keep damned hands off my friend!" says Pelin.

Brat's face loses some of its harshness for the first time, and the resemblance between siblings grows stronger.

"Thanks, Pelin. Good timing," says Jin.

"Looks like my sibling is now big bully."

"Brother. I'm your brother now, Pelin. Like I was born to be. And you're my—"

"Sibling," Pelin cuts in. "Stop fooling self, Brat. You're no better than any, worse than most. Instigating war against family just because you hate self."

"Didn't know you were still there, Pel, really."

"Not talking about me. Who took us in when dad kicked out? Or have you forgotten?"

"They used me, Pel. Used you, too. Tried to turn us into one of these," he gestures to Jin. "No morals, no sense, no idea how many people are destroyed forever because of some stupid idea that the world can't hold us all. It has so far, hasn't it?"

Pelin grabs Brat's arms, forcing him to look it in the eye.

"Stupid Brat. You know why world holds? Spreaders work hard. You been east of here? People live in old septic tanks. Used ones. Should have thanked spreaders you still can breathe. Now is too late."

# CHAPTER 24

↭

The "New Hollywood" had packed up and moved out of Albuquerque, and Sandy was doing the same. Glad as she was to be moving away from her constant worries about Jeremy, her mind balked at the thought of being more than a day's journey from the caves. Still, when the rumors became solid that the industry was moving north to the wind and water power of Wyoming, she began planning the travel paths and checking truck routes in case she couldn't hitch a ride on one of the industry vans. Speaking roles were more common for her now, and Marie had taught her enough Spanish that she could fake her way through the accent and get bit parts on the bilingual and Latino shows.

She hugged Marie again, hoping that Jeremy would stay away until she was finished packing. He had come home nearly every night since Sandy returned from welcoming Jin home—she'd found her door locked and her room undisturbed, thankfully—but he had managed to be absent when Lancaster came over. In fact, no one was there at all.

"You sure you have roommates? This place is quiet as a coffin," said Lancaster, looking around.

"Marie works eighteen-hour days in housekeeping, and Brooke only really lives here when she's between boyfriends. It was a nice arrangement until Jeremy came home," said Sandy.

"Well, all I can tell you is that he's definitely male, and could use a better deodorant," said Lancaster, wrinkling its nose.

"Thanks for trying," Sandy had said, and that had been the end of that.

Still, she had Rouelle's Rate single cued up on her pocketscreen, ready to blare at top volume with a single touch gesture. Soundwave would reach Albuquerque on its own soon enough, but since she had no idea where Jeremy spent his days, she couldn't be sure he was anywhere near a sound system. If he came home before she left for good, she might have to expose him to the deadly undertones herself.

She poked her head into the bathroom, checking for missed supplies. She couldn't remember if the pink bottle of hairspray had been hers or Brooke's, so she left it on the shelf and stepped into the hall. The front door opened and shut.

"Marie? Is that you?" Sandy called.

Her hand dived for the pocketscreen. The footsteps were too heavy to be Marie's or Brooke's. They staggered unevenly until she heard a heavy collapse and the scrape of furniture as the couch settled under the impact of Jeremy's weight. Home and drunk, at this hour of the morning.

She peered into the living room, just to be sure. Jeremy lay stiff on the couch, his hand clutching his chest in spasms and his jaw working.

"Jeremy?" said Sandy.

His eyes rolled toward her, begging for help. She ran to the kitchen and got him a glass of water, though she realized the instant she got back that he couldn't drink. She sat on the coffee table next to him and took one of his tightly clenched hands.

"Listen to me, Jeremy. Just breathe. Listen."

She unfolded her screen but swiped a different gesture, playing a song she used to calm down after a long day's work. She had also used it to slow her breathing the time she was nervous about her first role as a corpse, but she pushed that thought most of the way out of her mind and turned Jeremy's head back to face her.

"Do you want me to call an ambulance?" she asked.

He shook his head violently, which led to further spasms, and Sandy gritted her teeth at the pain when he squeezed her hand.

"You need to relax. I know it's hard right now, but you need to think of something that makes you calm. Listen to me."

She began humming along with the music, moving Jeremy's hand in a slight sway to the beat. Eventually, his breathing slowed, and bit by bit his muscles unclenched. He struggled to sit up.

"I don't think that's a good idea," she said.

She lifted his head just enough to help him take a sip or two of the water. The action reminded her of playing nursemaid to Jin, who had been just as insistent on trying to do everything itself. She smiled a little as she set the glass down. Ornery patients were her specialty.

"Can you tell me what happened?"

He couldn't. The story came out in fits and gasps, but all he knew was that he had felt fine, and then his heart started pounding and pain shot through his arms. He had made it home and thought he would get no farther than that again.

"It was a heart attack," said Sandy.

"No way. How old do you think I *am*?" said Jeremy.

Sandy sighed and went to get her bag. She set it down by the door then came back to stand beside him. The color was coming back to his face.

"Just consider it a warning. If you keep living the way you do, you'll die, no matter how young you are."

"What's that supposed to mean?"

Sandy looked at him silently, then went back to the door and slung her bag over her shoulder.

"I think you know," she said softly.

When she left, the door shut with a soft, final thud behind her.

## CHAPTER 25

Brat shakes loose from Pelin's grip.

"Come off it, Pelin. I can still breathe, it's not too late for anything. As far as I know, anyway."

He stares pointedly at Jin.

"Too late for spreaders," says Pelin.

"What you mean?" says Jin.

"Reason I followed," says Pelin. "To warn you. Don't know how you escaped before. Soundwave plague is deadly to spreaders."

Brat laughs so hard he drops to the pavement.

"All spreaders?" Jin asks.

"This country, all but you. Some in England, Germany, Australia. Rock version of music uploaded to general nets, dropped by fans. Big hit worldwide. Instrumental version, too."

Jin nods slowly, wondering if it should have asked Rouelle not to do its best on the music, but a mediocre song might not have gotten enough airplay to hit St. Louis, never mind anywhere else. There is no way to take the music back now, and Jin has to admire the balancing effects of the way Soundwave operates. The population will take a heavy hit across the globe, but those same populations will also lose the one control they had left. Their spreaders.

"Plague probably missed me because kept ghosting you," says Jin. "My brain chems were yours, every time."

"Or you're only spreader who truly keeps hate out of work," says Pelin.

"It can't hate if it has no feelings," says Brat.

"Has more feelings than you. Just doesn't throw them in everyone's face," says Pelin. "Must be very careful, Jin. Come home, please. And you, *sibling*. No place for you in caves, pumped silly with hormones, hating family, attacking friends. You'll die in plague too, your own fault."

"Pelin, let's help, maybe," says Jin.

"Help Brat? Why?"

"Because you don't want to kill. Because might come in handy." Jin turns to Brat. "Okay, no more spreaders, just like you wanted. Interested?"

"How long do I have to think about this fabulous offer?" says Brat.

"Until you feel heart attack begin," says Jin.

Pelin and Jin walk back toward the campus while Jin does some quick mental calculations. If Soundwave's mortality rate continues at nearly thirty percent, depending on how long the songs take for their popularity to fade, the population of the affected areas could reach the critical range again in as little as one or two generations, given the increasing water supply contaminants and decreasing soil productivity. Two generations to find and train enough new spreaders to cover the entire world. With no one but Jin with the experience to train and supervise the individual first spreads, assuming it even survives that long, the prognosis for the human race looks bleaker than ever. The Network's researchers might find ways to solve the resource problems by then, but that can't be guaranteed. Jin sits down at a table in the library and drops its chin onto its forearm. It isn't going to have a choice.

"Pel, want to listen to really bad idea?"

Pelin's eyes widen as Jin explains the concept of spreading an infertility plague.

"If Brat joins, we let him run propaganda. Plant suggestion in peoples' minds that God or planet or whatever people want to hear is holding back babies as message. Maybe he can spin in way that doesn't pit gens against each other," says Jin. It has little hope of this, but something must be done. Historically, human breeding programs have been rife with prejudice and short-sightedness. Even if it manages to avoid those pitfalls with its infertility plague, no one will believe it.

"Or against neuts," says Pelin, pulling Jin back into the conversation at hand. "You know they'd blame even if wasn't our fault. Truth is starting to leak out faster. If we can find way to make gens and neuts come together on this, maybe knowledge won't lead to hatred."

Jin shakes its head. "Need someone to hate. Someone to blame. We'll give them spreaders."

"How?" says Pelin.

"Say spreaders weren't part of Network. Better yet, no talk of Network. Have neuts come forward, saying Network is formed to repair damage done by small group of neuts who worked without others' knowledge or consent. Blame spreaders, with pictures and names so hate can be carried by dead neuts, not living."

"What if they trace infertility plague? Will discover Network lies, make hatred and distrust worse than if we tell truth from beginning," says Pelin.

"Won't happen. Infertility won't be Network. Please, Pelin. You keep this secret. I work with Brat if he'll cooperate, consequences in my hands alone."

"No, Jin."

"This is best chance. You go home, destroy any records of spread, eliminate supply closet, anything in labs not for positive medical purpose. Then go on as before, minus spreaders. Artists still create. Researchers, business, meds, teachers, everyone else keeps on with work. No one liked spreaders much anyway, won't be missed. May have to erase some research on brain chems, though."

"Need your help to find which records," says Pelin.

"No."

"You never coming home?"

"Make new home now. Minimize danger to others," says Jin.

"I'll stay. You might need friend. Don't trust Brat."

"Won't, yet, but must trust it soon or work without. Need you to deliver message to caves about destroying records. Besides, you don't like being away from home, remember?"

"Don't like being away from friends. Soundwave might kill you any day. You and Brat."

"Not self. Will spend some time in wastelands, planning. By then you have Rouelle release new songs, just music without deadly subsounds. New ones take over airplay, won't be so dangerous."

"Still might hear Soundwave song. Music that popular doesn't disappear."

"Probably. But I know songs, can distract self by ghosting. Also, test sound didn't kill me, probably because excitement over new project shifted brain chemistry out of danger zone. Now I have even bigger project."

Pelin stares at Jin for a long while, its eyes sweeping over Jin's face as if to memorize every line. Finally, it gives Jin a real gen-style hug and runs off without looking back.

An hour later, Jin begins its search for Brat. The pseudo-man is easy to find, sitting and waiting for it under a scrawny tree at the edge of campus. As Jin approaches, it sorts the difference between the scent of the real males around it and the scent of Brat's artificial hormones.

"You don't need my help with propaganda. You sell a pretty good story yourself," he says as Jin approaches.

Jin follows his eyes to the small figure walking off into the distance.

"Pelin tells me you're still planning to do the infertility spread," says Brat.

"Where you stand?" says Jin.

"Well, if the killing is really permanently done, I won't stop you. Not yet, anyway. Beyond that, I'm going to have to think about it. Was Pelin serious when it said I'm just waiting for a heart attack?"

"Depends on attitude. How much you hate and how far will you take? Unhappy won't hurt you, malice will. You've spent so long wanting revenge on Network, probably in high-risk category."

"Even if I'm not hating anyone at the moment?"

"Habitual brain chems leave trace residue. If you feel heart rate increase too much, get away from city or ghost a person not showing effects. I'll be in wastelands for few days, thinking. When ready, I'll return to library for research. Look there, tell me whether you'll help. I don't see you, will assume Soundwave got first."

Jin grabs most of its supplies from the hiding place in Belen and continues south. By the evening of the second day, it is deep enough into the wastelands for a fairly comfortable stay. It sets up camp in the carcass of a burnt-out van and focuses on the task of saving humanity from itself.

The question of the infertility plague makes Jin's mind feel as tangled as the junk heaps surrounding it. If anything goes wrong with the accompanying propaganda, those who breed will probably be encouraged to bear child after child unless they are killed out of jealousy. If their children are all fertile, the population is back to the saturation point in just a few generations. If the children aren't fertile, the human race dies.

More criteria line up in Jin's mind. The number of new children must be kept high enough to discourage interbreeding over the coming generations, and the balance between male and female must remain fairly even. Then there are racial, socio-economic, intelligence, and religious balances to consider. None of these can be changed or shifted to favor one group over another. There are so many factors to consider that Jin can hardly keep them straight without a screen.

It climbs out of the van and begins to pace among the broken electronics and twisted plastic around it. It should be able to solve a simple problem like this in its sleep, but its mind resists the whole idea. Taking away a gen's choice to breed is like taking away a neut's choice to study, to actively apply its intellect to improving the human condition. It shouldn't have to make this decision for them. It can't understand why they don't handle the problem on their own.

For four days, Jin sorts through the numbers in its head. Leaving one percent of the population fertile means ten thousand in a city of one million. Plenty for the gene pool and ideal for a sustainable population. But how to reach that one percent? And what about smaller cities and towns? Might have to allow ten to twenty percent in low-population areas. With just itself and possibly Brat to carry this out, there is no way to physically separate out a selected group while an infertility plague is unleashed on the rest of the population.

What it needs is to find something that naturally targets the select percentage without regard for social, ethnic, and other boundaries. Maybe some sort of existing benign disease it can use to neutralize the chemistry of the infertility. Or something potentially curable, where it can release a cure for the disease and for the infertility plague in a single treatment.

Jin kicks a rusted bumper with a soft thud of its shoe. Without the Network labs, it can't create the disease even if it figures out how. Maybe if it thought like a gen, designing this plague would be easier. The gens all seem to say that preserving more lives is better than bringing death to a few so those who live can live better. It isn't sure it can ever understand.

On the sixth day, Jin returns to Albuquerque. Its feet know where to go, even if its brain is too frustrated to think. The campus library may help it find a disease that will select the parents of all future generations. Details can come later.

The library stinks of body odor and dust. Even the smell of electricity and rare books can't cut through the reek of human flesh. Brat appears soon after Jin settles at a screen.

"You were gone long enough. Said three days," he says.

Jin smiles to hear that he slips into neut speech when he is upset.

"Said few, not three," says Jin.

"Well, what's the plan?"

"You helping?"

"It does look that way, doesn't it?" says Brat.

Jin explains its plan of targeting an existing disease—or possibly just a genetic factor—as their curing agent, but Brat's face hardens into its cruel look after the first few sentences.

"By targeting already diseased people you risk infecting the entire future of humanity," says Brat. "Just like a damned spreader," he adds under his breath.

"Heard that," says Jin.

"You were meant to."

"You have better idea?"

"There's got to be some other way of singling out the correct percent of the population. Physical characteristics, I don't know, things like Morton's toe or having one blue eye and one brown eye."

"Those both more than one percent, and select for items not random enough in population. But might be right track," admits Jin.

Brat begins a search for likely anomalies while Jin heads toward the stacks. The shelves are full of uselessly outdated books and pushy undergraduates who elbow Jin out of the way on the off chance that it might get to a book that they want first. Since printed books aren't allowed out of the library and some of these have not made it into the electronic archives yet, competition is fierce.

Brat's allotted two hours on the public screens turn up an equal amount of nothing.

"Has it occurred to you that if we limit ourselves to approximately one percent of the population, the whole human race will probably go down the tubes?" he subvocalizes to Jin so the students around them don't hear.

Jin waits until they are out of the crowd before answering in a normal tone.

"One percent is plenty. Half percent would be better."

"But the ones who are left fertile might not choose each other as partners. They won't even know they're still fertile because their partners won't be. Worse, if someone figures out who we left untouched, they may be forced to breed with each other. These aren't cattle, Jin. Hell, even a cow can refuse a mate if she wants to, just kick the bull and walk away."

Jin sinks into a chair. "Stupid. Sorry, of course is not right. Still thinking like disease, I guess."

"That's comforting," says Brat.

"Relationships don't matter so much with death. Hate this plague," says Jin.

"But you have no problem sending people to their early graves. Your brain is in the right place, but if you have a heart it's got a long way to go," says Brat.

"Why wouldn't I have heart? Because I'm spreader or because you think all neuts but you heartless?"

"Lighten up a little. I know neuts have hearts. I lived as one for most of my life. But you can't go around killing off huge numbers of people, then say you care about them and only did what was best. I remember, even if you don't, that you are the one who caused the plague which will probably end up wiping out one-third to one-half the population of earth. You can't tell me that's the action of a kind, caring person."

"You really believe I don't care?" says Jin.

"I'm sure you think you're 'bettering the human race' or whatever other lies you can tell yourself. I've heard that before, you know, in the trial of just about every serial killer there is. Maybe you even believe it," he says.

"You mean you never felt?" says Jin.

"Felt what?"

"You know. You tried spreading."

"I was brainwashed."

"If so, was by your own genes. Why do most gens want kids?"

"What does that have to do with anything?"

"Just answer," says Jin.

Brat looks out across the campus. "Some of them like the idea of a part of themselves continuing to survive after they're gone. Some just like kids, I guess. I don't know the exact reasons. I don't think many gens do either."

"Exactly. Part is what you say, psychological, but part is biological. The need for species to continue."

"Yes, I get it, but giving birth to a person and killing someone are not the same thing, even if you say they serve the same purpose."

"No, but biological imperative to have species survive is same. Gens fulfill need by having children, neuts by controlling population and trying to maintain healthy balance. Both do by teaching, creating medicine, studying life, but neuts are not natural breeders. We're natural control."

"That's the problem with being neuter. You know everything, but the rest of the world sees things differently. Maybe because neuts are wrong," says Brat.

"How?" says Jin.

"If you're such a public service, why did all the other spreaders die in your plague?"

"Possibly constant thoughts of killing, even without hatred, alter spreader brain chems enough to make them vulnerable."

"Aren't you afraid that neuts will turn against you now? You've killed people they knew, that they were friends with."

"They understand. Wasn't friends with spreaders, but I respected them. Sad they're gone, but no more so than for gens killed in any plague. Death is death, comes to all eventually."

"I can see you believe it. And maybe when the air clears from the ashes of their mass cremations, the people left behind will thank you. I wouldn't bet on it, though, not even within the Network," says Brat.

"Doesn't matter. Know I help, know where population would be without spreaders."

"That's the part I miss. The not caring what others think, or how they see me," says Brat.

"Hormones do that?"

"Partly. Combined with living among gens, seeing how they are with each other. You'd be surprised at the benefits."

Their walk takes them slowly around the campus, past men and women studying, laughing, talking, eating, arguing, and flirting. Brat watches them all, a half smile on his face. Jin watches Brat.

"What's better?" says Jin.

"Have you ever ghosted a person in love?"

"Sure. Feels good, but not worth giving up self for."

"I don't mean just the first rush. Over time, the lust and anticipation are followed by a deepening care and concern. Imagine that feeling of ghosting, but doubly powerful, to the point where you'd find yourself reaching out to touch another person just so you can intensify the contact. Not just touch, but to hold them, to need to be so close that you lose yourself in their skin."

"I understand," says Jin.

Echoes of that feeling come through in Brat's voice, making Jin feel the anticipation, the hunger.

"You don't. You can't," says Brat. "And I can't let that feeling be lost. That's part of what it means to be a gendered human. That and the uncertainty, the insecurity, the need for approval. It keeps them searching for more. Keeps them creative."

"Plenty of creative neuts."

"That's not the point. Their creativity is not in danger. Besides, I'm not just talking about art. I'm saying you have to allow gens to mate with their chosen partners, even if it requires leaving a larger percentage of the population fertile. Believe me, it's important."

"May take a while," says Jin.

"Good. Take all the time you need to make it something that actually will strengthen the human race in the long run. Take forever if you need to. In fact, I'd prefer it."

"Don't have forever. Library is closing soon. Should try more research, rest, think of ideas for tomorrow. Meet on lawn out front, figure tactics?"

"All right. When?" says Brat.

"Noon."

"So late? I thought you'd want to get an early start since there's so much work to do."

"Need time to get back into town," says Jin.

"Oh. Uh, where are you staying?"

"Don't know. Not abandoned building on east side of town."

Brat grins. "And why would that be? I think your old pack might still be there. I left it sitting out for someone more needy. A nice bag like that would make a fine place to carry all your worldly goods, wouldn't you say?"

Jin imagines some hungry person digging through the pack as if for treasure, tossing aside the too-small clothing but keeping the food, the bedroll, the canteen. It grabs Brat's arm, ignoring how the flesh relaxes after his initial surprise.

"Wait!" says Jin.

"What? Why? Oh, let it go, Jin. Let some poor beggar have your pack. There's probably nothing left in it anyway."

"Not that," says Jin.

Its heart is racing and its pulse is too high. It checks quickly, but nothing from the Soundwave plague is playing. That means the feeling is purely excitement.

"Have answer," it says.

"What do you mean, 'have answer'? Speak like a gen. Jin? What's wrong?"

It was wrong about Soundwave not being present. A song Jin recognizes begins crackling out of the speakers at a nearby drink stand. On top of its already increased heart rate, the undertones might be too much. It feels Brat's pulse begin to elevate.

"Quick. Ghost girl across lawn," says Jin.

They walk away from the campus, keeping pace with the girl and putting distance between themselves and the song. Even out of hearing distance, the waves still hit Jin, lingering in the air ten minutes after the tune is finished. The girl steps up into an apartment building and Jin releases the ghosting, switching its awareness to two men talking and laughing nearby. It motions for Brat to do the same. Finally, the waves die down.

Brat nods. "All right, then. Spit it out. What was this thing about your pack or whatever that was so important? Don't tell me there really was some sort of plague in it."

"No. Just made me think. Leaving objects for people to find. What if we release infertility plague to everyone, then leave antidote lying around on objects?"

"What kind of objects?"

"Any. Some antidote that absorbs through skin from object people would pick up, take home, share with mate. No specific target groups, let gens choose for themselves by chance. Use different objects so no one knows which cure. Won't even suspect."

"Yeah," says Brat. "It might work. Say a seashell or something. We can't guarantee that a person would share it with their partner, but they might. What about other people who touch it, though, visitors or friends?"

"Give chems short shelf-life. Might prevent mate from contracting cure, but must take chance. Try for objects gens like sharing."

"Like Valentine and anniversary cards."

"Perfect for wealthier demographic, but need other targets as well," says Jin.

Despite the increasing chance of success, it feels a heaviness in its stomach and lungs. The thought of so many living, breathing gens unable to get their bodies to respond in the way they know they ought to…it can't understand how this is better than death. It can't seem to understand anything about gens anymore.

# CHAPTER 26

Wyoming reminded Sandy a lot of Montana. Farms took up most of the habitable land, while the Rockies rose high to the West. Unlike Montana, however, most of the ranches and farms were self-sustaining, making everything they needed to survive and exporting nothing, trading only with neighbors. The separatist attitude and lack of any major industry aside from electricity left the state with the lowest population in the country. Sandy thought it was beautiful until she considered how hard the farmers must work and how much they probably had to do without. She touched her pocketscreen self-consciously. No wonder they grudgingly let the film industry in.

Slim and Lancaster shared a house in the foothills, complete with guest houses where any number of neut artists stayed when they came to work on projects. Slim had offered Sandy a place there as well, but she didn't want to remain dependent on neuter charity, and Slim wouldn't hear of taking money from her for rent.

"You could always pay *me* and leave it none the wiser," said Lancaster with a wink.

They were lounging by the pool, trying to fight off the day's heat. Lancaster had on its Heather persona, including a padded bathing suit and sarong to shield its identity from prying eyes.

"What would you use the extra income for? A second pool filled with chocolate?" said Sandy.

Lancaster grinned, waving its plate of cookies under Sandy's nose. She pulled away, shaking her head.

"Just watching you wolf those down makes me sick. I wish I had your metabolism," she said.

Lancaster adjusted its bathing suit with exaggerated irritation. "The price you pay for your womanly shape, sweetie."

"I'll trade you," said Sandy.

"Not on your life!"

"Well, not permanently. But I'd love to be able to just go wild for a day and not worry about fitting into my next costume or wondering if the makeup will cover the mountains and craters that break out on my face."

"Try strapping yourself into this getup just to go jump in a pool. Next time you and Slim head south, I'm coming with. I knew we should have gone for the tennis courts instead."

"Do you even play tennis?" said Sandy.

Lancaster shrugged. "Doesn't matter. We only have this much to stop people from asking questions. I got tired of the stories they told about our crowded little apartment."

Sandy turned back to studying her lines. The neuts' home was usually quieter than her own apartment, and they never seemed to mind her coming over when she needed to concentrate. She only had one roommate now and he seemed harmless, but he was always home, chattering on the phone to clients and friends. She could hardly watch a video anymore without listening to the added soundtrack of legal arguments punctuated with "Well, tell him that's not acceptable!" at regular intervals. Still, the place was paid for out of her own earnings, and she had the neuts' home when she wanted luxury.

Unfortunately for her lines, Lancaster was in a chatty mood.

"Listen to this! 'When will Liene and Lancaster tie the knot? Heather and Tom's nuptials are still in question.' Can you believe they're still running this stuff? You'd think people would be bored sick by now."

"I guess there's been a shortage of celebrity scandals since Soundwave took the worst offenders out. No one wants to hear another theory about the increase in heart attacks," said Sandy.

"They mention you in here too," said Lancaster.

"Really?"

"Little troublemaker that you are. Did you know you caused me to fly into a jealous rage by having a quiet dinner with my boyfriend?" said Lancaster.

It passed Sandy its pocketscreen. One picture showed her sitting with Slim in a restaurant, laughing. She recognized the dinner as the day they celebrated her first audition. Another picture showed 'Heather' looking pained.

"Jealous rage? That's the face you make when your bustier starts slipping," said Sandy.

Lancaster leaned in. "Oh, yeah. You're right. That probably would have made a better headline if I had something more underneath."

Sandy returned the pocketscreen. "Do you ever wish you could try out a gen body, just for a little while, to see how it feels?" said Sandy.

"No," said Lancaster, but it wouldn't meet her eyes.

Sandy waited.

"I don't need to," said Lancaster. "When I ghost you, sometimes I feel body parts that aren't there. Probably not the same way you feel, but you let me understand more of what being a woman is like than if I had the body without the mind that body was meant to be with."

"Me?"

"Of course, you. You know I ghost you fairly often. You said you didn't mind as long as I let you know when."

"I guess I just assumed you ghosted other women as well," said Sandy.

"Jealous?" Lancaster grinned.

Sandy jumped into the pool, making sure her splash was large enough to reach Lancaster's lounge chair. She tossed a few extra handfuls of water its way for good measure.

Lancaster dived in after her and continued the water fight. The tabloids were going to love this, if anyone was lurking nearby with a camera, Sandy decided. But she didn't really care. Being with Lancaster or Slim and spending long days at work kept the questions she didn't want to deal with housed squarely at the back of her mind.

Marie had sent her a letter to say that Jeremy had disappeared the week after Sandy left. Soundwave might have gotten him or he might have just run off; any number of other explanations could be true. Sometimes, things were better left unknown.

Still, when she was back in her own room, listening to the incessant phone conversations that crept through the cracks around her bedroom door, she wondered if Jeremy was dead from Jin's plague. She had almost been ready to kill him herself, just for her own peace of mind. She still kept Rouelle's songs cued up on her screen to remind her that she was as guilty as Jin in this spread. She could have warned Jeremy more specifically, could have told him why he was having a heart attack when his body was otherwise healthy. Yet she felt no regret, only a nagging self-doubt that wondered why she didn't feel worse. He wasn't one of the men who attacked her, and she had no real proof that he had committed crimes of any kind. But when she remembered how his eyes had mocked her, she got up and checked the bolts on the door. The world was a safer place without Jeremy and his kind.

She wondered if that made her brainwaves just a little bit more like his.

---

On her shoot the next day, Sandy ran her lines over and over while the gaffers and grips set up the shot. She shouldn't have goofed off with Lancaster so much, but nothing could be done now except cramming and hope.

"If you concentrate any harder, your head's going to explode."

She looked up to see a familiar mop of curly hair on top of a grinning man dressed in black jeans and a T-shirt. Tools hung off his belt loops, identifying him as part of the crew. After a moment's pause, she remembered his name. "Mark!"

"Nick," he corrected.

Sandy's hand flew to cover her mouth. She waved her script at him. "I'm so sorry. Mark's one of the characters in the last piece I did. I'm sorry. Nick."

He laughed. "That's okay. I'd ask for your name again too, but it's all over the tabs. You've been hanging with the A-list crowd."

"It's no big deal. Sl—Tom is a friend of a friend. He helped me get my first acting lessons, and Heather cheers me up when I get frustrated with this business."

"That's not really why I came to talk to you," said Nick.

"Why, then?"

He smiled. "To tell you that they're ready for you in makeup. Oh, and that you and I are going to dinner after the shoot tonight."

"We are?" said Sandy.

"In my world we are. It's a nice world. Want to come along?"

"You're strange," said Sandy, but she was laughing.

"I'll take that as a yes," said Nick.

She let him.

❧

"You're all pink and glowy," said Lancaster.

It and Slim were having a dinner for all of the neuts at their estate, mostly extras and a few techs that were working on the same film the "couple" was currently starring in. Phazy was there and gave Sandy its usual nod of acknowledgment.

"Things are going well?" said Slim.

"Very," said Sandy.

All heads turned toward her.

"Uh huh. You all can smell it or something, can't you," she said.

The others laughed, those who knew her more loudly than the newcomers. At least she had learned not to be embarrassed over her gendered feelings around them, for the most part, and although she knew the hormones she'd been pumping out in the weeks since that first dinner with Nick were causing the buzz, she felt giddy and almost proud of it all the same.

"Best drug around," said Phazy.

Several of the other neuts ghosted her and smiled.

"Okay, that's enough," said Slim. "You want to tell us about him?"

She wasn't sure she did, knowing she sounded like a teenager with a crush. Technically, she supposed that's what she was, but Nick said he cared for her, too. At first she had wished for a girlfriend to confide in, but here with the neuts, she was able to let everything flow, to tell them about Nick's humor and kindness, the way he looked at her that made her blood quicken and her brain go to mush. She didn't have to tell them that she worried it might be over too soon, that she was afraid of doing something stupid, that sometimes when he kissed her, she remembered men standing over her and the terrifying feel of losing layer after layer of her clothes.

They might not pick up on the specifics as they listened, but Sandy was certain the neuts who ghosted her would understand something of the conflict inside. She was grateful she didn't have to give voice to the words, to make her fears solid and real by saying them out loud.

Several hands reached out to touch her. Not invasive, just a moment of warm palm pressed to her shoulder, fingertips brushing her arm. The comfort she got from them worried her. What if she didn't know how to react to gendered kinds of touches anymore? Worse yet, she had no idea what she could tell Nick about her past and her friends.

"You'll be all right," Slim told her quietly when she left for the night.

"I wish I could be so sure," she said.

"You have plenty of time. I know you want to tell him about us, but you need to get to know him better first. I felt your doubts. Trust your instincts," said Slim.

"I know. It's just hard."

Slim hugged her then, and again she felt that invisible film that separated neuters from gens. She hugged it back fiercely, trying to send all of the warmth she felt toward it through that barrier, then left to go seek the warmer arms of Nick, whose barriers were only the ones she set for herself, to keep her secrets from spilling out like tears when he looked at her with just a hint of teasing in his gray velvet eyes.

"How was the party?" he asked when she stopped at his place on her way home.

He put down the game he'd been playing and led her into his room, the only place for privacy in the house he shared with six others, mostly crew members who worked for the same company he did. At least it was a real house, and though it was far from having a pool or even a yard, the stairs were comfortably worn, and it felt like a place that a family might have lived. Or might live one day in the future.

She settled into Nick's arms, drawing out the usual affectionate exchange so she could figure out how much to say.

"It's always good to see old friends, but I didn't know a lot of the people there," she said.

"I'm sure they were happy to get to know you," said Nick.

She smiled up at him. "Is that jealousy I hear? Don't worry, that's not something you have to worry about with this crowd."

"Hey, they got to spend time with you and I didn't. Of course I'm jealous."

"Well don't be. They mostly just..." Sandy wasn't sure where to go from there.

"Just what?"

"I don't know. People ate, they talked about their current projects. There were some crew guys there I think you might know."

"Did you tell them about your current projects?" said Nick.

"I told them about you, if that's what you mean. Slim was happy for me. So was Heather."

"Slim?"

Sandy stiffened. Had she really said that? She had. "Tom. Slim's a nickname that he asked me not to call him in public, and I forgot. Please don't tell him I said it, okay?"

Nick laughed. "Like I'm going to be telling Tom Liene anything other than, 'Yes sir, they're ready for you in five, sir.'"

"You kiss-up," said Sandy.

"Hmm, sounds like a good plan."

So he did, for a while, but Sandy pushed him away when things started to get too heated.

"What is it? Memories again?"

She had told him about the attack on the farm, how sometimes the remembered sensations came back to her at the worst possible times. He'd been great about it, so far, and she could tell he was trying to be now, but his frustration was clearly visible, and he seemed to be putting less effort into not letting it show.

"I'm sorry," said Sandy, and pulled him toward her.

*Let him have this*, she thought. As long as it lasted, she wouldn't have to speak. He pulled back for a moment, and she brushed the hair out of his eyes.

"What?" she said.

"You're not some kind of assassin, are you?"

"Why on earth would you say that?" She tried to laugh, but she wondered what he could know. About Jin, the Network, the plagues. Anything.

"Haven't you ever *watched* any movies, little rising star? Women with secrets are always assassins or spies. Then they sleep with a guy so they can get information or avoid giving any away."

"I've never played a spy or assassin. But I promise you, I'm neither."

He laughed at her sincerity, and his face lost the guarded look he'd worn since she came over. She leaned into him again, for herself as much as for him this time. Sometimes it was so easy to forget that he was barely older than she was, that both of them really still ought to be at home or somewhere near there instead of scrambling for work in a crowded hive of people who were all trying to do the same thing. She didn't stop him, even when the memories came.

They lay in darkness together a short while later, and she propped herself up on an elbow under the sheets.

"You're Mr. Mysterious too, you know," she said.

"Huh? How's that?" he said.

She watched him fidget for a while and then laughed. "It's okay, go ahead."

He smiled at her sheepishly and pulled on some clothes. She had only started sleeping with him the week before, and everything was still so new to her, but the one thing she had learned was that he always seemed to be fidgety afterward, and he wouldn't calm down until he had gotten up and usually had something to eat.

She lay back, waiting for him, feeling her own body slow down its systems. She wondered if the neuts had known she was sleeping with him—or if they knew she never had with anyone before. She pulled the blankets up tighter around her, trying to quell the embarrassment rising to her cheeks. She knew they would be as matter-of-fact about her activities as they were about any other biological function, but her nervous system was slow to get that message.

Nick came back in with a glass of water for her, wiping crumbs from his face with the back of his hand. She snuggled up to him, hoping she wasn't wearing on his patience, not sure how much or what parts to believe of the stories she'd heard about how men behaved after sex.

"What did you mean about me being mysterious?" he said.

"Just that you know more about my past than I do about yours," she said.

He shrugged. "What's there to say? I grew up in Albuquerque, never left until I came up here and found you."

"You make it sound like I'm the reason you came up here," she told him.

He smiled at her without another word, then reached up and clicked off the bedside lamp.

"Does that mean I can stay the night?" said Sandy.

He just put an arm around her, kissed her, and drifted off to sleep.

# CHAPTER 27

Brat grudgingly offers Jin a place to stay the night, if only to keep a hand in its plans. His apartment is a three-bedroom suite shared with a male college student and a married couple.

"Well, it's about time you brought yourself a lady home, Brett," says the college student.

He winks at Jin. Brat blushes and leads Jin into his room, shutting the door without introduction. Neither of them can help hearing comments from the living room.

"Are you sure that was a girl?" says the woman.

"Brett seemed to think so, and he's not the type to be bringing home young boys and shutting himself in his room with them," says her husband.

"And how would you know?" she says.

"I've seen him looking at Danny's girlie magazines, right Danny?"

Brat shrugs an apology. Jin wanders the room, taking in the smell of chemically altered sweat and sour sheets. For the first time, the thought occurs to it that Brat's fuzz of a beard might indicate physical changes on a much deeper level. It tries to ghost him, to feel if the hormones have given him some sense of vestigial organs, but Brat holds perfectly still until Jin has to admit defeat.

"As long as you're here, let's work," says Brat. "Do the objects that carry this fertility antidote have to be made of a certain material? Porous or plastic or anything like that?"

"Won't know until I figure chems," says Jin. "Just list any possible and we'll cut later. Try for anything people share."

They are still working when the morning sun begins to shine through Brat's olive-green curtains. Anything people might share with a partner goes on the list, from lingerie to a box of candy to an unusual rock that someone might find on the street, pick up, and take home. Brat looks down at their work and shakes his head.

"Jin, we have no spreaders, remember. How are we going to deliver a hundred thousand fertility-inducing flowers and unusual seashells to strategic locations throughout the United States, let alone anywhere else in the world? We'd both die of old age before we were even halfway finished. Especially if you insist on walking. They'll probably track us down and demand a cure for everyone before we get more than two states done."

"Wait," says Jin.

"Not again. What brilliant flash of insight do you have now?" says Brat.

"Better spread idea. Forget list."

"After you kept me up all night working on it?"

"Forget. Don't need objects person will pass on. Make cure invade salivary glands. Gens inclined to kiss chosen partners, yes?"

"Yeah. Okay, so that's how it spreads, and we can make the time limit a little longer. But here's a horrid thought: what if a rapist takes the cure. He might pass it on to a victim who could then become pregnant with a child from a man she despises, but she'd never be able to become pregnant by her chosen partner. That's more cruel than anything."

"True, but Soundwave reduced number of rapists in general. Can figure out some way to deal with others."

Brat is silent for a moment, digesting for first time that his hatred made his brain similar enough to a rapist for Soundwave to endanger him. He looks at Jin.

"We are probably the absolute worst two people in the world for this job," he says.

"We're only two. Back to work. Still need to spread cure to about one percent of population, let saliva glands take from there. Can keep some of list, but cut down."

"I still think the greeting cards are a nice touch," says Brat.

"Might be fairly easy spread, too, if we can hit distribution center."

"The post office," says Brat. "We're idiots for not thinking of it sooner. That's the classic method."

"What?"

"Forget all other plans. Forget the greeting cards, even. Ninety percent of the population uses e-cards anyway."

"Where you get statistics?" asks Jin.

"I made that up, but it's true—people don't send physical cards, but they do order packages. We hit the shipping companies and dose certain types of items, one for each portion of the demographic.

Jin feels the quickening flow of excitement. "Yes. Works for homeless, too, if we put cure on inside of boxes. Cardboard always useful for all socio-economic backgrounds. Best thing is we can always spread more."

Brat gives Jin an odd look, but Jin isn't paying attention. The scent of his hormones and the joint chemistry of their individual excitement over the project is already laying the groundwork for the chemistry Jin will use to make sure the cure is passed along. That eagerness and pleasure could be chemically reproduced, and if Brat is right, gens won't be able to help but share that with their mates. What it really needs now is a lab. An attack from multiple levels is the best way to ensure saturation for the initial infertility, before they release the cure. Food, water, air. The plague must trigger specifically to human chromosomes so there is no danger of cutting down other animals and devastating the food supply.

Jin sets that aside for the moment, forgetting its qualms and hesitation in the purity of theory. The mechanics of infertility are fairly easy. A chemical combination blocks the ability of the sperm and the egg to recognize each other and connect. Each one remains fine and healthy individually, but a slight change makes them believe they are incompatible. The hormones still balance, everything looks fine to the doctors, and there are fewer side effects than the drugs gens normally take for temporary infertility.

The plan for the cure is simple. The key to unlock the disease is built into the creation.

The initial cure must be absorbed through the skin. Unlike Soundwave, this one is all about direct contact, tactile sensation. Perhaps a pleasurable sensation, like Sandy described at Ocean Cave. Jin pushes the thought away, but it can't escape the memory of Sandy's hand playing just above the glowing crystals, the sound of her voice ordering Jin to touch them before it leaves the caverns, maybe for good.

It never did.

The initial excitement of discovery is gone, and the fact that it is creating a plague that will affect the entire human population makes Jin uneasy. It feels like it is plotting the death of all humankind.

It roams the city for a few days alone, trying to find a place where it can set up a small lab. There are plenty of abandoned apartments, thanks to Soundwave, but none where Jin can bring in supplies and work undisturbed. Then there is the question of acquiring the right chemicals without using the Network's contacts. Perhaps it should have accepted Bruvec's offer of more money for the trip.

"Brat, how you afford apartment?" asks Jin when they meet back at the university.

"I write. Manuals, mostly. Electronics, sewing machines, anything with instructions," says Brat.

"Just wondered. Might help later. Wanted to let you know I'm going back to caves one last time. Need to check something, say good-bye."

Brat looks relieved. "Well, you sure made that easy. Come on."

Brat leads Jin back to his apartment and into the darkened bedroom, ignoring Danny's raised eyebrows. The room glows a sickly green with the sunlight bleeding through the curtains. The bedclothes are a crumpled heap, just like the last time Jin was there. Then they move, revealing Pelin's pale face patched with dark purple bruises.

"You okay?" says Jin, kneeling beside the bed.

"Fine. Looks worse than feels. Just ran into trouble on way here. You lucky worst person you ever met was Brat," says Pelin.

"Some luck, that time," says Jin.

"Yeah, sorry," says Brat. "Pelin, turns out you won't have to tranquilize Jin and drag it back home by its hair."

"You'll come?" says Pelin.

"Decided I need to touch ocean crystals before Sand comes screaming after, maybe gets hurt."

"Brat didn't tell you yet? Is Bruvec, Jin. It's dying."

"So soon? Thought it had few years left."

"Was emptying supply closet. Dropped jar, hit with plague. Too weak to fight and didn't go see meds until too late. Has maybe few days left."

"Tell me rest on way home," says Jin.

During the ride, Pelin tells Jin that although Home Cavern supports the decision to let Jin carry the blame for the plagues and the infertility spread, the artists refuse. They insist on giving Jin any help it needs and will keep silence with the rest of the Network so the responsibility stays with a small group. If Jin doesn't accept their help, Slim has threatened to send Sandy to follow it everywhere it goes until it gives in. According to Pelin, Slim gave odds that Jin wouldn't last a week trying to work with Sandy's chatter. Jin admits it is probably right.

---

Bruvec lies still, looking tiny and frail and far paler than its natural skin tone should allow. The familiar white and silver of Home Cavern blinds Jin, but Bruvec's smile cuts through the dazzle. When it opens its eyes, Jin is glad to be home. Keri gives Jin a dirty look and stomps out of the room, her bare feet slapping the stones as if she wishes they were Jin's face.

"Ignore," says Net, gripping Bruvec's hand.

"Ker blames me? Couldn't be my plague. Mine act faster, all expired now anyway," says Jin.

"You gave order to clean out chems," says Pelin softly.

"True," says Jin.

"And you're only spreader left to blame," says Net.

Jin nods. Bruvec was like a parent to Keri, and she needs to give herself someone to hate for taking it away. Net, Pelin, and Jin stay with Bruvec for its last hours, watching the kindest person they know wither away. Its coughing silences any attempt at conversation, so they stand mute, lightly touching its arms. Net grips Bruvec's whole hand tightly in its own. Keri returns after only a minute, unable to stay away. She takes Bruvec's other hand, keeping as far away from Jin as possible.

Bruvec is cremated without ceremony, according to Home Cavern custom. Keri isn't the only one who sheds tears as the body is carried to the incinerator. Jin tries to remain stoic, not wanting to dishonor all other deaths in favor of Bruvec's, but it can't. If anyone deserves a spreader's tears, it is the neut who understood the need to spread and guided young neuts in their calling.

Jin takes one last look into the computing room, wanting to say good bye to Net before returning to the artist caves, but the old neut isn't there. The room feels oddly empty without it typing away at the corner desk. Jin waits for a while, preferring to stay in case it returns rather than risk upsetting Keri by looking around. It logs on and spends an hour skimming the news, not finding anything of real interest. Still no Net. Strange.

Keri is the only one in the kitchen.

"You," she says when Jin peers in. "Get out of here. You can starve to death for all I care. That guy in Albuquerque had the right idea."

"Just want say good-bye to Net," says Jin.

"You're too late. It went up top."

"Net? Up top? Why?"

Keri comes to clean the spot where Jin touched the table, spraying a ridiculous amount of disinfectant on the surface.

"It wanted to talk to one of the medics. Probably to find a way of protecting older people against dangerous plagues."

"Okay for others to die, not our own? You know that's not fair," says Jin.

"You're not even sorry, are you? And to think I thought you loved it as much as I did."

"No comparing, Ker. Did love. Do. Was accident, that's all. Anger won't bring back."

"It didn't have to happen. Bruvec had a good many years left in it. You said so yourself."

"You know it was weak, growing weaker fast. I'd hoped for few years too, but no one knows," says Jin.

"No one but you and your miserable spreader friends."

"You mean no one but me."

"Yeah, since you're so good at killing people you claim to care about," says Keri.

"Didn't kill Bruv. None of my plagues still active in storage," says Jin.

"Am I supposed to thank you because one of your plagues already killed off whoever made the one that killed Bruvec?" says Keri.

"You always knew I kill. Am same Jin now as then. So different when dead person is your friend?"

"When that friend is Bruvec, yes."

Jin leans against the entryway, not caring that Keri's finger tightens on the trigger of her disinfectant.

"When Net coming back?" it asks.

"Get out of here, Jin. Now. Don't ever let me see you around here again."

Jin sighs and turns to go, but Keri isn't finished.

"When I found Bruvec lying on the ground with that broken jar, I salvaged a sample of one of the others. If I see you around here again, we'll see how you deal with an unknown plague when it's thrown right in your face. Maybe you won't be so unfeeling when the accident happens to your own precious skin."

"Ker, get rid! You don't know how to adapt, outsmart plagues. Could kill self."

"Yeah, well I'll leave that one on your head too."

"No. Can't blame me for suicide," says Jin.

But it knows this isn't true. In this mood, Keri can blame anyone for anything, and Jin can't be sure it won't feel guilty itself. Someone else might have the skill to calm Keri down, to talk her out of her plans, but not Jin. Net will understand if it leaves without saying good-bye. It posts a note on Net's screen and leaves with Pelin for the artist caves.

"Any others feel like Ker?" Jin asks.

"None here. Probably some up top. Watch head."

Jin does not remind Pelin that it knows the cave route better than Pelin does. It could duck the stalactites with its eyes closed. It stops before climbing down the pit toward Ocean Cave.

"Be down in while," Jin says. "Not ready for others yet."

Pelin nods and continues down while Jin shuts off its lantern and breathes in the darkness. The cavern smells of earth, moisture, and minerals. Soothing. An insect crawls over its hand, tickling slightly. Maybe this is what being dead felt like back when bodies were buried instead of burnt. Jin hears a song bounce softly off the rock and realizes it is humming. The sound is comforting, though it can't remember how it knows this particular song. Probably something it picked up in Albuquerque.

It climbs down into Ocean Cave. Pelin has already gone beyond, either to wait in Painted Cavern or to tell the others they are back. Jin can't feel anything like Brat described, the sense of love as a longing to be part of another person. Still, its breath comes easier, and smiling and even humming are possible now that it knows it still has a home and friends. A secure place where people know it, and at least some of them still like it anyway.

Jin reaches out to the glowing crystals, meaning to hover and recall past ghosting like it always does. The purples are so deep it misjudges the distance. Warm minerals shock its skin. Sandy was right: despite logic, it had expected the crystals to be cold.

Jin holds its fingers very still, not wanting to break contact. After the initial surprise, a sensation of peace and well-being seeps into its body. It closes its eyes and traces the feelings from inside itself. Tiny amounts of various chemicals seep into its bloodstream from the fingertips, causing a sensation of ease. Of course. The crystals are neut-grown. The artist must have manufactured the chemicals they grew from and modified them to produce this sensation. Exactly the kind of sensation Jin was considering adding to the infertility plague. Even the initial spread could be a gift of peace and pleasure.

It analyzes the components within its bloodstream. Yes, a similar mixture could work without interfering with the plague's active chemicals.

Maybe it is getting too old for spreading. The sense of peace feels so good, so unique. Still touching the crystals, Jin pitches its own voice to match the low, steady vibration it feels.

"Bye, Bruvec. Love you. No more worries."

# CHAPTER 28

Keeping secrets from Nick was getting harder, and the more time Sandy spent with Slim and Lancaster to relieve the burden of silence, the more distant Nick became. He would look at her like she'd betrayed him when she refused to answer his questions, and he was growing more and more jealous of her relationship with Slim.

"I trust you when you say you aren't sleeping with him. What I don't get is how a girl who just recently came from Montana can be 'old friends' with a guy who's been on television for several years," said Nick.

"I told you, he's a friend of a friend. The people who took me in when my mother was killed are kind of its family."

"What did you say?"

"They're his family. Not blood family, but close enough."

"You said 'its' family. Not 'his.'" said Nick.

"I'm tired. I hardly know what I'm saying," said Sandy.

"You were fine a minute ago, and this isn't the first time you let that slip out. Talk to me, Sandy. Tell me the truth, for once."

They were sitting on the bench out behind the house, and Sandy glanced around at some neighborhood children, playing a game not far away.

"I can't. Not here. And these are other people's secrets I'm trying to keep, not mine," she said.

Nick stood up but didn't leave. "I'm asking you to cut the melodrama. I know whatever the secret is must be big and something about it bothers you, but I don't like that you don't trust me."

"I do," she said.

"No, you don't."

She felt like everything in her was swirling down a drain. Like the waters in the artist caves' baths: filtered, flowing, gone. She wanted to believe that Nick loved her. She wanted to think he was the kind of guy she could trust to accept her friends, but she'd seen too much in her relatively short life to really believe that was true. She'd seen her actor friends beaten because people suspected them of being gay, not even neut. The few that were suspected as neuts were the ones who ended up dead, and she only knew that because the Network kept track and had contacts in the morgues to keep the bodies quiet when they came through.

"Let me ask them," she said to Nick.

"Your friends Tom and Heather?"

She nodded, pulling out her screen. He said nothing when he left her alone on the bench, and she didn't know if he meant to give her privacy or was walking away for good.

She took a deep breath and called Slim, muttering half-silent pleas that it or Lancaster would pick up the phone and tell her what she should do. No one answered the house line, so she called Slim's personal number.

"Sandy?" it said.

"Don't be mad, okay? I think this is important enough to call you at work, but I'm not sure. Maybe you won't think so."

"Don't worry. What's going on?" said Slim, its features distinctly concerned on her small screen. "It's okay, I can talk here," it added when she hesitated.

"I think Nick suspects. I don't think he knows, but he's saying he can't take these secrets, and I accidentally called you 'it' instead of 'him' in front of him, and I guess I've done it before and he never said anything until now. I think I'm making a mess of things."

She thought she ought to feel like crying, but instead she just felt empty and cold, waiting for Slim's voice to fill her up, to tell her everything would be all right. Or to yell at her, curse her for ruining everything.

It let out an audible breath. "We knew this would happen at some point. With the spreaders gone, things are going to be changing fast in the Network. Might help to get some gens on our side."

"The spreaders are gone? What are you talking about?" said Sandy. "Where's Jin?"

There was a silence on the other end of the line.

"Slim?"

"I'm sorry. I thought Lancaster had told you. Jin's fine, though I'm not sure where it is right now. All hell broke loose in the last few weeks, and I guess we forgot to keep you updated. The spreaders are dead, Sandy, all except Jin. Soundwave got to them."

Silence clouded the air around her, waves of emptiness following Slim's last words. She hadn't seen Tei, had hardly thought of it, since it left her in Home Cavern. She couldn't even remember if she'd said thank you.

The phone she held was still on, and Slim was saying something. Words didn't matter. The tone was soothing, and sluggishly her brain started working again.

"I'm sorry. Is there something I can do?" she said.

"Not for now. I haven't heard from the caverns in several days. Lancaster might know more."

"I had no idea. I'm so sorry I opened my big mouth around here at a time like this," said Sandy.

"Times change. Why don't you bring your friend over tonight. I'll talk to Lancaster, see if we can ease him into the idea that we're just people, just trying to make a living. Is there anything I should know about him?"

Sandy's mind filled with irrelevant details, all of Nick's little habits and the bits and pieces she knew of his past. Nothing that would make his transition into the world full of neuters any easier.

"I don't know. I think he'll be happy not to have reason to be jealous of you. He says he isn't, but I think it's there. Either that or he thinks that you're more interested in men than in women," she said.

Slim shrugged. "He wouldn't be the first. And if he's okay with that, then the truth might be easier on him than it would on a gen who can't even accept that difference. Bring him by around nine. I'll let the others know to stay in the guesthouses. Lanky and I will be there."

"I thought you said never to call it Lanky," said Sandy.

"You can't. I can. The privilege of a long acquaintance. See you tonight."

"All right."

"And Sandy, don't worry. If he's not the one for you, another will be."

She wished she could ask it if it was sure, but the day was not about comforting lies. It was time for the uncomfortable truth.

She found Nick pacing irritably around the side of the house. He showed the same kind of restless energy as he did before he leapt out of bed, but this time she doubted he would be soothed by a snack, a couple of kisses, and some sleep.

"Will you come with me to their house tonight? At nine?" she asked him.

"Liene and Lancaster's?" Nick asked.

Sandy nodded. Surprise flared in his eyes, but he nodded back at her, then stood awkwardly staring at the ground. They had three and a half hours before they needed to leave for the house in the hills, and Sandy couldn't imagine them finding anything to talk about between now and then. Nothing that wouldn't set off another argument, at least.

She remembered Slim's words. Things change. But that wasn't always true. Some things were always the same. She felt some of the emptiness leave her as she reminded herself that she wasn't just some post-Hollywood aspire who depended on the approval of others to survive. She was a farm girl, tough and occasionally sassy, and she had learned early how to laugh when life—or an errant farmhand—dropped a whole pile of shit on her head.

Nick looked up at the sound of her laugh, defensiveness fading when she took his hand. She laughed so hard she could barely speak, and his confused smile in return made her want to pull him close, but they weren't really ready for that yet. Instead, when she could talk again, she said, "My mom was right. Being raised on a farm teaches you to deal with seventy-two different kinds of crap. I'm about to dump a seventy-third kind on you, so why don't we do something fun until then?"

He let her lead him back inside, where they dropped three hours' worth of their favorite shows onto her screen and just sat together, laughing occasionally, not touching, just behaving like friends. From time to time, Sandy caught him sneaking glances at her, pulling a little bit away. She felt she could almost have ghosted him, but she didn't need that kind of empathy to know he would stay, that he would trust her just a little while longer, and make his decision based on what Slim had to say.

She reached out, just once, and squeezed his hand briefly. He squeezed back, and she let go before he could consciously react. It might be her last chance.

She pushed that thought out of her mind, and by the time they made the long hike to Slim's estate, she had decided she was ready for a hundred and two kinds of crap. If Nick chose to give it to her, she'd take it and put it to use.

Lancaster answered the door with a hug for Sandy and a handshake for Nick. Sandy noticed it wasn't wearing any makeup, though its hair was still set in a feminine style. It also was without the shapers it used to pad its form, making it look younger and obviously neuter to Sandy's eye. Slim, too, was without any makeup. It greeted them both without touching them and led the way into the living room.

"I'm glad to meet you, Nick. Sandy's told us a lot about you."

There was an awkward moment where Nick struggled for something to say, and Sandy wasn't sure whether politeness or bitterness would win out. In the end, he simply gave Slim a bewildered smile and muttered something that might have been "thanks."

For a moment, he seemed more interested in the house than the people around him. Sandy followed his eye, realizing that the place really wasn't much bigger than his, but certainly more open, with views out of some of the windows creating a panorama of lights from the town and farms, and the relative lack of clutter that came from only two people sharing a home.

Something was missing, but Sandy couldn't quite put her finger on what. Perhaps just the lack of other neuts wandering in and out. The doors were usually open as the visiting neuts took advantage of the kitchen, screens, and the film library Slim and Lancaster collected.

"Anyone hungry?" said Lancaster abruptly.

That was the difference, Sandy realized. She had never seen the living room without a plate of junk food when Lancaster was home.

"Maybe something to drink?" said Sandy, glancing at Nick.

He nodded, and Lancaster disappeared. Slim looked after it with a slight shake of its head, and Sandy saw its lips move slightly. She wondered what it said, and if Lancaster could hear subvocalizations with its head in the fridge.

"Would you like to have a seat?" said Slim.

"Thanks," said Nick again.

Sandy looked from one to the other, but no one seemed to know how to start. She turned to Slim as Lancaster came in, handing out glasses of local juneberry juice to everyone and setting a plate of cookies by Nick's elbow. It kept none for itself.

"He wants to know about you. I didn't know what to tell him," said Sandy.

Nick looked horrified. "I don't want to intrude on your privacy, Mr. Liene, I just wondered why Sandy couldn't talk about all the time she spends over here."

"You can call me Slim. Most of my friends do, and mostly what Sandy does here is sit and talk," it grinned at her, "or listen, occasionally."

If Sandy had been just a little bit younger, she would have stuck out her tongue at it. She knew the Home Cavern neuts thought her an incessant chatterer, but the artists held their own in conversation, especially the topsiders. She offered the plate of cookies back to Lancaster.

"Can't. Stupid medics said I gained ten pounds since last time. Metabolism slowing down, I guess."

That explained the grouchiness. She hoped it wouldn't affect Lancaster's view of Nick. She took a deep breath, but Slim beat her to the words.

"Let's be frank. You're here because you caught Sandy referring to me as something other than male. It's true. I'm not. And I'm not the only one around, certainly far from being the only one in this town. We call ourselves neuts, short for neuter, because that's what we are."

It let that sink in for a while. They all watched Nick as he nodded slowly and took a sip of his drink with a hand that trembled slightly. A stunned look crossed his face.

"Hey, this is really good. What is it?"

"Just a mixer. Nonalcoholic, juneberries, crystallized honey, and some wildflower syrups thrown in," said Lancaster. It glanced at Slim guiltily, then took a defiant sip of its own drink. "You can't expect me to quit cold turkey."

The evening wore on, stiff and awkward for a while longer, until Nick seemed to settle into the fact that no one was going to drop anything bigger on him than they already had. Sandy let Slim and Lancaster handle most of the conversation, keeping careful track of what they told him and what they left out.

There was mention of an artist colony near El Paso, but nothing about the caverns or scientists, and certainly no mention of spreaders. Nick nodded and blinked a lot, occasionally asking a question. When Slim made an excuse to leave them alone for a minute, Lancaster followed.

Sandy put a hand tentatively on Nick's shoulder. "Nick?"

She wasn't even sure what to ask.

"If you want to know whether I believe all this, I'll let you know when I wake up," he said.

"It's not a dream. Neuts are real, and there are a lot of them around."

He shrugged. "Makes sense, I suppose. I never did believe those biology textbooks knew what they were talking about anyway; I just never had a reason to care. With so many people out there, there were bound to be a few mutations."

"They aren't mutants! That sounds like some silly movie monster. They've been around forever," said Sandy.

"I said mutation, not mutant."

"Sorry. I just tend to be a little—"

"—protective. I know."

He made the words sound like he thought it was a good thing. She searched his face, trying to read in expression what her friends could read in chemicals and vital signs.

"There's more to them, you know. Differences and things they haven't told you about yet. I don't want you to think I'm keeping more secrets from you, but there's just too much to get into all in one night," said Sandy.

"I trust you."

"Really?"

"Really. That doesn't mean I won't start asking questions again. But now I think I have some idea of what to ask."

Sandy jumped as she heard the back door slide open. She was certain she hadn't heard Slim and Lancaster go out that way. In fact, they had made a great show of tromping noisily up the stairs. Sandy had appreciated that, knowing they were taking themselves far enough away that she could at least have the illusion of speaking privately, though no doubt her words carried everywhere in the house to their sensitive ears.

A neut she only vaguely recognized came into the living room.

"Nick?" it said, eyes wide.

"Davis! What are you doing here?"

"Could ask you the same. I live here. Well, out back."

"He's here with me," said Sandy.

Davis looked back and forth between them, seeming to take a moment to read the space between them. Sandy looked back at Nick.

"Ah, so he's the one you've been on about," said Davis.

Sandy blushed. "You two know each other?"

"Davis runs the second unit crew," said Nick.

"Slim around?" said Davis.

"Upstairs, I think," Sandy told it.

She and Nick waited silently, listening to the footsteps and muffled voices. The silence wasn't awkward anymore, and she warmed at the thought of the long walk home alone with him in the dark, picking up where the relationship had faltered. A thunder of footsteps broke her thoughts before she could imagine the intimate details.

The three neuts came into the room with them, all eyes on Sandy. Slim took her hand, crouching down to eye level.

"Pelin just sent word. Bruvec's dead."

Nick tried to comfort her as well as he could, not truly knowing what was going on. She made arrangements to meet with Slim in the morning to get a ride back down to New Mexico, then cried with Nick's arm around her shoulder most of the way home.

"Do you want me to walk you back to your place?" he asked.

She nodded, needing the comfort of her own belongings and the smell of clean sheets wrapped around her. Nick walked her to the door. She intended just to hug him good night, but found that she couldn't let go.

"Will you stay with me?" she said, hoping it wasn't too much to ask. "Just as a friend, if you want."

"Is the power lawyer still at it all day and night?"

"I don't know. I've spent most of the last week at your place," said Sandy.

"Then I say we go in as loud as we can and both do our best to snore. Really loudly. All night long."

He took the key from her hand and let them in. Sandy wasn't sure how it happened, exactly, but she found herself hungrily kissing him, seeking comfort in a way only genders could do. *This is what I am*, she thought fiercely when guilt wedged its way in. Not neut, but gen. *I won't die in a cave, alone.*

She had no idea whether Bruvec had truly died alone, and Slim hadn't said exactly how, only that it had been sick. If it was too old to heal itself, shouldn't they all have known?

She felt Nick's body, warm and urgent, on top of hers. The spreaders were gone, Bruvec was gone, Lancaster's medics were making it change. But Nick was a gen—all gen, all man—and he made her feel safe. She gave in to that feeling, knowing the comfort was false. In the morning, she would have to face the truth that no one she loved was safe and that the only one who could protect her was herself. For tonight, she preferred the lie.

# CHAPTER 29

The sound of ragged, forced breathing causes Jin and all of the other neuts in the green room to look toward the entry door. Sandy follows their lead a moment later, just in time to see a wrinkled and weak figure collapse against the doorway.

"Net!" says Jin.

"Fine," says Net, brushing off Jin's assistance.

"What happened to you? You look awful," says Sandy.

Cook sets a plate of food in front of the old neut. Net takes a cautious taste, then refreshes itself more eagerly with a hint of a smile.

"What happened?" says Jin.

"Gens retaliated."

Net shows them a battered version of the same flyer Shaney showed Jin in St. Louis. The flyer was first spotted in the Southwest several months ago and had grown in circulation ever since. Net had been visiting a Network medic in El Paso to discuss Bruvec's death when some gens decided to act on the information.

A protest had been in progress when it entered the clinic, but Net thought nothing of it. There were always health care protests going on. Then the protest chants changed balance, losing several voices as men and women broke away from the group. That was the only warning Net and the medic had. The gens spread through the clinic, grabbing doctors and checking roughly for gender. The process would have been more of a bother to the gen medics than the neuts, except for the weapons the invaders carried.

"Saw them shoot Rheen," says Net. "Eerie silence. Muted guns. Ran to catch before it hit floor. Woman who shot it said 'It's not worth your time, old man,' and walked out."

Fortunately for Net, the gens didn't check patients and visitors. They found the other neut who worked at the clinic, and the execution was over. When the gunners left Net made its way to a public screen and sent out a warning, but it was too late. The gens had their own network, which struck simultaneously across the country. The Council was considering releasing another batch of Soundwave songs to target the clinic attackers. Net had come to find Jin and ask it to refine the plague for a more specific target group.

"No," says Jin. "Don't make this into war. If ever war comes between gens and neuts, neuts must lose."

Net shrugs, still angry.

"You know this, Net. Attackers took terrible action against group we all need, but strike back with Soundwave and others will just replace. Would need to send wave every few months, soon only people left are frightened or apathetic," says Jin.

"Do what, then?" asks Net.

Another set of straining lungs causes heads to turn again, and Miko runs into the green room with wild eyes.

"Man on way down!" says Miko.

"Where?" says Slim.

"Short route from surface."

So many people mutter and chatter in the background that Jin can't think.

"Quiet!" it says.

It can tell from their pleading eyes that no one wants violence here. Some look unconvinced that the man represents any danger, but coming so shortly after the attacks up top, Jin doubts he is just an explorer. It only has one hope.

"I'll go see," it says.

The short route to the surface starts just behind the kitchen. Cook leads Jin up until they hear footsteps and smell the combination of male hormones and sweat. There is also the faint sound of humming, which grows louder as the man approaches. Jin recognizes the song as one popular among Albuquerque students, probably the same tune it caught itself humming outside Ocean Cave. The tune is droned over and over, more like a morbid hymn than someone humming for pleasure. It has used the same technique itself to sound out passageways when it wants to move quickly through the darkness. It laughs, sniffing again to confirm.

"What's funny?" says Cook.

"Isn't man. Go tell others everything safe. I think. Just Brat."

"Brat?" says Cook.

"Ask Pelin."

Jin walks up the tunnel, humming Brat's tune. The song dies when it sees him. Huge circles hang under his eyes, and he has lost noticeable weight since Jin left him just a week ago. If he had arrived a few days later, Jin would have suspected him of trying to walk the whole way from Albuquerque.

"What's so funny?" Brat says when he sees Jin. "I heard laughing."

"You scared everyone. Make good bogeyman."

"Yeah, well, you won't laugh so hard when you hear what I did. The others will probably drive their paintbrushes through my skull, and with good reason."

"You do something besides flyers causing massacre of meds? Might be trouble," says Jin.

"No, just the medics. You heard about it pretty fast."

Jin tells him the basics of Net's story. He sags against the cavern wall.

"Yeah. I'm really sorry about that. I shouldn't have taken that jab in the first place. I knew that the medics helped everyone. At least I should've released an apology or something," he says.

"Wouldn't work. Retractions never effective as original statement. You started exposure. Only way now is forward."

They pause outside the green room while Brat prepares himself to meet the people he abandoned for so many years. All conversation inside stops when Jin pushes open the door. Pelin comes forward and touches Brat's hand.

"You here as friend?" says Pelin.

Brat looks around, avoiding all eyes but Jin's.

"Yes."

The room itself seems to release a breath. Everyone settles back in and food is passed around again, but the usual party atmosphere of the green room doesn't return. Brat remains silent, head down, letting the others ghost him and feel his remorse.

"Infertility spread on hold while we cope here," says Jin. "Soon gens all know about us. Med-killers won't keep secrets, and Net says they saw neuts with own eyes. Brat, must be your job. Come up with full exposé on neuts as if done by gen, but sympathetic gen. Release to big newspapers, magazines if possible. Slim, you have contacts up top?"

"I don't know if they'll accept this, Jin. They're show business contacts. They only deal in fiction," says Slim.

"That's good," says Brat. "Sorry, Jin, but I think I have a better idea. Do any of you know the technical side of filmmaking?"

A few neuts come forward. Among them are a director, a designer, and an editor. Brat's eyes flick back and forth as the introductions are made, and Jin can almost see the ideas forming in his mind. It hasn't ever had the chance to watch this rapid creative process in anyone but itself before.

"Great," says Brat. "Our project is a confession story. Mine. The gens would see through the sympathetic observer routine and be suspicious if we do it that way. What we want is an action-suspense movie, based on a true story. That will take the audience through the whole roller-coaster of a neut's life and leave them identifying with the enemy."

Slim grins. "You'll be needing some actors, then, won't you?"

Brat tries to smile back. "We'll start with my story of trying to spread and the years I spent trying to make up for that. Cut in mixed bits of other people, fictionalized, of course, with dramatic death scenes and—I'm sorry, the introductions were a little overwhelming. Where's Rouelle?"

"Here," says Rouelle.

"Could we get you to compose the soundtrack? Use Jin's charts to get the right emotions triggered at key points, maybe, but mostly you would have free rein. I think even without the chemical manipulation, your music will tug at the audience. Plus there's an added bonus of your bands' names. Use both Rate and that one that got a lot of airplay on the college stations."

"Neuro Pause," says Miko.

"Interested?" says Brat.

"Sure," says Miko.

Rouelle nods. "Hasn't been big group project in too long. Everyone else in?"

"Just one thing," says Slim. "Don't say 'based on a true story' anywhere in the film. It makes the audience suspicious, it's been done so much. Just release the film as is, then let interviewers ask about where the concept came from."

"What if they don't ask?" says Sandy.

"They always ask," says Slim.

"What if we don't get interviews?" says Pelin.

"Then somebody isn't doing their job," says Brat.

"Can I be in it?" asks Sandy. "I know I don't have that much experience, but I think I'm getting pretty good."

"A natural actress," says Slim, in a tone that is more teasing than approving. Sandy looks smug.

"Great. We'll hold general auditions up top, but I bet we can find you a part." Brat hesitates. "Would it be all right if I stay here while I work on the script? There are a lot of people in Albuquerque who aren't too fond of me right now. Even if I weren't born neuter they might use the current state of things as an excuse to do some damage."

"Really, Brat? Why would people not like?" Pelin asks, all innocence.

The group ghosts Brat again, sorting out his fears and motivations. With Jin and Pelin speaking for him, the vote decides that he can stay. He isn't the only one who is excited by the film project.

"Will you continue with hormones?" asks Pelin.

"Yes. I know it's odd for you, Pel, odd for everyone, but it reminds me of who I am, what I've done. Gives me a connection with gens that I'm going to need now more than ever in order to make this film something that will reach as many of them as possible and maybe even prevent an all-out extermination. Sandy, I want you to be the first to read the script when it's done. Give me the opinion of a real gen."

"I don't know how 'real' I am. I've chosen to spend a lot of my time with neuts and don't regret that decision for a minute."

"That's okay, it's your biology I'm interested in."

"Well, if the benefit of my feminine charms mean that much to you, I'd be glad to give it a read," says Sandy.

"All right, then. If someone will show me where, I'll get to work," says Brat.

Slim leads him off while everyone else stays to complete the gluttony Cook has forced upon them. Jin notices that Brat's features have lost some of the cruelty it first noticed about him, making him look more like Pelin than ever. Still, there is something about them both that gives the impression of harshness. Jin wonders if the look is genetic or imprinted by a rough childhood.

"Jin, you serious about putting infertility plague on hold until movie is finished?" says Pelin.

"Much work to do on film, won't have time."

"Not good to wait until everyone knows about neuts. Will take Brat time to write script. Long time before movie's done, even working fast. You said chem theory for plague is done, right?" says Pelin.

"Yes. Still need to actually put chems together, infect objects to deliver both plague and antidote. Without Network funds."

"You know artist funds will cover."

Pelin is right. It has nothing to do with the movie script or the filming, directly. For now, it has nothing better to do than work.

# CHAPTER 30

The dingy little trailer that served as a green room was a wasteland compared to the velour and wood of the artist caves, but nothing better was available to the low-budget production. A silence had been stretching between Sandy and Nick for several minutes before Nick broke it.

"You're absolutely sure you want to do this movie?"

"Of course! Why wouldn't I?" she said.

"There's already talk of backlash and blacklisting, and that's with hardly anyone knowing what the movie is really about," said Nick.

Brat pushed open the flimsy door. "He's not still trying to talk you out of this, is he?"

"I hate it when you guys do that," said Nick.

"Me? I was just making an educated guess," said Brat.

The feigned innocence was ridiculous, and Sandy saw no reason not to laugh. Nick had experienced enough of the neuts' eavesdropping ability during the beginning phases of production to become used to it, but he still didn't like it. Well, she didn't either, but she knew the neuts were just as unhappy about having to hear more than they wanted. She figured most of them tuned out everything that wasn't directly relevant to them.

She had brought Nick down for his first trip to the caverns after he'd read the script and agreed to work on the film. If the idea of spreaders bothered him, he didn't say. He just asked Davis if he could get a better spot on the crew and ended up as best boy, which Sandy knew had something to do with lighting. More importantly, the promotion made him happy. She reached for any happiness she could these days, between her horror over the medics being slaughtered and her worries about Jin.

Seeing it down in the caverns, the little spreader had looked smaller than she remembered, more worried, and a little skeptical about the film. When she had tried to talk to it, other people always seemed to mob around, asking questions, and Pelin set itself out as Jin's guardian, not letting anyone through when it wanted rest.

Back up top, things were uneasy. The rest of the world was starting to realize something was changing. Her actress friends in Wyoming stopped speaking to her when they heard about the project she was working on, and a few directors had taken her off their call lists without explanation.

Slim and Lancaster were getting fewer calls as well, though as far as Sandy knew, no one knew what they really were. "The Project" was muttered about in low tones around town, and anyone who outwardly supported it was tossed to one side of a great divide. Sandy was glad when the locations were cleared and the cast and crew moved down to Colorado to begin filming.

She rubbed the condensation off one of the small windows and looked out at the late spring snow that blanketed the ground before the ancient cliff dwellings of Mesa Verde. The light dusting was almost pathetic compared to the Montana snowdrifts she used to play in as a child, but she loved the pristine whiteness and the way the brown dirt poked through the melted spots, making the whole world look like the top of a glazed crumb cake.

"You can't melt the stuff by watching it," said Brat.

"She isn't trying to, she wants more," said Nick.

She turned and smiled at him, huddled around his coffee as if the trailer interior weren't seventy-nine degrees and humid.

"Well, she can't do that either, and we need the locations dry for the outdoor shots. I'm not sure how much longer we can postpone," said Brat.

A delivery truck pulled to a stop on the dirt road that ran past the haphazard assortment of personnel and equipment trailers that made up the production's headquarters. Sandy didn't recognize the people who got out, but they carried long cases that looked like tripods and lighting equipment.

"Nick, were you expecting more lighting crew to show up today?"

He came up behind her and looked past her out the window.

"I don't know. Davis would be in charge of that, and there's no guarantee he would tell me."

"It," Sandy corrected him.

"*He*, while we're up here, and you should remember that. Not all of the crew knows this story is real," said Nick.

"Really? The cast does, and we'll probably slip in front of the crew if they don't know. Shouldn't everyone involved be told?" She looked at Brat.

"The people who will be working here day-to-day are screened, and I think all of them know, but Nick's right. If we have new crew members coming in, best to be careful until we're sure. And a lot of the post-production crew we have lined up are from other companies. To them, this is all fiction."

"I thought the point of this whole movie was to let everyone know that you guys *aren't* fiction," said Sandy.

Brat's reply was cut short by a series of explosions outside. Sandy dived for the floor and Nick tumbled down with her, trying not to land on her but only partly succeeding. Sandy looked at him and saw her own questions echoed on his face.

"Brat! Get down!" she hissed when she saw the half-neut moving toward the window.

"The equipment trailer. They destroyed it. Everybody okay?"

The two gens nodded, but Brat wasn't looking at them. After a moment, his eyes focused again and he strode toward the door.

"No one was hit directly, but Lancaster got a chunk of shrapnel in the face. I'm going to make sure everyone else is all right."

He left, and Sandy helped Nick sit up.

"I keep forgetting he can do that. He seems like just a guy most of the time," said Nick.

Sandy grabbed the first aid kit and checked Nick and herself one more time. Other than being shaken and mildly bruised from hitting the floor, they were fine.

"Go on. I know you want to help Lancaster," Nick said.

Sandy blew him a kiss and ran to the trailer where Lancaster spent most of its time. People, both neut and gen, were already surrounding it, pressing gauze to its cheek and checking for other damage.

"I hear you make a good nursemaid," Lancaster said to her, wincing at the pain caused by moving its jaw.

"Let me see," said Sandy.

The wound wasn't deep, but the jagged edges were nasty and would take time to heal. She cleaned the wound as well as she could, dressed and patched it and told Lancaster to use ice to keep the swelling down.

"Just what I need. Another medic telling me what to do," said Lancaster, but its eyes were grateful.

"I think a cookie might help the swelling go down, too," said Sandy.

Replacing the equipment put them behind schedule, but the artists helped with the funding, and by the time they were ready to shoot again, the snow had disappeared. Nick wanted to track down whoever had planted the explosion, but Brat was adamant that they were to focus only on the film.

"No one was seriously injured, and I don't want this to escalate further," he said.

"No injuries?" said Lancaster with a pointed stare.

"Consider it a challenge for the makeup artists," said Brat.

"Why don't you let the wound show?" said Sandy. "Jin should have some battle scars. It's earned them."

"We're trying to create empathy, not pity," said Brat.

Lancaster nodded. It took its role as Jin seriously, though Sandy thought it was a little upset that Jin would have nothing to do with it, itself. She had tried to explain that Jin just didn't know how to be part of something like this, but Lancaster had waved her aside.

"Don't worry. I think I can play a neut without too much research."

So the filming went on, interrupted almost daily by some sort of protest or act of vandalism. Since she had only a couple of small, background scenes, Sandy had plenty of time on her hands, which she used to peruse the seemingly endless flood of angry letters and ignorant threats they received.

Some of the flyers they received worried her. She checked them against the Network archives and sent new ones to Net, though she knew she wasn't supposed to have contact with Home Cavern from above. Net assured her that it checked for all traces of tampering and observation. The old neut was surprisingly eloquent in writing, compared to the monosyllabic person Sandy had known.

> I am afraid what you are doing is changing the world faster than the world can handle. Be careful, young gen, that you don't find yourself trapped underground with us, buried alive and away from the sun you so admire. Your help is welcomed, but as our friend says, if the battle between us comes, gens are the ones who must live. Without you, we all die.

Sandy nearly wept, reading that letter. She could feel the cold of the underground computing lab seeping out of the words and Net's own self-imposed isolation bleeding it dry into the machines it loved so much. She hesitated to send it more letters and flyers as the language and accusations became more vehement in tone. Still, whenever she went a week without contact, Net sent her a query asking if everything was well and if the tide against neuters had slowed. There never seemed to be hope in the question, only the search for information and a personal concern for her.

Alone in the trailer that served as the production office, Sandy occasionally imagined tracing out the touch pattern on her pocketscreen that would launch Rouelle's plagued song. Usually, she kept the screen folded shut and thought of her mother and Jeremy and the countless dead from Soundwave, neut and gen alike.

On days like today, when she had read too much hate mail and sorted through flyers calling for genocide, she pressed the button. She listened to the tainted song as she read tirades that dripped with hate, contaminating the nets worldwide with words that could burn neuts or bludgeon them black and blue.

As angry as she got in response, the song never did more than increase her heart rate by the slightest amount, and that might have been only her own nerves. She read the letters again, trying to understand, the music looping around her in the warm, oppressive air.

"Is this where you hide all day?" said Brat, coming into the trailer.

He froze, breath caught and hands clutching the doorway. Sandy scrambled to turn the sound off, then pulled Brat outside, wondering how far they had to go to escape the sound waves. He took deep breaths beside her and pulled at her arm to slow her down.

"Wait," he said between gasps.

She supported him with one arm. "I'm so sorry! I wasn't thinking, I just needed…"

There was nothing really to say. He nodded, then shook his head, but she couldn't understand what he was trying to communicate, couldn't do anything but apologize over and over until he finally clamped one hand over her mouth and twisted its still-boyish face into half of a grin.

"Let it go," he said. "I know why you were playing that thing. I just wish I wasn't susceptible anymore. I thought I was beyond that kind of thinking."

"Jin says habitual brain patterns can take months, even years to change."

"I'm sure Jin said that in a lot fewer words," said Brat.

"Were you looking for me? I mean before I inadvertently tried to kill you?" said Sandy.

"That's the spirit. Joke about my imminent demise."

"I didn't mean it like that! I just—"

Brat laughed at her to prove he was joking, but Sandy still felt like apologizing.

"Actually, I *was* looking for you," he said. "We finished your last scenes yesterday. I know you might want to stay around because of your boyfriend, but if you have other things to do, you're free to go. You can't really be enjoying reading hate mail all day."

Sandy helped him back to the trailer, moving cautiously so he could test his heart rate and make sure the waves weren't still hanging in the air with their deadly tones. She had already been searching for work through local casting agencies, but she hadn't found anything yet. She had no idea if that was because of her work on Brat's film, or if the local markets were simply full.

Brat dropped into a chair.

"Nobody's going to watch this film, are they?" he said.

"Are you kidding? With this kind of controversy, you're bound to open to full houses and coverage in every major newsdrop," said Sandy.

"And picket lines, and people who buy tickets just to make a statement by walking out five minutes after it begins," said Brat.

"Which will at least boost your box office sales."

Brat smiled at her. "I have no idea how you can still be an optimist after all of this mess, and I have even less idea why you don't bug the hell out of a cynic like me."

"Well, we know it's not my feminine charms. The hormones you take can't be *that* strong," said Sandy.

Brat looked a little sheepish.

"They are?" she said.

"Not exactly. But I know I find you more attractive than I would if I didn't take them. I'm still neut, Sandy, but I think I understand how genders feel, at least some of the time."

"Then I'll use all of my charm to tell you this: I'm staying on the set. If you need me, I'm here. If I get an audition elsewhere, I'll let you know. But you're right about me wanting to be with Nick, and maybe I can do a little PR. You know, go out and talk to people about the film, build up some positive anticipation, that kind of thing," she said.

"Using your feminine charm?" said Brat.

"That and my boundless optimism," Sandy laughed.

"Be careful."

Brat left her alone then, with a pile of hate mail to help her remember exactly how careful she needed to be.

# PART II

# OUTCAST

# CHAPTER 31

The initial screening of Brat's movie is held underground. Hundreds of neuts from across the continent gather in the subterranean theatre, along with a few of the trustworthy gens who were involved with the filming. The gens gawk as much at the natural surroundings as at any of the neut artwork. They are slightly more discreet about gawking at the neuts themselves. Several of the neuts are just as curious, not having been around gens for years. They inhale with closed eyes, sorting the smell of real men and women from Brat's synthetic hormones and the aroma of Cook's food. The auditorium is packed.

Vats of popcorn with imported cow's milk butter pass from hand to hand. Cook has an arrangement with a farmer in Carlsbad and gets fresh dairy more often than most topsiders, but even to the residents of the artist caves, cow rather than goat butter is a real treat. Pelin and Slim sit to Jin's left, and three gen crew members are on its right. Sandy leans her elbows on the back of its seat, uncomfortably close, her scent mingled with that of the young man beside her.

Both of them bear small scars and fading bruises that tell of troubles they suffered at the hands of people who protested the film. Sandy refuses to speak of their cause, saying only that the protesters made their point and she made hers, then she shares a smile with the man beside her in a way that leaves Jin and the rest of the room completely outside.

All of that is forgotten when the lights dim.

Jin hasn't seen a movie since before it joined the Network. The technology has developed far beyond that of its childhood. The special effects are necessarily low-budget, but even so it wouldn't have guessed that the sunsets were synthetic if the gens at its elbow hadn't congratulated each other in whispers. The open starry night over the New Mexico desert is obviously a fake. Even on a clear night as far from city lights as possible, no one can see that many stars.

The images and Rouelle's score are so compelling that Jin hardly pays attention to the story. The underscoring fills it with such tension that it fears Rouelle may have used some of the Soundwave undertones until it realizes the film is at the point when Brat decides to try its first spread. The music has simply taken its anxiety and amplified the sensation without any loss of clarity.

Brat's story is so different from Jin's. Bruvec found Jin wandering the streets of Pueblo at age fifteen, already convinced that the human race was rapidly outgrowing the capacity to deal with its own waste. Even among the lo-loc residents, Jin was poorer than most, and the only things handed out for free were pills and shots to keep the area safe from epidemic diseases. By then, Jin had come to the conclusion that disease would make the survivors better off. Still, it took the pills, telling itself it needed to stay healthy to learn more, and maybe learn enough to help others. It was a natural spreader.

Brat was not. It agreed with the principles of spreading, but whoever trained it should have seen that it had no stomach for the work. According to the film, Bruvec did try to discourage him. With Brat being seventeen years old at the time, that only served to drive him onward.

The failed plague is full of Technicolor gore and anguish, with supporting music that brings cramps to Jin's stomach and bile to its throat. As the score fades away into a lonely scene of Brat's self-imposed isolation, the physical effects ease and are soon forgotten.

Jin isn't sure whether it likes the neut actor who plays it in the film. The scene where it shovels bugs into its hungry mouth, crying with relief, is too much. Jin never would have cried over the bugs. It didn't have enough fluid in its body to waste on tears.

Pelin and Slim reach over to touch Jin's arm with their fingertips and hush its disgruntled subvocalizations. Even Sandy, who can't hear the words Jin's throat just barely forms, pats its shoulder. Jin turns around to see liquid shining in her eyes.

"Sorry," she whispers, "you just came home so nearly dead that time."

Several others, gens included, turn to look at them with raised eyebrows. Jin pointedly watches the screen, and Pelin unsuccessfully tries to stifle a laugh.

As the movie progresses, the deaths from neut plagues become more peaceful, lulling the audience into comfort until they are hit full force with the medic massacre and the deaths of the spreaders in Soundwave.

"It had to be that way to let the audience know the enemy is really dead," Sandy tells Jin when the movie is over. "That's just movie language. If you want to really kill the bad guy, you have to leave no doubt in anyone's mind that he, she, or it is dead, no coming back."

The only "bad guy" left at the end is Jin. In the movie, it vows never to kill again and joins Brat in a crusade to educate gens and rebuild the natural lands. Credits roll over the image of it walking with Brat down a dusty road, the pack on its shoulder filled with plant seeds instead of death, a silhouette in the simulated sunset.

The room fills with cheers and chatter as the last of the credits dissolve into black. Jin tries ghosting a few of the gens, but it can't tell whether the satisfaction they feel is purely artistic, or whether the story of the film had an impact as well. Jin asks one of the camera crew for his opinion.

"As a social statement, I can't really say. I don't think it'll change the mind of anyone who is set on hating you all, but as a movie it's great, and the promoters seem to love that kind of contrived happy ending. The soundtrack sales alone will pay for the production."

"Hey, Jin," says Brat. "Lancaster wants to know what you thought of its portrayal of you. Besides the bug scene, I mean."

The gen Jin was talking to takes a step backward, nearly knocking over one of Cook's trays.

"You're the real Jin?" he asks.

"Kevin, allow me to introduce you to the real live Jin. Jin, Kevin," says Brat.

"I thought you were just a composite character with a few creative flourishes thrown in. But you're a real spreader?" says Kevin.

"Yes," says Jin.

"Well, former spreader," says Brat.

Kevin looks to Jin for confirmation, but it can't give him any. The part about it promising never to kill again was one of those creative flourishes he mentioned.

"Just doing what's best for human race," says Jin.

Brat laughs like this is some big inside joke. "Stop scaring the gens, Jin. This is a party."

Kevin looks at the other people chatting in small groups. Jin refrains from ghosting him, guessing he would find that invasive, but from the outside he looks like he desperately wants to be somewhere else. Brat grabs his arm, and with a pointed look at Jin, drags Kevin off to go meet the resident artists. The crowd swirls around, laughing and eating, until Jin feels them all like a pressure on its skin. If this were a city up top, it would be watching to see what kinds of food the people were selecting, calculating the percentages, and figuring out what to poison in order to get the rate of population drop and demographic balance it desired.

It decides on the lemon bars. That would average a fifty-two percent drop, plus or minus three percent, fairly evenly spread across the ethnicities present. Add a powdered tranquilizer to the sugary topping, then a slow-acting poison either in the filling or in the drinks so the combination results in a painless, rapid loss of all brain function. Of course, that would fill the theatre with bodies and probably slow the distribution of the film, but since it isn't going to create the plague anyway, the mental exercise remains devoid of corpses.

Slim puts a hand on Jin's shoulder from behind, smiling grimly when Jin jumps at the contact.

"Come on, I want to show you something," says Slim.

It leads Jin out through the corridors to the music studio and seals the door behind them. The sounds of the party abruptly cut off, leaving a slight ring in their ears.

"What's here?" says Jin.

"Peace and quiet. Now we can talk without every neut in the crowd listening. They were, you know. I caught at least twelve of them missing parts of their own conversations just to listen to you talk to Kevin. Then they were watching you stand there, watching the crowd. It's a good thing you weren't subvocalizing."

"You know what I was thinking?" says Jin.

"Anyone who knows you could figure it out. You were deciding who should die and how," says Slim.

Jin looks at it carefully, but there is no recrimination in its face. "Just theory. Wouldn't really do."

"Of course not. But do you want to explain to the gens down there that you were only plotting their deaths for relaxation? And a lot of the neuts don't know you either. Do you think they won't take personal offense to even a hypothetical intra-Network plague?"

"Wasn't going to tell them," says Jin.

"Jin, you need to get out of here," says Slim.

"Know. Only staying to be polite."

Slim laughs, and unlike Brat's forced joviality, this sound is true joy.

"Of course. You wouldn't be rude enough to leave, would you? Even if you have to entertain yourself with some theoretical fatal chemistry. So be polite and tell me what happened with the infertility spread. Did you get that worked out while we were busy filming your life story?"

"Done. Won't know results for while, but judging from birth rates since completion, not great success."

"Why?" says Slim.

"Didn't factor in Soundwave plague. Reproductive systems sense danger when plagues occur, biology tries to save species by producing more offspring."

"And what? There's something you're not saying."

"And problem with plague from start. Too many ways to overcome. Fertility restoration is triggered by brain chems found in those really trying to have children. That way people can have kids with chosen partner like Brat wants. Basically, plague just gives out free birth control to those who want, only they don't know."

"So anyone who wants kids can overcome the plague? Why bother spreading at all?" says Slim.

Jin's eyes flash for a split second, but it keeps its voice quiet and level. "This not just making someone's life end earlier than maybe natural. Taking away choice, altering living bodies—"

"You couldn't. Poor Jin. What's the change in birth rates since the spread?" says Slim.

"Down forty-five percent."

"That's great, isn't it? Maybe not what you hoped, but good."

"No. Plague doesn't make next generation infertile, so in one generation population booms again, fast as ever, maybe more."

Slim is silent for a while. It picks up a set of mallets from the marimba nearby and inspects them closely.

"We're not going to last much longer, are we?" it says.

Jin shrugs. "Don't know. Maybe we'll find way. But if not, deaths won't be quiet and peaceful like Brat's movie. Starvation, industrial poisons, suffocation, painful disease; these aren't like manufactured plagues. Lots of suffering."

"So how were you going to do it?" says Slim.

"What?"

"Down there, at the party. How were you going to clear out that room and give it a sustainable population again?"

"Told you, wasn't going to," says Jin.

"Hypothetically," says Slim.

Jin tells it about the lemon bars.

"You really do have to get out of here, for your own sake," says Slim.

Jin nods miserably.

"I'm serious. There are going to be a lot of people coming in and out of the artist caves while we get this movie going, and there will probably be more soon who are coming to stay. We're effecting a major change in the world, and we're going to have to try to maintain some kind of control over it until people settle into the idea of neuts. I don't think you want to be here for that."

"Won't," says Jin.

"Are you going back to Home Cavern?" says Slim.

Jin shakes its head. There is nothing at Home Cavern except for ways to create plagues. It needs to figure out a new way to help, something other than birth control and heart attacks. In order to figure anything out at all, it needs to be moving its feet. The movie got the ending right after all. Jin is going back up top.

# CHAPTER 32

The surface cities look the same as always. There are fewer people on the streets, but buildings and wastelands don't die so the landscape stays the same from a distance. Jin wanders through Amarillo first, dressed in the style of a poor young man to deflect potential suspicion. The heavy pants are uncomfortably hot, but any ambiguity of gender might invite trouble.

At first, Jin wanders without purpose. It roams through familiar cities and towns, observing how they have changed, and how much they are the same. In San Antonio, a few neuts have become publicly known since the release of the film, but most remain in hiding, feeling safer in anonymity. This is true everywhere Jin wanders. Colorado Springs, Las Vegas, Tucson. Heat and wastelands, cities and shacktowns.

After many months, it can feel its brain chemistry change. The Soundwave songs still play occasionally, but its heart no longer races as the undertones pass through the air. Through lack of practice, its own brain waves have stopped sending the message that it's a killer. Without that, it has no idea what it is.

Towns still connect minor cities to major ones, with wastelands in the interior, away from the highways. Even in the mild spring weather the fumes are awful. By summer the stench in some areas will be deadly.

Jin stops every now and then in towns where people are working on improvements. Just like its character in the movie, it pitches in and helps remove garbage or fills in any manual labor jobs made vacant by recent deaths. That usually earns it a meal and sometimes a night or two in a vacant apartment. Clothing and supplies are easily restocked from the former belongings of the abundant dead.

In eastern Oklahoma, Jin watches an elderly man drag a little cart behind him and ask for clothing and toys from the dead. The sign on his cart says "redistribution wagon" in crayon colors.

"What's this?" says Jin.

"What it says. Redistribution. I take clothing, toys, anything useful from abandoned homes, take them to the surviving poor in other towns. No sense in perfectly good things going into the waste piles."

"Valuables too?" says Jin.

"*These* are the valuables. What good's a solid gold candle snuffer to someone without a shirt on his back?"

Jin sees his point and decides to do a little redistribution of its own, moving some of the better-quality abandoned items from town to town until it runs across someone who needs them.

Near dawn one day in the middle of Kansas, Jin enters a nearly deserted shacktown. A few kids run wild in the overgrown gardens, but everyone else is gone. The smell of rotting flesh and the sound of flies are overwhelming, but Jin pushes its way through the weeds into the center of the town. Something isn't right. There can't have been that many people affected by Soundwave in one small town. It chases down the kid who looks oldest and grabs him by the collar.

"You stay away from me!" he says.

He doesn't look older than twelve.

"Don't worry. Won't hurt you," says Jin. "What happened to all adults here?"

"You got eyes, man? They're dead."

"How? Plague?"

"Some of 'em. Then these trucks come through one night, about thirty people with torches and guns. They shot some, burned some, left the wounded for dead. It happens pretty often around here, only this time there were a whole lot more of them. I hid. Got my sister out safe."

Jin follows his eyes to the bushes off to their right until the boy realizes what he is giving away.

"She's far away from here now. Mostly just me," he says.

"Already saw others. Told you, won't hurt. You help find sticks for fire? Bodies won't stink and invite disease if we cremate."

"My mom said the diseases were all gone, except the ones people give you on purpose."

The other children creep in closer, trying to hide in the tall prairie grasses. Jin can hear at least two of them breaking the dried stems, and a third set of lungs from one who moves more quietly than the others.

"Not entirely true, and rotting bodies not good to keep even without disease. Besides, hereditary diseases probably never be cured," says Jin.

"What's hereditary?" asks the boy.

A little girl pipes up behind Jin, the set of lungs it had noticed earlier but couldn't see.

"Means your parents give it to you, only by accident."

"Shut up Jenny. That true?" the boy asks Jin.

"Close. Means parents or grandparents somewhere had disease in them, even if didn't show. Shows up sometimes in kids. Hereditary means passed on."

The boy nods. "We'll help. Ceelie, Jenny, go clear a fire space near the biggest pile of bodies. Jimmy, fetch dried grasses, much as you can find, no green ones." He turns back to Jin, "Sorry, no twigs. Maybe you noticed, we don't have trees."

Dragging the bodies is heavy, dirty work, especially trying to carry over those few who fell on the other side of the freeway. Most of the corpses are bigger than Jin, though there are a few dead children as well. They have to use the remains of most of the wooden and cardboard shacks to get the fire hot enough, but they do the best they can manage.

"What happened to other kids?" asks Jin.

"Kidnapped," says the youngest boy, Jimmy.

That makes sense in a way that causes Jin to wonder if it should just stop trying to save the human race. With birth rates down, people just might kill and kidnap in order to get children of their own. Or to sell them to the people who can't have them.

"What you kids going to do?" Jin asks.

"What we've been doing. Eat, stay alive," says Throm, the boy Jin first caught. The sister he mentioned is Ceelie, a six-year-old with big eyes and curly black hair.

"I came thinking to clean up towns like this, get rid of shell homes, let land go wild. You okay with that or should I leave?" says Jin.

"We haven't been using the houses. The people in the trucks might come back any time."

"Doubt," says Jin, figuring they have probably died in Soundwave by now.

"Them or others like them. There's always more," says Throm with a shrug. "You could take the houses and some of the other things if you want to. What would you do with them?"

"Don't know. If adults here, would have taken some to wastelands, used some for better disposal system. Can't do that alone."

"You've got the four of us."

"Okay. But safer to work at night, hide during day," says Jin.

Throm rolls his eyes. "Yeah, we already figured that part out, genius."

They load all of the usable goods onto wheelbarrows and one small farming cart, then drag them into the tall weeds out of sight from the road. There are one hundred shacks in the town, seventy made from plastic septic tanks. They break some of these down to patch windows that were cut into others, then dig deep holes for the thirty patched units and bury them in the ground with their openings just below the surface. During the day, they hide and sleep, taking turns at guard duty.

With Throm the only one over age ten, they are not strong enough to make major changes. Jin's goal is just to get everything compacted, out of sight, out of the way of growing things. It stores clothing and other items the kids might need in the second-cleanest tank. The cleanest is set up to catch rain water.

They pile any furniture they find by the roadside, as far as possible from where they live. Ceelie likes to sneak out to the furniture drop at dusk and report what has gone missing.

"Three chairs gone tonight. Only the one with the broken leg's still there," she announces.

For her seventh birthday, Jin gives Ceelie a knife found in one of the old huts. Most other weapons disappeared with the first attack or later when town appeared abandoned. Throm found three knives in his searches, so Jin gives him one of its own from the caverns, and they agree to give the younger kids each one for their birthdays.

Jenny's tenth birthday comes late in July. She chooses the serrated kitchen knife with a blade as long as her forearm. The next day Jin finds her burning ivy patterns into the wooden handle, using a piece of broken bottle glass to focus the sun.

"Where you see ivy?" Jin asks, "Doesn't grow here."

"I haven't always lived here. Before I turned four we lived somewhere with an ocean, and I had an ivy patch and some ferns I used to play in."

She finishes one side and turns the knife over, not caring if Jin watches or goes away. She is always like that, living in her own world but observing everything around her. She is the only one Jin can't sneak up on.

All summer they break down and bury the septic tanks. In the end, they still have ten left. All other waste is shoved down into the buried tanks and sealed over. That is the most they can do.

"You kids want to stay around here or find town and people?" Jin asks again as the days start growing cooler.

Throm catches the others by eye, and they all nod.

"We'll stay here. Thank you for the help, but we don't trust people in cities, don't see any reason to go get ourselves kidnapped or killed. We have food here. Jenny's been drying some beans and stuff for winter, and we'll have enough clean water from snow. As long as we can keep warm, we'll be okay. Thanks again for the help."

At this, Ceelie looks scared. "Are you really leaving us now, Jin?"

"No. Not yet. If you're staying, can help build home for you. Easier to survive cold. You want?"

They all agree. Digging takes most of the early part of fall, as Throm grows taller than Jin and fills out with muscle and the first few hairs of a mustache. Jin smiles as it notices his scent change. The younger ones gain strength too.

Jenny sends Ceelie and Jimmy out to gather seeds from grasses and wildflowers to spread over the old town site, restoring the land to prairie. She is in charge of the garden since she does best there, and Jin shows her some edible plants she hadn't known about before. When farming work is slow, she helps dig the house.

They go as deep as they can and set three of the leftover tanks into the earth. One common room, two sleeping rooms. Small tunnels connect the tanks, supported by pieces of plastic all scrubbed as well as possible with prairie grass and newly collected water. The house isn't comfortable like Home Cavern or the artist caves, but the kids will be safe enough there.

"Maybe we should have one more room," says Throm, "in case other kids find their way back."

After another week of digging, scrubbing, and burying, they have a four-room underground house with a slanting tunnel to the surface and several small vents for fresh air, some of which are closable to cut their heat loss.

"Use all blankets, extra clothes to keep warm," says Jin. "Use farthest disposal tank as toilet. Never make cooking fire in house. Could make toxic fumes with plastic, besides smoke danger."

"Yeah, we know," says Throm. "Keep the fire away from the road, as little smoke as possible. I was going to put dry grasses down one of the empty tanks to store until we need it. Say, Jin?"

"Yes?"

"Would you like to stay the winter with us? You can have a room to yourself. We all agree that you shouldn't travel in winter. This area can get pretty harsh."

"No. You only have enough food stored for selves, barely that. I have places to go for safety. Will stop by in spring, though, so stay alive. Okay?" says Jin.

"All right," says Throm.

All four of the kids hug Jin, insisting it spend at least one more day before moving on. For a chilly October morning, the little house is comfortably warm, and Jin falls asleep quickly. It awakens near dusk with a sense of peace and eagerness. It leaves before the kids get up, their good-byes already said.

The next town Jin enters seems fairly well off for a lo-loc community, though it wonders if a few of the kids might be from Throm and Jenny's shacktown. It leaves a pile of clothes on the courthouse porch for the poor. A woman catches it there and insists on giving it food and water to take into the next town. She also calls her neighbors, and soon Jin has more to cart to the next town than before, a walking rummage sale. It spends weeks like that, moving from town to town, helping with small repairs, cleaning, any job that will earn it a place indoors on a cold night. It still has most of the money forced on it by Pelin and Slim, since it only buys an occasional meal. Everything else, it earns through work.

It hardly ever thinks about the money anymore. At first it considered leaving some for the kids, but they can't buy anything in the middle of the prairie. Going into a nearby town would probably get them kidnapped, or killed if Soundwave's effects faded.

But it could buy something for them. Dried food or more seeds for Jenny's garden. It opens up the hidden pocket in its pack, feeling for the lump of folded cash. It pulls the money out, along with a small scrap of unfamiliar textured paper.

Dear Jin,

Yes, I'm a snoop. We wanted to send you off with a surprise, so I figured your pack was a good place. Thanks for not using your money on us. Throm was mad for a bit but I figured you were saving it for something or someone else since we never saw you use it for yourself. Besides, the work we did will probably let us live longer than a few bought meals ever could.

Here are some seeds from the garden, carrots mostly, a few others. Spread them around to the other people you'll help. They might not have any to start with.

Be careful, be safe, come see us in spring.

Love,

Jenny and the Shacktown gang

# CHAPTER 33

"You're really not going home," said Sandy.

It wasn't a question anymore. The words were hardly even words, more like rocks piling up between them, as thick as if the miles of limestone already separated them where they stood.

"I am home, Sandy," said Nick quietly.

They stood in a small cavern about an hour's hike away from the artist caves. Sandy remembered the feeling of comfort she used to get from the wild caves between the traveled paths of Home Cavern, and she wanted to sit down and lean back against the rock, absorbing the cold comfort the limestone's solidity gave.

This wasn't a conversation that was meant for comfortable sitting.

"I know you love this place, but how will you work, down here? You have a whole life above. And sunshine," she said. *And me.*

Nick reached toward her as if she had spoken that last aloud, and she shivered. He was practically like a neut now, uninterested in anything but the occasional touch, able to read her emotions from her face as clearly as if she spoke them. Slim had told her that anyone with half a brain and an open eye could do that, but Nick's perception unsettled her. Young men were supposed to be slaves to their hormones, not keenly perceptive and contemplating a monastic life among the stones.

"If you want to leave me, then leave me. Just don't use this place as an excuse," she said.

"You have everything backward. I don't want to leave you, but I need to be here. I'd almost forgotten what it was like to want to do something, to be excited about a project. Then you came along, and I wanted you. Now I want this," he said.

"But not me, anymore."

"That came out wrong." Nick's hands twitched as if to reach for her, but he kept them still.

"You don't love me," she said.

"I don't know. Really, Sandy. I don't—"

"—know. You said that. You don't want to hurt me—you said that too. Damn it, half of me wishes you were just a heartless bastard who was dumping me for someone younger or prettier or nicer to you," said Sandy.

"No such person."

"You even sound more like a neut than a man."

At that, his eyes hardened. Ha, she had hit a nerve. Her triumph faded instantly as she saw the anger on his face. She didn't want to leave him this way. She had no stomach for hurting him, either.

"I'm sorry. I didn't mean that," she said.

"Yes, you did." He leaned against a wall. "Maybe you're right. Maybe I'm down here because I think life would be easier without you as a distraction."

He smiled to soften the words, and she smiled back. She knew quite well how to distract him by now.

"You won't stay with me," he said.

This was not a question either. As much as Sandy loved the neuts and the caverns, her life was meant to be lived in the sun and rain and wild press of humanity above.

"At least there aren't spreaders out there anymore. I won't have to worry about you dying in a plague," said Nick.

Sandy hugged him briefly and left, wondering how long it would take him to realize that he didn't belong among the neuts either. Not if he thought about the end of plagues with relief. Perhaps none of them belonged anywhere at all, not until they had carved out a place for themselves and made their own homes. The neuts had done that below, and she would come visit from time to time, but right now she had projects and prospects that were miles above her head, waiting for her to reel them in.

She lost track of Jin somewhere in Kansas. Work was coming in more frequently, although usually her days consisted of sitting around with a roomful of other extras, waiting to spend an hour on camera that would translate into ten seconds or less of finished film. If she was lucky. The work was easy, at least, and paid for a room that was temporarily all her own in a real house, plus an upgraded pocketscreen. She had four roommates, all females this time, though they were looking for another to share her room. She couldn't afford the doubled price much longer.

"She definitely needs to be female," said Mia, a waitress at one of the hi-loc restaurants. Sandy and the others frequently offered to take on Mia's chores for just a taste of the leftovers Mia brought home from work.

"Having a guy around here might spice things up," said Clea, another extra.

"No men. I'm the one who has to share the room," said Sandy.

"Not even if he's cute? If he is, I'll trade you," said Clea.

"No men," said Sandy. "Though it doesn't have to be a woman, either."

Clea looked at her in disgust, the others in confusion. She had made no secret of her involvement in the neuter movie when she moved in. She hadn't wanted to live with people who couldn't tolerate the idea of neuts in their midst. From the looks on her other roommates' faces, she could tell they didn't really believe neuts existed.

"Well?" she said.

The two remaining roommates, Diane and Lynette, looked at each other and shrugged. Mia pulled a halfheartedly resisting Clea back into the room.

"She can't stand to have a man in the house, but she'd share a bedroom with someone who's barely human," said Clea.

"You're the one being barely human," said Sandy. "Some of the best people I know are neuts. Practically all of them, in fact."

"Yes, we've all heard your Tom Liene and Heather Lancaster stories before. I still don't believe it. Are you sure Tom's not a man?" said Diane.

"I'm sure," said Sandy.

"What, did you hit on him and he turned you down?" said Clea.

Sandy just gave her a cold look. She'd been practicing that one, but Clea gave her the dead stare right back, and Sandy had to admit that the other girl's was better.

"Fine. It was just a suggestion. We'll find another girl. A neut would probably go crazy in this house anyway."

Clea snorted and stalked off. Sandy unfolded her new pocketscreen and went to her room. That was when she realized she'd lost Jin. It had only sent one or two messages to Pelin like it had promised, but although the Network had broken ties with the artist caverns in theory, Sandy still maintained contact with Net. The message waiting for her was unsettling.

> Our friend desires to lose itself, I think. There has been no word now in Colorado, Texas, or Oklahoma for seven days. With the loss of the medics, my contacts stretch no farther than that until east of the Mississippi or North of Interstate 90, and those I know beyond those points don't know our friend's face, for the most part. I'm afraid I can no longer help you in this, although I look forward to your updates from the world above. If you see it, tell it… just tell it that everyone here awaits the next chance to say hello.
>
> In gratitude,
> Net

A soft tap on her door interrupted Sandy's third review of the message. She shut the screen down, engaging the code to lock her files' privacy.

The tap on her door sounded again, slightly louder this time, and she called out "come in," not remembering whether she had left it unlocked.

Lynette came into the room, looking over her shoulder first and closing the door behind her. Sandy smiled at the shy girl. With her dark, curly hair and her slight roundness, Sandy often thought of her as a younger sister. One look at her face now told Sandy how wrong she was.

"Why say that? About having neuts here?" Lynette demanded.

"Because I meant it. I didn't realize you were one until just now," said Sandy.

"How did you know now?" it said.

"Well, for one thing, you talk more like one when you're upset. That's why you don't talk much, isn't it?"

"Easier with script. I can memorize, not forget the useless words. How else?"

"I guess I just never looked that closely at you before." Sandy squinted at it. "You pad yourself well, but there's just something about your face. Lancaster could probably show you how to do your makeup better. Half the time, I forget it's not a girl when it's in character."

Lynette looked mortified, which Sandy suspected was due to the idea of meeting Lancaster, not the comment on its makeup.

"Have you had any contact at all with other neuts?" said Sandy.

Lynette shook its head. "Didn't even know there were others. Not until movie. Doctors said I was wrong, tried to fix." It pulled down the collar of its shirt a little to reveal old scarring, stretched from growth. "Not padding. Parents paid for operation when I was fourteen."

"You poor thing!" said Sandy.

Lynette covered back up. "Other operations, too. And hormones. Stopped taking those years ago, mostly because couldn't afford. Now am glad. Head feels clearer. Feel like self."

"Can you ghost?" said Sandy.

"Ghost?"

She explained the procedure as well as she could, and Lynette's eyes widened.

"Used to do as child. Felt funny, so I stopped," it said.

"Would you like me to take you to meet some other neuts? Slim and Lancaster are out of town on a shoot, but there are a few crew members that I could introduce you to," said Sandy.

Lynette pulled away. "No!"

"Why not? If I had been…oh."

Her eyes dropped down to Lynette's augmented body and she understood. Still, the poor thing needed some help.

"I have a better idea. Come with me."

"Where?" said Lynette.

"We'll go see a friend. I hope he's home."

Lynette backed up into the wall.

"You'll be fine, really. Brat knows more about being in between neut and gen than anybody," said Sandy.

Lynette was still hesitant, but Sandy convinced it to come along. They were mostly silent for the long walk into the center of town, where Brat still insisted on surrounding himself with the densest saturation of humanity. Occasionally, Sandy whispered reassurances to Lynette in a voice only a neut could hear. She also called ahead to Brat, leaving a message that she had someone for him to meet, hoping aloud that he would be home by the time they got there.

They had to wait half an hour in his lobby until Sandy finally got in touch with him and he agreed to come right home. On seeing Lynette, he nodded to Sandy and ushered them both into his apartment. With casual hellos to his roommates, he took them into his room and immediately tried to set Lynette at ease. It took hours for the altered neut to become comfortable enough to even look at Brat, at which point he asked Sandy to give them some time alone.

"Are you okay with that?" asked Sandy.

Lynette still looked like a frightened child, but it nodded, and Sandy knew better than to mistake it for fragile and defenseless. If it trusted its instincts, it would do all right. The operations wouldn't have slowed its thought processes, and Brat could certainly teach it to take care of itself.

The words "trust its instincts" echoed in Sandy's mind. Slim had told her the same thing, but she hadn't been able to use that with Jeremy. Or maybe she had. Her instincts had told her not to trust him, and his reaction to Soundwave proved her right. But instinct was also why she sat with him and soothed him before leaving him to get on with her own life.

Her instincts now told her that Jin needed help. Somewhere out there, it was lost and alone, and as much as it might want things that way, there were too many dangers for one small neut to face every day alone.

She walked home quickly and locked her bedroom door behind her. Then she called up maps of the United States on her new screen, following the route reported by Net's contacts as Jin wandered north and east from the caverns.

"Oh, Jin," Sandy said to the walls of her room. "You went back there, didn't you?"

Of course it had gone back to St. Louis. Like a child who couldn't leave a scab alone, it was going to pick at that wound until it bled. She hoped it knew what it was doing. She hoped she was right about what she had to do.

She packed a week's worth of clothing and left money for bills with Diane.

"I'm heading to an out-of-town shoot for the next few weeks. If you guys find a roommate, tell her she can have the right side of the bedroom closet. Or if it's a guy, I'll take Clea up on that offer to trade."

"You're leaving right now?" said Diane.

Sandy hesitated. "In the morning. Sorry, I'm just hyped up to go. Has Lynette come back yet?"

Diane had a strange look on her face. "She just called. Said she tried to reach you, but you didn't pick up, and to tell you that your friend had offered to let her stay the night so she didn't have to walk home across town by herself."

"Good," said Sandy.

"Your friend is a guy, right?"

"What makes you say that?" said Sandy.

"Just the way she sounded. I've never known Lynette to even look at a guy before. She actually sounded excited."

Sandy grinned. "Then I'll let her tell you whatever she wants to say. If I'm gone before she gets back in the morning, tell her I'll call in a day or two."

"So what's the shoot?"

"Which shoot?"

"The one you're so hyped to go on that you have your bag slung over the shoulder of your pajamas," said Diane.

"Oh, that one. I'm not sure yet. I think it's some sort of action-adventure."

Diane laughed at her. "With you as the swashbuckling heroine, no doubt."

"I don't know how much swashbuckling there will be, but I'll play the heroine if anyone will let me."

Diane laughed, then sobered. "Be careful out there, Sandy. There are a lot of people out there who would love to take advantage of a girl like you."

"Like me?"

"Innocent. You may not be exactly naive—yes, I heard about some steamy affair with a crew member, and there are rumors he wasn't the only one—"

"I never—"

"It doesn't matter. You just give off this sense of young-and-innocent. I think sometimes you forget how vulnerable you really are."

*Never*, thought Sandy, but she thanked Diane anyway and crawled into bed. For the first time since the incident with Brat, she listened to the Soundwave song again, all the way through. She still was immune to the plague's effects, but she knew all too well that the fiercest kind of danger was the individual human kind. Just because there were fewer attackers out there now than there had been not too long ago didn't mean she didn't have nightmares sometimes of a cold henhouse floor and a view through the chicken wire of the look in her mother's eyes before she finally closed them for good.

# CHAPTER 34

Jin didn't mean to return to St. Louis, but once it stepped onto the shoulder of I-70, its feet never veered to the north or south. It carries nothing but itself and its old travel pack into the city on a too-bright February morning.

The snow, still clean, sends sunlight dazzling off in all directions. Flyers posted in several places, along with the city's electronic screens, advertise for the local volunteer relief corps. Jin goes to the listed address, but no one is there so early, so it rests on the porch to wait. This is the first city it has encountered with an organized relief effort. The place seems clean. No corpses rot in the streets to add their stench of decay to the city stink. Even the wasteland odors seem muted. Other than the sidewalks being emptier than on Jin's last visit, the city looks the same.

A redheaded man stomps up the steps past Jin, knocking snow off his boots.

"Can I help you?" he says.

Jin has to remind itself to return his handshake.

"This place to volunteer for relief?" it says.

"Sure is. Just give me a moment to get the place opened up. We don't usually have people waiting in line."

He unlocks the door and flips some switches, filling the room with light and a mechanical hum.

"It'll take a moment for that heater to kick in. Have a seat. Any experience with this kind of work?" he says.

"Yes. Been traveling around, helping where needed. Cleaning, building, cremation, anything."

"Not squeamish, are you?"

"No. Dead is just dead. Sometimes messy, nothing frightening."

"That's good. We take any help we can get, but a lot of people don't want to get their hands dirty. I'm sure we can use your experience."

"Haven't worked in organized effort before," says Jin.

"That's all right. Most of us haven't, until now. Just follow the directions of your volunteer coordinator and you'll do fine. There's a group run by a woman named Margaret meeting near the zoo this afternoon. They're cleaning out some apartment buildings nearby. Would you believe one of the buildings is completely empty?"

"All dead?" asks Jin.

There is no way Soundwave could have done that.

"About half. Some from the wave of heart attacks, then we had a bit of bad business with some vigilantes coming through. Most of them died just after killing the people who lived there."

"What about people not killed?" asks Jin.

"Mostly scared off by the violence, I think. They just moved out. I can't say I think it'll do them much good. Nowhere's safe anymore."

Jin is pretty sure he is right, despite Soundwave's effectiveness. "When does volunteer group meet?"

"One thirty. That ought to give you time to get some lunch first, if you like. We provide sack lunches for volunteers when we can, but it's usually a choice of peanut butter or peanut butter. There's a passenger stop right out front here where local delivery trucks will often pick up passengers for a little extra cash. I think there's a pet food truck that runs that route and usually has a few extra spaces. Good luck, and don't hesitate to let me know if you need anything."

Jin thanks him and leaves, ignoring the passenger stop. There is plenty of time to walk, maybe even enough to get a real lunch.

A little before one thirty, it joins a group of people gathered by the cardboard volunteer sign on the south side of the zoo. Most of them seem to be regular volunteers, with only two other first-timers besides Jin. One of the regulars is a neut. It hasn't particularly tried to disguise itself as one sex or the other.

Jin catches its eye and asks subvocally, "Safe to be neut here?"

The neut finishes its conversation with some of the gens, then comes over to Jin.

"I'm A.J. Margaret should be here in just a minute. You experienced?"

"Some," says Jin.

"Good. Looks like you can handle rough work." It faces away from the group and drops its voice so only Jin can hear. "People here mostly okay with neuts, but let them get to know you some before you tell. Be glad Margaret's daughter isn't coming today. She hates neuts."

"Plague deaths?"

"Yeah," says A.J.

"I'll remember," says Jin.

"Good. There's Margaret. The one in orange coat."

Jin shuffles to the back of the crowd as a familiar-looking older woman approaches.

"Hi everyone, sorry I'm late. Let's see, Randy said we had a few new people out here today, where are you?"

Two men step forward.

"Good to have you with us," says Margaret. "What are your names?"

"Marik," says taller, dark one.

"Lance."

"Hello, Marik and Lance. We should have one more. Don't be shy."

There is no backing out now. Jin takes a deep breath and steps to the front of the crowd.

"Hi, Mrs. Lewik."

Margaret's eyes widen. She glances guiltily over her shoulder, and Jin notices A.J. watching the two of them with narrowed eyes.

"Ji...Jen?" says Margaret.

The others resume their conversations quietly, leaving Jin and Shaney's mother some room to talk. Most of them still listen, pretending not to.

"I had no idea you were back in town," says Margaret. "Be glad Shaney isn't here today. I'll tell you about it later."

She leads the group across the street to the abandoned apartment building, delegating jobs as they go. New volunteers are paired with the more experienced help, which Jin suspects is to discourage thieves as much as to teach the newcomers what they need to know.

"Janice, I think I'll take Jen with me today and let you work on the third floor by yourself. Jen, we're fourth floor, sort and sweep," says Margaret.

For a while she works in silence, and Jin follows suit. They sort the leftover clothes by condition and pool any money and "valuables" for donation to the appropriate charities. Furniture is sorted by condition for donation or recycle and nonperishable food items are boxed for the food bank. Too much of the food has already perished, so they pack it in compostable containers. The tenants from the first apartment they clean evacuated rather than dying there, so there isn't much left except rotting food, stink, and dirt.

"Do clothes go straight to poor or resold?" asks Jin, hoping to find a safe topic.

"Children's clothing is all donated to needy families, free of charge. Some of the nicer clothing is sold at low prices to raise money to assist other poor people. Same with the valuables and furniture. The food is donated, of course."

"Adults might need free clothes too, especially coats. And blankets," says Jin.

"They get blankets at the shelter. That's where most of these will go. We tried handing coats out there too, but people wouldn't take them."

"Pride?"

"Pride," says Margaret, her tone an unreadable mixture of emotions.

She starts scrubbing the kitchen, her back to Jin as it sorts through the cabinets. At first, Margaret's sponge cuts sharp streaks in the accumulated grime. After a while, the dirt just smears.

"Jin, why are you here?" she says, dropping the gendered form of Jin's name now that no others are around to hear.

Jin consults the top of a cereal box for an expiration date. "Don't know. Set out helping shacktowns I saw on interstate after last trip. Road leads here."

"Shaney blames you personally for Jason and Dale's deaths, you know. And everyone else she's known who died. What did you tell her when you two were together?"

"Some truth, some fiction. She's right. My plague did kill Jason and Dale. Didn't know during spread, of course," says Jin. Margaret doesn't seem to have trouble following its stilted speech patterns, so it relaxes into the conversation. Maybe she remembers the way Jin spoke as a child, before the teasing began.

"Oh," says Margaret, the most she can manage at the moment.

"Wouldn't have mattered, though," says Jin, hoping that Margaret will turn around and look at it again. "Can't let personal feelings get in way, no matter how hard. She might be right about other deaths, too. She didn't know when I left."

"No. She started getting suspicious about all the heart attacks, but it was after she saw that movie about you that she became convinced. Why did you let them use your real name in that thing? You're smarter than that. I always thought you were smarter than the whole lot of us, though you're doing your best to prove me wrong. You should have used a pseudonym, at least."

"Figured time for lies was past. Lied to Shaney, sorry about that. Told her I didn't kill."

The sponge stops moving, and Margaret stands perfectly still. Jin can ghost her breathing, but no more.

"Why, Jin?"

"Didn't think truth would help. Not trying to hurt her, just wanted to help."

"This is helping, Jin, this work right here. Getting your hands dirty and ending up with something clean, not streets filled with bodies, mass cremations, funeral bells every day. Not my daughter on my doorstep at midnight with her husband and son dead, another son half dead in her arms. How could you think that would help?"

Jin wonders if it should have Brat make a flyer, maybe another movie, so it can stop needing to convince people of the danger that is in front of their faces if they would just stop hiding behind their fears and do the math. Can't they smell the bacteria in the water, feel the wastelands pressing in?

"You saw movie. Don't kill anymore. Promised only constructive help for now, like Brat says. Made promise for people I care about," says Jin. Pelin wouldn't let it go up top without making that promise.

"But you don't believe in it?" says Margaret.

"I feel pain when friends die, too," Jin says softly.

"But you do kill them anyway."

"Don't expect you to condone, but plagues help survivors live longer, better. Rather have million humans die, including self, than watch whole race go insane. Soon we'll kill each other for last scraps of food, clean water, air, maybe just because we can."

Margaret finally turns to Jin, her eyes full of sadness rather than hate.

"Yet some of us prefer even an insane life to none at all. Oh, Jin. I can see how earnest you are, how honest. But I just don't think the world is ready for you, honey. Stay retired. And stay away from Shaney. She's wary of all neuts, but you she hates with a passion," says Margaret.

"Yeah. Other neut in group said she won't stay if it's here."

"Poor A.J. It's a wonderful help. Decisive, and a strong worker. But I always have to schedule ahead of time so it and Shaney never work the same shifts. Hand me that clean sponge, will you? This one's no good anymore."

She climbs a stool to clean strange colors off the wall near a high cupboard.

"Sorry about your grandson and son-in-law," Jin tells her. Ghosting reveals some anger, but mostly a sensation Jin can't quite name. Margaret notices Jin watching her.

"I don't hate you, Jin," she says. "I don't understand you, and I'd rather not think about what you just said, but I don't hate you. I can't."

Compassion. That is the sensation Jin feels.

"Don't understand me, but understand why I did?"

"It's not something I can understand. But I know you aren't what Shaney thinks you are."

Jin isn't ready to hear what Shaney thinks of it.

"I just want—"

"Jin, the world isn't going to care how many times you explain yourself, or how well you do it. The next several generations are going to remember your name as the thing that could have killed us all."

"Yeah," says Jin. It's still learning that, still trying to understand that point of view. "But I do help now, several towns. Kids and adults now have chance of living better because of my help. Even if some hate me, can't hate that," says Jin.

"Maybe not, but they won't trust it. I don't trust it. If you believe you need to kill all these people, how can you also help them survive? It doesn't mesh."

"That's because when you see my work, you see corpses as end result."

"You don't see corpses?" asks Margaret.

"I see those alive having opportunity for better life. Even if homeless or hopeless now, future generations benefit."

"You're right, I don't see that. Oh, I see the logic in it, but human beings don't operate on logic alone."

"Know. Don't understand why people don't just look around, see world, limit selves to one kid per couple. I've read all explanations, still don't understand. Not built for, maybe."

Margaret gives a short, humorless laugh. "No, I guess you aren't built for it. But even those of us who are don't really get it.

But you can cheer up a bit. I read in the paper the other day that our national birth rate is down about fifty percent."

Jin packs its boxes in silence. Margaret turns to look at it, her rubber-gloved hands on her hips.

"Oh, Jin, you didn't." She stares. "You did. Jin, this has gone way beyond too far! Get this through your head right now: you are not in charge of other people's destinies. Not mine, not Shaney's, not some stranger across town, and certainly not the entire human race. Damn it, Jin, your so-called helping is nothing but interfering with people's lives. If you can't understand that, then maybe you need to just find a private place somewhere alone while you let the rest of us live in peace."

"Padded cell, you mean," Jin says.

"Something like that," says Margaret.

The work continues in silence for a while. Jin doesn't understand gens at all. They say they want to improve their world, but they want to stop anyone who is trying to help.

When Margaret's intense scrubbing finally slows a little, Jin tries again. "You see what's going on in world, Mrs. Lewik. Margaret. I know you see. If could help, what would you do?"

"What I did do. What I am doing."

"Cleaning buildings? Sorting donations?"

"That's what I do now Jin, because I can. It's not my whole life. I limited myself to one child. I hadn't planned on having any, really. But Shaney came along, and Van and I raised her as best we could, never had another. Like your parents. They never had any others but you."

"Thought maybe they were afraid to have another like me," says Jin.

"Your parents didn't understand you but they did love you. I know both your parents cried for days after you left. Eventually, they settled into it. We all knew you could take perfectly good care of yourself."

"They still alive?"

"No. They moved to Florida a few years after you left. Both your mom and dad died in a terrible hurricane, trying to help a couple who couldn't find their way to a shelter."

Jin tries to picture the parents it knew out in a hurricane. It can't.

"I guess saving humanity from itself is just in your blood," says Margaret. "Come on, we have thirty more rooms on this floor alone, and at the rate we're going we won't get even two more done before dark."

Storm clouds move in around four o'clock and completely cover the sun, plunging the building into twilight. The smears and stains all blend together in the darkness.

"I guess we'd better gather the troops," says Margaret.

Jin joins the rest of the crew in carrying box after box to the curb. The few lanterns and flashlights among them are set to light the stairwells, making the building feel cavernous and comfortable. The smell of dampness in the cold air adds to Jin's feeling of being at home.

"Okay, stuff for the shelter goes in the rental van, thrift store goods get split between Kien's wagon and Leroy's truck. Anything that won't fit we'll lock in the manager's office until tomorrow," says Margaret.

Jin hands off boxes to the truck loaders; it feels the temperature drop. Leroy loads and unloads the truck twice, trying to fit more than physics will allow. Apparently this is nothing unusual. People smile indulgently and help him unload, then tell Margaret good-bye and whether or not they'll be in tomorrow. Leroy is stuck doing the third reload alone.

"Need hand?" says Jin.

"Nah, I like doing it better myself. I've got a system."

His system seems to consist of standing back, nodding to himself, repositioning each item twice, then more nodding. In the end, the truck holds less than the first time. Jin takes the leftover chair and box into the building manager's office and picks up its pack.

"Were you planning on coming in tomorrow? Or any other day?" says Margaret, looking up from her inventory.

"If not problem, sure."

"Shaney never comes in before three because of school. I guess you could come any day as long as you're out of sight by then. She's scheduled in for the rest of the week."

"School? Teaching again?" says Jin.

"Yes, though she now carefully avoids telling people why she went back to it." Margaret rubs her eyes and stretches. "I guess I wish you were all bad, Jin. Then I could just hate you like she does. Instead, I have to see the good you've done her, and the help you are here and probably other places I've never heard of. You overwhelm me. And then I think of the little kid you were, how close you and Shaney were for that little while."

"She was good friend," says Jin.

Margaret shakes her head. "Go home, Jin. Go wherever you're staying the night. Show up tomorrow or not, your choice. I hope you'll understand if I just don't want to think about you any more tonight."

The next day, Margaret puts Jin with some other workers, and the day after that on its own. Sorting clothes and scrubbing sinks leaves plenty of thinking time, and Jin finds itself thinking about its parents more than it would like. Jin tries to concentrate on the cleaning, but it can't help hearing the sounds of the city around it and the people talking and moving on the other floors of the building. Too many people. Not yet, but soon. Another generation. At a quarter to three in the afternoon, it leaves by the side door just in case Shaney shows up early.

Jin decides to stay only a few more days, long enough to finish out its assigned floor of the apartment building. Spending money on hotels is too strange, but it doesn't feel right asking if it can stay in one of the apartments, and the other empty buildings around town have similar crews working on them.

This assembly-line cleaning is no good, anyway. It would rather sweat for days digging a home for children than scrub an empty building where only half of the goods they salvage actually get to the people who need them most. Too much is simply carted out to the wastelands and dumped, or worse, flushed down the drains.

An image of Pelin comes into Jin's mind, along with an ache in its throat. The sound of Slim's laugh, Brat's cruel-kind eyes. Sniffling cold air is no help. Jin returns to its hotel, which reminds it of the trip out through El Paso with Pelin. It misses the warm steam of the bath in the artist caves, the fresh taste of growing plants, and Cook's nourishing food. It even misses Keri's temper tantrums and the purity of Home Cavern. It misses Bruvec, always.

Lost. That's what the feeling is. Doesn't matter anymore what the next step is in humanity's great suicide attempt, because this time Jin won't do anything to counteract the self-destruction. And Margaret says *it*'s overwhelming.

Jin thoughts fall into dreams as it collapses on the hotel bed. It is talking to Rouelle, but Rouelle's answers don't match its questions. Keri forgives it but feeds it poisoned food. It detects the poison and chases through its body in search of the key to cancel death, only Keri didn't include a key.

The strangest part is that the dreams don't really feel like nightmares. Full of frustration, yes, but no terror, no fear of death or loss. It just wants understanding, but there is none to be found.

Jin wakes late in the morning, cramped and aching. It finds itself checking out of the hotel before realizing it has a plan. No more wasting time in St. Louis. It should never have come back. The answers aren't here, or if they are, Jin can't find them. It decides to stop by the apartment building on the way out of town, just to say good-bye. It owes Margaret that much.

She is knee-deep in books when Jin arrives, stacking them in piles around her. Library, shelter, thrift store, and any that teach practical tasks in a separate stack for the volunteer corps. She pushes away the gray hair that has fallen into her face and looks up. Jin is disappointed to see that its presence makes her nervous.

"Hi, Jin. You're early. I was just about to go over to the zoo and gather up the volunteers."

"Just want say good-bye. Thanks for letting me help."

"We let everyone help."

"Didn't need to let me."

She puts down a book and looks at Jin steadily.

"I do hate a part of you, Jin, but I know there's more to you than that part. Sometimes—"

She stares past Jin. It knows a woman is approaching, but had figured she was just another volunteer. From Margaret's look, Jin can see that it won't get out of St. Louis quickly and quietly this time.

"Mother, what is that *thing* doing in here? I knew you were letting some of them help, but this is too much. Jin, get the hell out of my city."

Jin can't help smiling, thinking of the time it heard those same words before, yet later the one who said them had become an ally, even a friend. Shaney doesn't appreciate the smile. She shoves Jin down the hall with surprising strength. Jin tries to block the blows without hurting her, but it is used to fighting for its life. Passive defense is harder than it expects.

"Stop, Shaney. Was just leaving," says Jin.

"Damn right you're leaving! Cut to bits in a box if I have anything to say about it!"

She continues to slap and punch, but weakly. Sobs ruin her aim. Jin accepts a few bruises on its arms, protecting the important parts until Shaney wears down. Margaret motions Jin aside and gathers Shaney into a hug.

How can gens enfold each other so easily? The embrace looks awkward and uncomfortable. Just watching makes Jin's skin crawl. Only through ghosting can it understand a glimmer of why they need this, but it prefers its own methods of contact, the feeling of Bruvec's, Pelin's, or Slim's fingertips on its arm, sending the faintest warm tingle of comfort.

Margaret talks quietly to Shaney, crooning with comfort, trying to convince her daughter that Jin is still a human being. Shaney turns.

"But you still don't get it do you? Even though you've stopped killing people, you just don't see that what you were doing is wrong. You are the closest thing to pure evil I have ever known."

Jin is shocked, and lets the feeling show. It knows people think that what it does is wrong, but evil? Evil is something so remote, so far from human that it is incomprehensible.

The tears startle Margaret and Shaney only a little more than Jin itself. It stands in the doorway, head down, two tears escaping to spot the dust on its shoes. Like talking to Rouelle in the dream, it speaks a different language from Shaney, carrying on a different conversation. Only proximity makes them look like they are talking to each other. Jin turns around, not wanting them to see its pain, even knowing that they can't and wouldn't ghost it and take the pain into themselves.

"Don't worry," it says. "Won't come back."

"It's bad enough just knowing you're out there somewhere," says Shaney.

"Hush, Shaney," says Margaret, pulling her daughter back into her. "Even if you hate it now, you were friends once. Jin, haven't you done anything really good with your life? Tell Shaney. Anything. Don't leave her haunted."

The request is put mildly, but when Jin turns back around, Margaret's eyes are pleading for it to rescue her daughter. Jin sets its pack down and reaches into a pocket.

"One thing, maybe. Maybe you won't like, but can't hurt you."

It opens its hand and pulls back an oil-proof cloth to reveal a purple crystal. The color isn't quite right. Too much exposure to daylight has washed out some of the vibrancy, but the rock is grown from the same chemicals as the crystals in Ocean Cave. It holds the crystal out to Shaney.

It had decided not to use the pleasure-inducing chemicals in the infertility plague, not wanting to drug people into submission. But the experiment in controlled tactile mood enhancement was a success, and it keeps one crystal in its pocket just to know it can have access to the crystal's pleasure if it needs to. Some odd notion of touching it in its last moments if it dies on the trip, just to make Sandy happy if its body is ever found.

"So you found a pretty crystal. Big deal. This makes up for death and destruction? You aren't worth the skin you drag around," says Shaney.

"Touch," says Jin.

Shaney looks from Jin to her mother, but Margaret's face is simply waiting. Jin holds the crystal steady until Shaney reaches out, hesitating slightly just before she touches. Jin wonders if there is something inherent in the crystal's properties that causes the hesitation. Maybe someday it will be able to study again and find out. Shaney finally touches the rock, then shrugs and pulls her hand away.

"So what?" she says.

Then her face shifts with confusion, as if she is listening hard for some tiny internal sound.

"Let me see that again," she says.

Jin still holds the crystal outstretched in its hand. Shaney strokes a clear purple facet.

"That's amazing," she says quietly.

She won't look Jin in the eye. When she finally pulls her hand away, her eyes are closed and her face more relaxed than Jin has ever seen. It offers the crystal to Margaret. She glances at Shaney, then puts out her hand. Slowly, with only the slightest pause before contact, she caresses the crystal with delicate strokes, like a child trying to pet a ladybug.

"Did you make it somehow?" asks Margaret.

Jin nods.

"How can that be? Does it affect everyone this way?"

"You used to help me grow crystals when I was a kid, Mom," says Shaney. "Remember? Charcoal and bluing or something like that."

"Much the same," says Jin. "Different chems, though did some experiments with charcoal. Artists grew long time ago in place near where I live. Phosphorescent room with crystals and glowing lichen. I analyzed chems, created own version."

"So you're a scientist now, too. Great," says Shaney, the peace of the crystal wearing off quickly. "I still say 'so what?' That's a nice crystal, it makes people happy. So you go around and give one to every person whose friends and family you've killed, then what? Do you think they want to be mindlessly serene? They want their families back!"

"Crystal isn't cure, isn't apology. You wanted to see something good from me. That's all. Crystal is good," says Jin.

Shaney and Jin stare at each other, not speaking. After a while, Jin shrugs and turns away, lifting its pack to its shoulder. "Shaney, hope you give A.J. chance. It's not me, no need for hate. Have good life, best you can. Won't come back here, ever."

It walks down the stairs and out the door, trying not to, but straining its ears anyway, hoping that Shaney can forgive it, at least enough to say good-bye. The farewell comes from Margaret, instead. Her whisper is so low Jin knows the words are not intended for Shaney's ears, maybe not even for its. It whispers back, knowing she won't hear.

"Good-bye. Thanks."

It doesn't know what it is thanking her for. Listening, maybe. Letting it help. Treating it as human. Jin leaves the whisper trailing behind as it steps back into the grainy city air and, step after step, leaves its childhood home one last time.

# CHAPTER 35

Three weeks of searching turned up nothing, and eventually Sandy had to go back to work. While she was on set, she constantly searched the newsdrops and her limited Network access for any sign of Jin. She started taking any days off she could afford to head down to the artist caves.

Lynette asked Sandy if it could come with her on her next trip below.

"Of course! Are you sure you're ready?"

"Ready as you are," said Lynette.

"I doubt that. I've been dying to go since the last time I got back. I just wish there was news, or something I could do."

"Not entirely true." Lynette's eyes held level with hers.

"I've been subvocalizing, haven't I?" said Sandy.

"Little. And scent changes."

Sandy flushed a deep red, trying to remind herself that Lynette couldn't help noticing the things it noticed.

"Want to talk?" it said.

"Not really," said Sandy, "but since I can't seem to help myself, you'll get an earful anyway. Let's go somewhere else."

They walked outside for a few blocks in silence. Sandy led the way through neighborhood streets that were once a state park, stopping only when they got to the place where the Popo Agie River cut through the town in a defiant statement about the forces of nature. The water crashed loudly over its shallow bed of rocks, but Sandy was certain that Lynette could hear her.

"You smell Nick on me, don't you?" she said.

"Smell man," said Lynette.

"Normally, we're not like that. Every time I go down there, everything's strange and awkward and we agree to be friends. I've even dated a few other guys, which Diane obviously heard about somehow, but I need to be with someone who knows about neuts. I'm just no good at secrets."

"Kept mine," said Lynette.

"And I will, still. I keep others, too, some of which you'll probably learn when you go down there if Brat hasn't told you already. But I hate not being able to talk to the people I'm close to, and I have too many secrets to be close to anyone I don't already know I can trust. If that makes any sense at all."

"Does. Some."

Sandy laughed a little, but, to her own ears, the sound fell flat.

"You remind me a little of someone," she said.

"Neut?"

"Jin."

Lynette stopped walking. Sandy looked back at it, waiting for an explanation, but it was silent, and in the overcast day she couldn't read its eyes.

"You think I'm like killer?" said Lynette.

"That's not what I said. Jin is...I miss it. That's why I keep going back down there, not for Nick. It's quiet, like you, and gets right to the point. That's all I meant by that."

Lynette continued walking again, and Sandy kept pace beside it.

"You still want to know about me and Nick?"

Lynette nodded.

"I don't know if I can describe it. A gen thing, I guess. When you were taking the hormones, did you ever feel that kind of attraction to a person that seemed almost irresistible, like your brain was flooded with signals telling you 'this is the one, this is right,' and even if you knew it was biochemical soup, you still wanted to be with that person, to see if maybe it was more than just biology making you feel that way?"

"Hormones made me feel confused. Sounds like not as confused as you."

"Maybe not. But that's what happened when I was down there last time. I don't know if this time will be different, if we'll stand there embarrassed or run to each other or maybe pretend the other doesn't exist."

"Sounds complex. Maybe someone should make anti-hormone; help gens be less confused."

"Don't even think that, or someone's going to lynch you. I'll take the confusion any day—and the hours to gripe about it later. It's funny. I understand being female pretty well, and I think I understand neuts, but I don't think I'll ever understand men."

Lynette looked up at the sky. "Getting dark."

"Nothing ever really gets dark around here. Just wait until I get you into one of the wild caves with the lanterns shut off. Then you'll see darkness."

"Maybe," said Lynette, and Sandy thought she saw it shiver.

She wondered if it was going to back out of the trip after all. It had already threatened to, several times before. If it did again, she wouldn't force the issue. She looked out across the twilight as they made their way home, looking forward to the long climb through the darkness and the warmth and light at the end of that climb. As always, she hoped to find that one familiar face among the neuters gathered there, the one person she trusted to say exactly what it thought, nothing less or more.

To Sandy's mild surprise, Lynette didn't back out. She coached the neuter through the dark passageways, grateful that the route they were taking didn't require any of the tight, wriggling crawls that dotted the path from White's City to Home Cavern. Lynette seemed okay with the darkness and depth, but Sandy suspected it had a mild case of claustrophobia.

Slim greeted them before they got to the green room door, and Sandy gave it her now-customary brief hug. Lancaster was just inside, munching from a plate of wilted vegetables and not looking very happy about it.

"Any news?" it asked her after she introduced Lynette around.

"I was hoping you would have some," said Sandy.

Lancaster shook its head and offered the plate to Lynette, who simply gawked.

"You mean you didn't tell her who I was?" said Lancaster.

"I did," said Sandy, elbowing Lynette to close its mouth.

"Sorry. Just...didn't really believe. So many neuters here."

The others laughed. There really weren't many around at the moment, just the usual gathering of musicians and artists, plus a writer or two sitting alone.

"They're usually nocturnal," said Sandy nodding at the latter in a stage whisper.

"How you tell, down here?" said Lynette.

"Technology," answered Slim. "Come on, I'll show you around. Sandy, there's someone over there who wants to say hello."

Sandy looked around, expecting to see Nick. Instead, a neut with thin, limp hair pulled back into a ponytail, wearing almond-shaped glasses beckoned her over.

"Yes?" said Sandy.

"Heard you're famous actress now. Should have been artist's apprentice. Such waste," it said.

"I'm hardly famous, and I'd make a lousy artist, I think. I can barely draw a stick figure."

"Not draw, sculpt! Of course, might talk too much."

She looked at the neut more closely. "En?" she said.

It looked over the tops of the glasses. "Took long enough."

"En! I hardly recognized you with the long hair and glasses, not to mention the light. So, have you made any convincing fake rocks lately?"

It shook its head. "Just thought you'd want to know—company abandoned project. We had to change cavern route two more times, then scientists decided rocks were unstable and went looking somewhere else."

"Good. At least you won't be making friends with tanks of toxic goo anytime soon," said Sandy.

"More worried about gens than waste," it said.

Sandy caught a flash of a familiar figure out of the corner of one eye. She turned her full attention to En, hoping it wouldn't notice how her blood pumped faster and her stomach seemed to creep upward toward her throat.

"Why don't you show me what else you work on?" she said. "I'm sure you do far more interesting sculptures than a passageway full of altered rocks and scent-absorbing dust."

"Rocks interesting too," it said, but it seemed happy to lead her out into a section of the tunnels she had never been to before.

She kept track of the path as well as she could, but forgot all about that when she stepped into the sculpting studio.

The studio took her breath away. One entire wall was carved into human forms—male, female, neuter, and combinations of the three. The rock was polished smooth and glazed with a color-shifting finish that took on warm or cool hues depending on how the light hit it. Not until she was standing quite near did she realize how huge the figures were. Nearly twice the size of real humans, they towered over her with such perfect proportion that they might have been cast from live models of giants.

"Now I know I could never have been your apprentice. This is amazing," she said.

The rest of the work in the room was equally impressive. Clay, metal, and glass sculptures of all sizes were set where a person could walk around them, viewing from all angles the shapes and shadows of the forms. Side caverns held the works in progress of many individual artists. En showed her its own, an abstract of sharp angles jutting out of deceptively smooth curves.

"Called 'Jaws of Our Time,'" it said.

"It's beautiful."

"Everything's beautiful down here," said a male voice.

"Nick. You followed us," said Sandy.

"You avoided me," he said.

"Thank you," she said to En.

It bowed its head slightly in acknowledgment and gestured her toward the entrance. It stayed behind while she walked with Nick, though she suspected it was probably listening.

"You keep coming back here. Why not just give in and call it home?" said Nick.

"I'm not coming back here for you, or this place. I'm coming for Jin," said Sandy.

"Jin isn't here."

"Not yet, but someday it will be," Sandy insisted.

Nick said nothing.

"You were the one who left me, remember?" she said.

"Not because of you," Nick reminded her.

"No. Because of you. Because of who you are. Maybe you really do belong here—you look good, and you seem happy. But last time I was down here was a mistake. It shouldn't have happened," said Sandy.

"That's not true."

She stopped walking and looked at him. Reached out and touched his face, watching his eyes light up when she did. She hated to put that light out, but she had to, once and for all.

"I'm sorry, Nick. You're right, I'm glad we had one last night together. But it's over. We live, literally, in different worlds. I'm moving on. You should too."

He pulled away and walked into the darkness in silence. She tried not to feel too bad for hurting him and found that she really didn't. Mostly, she was just relieved. And somewhat lost, as well.

"En?" she called softly, then a little louder.

"Wasn't eavesdropping," it said, coming down the tunnel toward her.

"No, it's not that. Could you show me how to get back to the green room? I'm not familiar with this part of the caves."

It led her on a path that didn't look quite like the one they had come through before. When it ended in a dimly lit corridor near the living quarters, she understood. Nick had thought they were going back to his room, had been leading her there either unconsciously or consciously. Somewhere inside, she had known it too, as unfamiliar with this part of the caverns as she was. Maybe she was getting better at reading other people's emotions. Or maybe he was just following the well-established patterns of his brain chemistry.

At this point, it didn't matter. She turned toward the more populated areas, finding her way easily now that she was back in familiar territory. En disappeared somewhere behind her, but she hardly noticed. She couldn't keep coming down here, letting Nick believe that something more was between them. If Jin wasn't going to let them know where it was, she was just going to have to remind it where its friends were, and she had a growing idea of how to be heard.

# CHAPTER 36

The roads seem more barren as Jin leaves St. Louis. Dust kicks up with every step, and grass stalks break with depressing crunches under its sneakers. It feels a chill deep inside that the cold, hard limestone beneath the desert has never caused. Without a functioning mind to guide Jin's feet, they automatically head toward south and sun. It follows the Mississippi River as much as possible, foraging for food and hiding in the wastelands along the way, avoiding all human contact.

The heat and humidity of Louisiana finally make Jin's synapses fire faster, and it decides to see if Baton Rouge still has a public library. Perhaps there are edible plants native to the area it should know about, maybe even try out in one of the lo-loc restaurants. It hasn't touched its money in a very long time.

After half a day of wandering, Jin finds the library in a thriving lo-loc area with plenty of home and restaurant gardens. A familiar picture catches its eye as the public screens at the top of the library steps slowly scroll through the national news.

Shaney's hatred must have kept her memory sharp, since the sketch of Jin accompanying the news is little different from the face it last saw when cleaning mirrors in a St. Louis apartment building. Jin tugs its hair over its eyes and pulls its hat down tightly before stepping closer to read the scrolling text as it repeats.

Man? Hunt

Special Agent Simone Burwaltz of the FBI declared last Monday that the Bureau has decided to take official notice of the claims that the plagues which have erupted in

> our cities for the past century are the work of a group of genderless human beings, one of whom is still at large.
>
> Agent Burwaltz stated in a press conference earlier this morning that reports of this person appear to be correct, though analysis is still being made on the current threat to society. A warrant has been issued for the arrest of Jennifer Bronwyn Morales, commonly known as "Jin" or "Jin Bruvec."
>
> Fueling the FBI action is a St. Louis woman, Mrs. Shaney Lewik Anderson. According to Anderson, who knew the perpetrator as a child, "It has no morals whatsoever, and would as soon kill its best friend as its worst enemy."
>
> Mrs. Anderson allegedly received a visit from Jin earlier this year, in which the suspect confessed its crimes with no remorse. Margaret Lewik, Mrs. Anderson's mother, was the only other witness to this confession.
>
> "Jin is a very confused person, yet at times brilliantly intelligent. At this point, I think it is more of a danger to itself than anyone else," said Lewik.
>
> The FBI is offering rewards for information leading to the apprehension of this criminal. Contact Clark Severoud at the number below if you have any information that may lead to the apprehension and arrest of this dangerous suspect.

Jin considers taking its chances inside the library, but a few new edible plants aren't worth the panic that rises when it thinks of being trapped in a prison cell with gens so close they are living one on top of the other. It turns on the well-worn ball of its foot and heads away from the river and the city. Every public screen it passes on the way out of town seems to be showing its face, and only its overgrown hair and broad-brimmed hat protect it from the public cameras and passersby.

Far into the decaying garbage heaps, sheets of moss hang off the piles of refuse like shawls. Bugs create miniature storms at dawn and dusk. The warmer climate feels good on Jin's body, but its mind is cold and numb. It huddles with the bugs and discarded household items, the only way it can think of to avoid anyone who might be hungry for an FBI reward.

In spring, Jin returns to Kansas, hoping to find a welcome among the shacktown children. It approaches from the south, cutting through lo-loc farms and wastelands rather than following the highway. Bulldozer noises echo for miles across the prairie as Jin nears the site of the former shacktown. Work crews that rebuild towns don't have access to heavy equipment, not unless an area is slated for a new hi-loc development. Jin tries to picture one going in where the septic tanks are buried beneath the prairie. The sounds grow deafening as Jin gets closer, keeping low to blend with the swaying prairie grasses.

When it hears the shouts of the workers over the machinery noise, it drops to the ground and shades its eyes. This is no hi-loc division. Backhoes and hand shovels work together to excavate the earth, and trucks marked with the symbols for various types of nonrecyclable plastics wait to dump their wares as soon as the digging is finished.

Jin tries to find the chemical sensations of anger or sadness that these workmen are where Jenny's gardens should be. Mostly, it just feels tired and alone.

Again its feet turn south, this time to northern Texas. After two days in a lo-loc subdivision, a neut approaches Jin on the street. It's dressed like a man, but the build is a little wrong and it lacks the telltale scents of testosterone and androgen. Jin continues walking past, but the other stops and grabs its arm.

"Jin?"

Jin just stares back. It hasn't answered to its own name since leaving St. Louis.

"Aflin," the other neut introduces itself. "Helped you test plague once."

"Oh." Jin pulls the memory from deep within its brain. "Researcher, Sand's friend. Hi."

Aflin pulls out a pocketscreen, keeping a grip on Jin's arm. It begins entering numbers with a grim look on its face.

"Why?" says Jin.

"They get you, maybe rest of us go free, gens stop killing us," says Aflin. "You understand. Greater good."

Jin notices a scar on its forehead and cuts along the backs of its hands. It speaks into the screen, then uses the controls to snap a photo of Jin from the local traffic cameras. It waits, grip firm, as the faint music of a government hold function plays.

"Won't stop with me," says Jin.

"Maybe not. Why you care? Death no big deal to spreader."

But death is a big deal. For months now it has wandered, killing itself slowly, but the death of one former spreader won't even slow the inevitable at all.

"Won't let you do this," says Jin.

"Don't look like you have muscle left to stop me," says Aflin.

The pitches in the hold music are intended to be soothing, but they have the chords all wrong. Jin stirs its rusty vocal cords, completing the note combinations until it feels Aflin relax its grip.

Two years ago it would have taken the opportunity to run. Now, it won't get ten yards before the other neut catches up with it. Aflin is younger, stronger, faster, and in better health. And it knows what it is fighting for. Jin just has Shaney's voice in its head to drive it, talking about worthless skin.

"Hang up, Aflin," Jin says, then continues humming.

The smooth tones of a receptionist hang clearly in the dry air. "Thank you for holding. Am I to understand you have a positive ID concerning the whereabouts of a wanted criminal?"

"Jin Bruvec," says Aflin.

"One moment please."

There is one safe place left in the world for Jin, but the nearest entrance is hundreds of miles away.

"Please state the location of your sighting as specifically as you can," says the voice on the phone.

"Dalhart, Texas, outside of the Landry-Irons building on the northeast side of town," says Aflin.

"Are you certain that the person you've seen is the person wanted for questioning?"

"I've met it before," says Aflin. "I have photo confirmation if you can tell me where to send it."

"I'm Jin," Jin says into the screen in disgust. "And leaving."

It twists out of Aflin's grip, using brain power more than physical strength to stay ahead of Aflin through the maze of buildings. Parking garages are good for hiding but not with professionals coming after it soon. The FBI won't give up after looking under a few cars. Jin dodges to the right down an alley instead. Aflin doesn't have Jin's experience in sounding ahead, so it hesitates and stumbles while Jin gains a longer lead.

"Stop humming!" screams Aflin, and Jin hears the sharp echo off the last syllable. Dead end ahead.

"Sorry," Jin says, rebounding off the wall and running straight back past Aflin, knocking it to the ground harder than it would have liked in the process.

Politeness doesn't matter. Survival is key.

Tires pull up without sirens or lights, but the shearing sudden stop of a police car sounds the same anywhere. Jin hears every command, every footstep and question as they canvass the area and eyewitnesses point the way toward Jin.

Keep moving, one foot, then another. If the authorities were smart, they would seek out neut recruits to sound out criminals on the run. Jin wonders if Brat has found a way to distract people from that truth with other movies or his all-too-effective literature.

The gen nearest is a local cop, not a federal agent, and she's not much bigger than Jin. It contemplates pulling the same trick on her as it did to Aflin. She hasn't seen it yet, and it has enough strength. But a much larger male cop comes up behind her, gun drawn and pointing far too close to Jin's direction.

Jin is tucked into a space between the back of a building and a chain-link fence. It could climb the fence, but any sudden movements will rattle the links and send the cops running right to it.

The wind makes the decision for Jin, blowing up with the rattle Jin tried to avoid. Without consciously deciding, it hops the fence and drops into the thick weeds in the lot beyond, kicking over toys and cartons in the rush to get away. Only the incompetent hearing of the gens lets it make its escape, but now that they know it's in the area, Jin can't waste any time getting home.

By dawn, it begins to feel lightheaded. The only place to sit nearby is the doorway of an empty shop, but Texas has strict vagrancy laws, aside from the manhunt going on. It sits anyway, only because if it doesn't it will fall in the street. Its head hangs down and it tries to catch its breath, but its heart feels three sizes too big for its rib cage.

"Here. You need this more than I do."

A man, dressed for work, holds out a sandwich in front of Jin's face. A mechanic of some sort, judging by his uniform.

"No thanks. I have food," says Jin, trying to keep its face hidden.

"Then for God's sake, why don't you eat it? Look at yourself. You're about as big around as my little finger."

Jin smiles weakly. Its heart is still pounding too hard, and it will be sick if it eats now.

"Just need to rest first. Then I'll eat."

The man takes a bite of the sandwich himself. "This isn't the best place to rest," he says around a mouthful of bread and something that smells like bologna.

The smell nauseates Jin.

"They'll pick you up for loitering quick as anything around here," he says.

As if to prove him right, a cop strolls up.

"Is this person bothering you?" he asks the man.

"Nah, officer. My friend here was just feeling a little woozy and had to rest for a minute. We'll be continuing on our way in a sec, you'll see."

The cop glares at Jin. "All right. Consider this a warning, though. We don't tolerate vagrants here."

"I understand," says Jin, watching the cop's shoes for any tension that might indicate he recognizes it.

The effort of speaking takes most of Jin's breath. If the whole state is like this, it will have nowhere to sleep even if it has gotten past the FBI search perimeter. The wastelands are more than one day away in its current condition, and the money it has left isn't enough to stay in hotels all the way home, even if it dared to check in. When Jin's heart rate slows enough to eat, it pulls a package of crackers out of its pack.

"That's good," says the man, his sandwich finished. "You really ought to get some real food in you, though. Those crackers won't do much more than keep you alive. You ought to enjoy what you eat."

He pats his stomach bulge and laughs. Jin stands cautiously, still hiding behind its overgrown fringe of hair. Yes, its legs will hold. It lets its pace slow a bit once the cop and the man are out of sight and eats a few more crackers while walking. It should have enough money for a real meal and a good night's sleep in a hotel, and that may make the difference between arriving home alive or not at all.

There is no time to exchange work for clothing, so it picks out some thrift store items slightly less threadbare than its own and pads itself here and there to look female and therefore innocent, or at least more innocent that a neut looks to a gen. It has no practice with the current makeup styles women favor, but it does its best with the help of a magazine, then counts out the rest of its money. There is enough. It checks into the cheapest motel available, a kind of dormitory for travelers hoping to avoid the vagrancy police. They accept cash and don't require any sort of identification.

After showering and reapplying its makeup, Jin feels vaguely human for the first time since St. Louis. The padding is awkward, and the smell of the face paint makes its eyes water, but its brain is clear enough to notice the hunger ache. It looks in the mirror and sees a young woman, but not the daughter its parents would have wanted. The bones at its wrists and hands are far too prominent. Cheekbones, too, like a skeleton with a ghost costume on. Too many days of sun have made its skin leathery enough that no one would call it "kid" anymore. Still, it looks younger than most gens its age. And it looks nothing like the picture on the "Wanted" poster.

The pack will have to go. Jin didn't buy anything a girl could carry without drawing attention, but the money and some crackers fit into its pockets, and the rest of the necessities tuck into its shoes and socks. Traveling lighter than ever, Jin walks into a lo-loc restaurant and tries not to look over its shoulder.

"Just give a holler or a wave when you're ready to order. We're pretty casual around here. Heck, we even have a vegetarian dish," says the woman who seats it.

The sound system in the restaurant is up too loud, but the food smells wonderful. Jin orders a half rack of ribs, not caring if they're cow, pig, or camel, and settles into transferring the meat from the roasted bones to its own. Halfway through its meal, the owner pulls up a chair and asks how everything is.

"Haven't had food this good in year and a half, maybe," says Jin, trying to pitch its voice in the same range as the other females in the room.

The owner laughs, clapping Jin on the shoulder a little too hard, but it isn't exaggerating.

"Well, let me know if there's anything else you need," he says.

A feeling of overwhelming loneliness creeps over Jin as it licks the sauce from its fingers. It reaches for a napkin and pushes the plate away, noticing others doing the same thing throughout the restaurant. People wring their napkins, chew more slowly, or stop eating and look pensive. Even the cheerful waitress leans her chin on her hands at the counter. Jin can almost hear a voice, like a person speaking too far away to make out the words. Like the voice of a friend. It tries to place the sound, but the music is still too loud and gets in the way.

Jin forgets the other voice for a while and listens to the song. Organ tones like Rouelle's give the chords their melancholy sound. Guitars, bass, drums. Possibly Miko's drums. Jin can't tell. The singer is definitely female. Could be Sandy, could be anyone. It realizes it doesn't even know if Sandy sings. The lyrics could be any pensive rock ballad, but there is something too familiar, and once Jin tunes in to the music, the other voice in the background becomes clearer.

Subvocals under the music. Slim's voice, asking Jin to come home. Jin waves the waitress over when the song is finished.

"That song just on—how old, do you know?" asks Jin, then realizes it is neglecting to use gendered speech patterns. It hopes the waitress and the owner were both too distracted to notice and vows to be more careful.

"That's a good question. I know I first heard it driving my kids to school 'cause I had to pull the car over to find a tissue, and I never cry at some old sappy song. That was about three months ago, but unless it's a local band it could've been out a while before it even got into our mix. I'd guess it came out anywhere between four and six months ago, maybe longer. It is great, isn't it?"

Come home as soon as you hear us, Slim had said in the undertones.

Jin heads straight to the nearest local passenger pickup from the restaurant. No more nonsense about needing to walk. The costume would make lengthy foot travel nearly impossible. All of the traffic going toward Whites City has left for the night, according to a hand-printed schedule on a cardboard shipping box at the stop, so Jin memorizes the pickups for the next day and makes sure it has the customary amount of cash, then heads back to the hotel. Sleeping is hopeless. It paces the floor until the other tenants complain.

It can't do anything but wait. No use passing the time by thinking. It has been doing that for a year and a half with no results. The only important thing is to get home. If it were walking, it could be nearly two hundred miles closer by sunup.

No, those days are long past. It looks down at itself, knowing that under the nightshirt, the hard muscles in its legs are knotted around the bones with no padding of fat. In this condition, it would be lucky to get twenty miles. One good meal can't erase months of neglect. Sandy will be mad when she sees it.

Jin sleeps for two hours, finally, just as the sky begins to gray, then is up and at the pickup point long before the city is fully awake. It catches a ride on an electronic components delivery truck all the way to El Paso, sleeping fitfully for most of the ride home.

## CHAPTER 37

The short route from the surface to the artist caves is steep but easy to climb down. Jin relies on its ability to follow the signs of use and stay on the otherwise unmarked path that should lead it straight to the artists' kitchen. The route it took with Pelin would have meant less above-ground travel, but at least this way it can ask Cook for something to eat before getting caught up in greetings.

No one is in the kitchen, and no sounds reach Jin's ears from the green room beyond. The chemistry of fear drips into Jin's system as if injected from an external syringe. It races through the tunnels as silently as possible, keeping to the shadows.

Clothing and personal items are all sitting out as if waiting for their owners to return and continue some interrupted activity. Books are propped open midway through, artwork left out half finished. There are no signs of a struggle, but no signs of life. Every now and then Jin catches the lingering scent of gens. The female scent could be Sandy, but the male hormones are real, not just Brat's synthetic mix. The vibrational signature of human loss seems to echo from the walls, but that might just be in Jin's veins. There is no one to ask or to ghost and find out.

There is no time for sadness. It checks the recording studio in case anyone is hiding in the soundproofed room. The lights are on and music is out on stands, but there is no one home. At least Rouelle had time to cover its instruments before leaving. Jin slowly follows the tunnels back down to the kitchen.

The coolers are full of prepared hors d'oeuvres as if ready for a big celebration, and the food looks fresh. Blood beats heavily in Jin's throat. They can't be far ahead.

The fastest route to Home Cavern is through the auditorium. Jin slows to a creeping pace in the darkness of the backstage tunnels, gaining control of its pulse and breath. It should have realized this would happen. Too many people were getting to know the cavern's location. Secrets can't be kept forever.

A fresh gen scent hits Jin as it approaches the entry to the stage. Multiple gens. Men, women, even a few children. The strength of the scent says they are still nearby, yet everything is silent. There is no blood smell, no death smell, no stink of fear. Nothing except a soft hiss, like a hundred small winds blowing together. Breathing.

Jin peers through the back curtain onto the stage. The whole artist community is gathered on the floor, plus many people Jin doesn't recognize, including several gens. A few might be the gens it met at the screening, but it is sure at least a few of them are not. Everyone is amazingly silent and still. They form a huge circle around the stage, a candle in front of each seated figure. The small flames are the only light present, and they flicker slightly with the wind of all that breath.

Jin hesitates, not wanting to intrude on the unfamiliar ritual. Most of the people have their eyes closed, but the sound of Jin's irregular breathing distracts the neut just in front of it. It waves Jin in without looking and inches over to make room. The whole circle adjusts to compensate.

Jin feels awkward being the only one without a candle, but that can't be helped. Instead, it tries to settle into the group breath pattern, grateful its friends are alive and safe, even if they are acting strangely. It opens its eyes every now and again to keep from falling asleep. A few of the others seem on the verge of nodding off as well.

Pelin and Slim sit together about a third of the way around the circle. Three gen kids are next to Brat, straight across the floor from Jin. It squints against the shadows. Yes, they look like the shacktown gang minus Jenny. Jin can't help letting out a sigh of relief, but it controls its exhalation to blend with the pattern around it. At least three of them survived. It hopes Jenny is either happily tending a garden somewhere or peacefully dead, not living a life of abuse and pain somewhere above them.

The silence creeps on for half an hour. Jin settles into the comfort of darkness and friendship, feeling the residue of its earlier panic wash away. Someone will explain the ritual later. For now, being home is enough.

Finally, Brat lets out an audible sigh, and after a minute, three more. People begin to stir and the breathing becomes more scattered and fades into the background while sounds of shuffling fill the room. Some people stretch out their legs and backs, but still no one speaks. When the room returns to stillness, Brat takes his candle and stands.

"Thank you all for coming down here to honor our friend. While it may still be alive somewhere, we have had no response for so long that we fear the world has claimed the last member of a profession, a tradition, which may well have saved the human race several times over. Though many hate and fear the name of 'spreader,' those gathered in this room today know of the great compassion and unyielding strength in those who bore that name. We gather today to honor all spreaders; may they know the kindness of the rest they brought to many. May they who are hated and reviled by many accept the love and mourning of those few who knew, and who miss them."

A few people among the crowd with religion murmur 'amen' and other comments. Most just nod. Jin wonders when Brat started talking like a nutcase. This is the same person who left it to wander starving in the desert?

"Today we honor the spirit of one spreader in particular, the only one whose fate is yet unknown to us. Having had so much time elapse without word, I regret that we must accept the possibility that Jin, also, has found the only peace its soul may ever know. Jin, wherever you are, we send you our love. We miss you, and we ask that if you live, you return to us soon."

"Okay," says Jin.

It can't think of anything better, not that it would have had time for a speech anyway. The entire crowd swarms over.

"Watch candles!" shouts Pelin, beating a small flame out of Jimmy's pants.

"Lights!" says Rouelle.

The overheads come on, washing the stage in a glow that leaves everyone blinking and rubbing their eyes. Ceelie pushes her way through the crowd and inspects Jin carefully.

"Yeah, it's Jin. It's too skinny, though."

Sandy laughs and picks her up. Others press in closer, asking questions, touching Jin's shoulders, telling it how tired and undernourished it looks. The entire crowd drifts into the larger social room behind the green room, carrying Jin with them. Within minutes, Cook's food is piled high on the tables and disappearing almost as fast.

"So, how long have you been here, Jin?" says Brat.

"Not too long. Sat in circle for while. Nice speech, though some sounded familiar," says Jin.

"I may have borrowed a word or two from other sources, but only because I wanted the very best," says Brat.

"You'd make good salesman. Since when you like spreaders?"

"Since about six months ago when we still hadn't heard from you. Pel and I thought for sure you'd gotten yourself killed."

"No such luck."

"Come on, Jin. You know I'm not like that anymore," says Brat.

Jin looks carefully, but his eyes are sincere, and he seems genuinely happy to see it.

"Good to see you too," says Jin.

As soon as it sits on a couch, Pelin places itself on one side of Jin and Slim on the other. Brat and the kids take the couch across from them. Anyone else who can fit crowds around to ask questions and hear of Jin's adventures. There is not much to tell. It skims over the account of St. Louis without mentioning Shaney. Pelin's eyes widen slightly when it mentions the city, but it says nothing. Sandy elbows Brat, giving him an I-told-you-so look, which he ignores. Any time Jin stops speaking for even a few seconds, Slim or Brat shoves food in its mouth while Sandy keeps them in fresh supply.

"Okay, enough. Be sick if keep eating. Tastes great, Cook, but body isn't used to so much," says Jin.

Rouelle and several of the other musicians bring their instruments down and provide the party's entertainment. A few people begin to dance. Mostly gens, at first. The topside neuts join in after a while, then some of the locals.

"You dance, Jin?" asks Slim when it comes over to rest between songs.

"Trying to think. Maybe taught some dance in elementary school. Some folk kind, maybe. Never did after, so wouldn't know steps."

Slim laughs and gestures at the crowd around them. "This kind of dancing isn't taught, just felt. And fun."

"No," says Jin.

"You should try it sometime. You never know, you might actually learn to enjoy yourself for a moment or two. But wait until you have a little more meat on your bones, or Sandy will have to play nursemaid again."

Slim joins back in the dancing, twirling Sandy around and then letting her twirl it. Jin watches them mingle with the other neuts and gens, all swirling to the rhythms and pleasure-inducing tones. Pelin returns to join it in silence. Jin moves just enough for Pelin to ghost it, and after a few moments of shared being, Pelin leans back, satisfied. Throm works his way through the crowd to join them, with Ceelie and Jimmy not far behind.

"Jenny's dead," says Throm.

Jin nods. "How?"

"Some guys drove by one day, stopped their car to take a leak or something and wandered into our field. Jenny was out pulling weeds, and I guess she figured that getting the garden ready was more important than hiding. They saw her and decided she was just about old enough to look good."

Throm's lip curls into a disgusted sneer.

"She did great, though. I got there right at the end. She had already cut up two of the guys pretty bad, and the third one was bleeding from his nose and one eye. He had her knife by then, though. Don't know how he got it away. He had his pants down and was trying to take hers. I told Ceelie to fetch my knife, then yelled at the guy to distract him. It caught his attention long enough that she was able to take back the knife and cut his damned prick off."

"I got Throm's knife as fast as I could," says Ceelie.

Throm puts a protective arm around her. "You did fine. So Jenny puts that guy out of the rape business forever, but now the other two are pissed off enough to quit moaning about their cuts and come after her. She yells that they'll never get her alive, and if they were sick enough to want her corpse she hoped they got all the old diseases. They were about to grab her when she stabbed herself. Three times before she was too weak to do anymore."

Ceelie nods, her eyes red and brimming. Throm hugs her tighter and she snuggles into him.

"Ceelie got back with my knife just then, tossed it to me, and caught Jenny as she fell. I think that stopped them more than my knife. Watching a kid Ceelie's age trying to protect a dying ten-year-old, I don't know, maybe it kind of made them see what pigs they were being or something. They got kind of spooked and drove off. We couldn't afford a big enough fire to burn her body."

Throm shrugs, but Jin can see the tears he blinks back.

"We had to bury her," Ceelie finishes for him.

"Like garbage," says Throm, his voice barely a whisper.

"People used to always bury dead, not burn them," says Jin. "This way Jenny can feed plants. She would like."

The homecoming is so overwhelming that Jin can't process Jenny's death. It doesn't want to tell them about the wasteland now disturbing Jenny's gardens and her grave.

"Why didn't you come back?" says Ceelie.

She climbs into Jin's lap, eliciting smirks from the others. Jin stiffens but doesn't push her away.

"Did. Sorry was too late. Own fault, not keeping track of time. Checked in later, nobody home."

"After Jenny died we were afraid people would come looking for us. We went looking for you and found Brat instead," says Throm.

"Where you go looking?" asks Jin.

"Here, of course. Jimmy had seen the movie about you, so we figured from the fact that you walked home from Albuquerque that you probably lived somewhere around Carlsbad Caverns."

"Didn't know you knew I was same Jin. And movie had me walking north to Mesa Verde."

"Yeah," says Brat, joining the group. "We had to pay plenty to get Mesa Verde to let us film there. Even more when they found out what the film was about."

"We knew you wouldn't give away your real location in a movie," says Throm. "We looked on the maps for any place a lot of people could live underground."

"You were so good with tunnels and stuff, we figured you were used to it," says Jimmy.

He has a pile of grapes in one hand and a sandwich as big as his head in the other. The grin on his face dazzles the room.

"You like here?" says Jin.

"It's great! I've never seen so much food. I told Cook I'd be its personal tester, so if it ever wants to try new recipes I'll eat them and let it know what I think," says Jimmy.

Jin takes one of his grapes. "You walked here?"

"Like we could afford a ride," says Throm. "We took what we could from Jenny's garden, stuck to the wastelands as much as we could, and took turns guarding while the others slept. We know how to keep safe, remember?"

A few hours later, when the topsiders are mostly gone, someone suggests moving to the baths. Jin has been aching to go ever since it found that the others were all right, but it hadn't wanted to make the suggestion with so many gens around. They were sometimes funny about things like that.

Only one excuses herself, saying she is too tired. The others are enthusiastic, grabbing what's left of the food trays to take with them. Jimmy sheds his clothes at light speed on the way to the water and leaps in with a holler and a giant splash.

The rest of the group is a little slower. Jin sinks into the river, feeling the dirt of its journey wash away. Work-sweat and fear-sweat all carried downstream, filtered out, gone.

Sandy joins it after a while, clad in a dark blue bathing suit that seems to catch the eye of her boyfriend, but Jin can almost see the tension between them and isn't surprised when it learns that whatever was between them is over. That doesn't matter. Sandy looks good, healthy, and more confident than it remembers.

"Song that called me home," it says. "Your voice?"

"My vocal debut. Rouelle tells me it had to modify the tones a little, so I shouldn't ever expect to go on tour without some intensive lessons, but that's not why I did it," says Sandy. "I just wanted you home."

"Why? You don't live here now. Don't need me," says Jin.

She meets its eyes squarely, and for the second time since meeting her, Jin is reminded of its mother. Not just its own mother, but Margaret, too, the look on her face when she held Shaney as the younger woman broke down from all that life—that Jin—had heaped on her. A different kind of love than Brat talks about with his hormones and his ghosting, but one that is strangely familiar to Jin.

Sandy reaches out slowly and brushes her fingertips over Jin's knuckles. When it returns the gesture, her eyes twinkle, and without a word she smiles and swims away.

Pelin swims over to sit nearby. Jin clearly remembers a time when that would have made it cringe. Now, it touches Pelin's shoulder, just gently, a little stroke like Margaret feeling the crystal.

"Sorry I didn't contact you, really. Too caught up in own head, guess. Still trying figure who I am now," says Jin.

Pelin nods. "You saw Shaney."

"Yes."

"Want to talk?"

"Not much to say. She hates me, probably always will."

"But you were helping," says Pelin. "Couldn't she see?"

"Doesn't matter. To her, I'm killer of husband, children. I am most evil thing she knows."

"Not evil, Jin," says Pelin.

"No. But maybe Shaney's partly right. Margaret, too. Others up top. Maybe world doesn't want my help."

"What then? Let human race wash down drain, maybe few of us down here survive, protecting selves without helping others?"

"If they choose. Maybe they'll figure out on own. Some have already," says Jin.

"You know they won't. Not until too late."

"Like you say, I know. But Pelin," Jin pauses to deepen its breath so its voice doesn't break, "they choose life for all now, death for all later. They know death's coming. Hope to put off until old age, but concern is for selves, own children. Not whole race at large. We keep doing what helps survival; all they see is failure to protect families."

"I see," says Pelin.

Friends and family splash around them, celebrating. They are finished mourning the death of the spreaders. Pelin and Jin let their tears run into the water, mourning the end of the human race.

"Won't happen too soon," says Jin. "You and I maybe dead before."

"That supposed to comfort?"

"Seems to, for most. Funny how all want to be safely dead before death comes. Would you sacrifice self to save race?" asks Jin.

"Thought about that my one time spreading. Wouldn't kill self to make one less body. Be replaced before corpse is cold, many times over. If Soundwave had taken me along with others, would have been okay. What you think if I died in Soundwave?"

"So many dead," says Jin. Pelin waits patiently. Jin imagines watching it die from the music it ordered from Rouelle. It remembers how glad it was when Pelin seemed unaffected by the sounds.

"Your death I would mourn. Mourning for friends, respect for strangers, compassion for enemies. Don't miss them, would have missed you," says Jin.

"But wouldn't have stopped plague," says Pelin.

"Plagues always designed not to be stopped by anyone other than person affected. You know. Protects spreaders from that decision."

"But would you? If could," says Pelin.

What does it want Jin to say? "No. Would have hurt, watching. I'd stay with you until end, hoping to give comfort. Would let you die."

Pelin smiles. "Thanks, Jin. Love you too. Just don't let self die so easily, okay?"

"Can't. Instinct won't let me."

"Certainly have tried. Sand promised not to say anything today, but tomorrow you'll get lecture for hours on being too thin, staying out too long, not taking care of self."

"Fine," says Jin. "Sand will enjoy. She thinks I'm personal project."

"Now just need to find you a new project," says Pelin.

The lighting fades around them into simulated sunset with changing cloud patterns and a color that makes Pelin's face glow through the curtain of steam. Jin watches its friend appear and disappear as the vapors rise. It smells the gens around them and the warm, growing earth.

It is dead to the world above them, it realizes. It can never go back, not just because of the people searching for it, but because it can't bear to see the crowded streets and reeking wastelands and do nothing about them. Shaney will be happy. She buried it after all.

Jin reaches up to the riverbank and pulls its crystal out of the pocket of the crumpled clothing it left lying there. The chemicals weren't hard to develop, and down here it will have access to anything it needs. Net will provide computer access with or without Network approval, and it already has all the research it needs to make chemically induced sensations of the full variety of human emotions. If it can grow crystals that portray the full range of human experience, then maybe someday, even if the species is long gone, some new intelligent life form will repopulate the land and discover the crystals. They can touch them, study them, and know what the creatures that called themselves humans once were.

Pelin floats closer, its face parting the steam next to Jin.

"What you thinking?" it says.

"Thinking maybe time to become artist," says Jin. "Want to help?"

THE END

# AUTHOR BIOGRAPHY

Deb Taber is a writer and editor specializing in speculative fiction. She was introduced to Pierre Breton's T*he Secret World of Og* and Norton Juster's *The Phantom Tollbooth* before she could fully speak, so it should come as no surprise that her inclinations to write and edit bent the way they did.

Now, she edits professionally as a freelancer for publishing houses and individual clients, lending her editorial eye to everyone from first-time novelists to best-selling authors. She is working on developing detachable eyestalks to facilitate this procedure.

When not reading others' work, she spins her own stories out of the Pacific Northwest dampness in a coffee-fueled frenzy, exploring the murky and tortuous recesses of human and inhuman nature. Her fiction has appeared in *Fantasy* magazine and various anthologies. Find out more at debtaber.com.